C000103542

CAGE of the CURSED

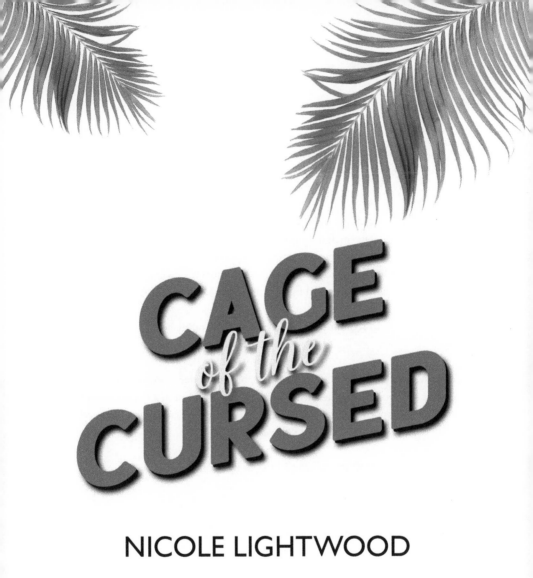

CAGE of the CURSED

NICOLE LIGHTWOOD

CALADESI
PRESS

Cage of the Cursed
Legacy of Light Series Book One

Copyright © 2023 Nicole Lightwood
All rights reserved.

No part of this publication may be reproduced, distributed, or transmitted in any form or by any means, including photocopying, recording, or other electronic or mechanical methods, without prior written permission of the publisher, except in the case of brief quotations embodied in critical reviews and certain other non-commercial uses permitted by copyright law.

To request permissions contact the publisher at
hello@caladesipress.com

This is a work of fiction. Names, characters, business, places, events, and incidents are either the products of the author's imagination or used in a fictitious manner. Any resemblance to actual persons, living or dead, or actual events is purely coincidental.

Cover Illustration and Interior by Nicole Lightwood

Library of Congress Control Number: 2023916564
ISBN 979-8-9881418-1-5 (Paperback)
ISBN 979-8-9881418-2-2 (Hardcover)
ISBN 979-8-9881418-0-8 (Ebook)

First Edition November 2023
caladesipress.com

Published by:
Caladesi Press LLC
Lawrenceburg, Ky, 40342

For Daniel and the Wildlings

CHAPTER 1

NOTHING REMINDS PEOPLE of their own mortality more than death.

The authorities haven't confirmed if the murder took place on the island or the mainland, but it hardly matters. People are terrified. The perfect reputation of safety is now questioned. A community where we leave our doors unlocked and people live without fear of their kids roaming the island—it's now all challenged.

The morning air is heavy with the crisp scent of the ocean. Salt clinging and fragrant on the mangroves that line either side of the channel. The rising sun sets the ocean to sparkle and turns the inter-coastal into a mirrored surface of glimmering gold. It sings of something ancient and magical. Dolphins slice through the clear water not yet turned up by boaters, enjoying the warmer current flowing through the channel and hunting the low tide meals. Palm trees filled with wild parrots chatter happily in the new day.

I breathe it all in through the open car window on our way to school, letting the familiar scents dull the near-constant ball of nerves behind my breastbone. The island of St. Sierra is famous for

its white sandy beaches, palm tree-lined streets, mansions by the sea, and according to the big turquoise sign by the pier, the best grouper sandwich in the USA. Now all anyone can talk about is the dead girl found on the beach.

It's been difficult not to watch the news and speculate on the details. It's been over a year since the nightmares stopped, but the dead girl on the beach brought them back up from whatever dark place my mind keeps them. Mostly I dream of all the embarrassing things I've said or done, or vines and roots that come up from my bedroom floor to strangle me, but lately, all I see is her body stuck in the shore break.

In my dreams, I stand on the shore watching the ocean try to decide if it wants to claim her for good or not. I know she's dead before I even reach down to feel her pulse. I don't tell anyone that the dead girl wears my face.

The sound of mom clucking her tongue brings my attention to the unusually long drop off-line, as most of us are within walking distance of the school. Her concerned gaze travels over to me, but she holds back any conversation on the subject for now.

Kat exits her mom's car a couple of vehicles ahead of us. Her wavy brown hair flares out as her hip knocks into the car door, slamming it closed. I see her mom call out the open window, to which Katerina flippantly waves her off on her way to her favorite post under the colonnade.

I reach for the door handle, but mom's voice stops me. "Maybe you shouldn't walk home today." She bites her lip. "A quick wait in the school office. I can be done with work by four-thirty tops."

I make a face at the prospect of sitting with the school secretary, giving me the stink-eye for keeping her late. "It's a ten-minute walk I've done a million times. I'll be fine."

"Keep your keys in your hand and the phone in the other." I give her a questioning look and she shrugs, making a thrusting gesture with her fist. "You can use them to stab someone in the eye."

"Ew. Who suggested that? Dad?"

She gives a noncommittal shrug and says, "Just text me when you get in the house."

"I know, I know," I blurt, glancing out the window. We're holding up the line. My stomach clenches with familiar dread, the anxiety building. Mom jerks her chin to the door, releasing me.

Kat is staring at the student parking lot like a hungry panther as I walk up. Her long legs make the Shorecrest gray plaid skirt look as if it's breaking regulation, her pale blue shirt not far behind.

Her clever eyes flick to mine, giving me a sly grin. "You ditched the colored contacts?"

I touch my eyelid reflexively; missing the subtle weight I've grown used to these past few years. "Yeah, and I already hate it." I rock back on my heels and nod toward the student parking lot gate. "Waiting for someone?"

"Window shopping," Kat grins and turns her attention back to the students, or more accurately, the boys, coming from the parking lot and the drop-off line.

"Nothing good then," I say, as most of the boys at Shorecrest are idiots.

Kat waves away my pessimism before her eyes move along to follow a junior boy a grade below us. He throws her a nod before disappearing through the open gates. "Speaking of yummy," she says, her attention pulled from the parking lot. She grabs my arm, giving me an imperceptible start. "I heard you have Ash freaking St. Claire in your first period."

And in Latin, I add silently, not wanting to hear about how 'lucky' I am. Kat lets go of my arm. "I'm so jealous," she huffs. "I would kill to have him in one of my classes this year."

"Don't murder anyone for his benefit," I mumble. Blondie wouldn't notice it, anyway.

Kat goes to hit my arm playfully, sees me wince, and pretends she doesn't. My friends are good about that, not calling attention to my nuances. I used to jump whenever anyone touched me. Before I got better at hiding it. It's not that I hate it, I mean, but it always makes me feel as if I'm being jolted from the inside. Every cell screaming, alert, alert, alert. Run, run, run.

"So, what's he like?"

"How would I know?" I shift on my feet. "He doesn't talk to mere mortals like me."

Talking about Ash St. Claire makes me feel as if my body is also screaming, alert, alert, alert. Run, run, run. I could say that about a lot of things, but St. Claire is high on my list. Shorecrest Academy is peppered with the Western Crescent Elite, along with a few mainland transplants, so it isn't the first year I've had blue eyes in any of my classes. It *is* the first year that Katerina Montez is single and has a keen interest in him.

It's also the first year I get a strange buzzing in my veins and stomach whenever he's around. The first year I silently admit I kind of like his face. That's the problem. Boys from the Western side of the island are trouble, and I despise anything in the same universe as trouble. I like rules. Boundaries. Kat is all about breaking down both.

"One day you're going to have to talk to boys," Kat says.

"I talk to boys," I frown.

"Really talk to them, Echo. He's Ash freaking St. Claire. You can't tell me you don't think he's cute."

"I do not." My unhappiness with this conversation deepens.

"Liar." Kat smirks, her red lips curling at how full of it I am. She clucks her tongue with a sigh. "I guess no one can compete with your first love."

My heartbeat quickens at the direction this conversation is going. Desperate to change it, I blurt, "I have Adam with me in the library."

Kat wrinkles her nose and asks, "Does Meredith know?"

I nod. I didn't want to remind Meredith of the feelings she tried all summer to forget, but not telling her was worse. Last year Adam was there for the shopping trips, the beach, and the Saturday girls' nights, with his corny jokes, big grin, and chocolate eyes. Driving us around in his truck that smelled like cut grass, surfboard wax, and fishing lures—and then this summer he was gone. Their breakup was as sudden as the vacuum it left in our lives.

As quaint as the island is—we barely saw him. At first, I thought it was a good thing, but it was heartbreaking to watch Meredith quietly looking for him around town. Meredith is very good at swallowing down her pain and watching her eat this hurt Adam caused made me hate him just a little.

"Have you talked to him?" Kat asks checking the polish on her nails.

It's just us in the Library, but my plan for the rest of the semester is to keep our interactions to a minimum. I get defensive on Meredith's behalf when I see him, but it's a confrontation Meredith should have. If she wanted to. When he broke up with her, she let him go without a fight. It would surprise anyone who knows her, but I don't think I would do things any differently. I can't even talk to the boy I like, let alone fight for him.

"Not really."

"Talked to who?" Meredith asks from behind me.

I give a guilty start, but I'm already kind of jumpy, so she doesn't seem to notice it's because we were talking about her ex. Her smile wouldn't be so bright if she had.

Meredith turns that ultra-white smile on Kat, whom as smooth as ever, throws me under by saying, "Just Echo's dream-boy."

My face turns uncomfortably warm, and I turn to glare at Katerina, who ignores it.

"I heard you have him in a couple of classes," Meredith coos, smoothing down the high-waisted version on the Shorecrest gray plaid skirt.

"A couple?" Kat turns her full gaze on me, her eyes flashing. "You said you didn't have him in any?"

I, unfortunately, do *not* have Alex Carter, the focus of my late-night sleepover confessionals, in any classes this semester. Meredith innocently blinks at me with her brown eyes when it clicks who she's actually talking about.

I scoff. Wretches all of them. "Oh, please. St. Clare, um no," I say with an exasperated roll of my eyes.

Meredith laughs, wrapping one of her tight curls around her finger. "You said he makes you feel tingly."

Kat arches her thin brow, but her smile is as ecstatic as ever.

"I actually said buzzy. *Buzzy.* Like being stung by sixty-thousand bees. Anaphylactic shock." I swallow down the urge to flee from this conversation, as it would only give them more ammunition to tease me.

"So Ash St. Claire makes you feel buzzy, and Alex Carter makes you feel all tingly?" Kat tilts her head, tapping a red nail on her matching lips. "Sounds like you're crushing to me..." Kat flashes a grin. "So which boy haunts your dreams, Echo, Alex Carter or—Ouch," Kat yelps, turning a sharp disgruntled look to where Meredith pinched her.

It registers slow like molasses, the group of boys passing next to us on their way to the front gate. Dread spreads from my center and up my arms, making my scalp prickle. Kat's mouth snaps closed; her fingers press on her lips as if she could take back her words.

"Don't look," Meredith whispers, but it's too late.

Alex Carter is a few feet away, his best friend Tyler beside him on their way to the front gate. I quickly glance at my shoes, feeling my face get hotter than midday in July.

"Do you think..." Kat trails off as Alex glances over his shoulder at us.

A big grin splits Tyler's face as he pushes Alex towards us, towards me. "Go for it, man."

Alex rights himself right before he would have collided with me. "Sorry," he says, looking apologetic. He pushes a hand through his sandy brown hair, glancing over his shoulder at Tyler.

My face is burning hot, the nerves in my stomach now a CAT 5 hurricane. I know people are moving past us heading through the gates, but I am hyper-focused on Alex's brown eyes and his shy grin, and his lips hovering between speaking and silence.

He takes a step towards me, close enough that I can smell his cologne. The intense way he is looking at me has my heart destroying my rib cage.

"Hey," he says, eyes narrowing. His gaze dips, devouring me from my feet back to my eyes.

He opens his mouth to say more, but Tyler jostles his shoulder, pulling him away. "Come on, flirt later."

It effectively releases Alex from whatever trance he was in. "See you around," he says, giving me one last look over his shoulder as they walk through the gates into school.

I count to five before I say, "Just great Katerina." I blow out a long breath. "Thanks for that."

Meredith chews her cheek, staring after them. Kat gives me an apologetic look. "Well, on the bright side, Alex finally knows you're interested."

If you were to manifest one of my nightmares, Alex finding out I have a crush on him would be one of them. My old friends of anxiety and panic war with each other as Kat tries to apologize.

I raise my hand, cutting her off. "I'm going to be sick." I pinch the bridge of my nose, as I say, "That gossip lush Tyler is probably texting the entire school right now."

Meredith chews on her bottom lip. "It's probably not that bad..."

Kat laughs, shrugging her shoulders. "Tyler has bigger things to worry about. I heard he's on Academic Probation for sports."

Meredith grimaces. "Yikes."

I keep my head down as we walk through the gates, feeling like everyone's watching me already. When we get to the crossroads between the English building and Science Labs, Kat's smile becomes a little too saccharine. "Let's walk Echo to class."

"No way," I say, shaking my head.

Katerina loops her arm through Meredith's and the two of them lead the way to my first period. They strategically stop to get a good view through the open classroom door to gawk at St. Claire. He's lounging at his desk in the back row, a book propped up in one hand while his thumb distractedly taps on the desk as he reads.

"Oh," Kat coos, dancing away from the door. "So studious."

"Just what you need, a literary man." Meredith bumps her hip into Kat's, giving me a toothy grin.

"He can read me bedtime stories." Kat gives Meredith a conspiratorial look.

The first bell rings, thankfully cutting off the rest of their objectification. Meredith quickly kisses her fingers, throwing them out to us as a way of goodbye as she dashes to her class across campus.

Kat, not being able to resist, gives me a wink before she goes. "Tell him my name," she says. Her laughter follows her down the hall.

My battered heart almost gives out when I turn to enter class and see St. Claire's piercing blue eyes fixed on me. It kicks up the beehive in my chest and I scowl, feeling sour.

The last row has always been my respite, the only place where I don't feel like everyone is watching me and St. Clare has the audacity to sit in the back in both the classes we share. He lounges in his seat, looking casually unaffected by the world as usual. He puts away his book as I slide into my seat next to him.

There's a vibration coming from his pocket and I panic for a second that it's already Tyler telling everyone about my crush on Alex, but remember that Ash doesn't have many friends at school. As far as I know, it's only Adam Woo, Meredith's ex, but there are plenty of rumors about how he spends his time outside of Shorecrest.

Not that they're credible sources, but there is definitely something strange about St. Claire. In all the months Meredith dated Adam, she rarely saw him. We hung out with Adam plenty, but Ash was conveniently unavailable. Meredith blames him a little for the breakup. I don't know if it's true or if she just needed a target for her pain.

I chew on the end of my pen as he slides his phone back into his pocket. Kat wants me to use my proximity to St. Claire to get her a way to his heart, but I'd rather stand in front of the entire class in my bathing suit and recite the alphabet while holding my tongue.

Charity Harmon glances back, her eyes flicking between the two of us while she idly plays with her pencil. She whispers something to Emma beside her and the two of them bend their heads together at something on Charity's phone.

My stomach clenches.

Charity hasn't been shy about letting me know I'm her least favorite person—with little shoulder bumps in the hallway and whispered laughs in my direction with her friends. If she found out I liked Alex too, she wouldn't be quiet about it.

I sigh in relief when I see they are looking at homecoming dresses and not an incrimination message from Tyler. No one is talking about me. Still, it feels like the universe is watching me.

I am aware the prisons I make for myself are mostly in my head, but it doesn't stop, doesn't change my screwed-up brain from making them. I'm thankful that they're small cages and not the big black voids that they used to be.

It's getting better. I am better at hiding it.

CHAPTER 2

ALEX CARTER IS leaning against the lockers outside of my third-period Latin class talking to Charity. I would have known he was there even before the angry hornet's nest in my belly. There is something charismatic about him that demands attention.

He pushes off the bank of lockers and calls my name. "Hey, it's Echo, right?"

Everything in me is screaming like I hit the panic button inside my brain, but instead of igniting into action, I am frozen.

"Maybe?"

He laughs like I said that on purpose. "Sorry I just took off this morning. Tyler and I had a thing."

This is the most I've talked to him in two years and I have a powerful urge to flee, but then I hear Kat's confident voice in my head telling me not to let an opportunity slip away.

"It's fine," I say, even though Tyler laughing at me still burns in my thoughts.

Alex rubs a hand on his neck, looking apologetic. "And sorry, if I was a little, um, intense this morning. I freeze when I'm nervous sometimes."

"Oh?" I shift from one foot to the other. The hint, even a little, that maybe he was just as nervous talking to me brings warmth from my belly to my toes.

Someone calls his name and when he looks away, I use the distraction to absorb the way his uniform fits him. I snap my eyes up to his face when he turns back to me.

"We don't have any classes."

"No, we don't." Our conversation is not funny, but my mouth keeps wanting to grin.

Goosebumps spread along my skin, and that hum starts. Alex's eyes narrow behind me and I use the momentary distraction to school my face.

"So, um, hey, what lunch do you have?"

"Second." *The same as you.*

He takes a step toward me, and I reflexively take a step back. He notices. His eyes flick behind me. My stomach cramps with dread. *Apologize. For what? Anything, say anything.*

I open my mouth but Alex is already saying, "So, hey, I better get to class, but I'll talk to you later?"

"Oh, sure, okay." I fumble with something to add, but his attention is already down the hall.

I watch him walk away before I realize I've been standing in the middle of the corridor. When I turn around, St. Claire is staring at me. He has his phone in his hands, and his brow arches in amusement. Mr. Hanson forbids phones in class, even going so far as confiscating them until you're finished with detention.

Embarrassment creeps over me, souring my mood. "You must be so popular," I say, eying the phone, remembering how it buzzed most of English.

His gaze flicks down the corridor knowingly. "You too." He makes an elegant gesture for me to go before him into class.

I inwardly roll my eyes at his semblance of chivalry, but at the risk of being late, I oblige, turning to enter the classroom—I freeze in the doorway as all eyes are on me. With mortifying clarity, I realize they had a front-row seat to my conversation with Alex. The late bell rings and I think I might die here.

Charity glares at me with the pencil eraser between her teeth. The look she's giving me is probably because of my earlier proximity to Alex, but at that moment St. Claire puts a hand on my lower back to urge me forward. It effectively unfreezes me and I head to my seat.

Mr. Hanson gets up from his desk with a flourish. "Now that you're done holding up class," he says in our direction. "We can begin the lesson."

AS SOON AS THE bell rings, the class erupts in noise as we pack up and flee towards the door. Mr. Hanson has that effect on people. I try to hang back, but Ash and I still make it to the door at the same time. He encourages me to go first. I resist giving any reaction as I walk ahead of him through the doorway.

The hallways fill with the excitement of the lunch crowd. Boys jostle friends, girls talk more animatedly, their steps slow without the overbearing late bell. I decide to take the long way to lunch, as the activity in the halls feels more overbearing than usual.

I can feel someone watching me and when I turn I see Charity behind me, her eyes narrow on mine with a look that turns my blood cold. I frown, turning forward. The hallway feels claustrophobic and I decide to cut through the science building for the path behind the library. This time of day, it should be empty. Giving me time to breathe.

The ground goes out from under me as I hit the floor hard. After the initial shock wears off, I realize I was pushed. I slowly get to my feet. My palms hurt, and it's painful when I reach down to grab my bag.

Charity stands in front of me, a satisfied smile on her face. I eye the deserted hallway and swallow to find my voice.

"You pushed me?"

"Maybe you're just clumsy?" She steps forward and I back up into the wall behind me. A malicious grin splits her face at my reaction.

Charity's smile grows more poisonously joyful. "Jumpy."

I like to avoid confrontation when I can, but I've never considered myself a coward.

"What's your problem?" I ask, my heart thumbing inside my chest.

Charity appraises me with deliberate slowness. "Poor little Echo, scared of her own shadow. It must be miserable being you?" Her face twists into disgust as she continues, "Everyone knows about your unrequited crush on Alex."

My small intake of breath gives her too much satisfaction. The bell rings over head and my eyes dart down the hall waiting for the doors to open but everyone in this wing has been dismissed for lunch.

"Call for help," she says, mirroring my thoughts, "like anyone would believe you."

Her father's an attorney in the city on the mainland. I've heard Meredith's dad mention him a few times. *'You go to school with Benedict's daughter. They call him the jackal. Thank God he's on our side'.*

Charity could be a jackal in this moment. Teeth and fangs that bite. The apple doesn't fall far from the tree.

"What do you want?" I ball my hands into fists. Something dark uncoils at being pinned by a girl only a little bigger than me. Trapped. Always a prisoner.

"You want to know what Alex and Tyler say? You're the last on their list. Alex's just messing with you for fun," she says with a smirk. "Just another game they're playing."

"Careful—sounds like jealousy," I say. It's false bravado, adrenaline, or stupidity fueling me on.

I put my hand on the wall to steady myself as the ground shifts.

Her expression sours, and for a moment she wears the face of my nightmares.

"What's wrong, having another freak-out?" Charity tugs a strand of my hair before I can swat her away.

Fire blazes in my veins. The hallway narrows as my heart jumps into my throat. I feel dizzy and close my eyes to stop the spinning.

When I open them, Charity is laughing. She plays with her necklace, one of those cheap yellow crystals they sell at the mall, as she says, "I was joking. Don't lose it."

"Leave me alone," I hiss at her.

Charity takes a step forward, fists clenched like she wants to hit me, just as a door bangs further down the hall. We both jerk towards the sound, footsteps coming from around the corner.

"Watch your back, Echo." She spins around with a whirl of her hair and pushes through the science building doors.

Her exit echoes in the empty hall.

I lean my head back against the cream painted brick. After a moment, I push off the wall. My hands are shaking and my legs are heavy as if I'm wading through water.

Charity feels threatened by anyone that doesn't fit her narrow view of what the world looks like, but I never thought we'd clash in violence. I thought I was the type to defend myself, but I felt powerless.

I brush a hand over my face as Charity's words taunt me. I know I shouldn't believe her, but sometimes your heart and your brain have conflicting ideas and the war they make inside of you won't leave room for rational thought.

The hallway darkens as I make my way toward the back exit. I close my eyes to adjust to the blinding sunshine and when I open them again; I see the haunted woods of my dreams. The trees reach their branches towards my feet to snake around my ankles, pulling me into them and devouring me.

The ground shifts from solid to sand-like water, sucking me down. And like in my nightmares, I crawl out, dumped onto the shore. But I am still at school.

The walkway is empty, but it won't be for long. I push myself up and turn towards the old art building and an unused bathroom where I can hide and call my mom.

There's a quaking, electrified feeling that's still running through me, and my chest feels tight. I haven't had a panic attack like this in months. I wanted to believe they stopped.

My breathing gets tight, and my blood vibrates. I close my eyes and push it down. Breathe—focus on breathing. My head is splitting open. I try counting out the breaths. It usually works, but my heart is still trying to break free of my chest.

I pull at the collar of my shirt; the humidity suffocates my skin an electrified wire. I dig out my phone from my backpack as I take the shortcut, turning off the colonnade onto the dirt walkway.

Something is wrong.

My veins are humming, and my blood is too warm.

My vision shifts like I am seeing all the seasons through a flip book; the hallway in summer, in fall, in winter, in spring, and then I am falling.

My hands dig into the patchy grass and sandy dirt as energy pours through my veins, filling every cell and remaking me.

My fingers are burning with a light all their own.

It spreads up my hands, veins bright like lava. Sparks dance from my fingertips, flickering over the sand like Fourth of July sparklers. My breath gets caught in my throat as I stare down at the hallucination.

"Echo, are you alright?" Adam Woo's voice snaps me out of my daze. He reaches down to help me up.

I recoil back. "No, don't touch me," I warn, not sure if I'll hurt him.

His eyes widen as he sees my hands, but he doesn't look frightened. It must be the opposite of what's on my face. He bends down, one knee on the ground, and glances around the hallway, "Someone might see you. Can you turn it off?"

I look up at him with watery eyes. "No. I... I can't make it stop."

This reminds me too much of a night at Meredith's thirteenth birthday party. Maybe there were too many people, and I pushed myself too fast. I ignored the signs and the feelings. I just wanted to be normal. I thought I could push it down, and bury it. I thought I had it under control.

That's probably the memory Charity has. She was there. A lot of kids from school were. Not everyone saw my panic attack, or that Meredith and Kat helped me upstairs, but I'm sure people talked about it. That night I was sitting on the floor of Meredith's bedroom, her thick white carpet soft on my toes as I cried and confessed to them too that something was wrong with me.

Adam slides his backpack around, quickly pulling out a sweatshirt. He drops it on my hands. The light now hidden, I let out a relieved breath.

"I know a place we can go. Can you get up?"

I nod and shakily rise to my feet, letting Adam lead me to the rear entrance of the library, careful to keep his sweatshirt covering my hands. We enter through a plain metal door instead of the grand archway and columns in the front. A blast of cold air hits me, chilling my clammy skin. We turn right down a hallway instead of the main room, which is never empty during lunch.

I follow Adam to a plain door with a sign that says no admittance. He smirks when I ask if we're going to get in trouble for going inside. He pulls open the door, revealing a dark room. It has a musty smell of forgotten things. Adam uses the flashlight on his cell phone to reveal a path through a stack of plastic chairs.

"Is there anyone you can call to help you?" he asks, making his way through the room. "Your parents maybe?"

I shake my head no. I've already put them through enough. When all the times the noise and crowds were too much for me, I don't want to add glowing hands into the equation.

I lift my cloth-bound hands. "I don't even know what this is."

Adam searches my face, then he runs his fingers through his hair. "Okay. I know someone who can help."

"You 'know someone'?" I ask.

He makes a non-committal grunt as his fingers move purposely over his keypad. After he sends his message to this mysterious someone, he turns, sliding through a space between an old audio video cart and a stack of dark blue plastic chairs. I follow behind him, my curvier hip catching the corner of the entertainment cart and making the wheels squeak. Adam reaches over me, holding it steady so I can slip past.

There's a break in the clutter in the back of the room wide enough for Adam to open a door. It looks no bigger than a closet and I'm about to tell him I'm not getting into a four-foot space with his six-foot self when his flashlight carries down the wall and reveals a bend. I follow him around the odd little L-shaped corner into another room. Adam pulls the metal string of an old light bulb fixture in the ceiling. It flickers to life, casting the room in a dusty yellow glow.

Long skinny tables hug the walls with funny-looking equipment under black canvas covers, chairs tucked under them. There's a stack of dark green trays under the table, and a floor-to-ceiling cabinet in the corner. Dust covers almost everything except one bare table in the middle of the room. A chair pulled out as if waiting for someone. The room has a slightly haunted feeling that makes me shiver.

"It's the old darkroom. Practically forgotten," Adam says. "No one should bother us here."

I move my gaze away from the dustless table. "Do you hang out here often?"

Adam leans against a table, crossing his foot over his ankle. "Sometimes, but it's not really my—"

Movement in the shadows catches our attention as a figure comes from around the corner.

Adam doesn't look surprised as Ash St. Claire steps into the light. His light blond hair looks golden under the antique bulb, mused as if he ran here. For a moment, a bright light glows around him before I blink and it's gone. His ocean eyes keenly take in the scene, shifting from surprise to suspicion.

"What's going on?" Ash asks, fixing his hair.

Why would Adam tell St. Claire? My heartbeat thuds harder, my face warming. The room darkens at the edges and little pinpricks dance in my fingers. You could explain it away as a trick of the old dusty bulb, but a faint glow shows through the sweater fabric.

I gape at Adam. "What is he doing here?"

Adam lifts his hands in a placating gesture. "It's okay Echo, he can help."

I glance at Ash. His eyes lift from the sweater to my face, and his head tilts. "I can?" he asks at the same time I say, "Him?"

Adam shrugs and says almost sheepishly to St. Claire, "It seemed like right up your alley?"

St. Claire's eyes travel over me like an appraiser trying to find the value of an object. "Well, what kind of help can I provide exactly?" He puts his hands in his pockets, a simple thing that he makes arrogant.

Adam gives me a sideways look before he says, "I found her behind the library. Her hands were glowing."

"Adam," I hiss. I'd pinch him, the traitor, if I didn't need to keep my hands covered.

He turns that apologetic smile on me before telling St. Claire, "I don't think she knows what's happening to her, and I thought, well, you could help?"

"Oh, that alley," he says, a soft chuckle as he shakes his head.

I frown at the cavalier way they talk about this strangeness that's happened to me. My fingers strangle the knit fabric around my hands, and I turn my displeasure on Adam. "Is this some kind of joke?"

"Dude," Adam says to Ash, giving him a pleading look.

St. Claire sighs up at the ceiling. Some tension around his shoulders deflates. "I can't help if she doesn't want me to." Ash pivots his body towards mine. Again, his crystal blue eyes assess me much deeper than the surface.

Butterflies fly around the ball of nerves in my stomach. "Stop looking at me like that," I tell him.

He arches a brow. "I'm looking at you like you're looking at me." The corner of his mouth lifts. My face warms as he adds, "I'm here because Adam told me he needed my help. If that's not the case..." He glances at Adam, who gives him a 'try harder,' gesture.

"How, exactly, can *you* help *me?*" I ask him.

Ash inclines his head to the sweater covering my hands. "We can start with your hands."

I turn a skeptical eye on him. St. Claire doesn't look like he'd know how to stop freakishly glowing hands, but neither am I the type to have them. I glance over at Adam, who gives me an encouraging smile. If Adam trusts him, then maybe I should too.

"May I?" he asks, taking a step forward.

I give a small nod. I watch him untangle the knit fabric from my hands, my eyes trailing up the sleeves of his crisp white button-down, folded up to his elbows, showing the tanned skin of his arms. My gaze slides to the Shorecrest Academy sweater vest that flatters him in a way that fails some of the other boys at school.

He gently inspects my hands, turning them over. No trace of glowing light. I flex my fingers, the dusty darkroom air cools my clammy palms, and let out a relieved breath.

"Looks like you're under control now," he says, taking a step back and sliding his hands into his pants pockets.

"How did this happen to me?" I whisper, not expecting St. Claire to answer.

"You were born this way."

I give him a sharp, incredulous glare. "That's stupid. Wouldn't I know if I was born like this?"

"Not if you were a Quiescent," he says matter of fact. "Did your parents tell you about Siphons? Ever notice anything strange in your family?"

I narrow my eyes at him. "Of course not. There was no 'hey Echo, your great grandmother's hands light up, it skips a couple of generations, but don't freak out if it happens to you' conversations."

Ash's expression is patient, but his height feels condescending, especially the way he tilts his head down to look at me. "Okay," he drawls. "Then I'd take an educated guess you're a Q."

"I'm supposed to know what that means?"

Ash slowly takes in his bottom lip, holding it with his teeth. It draws attention to his mouth and I scowl.

He comes to some decision before he says, "Quiescents are latent Siphons, a diluted genetic line," and before I can ask he quickly continues, "Siphons are people who can wield an energy source called the Light, and use that energy in different ways, what you might think of as magic."

St. Claire delivers it as facts, the words familiar on his lips as if he's reading it out of a history book and not something he's made up on the spot to mess with me. But still. Glowing hands, people with some sort of magical abilities? This can't be real.

I take in a deep breath. "Right. Sure."

Ash straightens. "You don't have to believe me, but how do you explain what happened?" He turns to Adam, the look he gives him saying 'see, I told you.'

"How do you know about this... stuff?"

"Because I do," he says with the bored indifference I associate as a permanent addition to his personality.

"Is that what you are? A Siphon?" The word feels silly in my mouth.

"No," he says, hard, final.

"You're real helpful," I say. My turn to give Adam an 'I told you so' look. "How do you believe any of this? Please don't say 'you just do?'" I try to mock St. Claire's deep voice.

Adam doesn't look perturbed by my sour mood as he says, "I've seen things you wouldn't believe, Echo. Trust me." And then he adds with no hint of doubt, "Everything he's saying is true."

"What things?" I ask.

I miss whatever look Ash gives Adam to make him say, "Uh, I can't say."

"Sure." I purse my lips as I look over at St. Claire, who pinches the bridge of his nose, the first sign that his cool armor is breaking.

"I'm trying, okay, this is—" he waves his hand airily in my direction, "difficult for me."

I rock back on my heels. "Okay. Why is this happening to me now?"

"Families can go generations without knowing they have Siphon blood. There's usually a trigger that awakens Q's. Stress, or a traumatic event."

"I'm always stressed." Ash's eyes flick to mine and I close them, shaking my head. "No. There has to be something else." I open my eyes to find St. Claire still watching me. I clear my throat.

"Well..." Adam says, looking at Ash.

A silent conversation quickly wages between them, ending with Ash sighing. "Some Siphons can attach intentions to certain gems, crystals, or precious stones; called Curses. But a curse in this case is very unlikely." His gaze roams over me as he says, "They have to touch your skin to work properly, and it doesn't look like you're wearing any jewelry. Unless you've got it somewhere unconventional."

I ignore his curious probing and ask, "There are curses now?"

Ash rubs a hand down his face before he tells me, "They are extremely volatile and outlawed for a reason."

"Okay," I say slowly, looking at Adam for any sign that this is one stupid prank. "But what do I do about this?" I hold out my hands.

Ash checks the time on his watch. "Make sure it never happens again."

"Real helpful."

"Q's aren't powerful, so next time it happens, breath through the shock of it and it should go away. If you can stay out of trouble, you should be fine."

"I can't believe we are having this conversation." I raise my eyebrows and he lifts his hand in a take it or leave it gesture.

"I don't make the rules, I just follow them."

We all look up as the bell rings, muffled from somewhere outside the darkroom. Adam slides off the table.

Ash claps his hands. "Since it looks like everything's cleared up..." He points his thumb behind him and turns around with it. Adam follows him out. Their voices drift around the corner. I catch a snippet of Adam apologizing for Ash missing lunch and Ash assuring him it's fine. I feel bad for how frosty I was to St. Claire, but he wasn't exactly warm himself.

I snatch my backpack off the floor and study my hands once more. How easy it would be to believe it was all a hallucination caused by my anxiety? If Adam hadn't seen it as well.

When I enter the hall outside the storage room, Adam is standing there waiting to hand me my phone. I thank him, grateful it's not broken.

The hallway is eerily quiet, and I lower my voice. "So, how long have you known about this stuff?"

"Um, around the last thanksgiving break, I guess," his voice is soft with secrets.

I frown, remembering around that time Meredith quietly confessed she thought he was hiding something. Adam and Ash have been friends for a couple of summers, but St. Claire wasn't included in the package when Adam and Meredith dated. St. Claire kept himself separate, and I always thought it was because he was a huge elitist, but maybe there was another reason involving Siphon and secrets.

I slow to a stop, and Adam stops with me. "And this stuff is for real?" He gives me a look, and I say, "I know, I know, the girl with the glowing fingers." I wiggle them for emphasis. "It's just... St. Claire," I say a little witheringly.

Adam gives the floor a small smile before turning it towards me. "You know, everyone gives him a hard time about who he does or doesn't spend his time with, where he lives..."

"You're not giving me the speech about how misunderstood he is, are you?" This time I do put my hand on my hip.

Adam shakes his head with a small laugh. "It's not about money, it's about character," he says. "There's so much judgment at this school because he's not sticking to the typical Shorecrest persona." Adam raises a brow at me. "I didn't expect you to be one of them." I stare at my shoes, my face guiltily warm. Adam taps the wall next to us, a quick rap of his knuckles, "I know he seemed bothered, I mean, I put him on the spot, but he's actually really shy."

I can't stop the incredulous scoff that comes out of me. Adam shakes his head, and his amused smile shows the dimples in his chin. "Sorry," I say, feeling bad for insulting his friend. "It's hard to believe."

"Well, maybe you shouldn't be so judgmental." He grins at me as he walks down the hall.

"I'm not—"

"I know. I get what's going on," he says with a little too much mischief for my liking.

I didn't think my face could feel any hotter. I scowl, but before I can work up what to say to all of that; he spins on his heel, heading towards the librarian's desk where the teacher's assistants check-in. I follow behind, but much slower, my feet heavy as the reality of what's happened settles in. All that's changed in thirty minutes. If Adam and Ash are telling me the truth, then what does it mean for the world as I know it?

What does it mean for me?

There's a flutter in my chest. It whispers that things are happening. Fear moves through me. I'm not sure I'm ready for my world to change.

It's surreal watching your hands light up like glow sticks and finding out two boys from school have insider knowledge about a secret magical underground that I may either be the victim of or a part of it.

Adam and I stand side by side as Mrs. Velasquez doles out duties for the hour.

Adam was always good at looking at you like you meant something, even if you didn't. And he's very good at looking at you like he didn't just save you from some magical curse, as you embarrassingly freaked out.

He's got a new haircut since last year, and it looks like that last bit of softness in his face is gone. I can see why Meredith enjoyed looking at his face so much. And even though I'm mad at all boys right now, I can also see why Meredith fell in love with him too.

After I was done with the copier, I sought him out in the stacks, re-shelving books.

I want to ask if this secret thing that involves St. Claire is the reason Meredith and him broke up. If it drove them apart, but when I finally get a moment alone with him, I ask, "So what's the deal with St. Claire?"

"What do you mean?" Adam licks his lips, casting a cautious glance at me.

"Why does he know so much about this?"

"He told you..."

"The bare minimum," I say. "I know there's more."

Adam concentrates on the book in his hand, but I doubt he's interested in crocheting for beginners. "That's not really my secret to tell," he finally answers.

"So there are secrets, then?" I take a step forward, grabbing a cupcake decorating book and shelving it.

Adam casts me a withering look before he organizes the remaining books on the cart.

I mirror him on the other side. Separating the biographies from the classics.

"Why did he tell you?"

Adam shrugs. "Keeping secrets wears on you."

"So he needed to confide in someone he trusts?"

"Maybe."

"Are you a Siphon?"

"No," he says with a laugh.

I chew my lip, picking the edge of a smiling mochi sticker someone decorated the cart with.

"Have you ever seen one?"

Adam pauses while arranging the books. He glances at me and then back at the books. "Yes."

I lean in and lower my voice. "What happened? Who? Is it someone at school?"

Seeing magic on someone else would make what happened to me earlier even more believable.

Adam glances at me sideways. "You know what a secret is, right?"

"Yes." I say. "Come on, Adam."

He blows out a breath, pushing a hand through his hair. He leans down, meeting my hopeful eyes. I can feel the nerves in my belly jumping up.

If there really is this secret magical world, I need to see it. I want to know all about this secret world Adam is privy to and where St. Claire fits into it. I want to know if there's a way that Adam can be with Meredith and keep his secrets too. Maybe I can fix them, but maybe it's not for me to try. What if this secret goes deeper than I know and the second time around would destroy her?

What am I? Where is my place in all of this?

"Go ask Ash," he says, pushing the cart away from me.

I snatch a copy of the tempest off the cart and head around the corner to shelf it. I keep my thoughts and my meddling to myself for the rest of the period.

CHAPTER 3

I TOSSED AND TURNED all night, my body restless and raw. Dreams of glowing trees, their roots stretching out to me, to my fingertips, of boys with blue eyes and smarmy lips telling me secrets I can't remember.

I foolishly tried searching the Internet, but this is not like the movies where a few quick clicks pop up some obscure Latin prophecy telling you exactly how to save the world. There was no convenient explanation of what happened to me on any search pages except a growing list of conspiracy theories and some interesting reading on a popular fan-fiction site.

I am convinced that Ash freaking St. Claire is a sadist with his story of curses and Siphons. Maybe something he and Adam cooked up to mess with me. But no, I tell myself, Adam isn't like that.

All these things churn in my head as I get dressed for school. My button-down feels scratchy against my skin this morning, and there's still some of that restlessness from last night, making me fidgety. A spasm in my muscles that I can't quite stretch out.

I'm rinsing out my oatmeal bowl when mom comes back downstairs. When she sees me watching her, she sighs and shakes her head.

"Please," I beg.

She grabs her cell phone off the charger and takes in a deep breath. My shoulders slump at the oncoming lecture.

"You're not sick," she says, "you're not having an attack. What's the problem?"

My nails rap on the counter as I decide if telling her what I'm really thinking will help the situation or not. That yesterday my hands began to magically glow and perhaps it's all a stressed induced hallucination. That I imagined the entire conversation with the most unlikely boy at school because earlier that day my crush overheard I liked him, and Charity got possessive over him.

My parents already have enough of the everyday me to worry about. "Um..."

"Is it about that boy?" She purses her lips. "Echo, it's not healthy to avoid every uncomfortable situation in life."

The image of St. Claire's arrogant mouth and incredulous eyes fills my vision. I tug on my shirt, the collar feeling tight. "He's just so annoying."

Mom smiles, a laugh in her mouth. "Since when? You've been fawning over that Carter boy since freshman year."

Oh. *Right.*

I look at my shoes. "No, I meant another one."

Mom lifts a thin blond brow. "There's another one?"

"No—" I let out a frustrated growl. "Forget it."

"Echo..." She reaches out to take my hand but stops when she sees me pull back.

She's gotten very good at hiding her disappointment, but I can still see the sadness in her eyes. It's not that no one can touch me, I only prefer it to be on my terms.

Her hand curls on the surface of the counter. "A minor embarrassment is no reason to miss school," she says. "Unless he's harassing you?"

I shake my head. "No, nothing like that."

"Good." She smiles, but her mouth quickly slides into her no-nonsense one. "Then school it is."

MEREDITH IS SITTING ON the three-foot garden wall by our spot under the colonnade when I get to school. A row of arboricolas and azaleas are behind her. Her foot is tapping lazily to a song I can't hear.

"Hey." She smiles, pulling out her earbuds when she sees me. Her face molds into concern. "Did you stay up all-night binge-watching your superhero show again?"

"Do I look that bad?" I stop and tug on my messy bun.

"No," she lies. "Still thinking about Alex?"

"Not the highest on my mental anguish list, but it's up there."

A minute later, Kat saunters up. She gives me a long once-over. "Did you stay up all night stalking Alex online?"

"No," I say sourly, and adjust the straps on my messenger bag. "Am I that predictable?"

Meredith and Kat share a guilty shrug, but my attention wanders to Charity and Emma walking toward the gate. Charity's icy gaze slides over the three of us, and then she leans in to whisper in Emma's ear. Whatever she says makes the other girl look over her shoulder at us and laugh.

Kat and Meredith are exchanging harsh whispers between them, and they miss the whole thing. I'm not sure if I'm grateful or not. Every time I open my mouth to tell them about what happened with Charity, the words get stuck in my throat. I don't want to talk about how Charity warned me off Alex, or hear how I should have punched her in the mouth, or have them think it rattled me so much that it's the reason I ditched lunch. I cannot have that conversation lead to the real reason I wasn't in the cafeteria.

I try not to look for St. Claire when I walk into class, but it's like my eyes are magnetized to him. He's reading a book again, his eyes never leaving the page.

Yesterday feels like a dream, gauzy around the edges. The details are there, but my mind is having a hard time putting them in my current reality. The one where Ash freaking St. Claire told me magic is real. Where I saw it pouring out of my fingertips. What if everything he told me is true?

I stare at my hands under the desk, but there's nothing unusual about them except the chipped glitter nail polish. But that's more Kat's annoyance than mine. She's always offering to repaint them.

Nothings happened sense, maybe it was one of those curses he was talking about.

I let out an indignant huff.

"Hey," I say, pitching my voice to the boy beside me.

He lifts his head up, his brow arched. "Yes?"

There's something about his tone that narrows my eyes.

"About yesterday—"

"There's nothing to discuss," he cuts me off, pitching his voice even lower, "I'm not the liaison to every wayward Siphon on the island."

The memory of all the times he was conveniently busy whenever Meredith told Adam to invite him along flashes through my thoughts in the split second I take to blink at him.

"I didn't ask you to be," I practically growl.

"Good, then we have an understanding," he says, leaning back.

I slap my notebook onto my desk as the bell rings.

If Ash freaking St. Claire wants to pretend that the conversation in the darkroom never happened, then so will I.

I don't know what it is I'm feeling but relief isn't it.

CHAPTER 4

I FEEL LIKE I'M being watched.
A lot.

I feel it when I'm forced to sit anywhere besides the back of the class, in a quiet store or when I'm in a crowd. That creeping warmth spreads through me, making my skin prickle, and has me turning my head to find that it's only my imagination.

The same icy tickle spreads over my scalp as I enter the park across from the school.

Dad says Venetian park reminds him of the old Florida before the hotels and condos and every strip of coast became covered in brick and asphalt. Hugh oak trees with tendrils of moss stand watch among the native palm trees. The grass is that dark green of August, with patches of white sandy soil scattered throughout. You can smell the salt in the air from the channel on the west side of the school. It mingles with the earthy scent of the freshwater lake in the park.

Egrets, with their long legs, wade along the bank patiently waiting for fish. Turtles sun themselves on a felled tree in the water. A Muscovy hen peeps to her row of ducklings on their way to fallen scraps around the picnic tables, and the round eyes of an alligator watch them all from the middle. Waiting.

There's a playground near the entrance where little kids, their chubby faces smiling, swing while their moms push and chat. A man walks his dog towards the dog park and a couple of cyclists slow as they turn off the bike path and into the parking lot. They stop at their car, unbuckling their helmets and taking swigs of their water.

None of them are watching me.

I turn onto the shortest trail towards my neighborhood. The soft noise of the playground fades; replaced by the rustle of animals and the quiet flutter of birds flitting back and forth in the treetops. I absorb the sounds of squirrels digging at the base of the trees and chasing each other around the tree trunks, trying to steal each other's finds, and the soft steady rhythm of my shoes on the pavement.

Afternoon light flits through the trees, casting shadows and dappled light on the ground. I pull out my cell phone and headphones. The melodic voice of a rock song cover my parents used to listen to fills the quiet. Music can sometimes distract me from my thoughts, or the intense feelings. I enjoy the serenity of my walks home from school. The music, the trees, and me.

I reach the crossroads where the bike trail intersects the hiking path. Big red signs warn you; Danger, look before crossing, with a little graphic of a walker getting annihilated by a speeding bike. I turn to make sure the path is clear and see someone behind me.

They're wearing dark jeans and an oversized black sweatshirt, the hood pulled over their heads casting their features in shadow. I'm sweating in my light blue uniform shirt and plaid skirt in this oppressive humidity. It's an odd choice for afternoon jogging in the park unless they want to get heatstroke. It's giving off serial killer vibes, especially with the murder a few weeks ago.

I see the dead girl's face. Not the graduation photo with the heart necklace that accompanied every news report, but the one in my nightmares where her eyes are picked clean by sea life. I pick up my pace.

There's nothing posted that you can't walk on the bike trail and it's the quickest path toward the back exit that backs my neighborhood. I tense when the creeper doesn't take the fork that leads to a smaller lake—very picturesque, with large willows sweeping the water, and a set of bathrooms—the dread rising in my gut.

Okay, breathe, *it's fine.* It's probably nothing. Just a coincidence they're dressed like a stalker.

When another trail comes up, even though it'll loop me around and I'll have to double back, I take it. My heartbeat ratchets up when they turn onto the same path.

It's not fine.

A summer breeze picks up in the trees, bending them one way and then another. Dead leaves travel along the ground, racing away from me. The air shifts like right before a storm, but when I glance up, the sky is sun-bleached blue.

Sweat glistens on my skin from the heat, and the uncanny feeling of fear. A clawing, choking feeling grips my throat and I try to breathe through it, but my skin burns. My vision wavers, like right before the world turned weird, and my hands glowed.

Not again.

I don't care how stupid I'll look, I spin around and shout, "Stop following me!"

They stop on the path looking like a modern grim reaper. Waiting. I expected a middle-aged man to push his hood back and ask what is wrong with me, that maybe it was someone from Shorecrest and we'd laugh about it later. None of those things happened.

I am not a strong runner, but when someone chases you, you run. My backpack bumps along my spine, and sweat drips down the side of my face, but I push my legs harder, wishing that I had taken Meredith up on her invites to go jogging.

I take the trails at random, forgetting which one's lead to bathrooms and hopefully people and which ones are taking me in a circle around the lake.

A frightened squirrel darts away from the base of a tree up ahead. I can feel the hairs rise on the back of my neck like fingers reaching out to grasp my backpack and pull me down. The humming in my blood gets stronger, my pulse is like an airplane engine, and there's this overwhelming sensation that something bad is going to happen.

I jerk a look behind me and scream. A hand grabs my backpack, pulling it from my shoulders.

My fingertips prickle first, and then the overwhelming sensation that my blood is on fire, but I don't stop running.

I collide with solid steel covered by smooth skin and fall backward hard, yelping from the surprise and pain of it all. I see a hand coming down; the voice muffled over the ringing in my ears.

My hands burn where they rest in the sandy soil. A tree cracks from somewhere in the bushes. The hairs on my arms are rising. I barely have time to yell, "No, don't touch me!"

That's when everything explodes.

I WAKE UP IN someone's bed.

A patch of sunlight shines on the soft gray-blue duvet cover beneath me. My throbbing head rests on a pillow that smells like lavender, salt water, and sunshine. I stretch my fingers out to the triangle of light. I remember the pain. It seared through my veins. A track of lava spread throughout my body. I remember screaming and I remember the light. I do not remember how I got into this bed.

I sit up experimentally, half expecting to feel dizzy, but everything stays where it should. It's cool in that artificial way that air conditioning does to a room, and it has that clean scent of clothes fresh out of the dryer. The furniture is really old or made to look like it. Complementary and sparse except for the bookcase in the corner. It's crammed full of books, both new and old, with a few titles

I recognize. There's a bathroom with bright white tile and a closet on the left side. The end tables beside the bed are empty except one holds a mercury glass lamp.

I carefully slide off the tall bed. The carpet is thick under my shoes as I softly step to the dresser where some personal artifacts rest in a fabric-lined tray. There are two expensive-looking watches and a charging place for a phone. My backpack is missing.

I press my ear to the door seam and listen, but all I hear is quiet. I turn the doorknob and quietly step through to another room. It looks like a living room with a plush leather couch in front of a flat-screen television mounted to the wall. A minimalist cabinet sits below it filled with game systems, speakers, and a collection of games.

The room is bright with sunshine coming through the wall of glass that makes up the right side of the room. Maybe I'm in a condo on South beach. I don't go onto the balcony, but I can still see plenty from where I stand by the glass. Below is a beautiful stone patio with steps leading to a lush green lawn, and another set that takes you to a crystal clear rectangle pool. At the edge of the backyard is a stone privacy wall and the ocean beyond. It has the spacious feel and decadence of the Western Crescent.

I scan the room for details, but it's void of identity. Even Meredith's well-kept room shows signs of the person who occupies it. Until I notice the closed laptop on the desk by the door. I walk towards it, my hand on the metal surface, when I hear footsteps coming down the hall outside.

I grab an industrial-looking sculpture off a shelf as the door opens. I swing, but a hand grabs my arm before I make contact.

"What the hell?" he asks, surprised.

I let Ash St. Claire take the statue from me and give him a hard shove, knocking him off balance. "What are you doing here? Were you following me in the park?"

"What the hell?" he repeats, taken aback. Quickly recovering, he says, "I freaking live here."

He places the statue back on the shelf with a moody glance in my direction. He's dressed in a tank top and running shorts, with one earbud still in his ear.

Seeing him out of the Shorecrest uniform temporarily unnerves me. The presence of so much tanned skin and the tight cut of his clothes has my stomach doing weird little flips. I turn back to the room once again to see if maybe I had missed some evidence that this place belongs to him and realize I don't really know much about the aloof boy with strange secrets to see any trace of him anywhere.

"Why have you kidnapped me?" I demand.

He shakes his head with a soft laugh more to himself. "I did not kidnap you," he says, leaning a hip against his desk and crossing his bare arms over his chest, accentuating his muscles. He nods towards the half-open door. "You can leave anytime."

"Then what am I doing here?"

"You fainted." His eyes narrow on my surprise. "When I went to help you up, boom, like touching a live wire." He pushes a hand through his hair. "I couldn't call the paramedics and risk you killing someone. And I don't know where you live, so I chanced your annoyance at waking up in my bedroom and brought you here." He cast another moody look my way. "Clearly, I should have left you in my car."

"Well, thanks for not leaving me."

Ash's lips flatten, his fingers tapping a rhythm on his arm to my heartbeat. He lifts off the desk, and I take a step backward. He absorbs my reaction before he reaches over the couch for my backpack.

"Oh. Where did you find it?"

"A few feet from where we collided."

I unzip the front pocket, pull out my phone and let out a small breath that the screen is still intact.

He watches me search my bag, digging through the pockets. "Looking for something specific?" he asks, with one brow arched knowingly.

The bag is empty of any cursed rocks. I remember the ground moving; the trees bending at odd angles. I feel foolish now that the threat of danger has passed. I slowly meet his heavy gaze.

"It happened again, like at school, but different," I say, wrapping a hand around my middle. "Someone was following me and I panicked. I think they were chasing me, they grabbed my bag—" I reach behind me as if I can still feel the straps pull from my shoulders, "then I ran into you."

I don't like the way he's looking at me, brows furrowed. I shake my head. "Maybe it was nothing."

"Did you see who it was?"

"They had a hood pulled up so I couldn't see their face."

"That explains why you electrocuted me," he muses, brows still pulled down in thought or doubt.

I give him a slow perusal, looking for injuries. "You look fine."

He grins, showing a dimple in his cheek and says, amused, "It's very difficult to hurt me."

I ignore the rising warmth to my cheeks and say, "I don't have time for your cryptic crap, St. Claire. You made it clear you're too busy to help me." I thrust out a hand toward him. "Why bring me here? You could have asked Adam where I lived?"

"Did you want me to tell your parents about what you can do?"

"Okay, point to you."

Ash sighs, pushing a hand quickly through his hair. "Echo, I'm sorry." He takes a half step toward me. "Understand where I'm coming from."

I straighten, but I still have to lift my chin to search his eyes. "And where is that?"

"My life is complicated," he says, his words just for me. "I try very hard not to bring others into it. I've already complicated Adams..."

My arms uncross with interest, waiting for him to elaborate, and when he doesn't, I ask, "Like how?"

"I know I brushed you off before, but—" I open my mouth but he rushes on, "I want to help you."

"How can you help me Ash, how?"

He turns his face away from me, closing himself off. I can see the version of him from school sliding back into place.

I'm prepared to leave when he says, "You asked me in the dark-room how I know so much about this." His eyes stay fixed on mine. "My family are... Protectors of humanity, called Domini. My father, his father before him, we uphold the Lar'iel. It's a kind of law—"

"What is that?"

"Like when Siphons—"

"No, stupid. What is a Domini?"

He blinks at me. "Oh." He reaches over and adjusts a statue that doesn't need adjusting. "The Domini keep Siphons from abusing their powers and hurting people."

"Like the magic police?" I smirk.

One side of his mouth twitches. "Like the Domini."

It sounds a lot like the magic police. "And that's what you are?" I ask tentatively.

"Something like it," he rubs the back of his neck, "or I will be someday." He stares out the glass windows behind me.

There's something tickling along my skin, fluttering in my stomach. Until a few days ago, the possibility of magic and glowing hands was fiction. What else is there lurking right before my eyes? I bite my lip before I ask, "Do you have powers like Siphons?"

Ash's attention shifts back to me. His fingers tap on the top of the statue, his expression conflicted, almost pained. Finally, he says, "No, but we are stronger and we eventually become... indestructible. Immortal." He lets the last word drop into the silence.

His running clothes show an awful lot of skin, broad shoulders, muscular arms, stronger than most boys at school, and an indent of his thigh muscle above his knee I've seen on some runners. Nothing screams indestructible, but he's definitely not fragile.

"You're immortal?"

"Not completely. Yet," he says. "The age of immortality varies among my kind, but the shift usually begins in our teens. We start by getting stronger, and our bodies can heal faster."

"How old are you?"

"Seventeen."

"Like a real seventeen or I stopped aging three hundred years ago and keep repeating high school kind of seventeen?"

Ash's brows lift, and his lashes flutter with incredulity. "Actually seventeen. Why would I go through high school again if I didn't have to?"

"Huh." I turn his words over in my head. "So..."

"So," he says. "If I were human and had touched you in the park, I'd probably be dead."

I blow out a surprised breath. If he was human. He'd be dead. I swallow all the implications down, and walk to the glass doors. The view is spectacular; a panoramic view of the emerald green ocean, sparkling with the early evening sun.

It's exactly what I would have thought St. Claire's backyard to be. The rest of him is not what I would have thought. Ash is full of surprises and mysteries, and I feel there are a few more hiding behind that pretty face.

Ash slowly walks up beside me. We watch the ocean in silence.

"You're sure I'm one of these Siphons?" I ask, holding on to the last thread of hope that this is something else.

"I do."

I keep my eyes on the sea when I ask, "Can I stop what's happening to me?"

There's a slight pause before he says, "No, but you can learn to control it. I'll help you."

We turn so we're facing each other. "I don't want to hurt anyone," I admit. I think about what he said earlier, and I weigh his words with the concern on his face. "You said there were Laws?"

He nods.

"What happens to a Siphon that hurts someone?"

"The sentence depends on the severity."

"What if they kill someone?"

"The punishment is death."

"What if it's an accident?"

I see his throat dip. "We need to make sure that doesn't happen."

There's a cold weight in my stomach that raises the skin on my arms. I rub them away. What am I getting myself into? I give a quick nod of understanding. "Why are you helping me now?"

Ash pulls out a set of keys from his pocket and twirls them around his finger before catching them in his palm. "You don't have anyone else who can help you, and things are escalating." I cross my arms over my chest and he frowns at them, turning towards the ocean. "Plus, you're Adam's friend."

I search the angles and curves of his face for a moment before I turn back to the spectacular view of the sea.

Ash stares at the keys in his hand, his thumb rubbing their teeth. "And I don't want you to get hurt."

"You don't want me to get hurt or you don't want me to hurt someone?"

"Both," he breathes, an admission.

I suck in a breath. "Okay," I say, letting it out and pushing down the sudden urge to cry. "So, where do we begin?"

ASH LEADS THE WAY down the hall into a brightly lit overpass that connects the main house to the garage.

"The library." He says, sliding his hands into his pockets. "My father has quite the collection."

"That's nice." I give him a puzzled look, and he chuckles to himself, probably at how weird he's acting.

"What I mean is, we can start there, go through what we have on Siphons, figure out what's happening to you."

I rake my teeth over my bottom lip. "At your house?"

He nods, a little uncertainly. "I can't lend them out, security reasons—"

I hold up my hand. "I get it, it's just—I can't believe this is happening. It feels surreal."

"I know this is a lot." He flicks on the stairwell lights before we enter, giving a nod that I should follow. "It's just this way."

As we descend the steps, the garage lights flicker to life on their own, revealing a large room full of neatly parked cars in their respectable bays. Ash strides towards the black classic car he drives to school, unlocking the passenger door. The word Chevelle shines in silver along the side.

Inside smells like leather, the ocean and a hint of oranges. Ash's expression is neutral, civil as he takes his place behind the wheel. My stomach flutters with familiarity.

"Wait, you carried me up to your room?"

"Yes." He presses a button and the garage door slides open.

"Your parents weren't suspicious of you carrying a body upstairs?"

"My parents weren't home." He starts the car, the engine rumbles to life, a beast awoken from sleep.

"That's still weird."

He gives me a pointed look as he smoothly shifts into reverse. He elegantly backs out of the garage and onto the main driveway, heading towards the road. The iron front gates slide back into the privacy wall before we've even reached them. Ash slows, checking for cars before pulling onto the cobblestone roads.

Ash lives on a crescent-shaped piece of land off the main island called the Western Crescent. This part of the island is painted with meaning and elegance. You can see it in the quaint brick roads uneven with age and too much character to replace, in the deliberately constructed parks with filigree iron benches, dripping with exotic plants, their flowers a performance of their own.

Most of the homes we pass are Renaissance and Roman-inspired with a few Mediterraneans thrown in. Tall queen-ann palms stand sentry in the manicured yards on extra large lots that either back the intracoastal or the ocean. Every other house has a stone wall and iron gates like the St. Claire's.

Ash's fingers tap nervously on the gearshift as we wait at the four-way right past the small bridge that connects the W.C. from the island. The only conversation is when I give directions to my house. He turns off Evergreen into my little neighborhood a few blocks from the bridge. I don't live far from him, not really. I could probably ride my bike to his house in fifteen minutes. Not that I would.

Ash pulls into the empty driveway. My parents should be home any minute and there will probably be a conversation about why I'm sitting in a boy's car. In fact, I can think of two other people who would like to have a conversation about why I'm sitting in this particular boy's car.

I'm not sure how I would explain it to my friends. I can hear Kat's inquisitive tone in my thoughts, pushing me for answers. *He doesn't just give people rides home; he doesn't even talk to anyone. What's going on Echo? Do you like him now or something?*

Their suspicion and inevitable hurt when I don't give them answers that make sense. The right ones, anyway. No story seems believable. I can hear their voices clearly in my head. It hasn't even happened, and I already feel the assault of questions and answers I can't provide. Denying anything is saying something, and I can't produce the truth.

Even if they can get past the really hard-to-believe bits, a part of this story isn't even mine to tell.

St. Claire keeps the car idling but shifts towards me as if he wants to say something. The cool air from the vents raises goosebumps on my bare legs. I fidget with the hem of my shirt as I blurt, "Let's not tell anyone about this."

His brows lift but he nods in agreement, "Of course. And you won't tell anyone about me?"

"I'm pretty sure everyone at school already knows you exist."

"I mean about—"

"I know what you meant." I flash a grin. Who would believe me about the immortal thing? "And yeah, this," I motion between us, "is going to raise a lot of questions that I can't answer. I don't need to add any more complications to my life. So we can't tell anyone we're hanging out, okay?"

Ash shifts. "We can tell them we're studying. For school." He says it as if it's so easy.

I scrunch up my eyes. "No, no, no, there is no just studying. Trust me, okay, you attract a lot of attention." I roll my shoulders. "And I don't like that kind of attention." I shudder, thinking about not only my friends' reactions and questions, wanting me to introduce them, asking Ash to sit with us, and the tense conversations as they probe him for details of our friendship but all the extra eyes on me at school. No, no, nope.

Ash shrugs. "Whatever you say. I'll pretend I don't know you."

"Well, don't be stupid. We have class together." I point at him, "but don't tell anyone I was at your house, or that you gave me a ride home. Ever." I gesture to his obvious metaphor of a vehicle. "Or that I'm coming over—keep it to school stuff."

I grab my backpack off the floor and open the heavy car door, but turn back to say, "And let's keep our distance at school, in case anyone gets the wrong idea."

A smile slowly teases up one side of his mouth. "Okay," he drawls.

"Okay. See you tomorrow." I quickly close the door and hurry up the front steps, rushing into the house before my legs wobble. I lean back against the front door and let out a long breath. What have I agreed to?

CHAPTER 5

I WASN'T IN A hurry to return to the place where I was being followed the day before, but it was the easiest meeting place.

Ash's black car sits sleeping under an enormous oak tree in the back corner of the parking lot near the dog park. There are only a few people from school who take the shortcut through the park, and they wouldn't have a reason to be all the way over here.

I take in a deep breath and walk towards his car, looking over my shoulder the whole way. His tan arm hangs out the driver's side window and the sight of it causes my stomach to clench with the reality of what I've agreed to.

I take in a deep breath before I open the passenger side door and toss my backpack into the backseat.

Ash's eyes slowly lift with the laziness of a balmy afternoon. "I could have picked you up." At my narrowed eyes, he adds, with a hint of exasperation, "A few streets from the school, or whatever."

"It's fine."

He turns his frown towards his windshield, squinting at the sun. "Do your parents know you're coming over?"

I laugh. "I told them we were going to study. Don't worry, you're not kidnapping me." I give him a look that has him shift in his seat.

"You're not worried it'll get back to your friends?"

"My mom's cool. She won't say anything."

Ash taps on the gearshift before he starts the car. Sweat drips down my back and I turn the air vents to my face to take some of the flush off me. He takes Hawthorne driving past the school. I slide down in my seat; the seatbelt digging into my neck. He glances at me out of the corner of his eye. I fidget with my ponytail as the silence stretches.

He arches a brow as he stares down at me. "My windows are tinted. No one's going to see you."

I slowly slide back up as the car moves forward. "Hopefully." Ash's hands tighten on the steering wheel, his stare too intense on the stoplight. "What?"

"Nothing," he says.

"You're giving me judgy-eyes."

"I am not."

Ash's brows are a little too broody towards the road as we get moving again. I give him a dramatic *I-told-you-so* look, and he says, "It's… I've never had someone so embarrassed to be seen with me."

I sigh and pick at the skin around my nails. "You don't know what it's like. Us suddenly hanging out," I make a gesture to imply the entire island, "people will talk, they'll make up their own conclusions."

His hand moves to the gearshift. It's a natural, graceful act. "What conclusions are you worried about? That we're friends?"

I give him an incredulous glare. "You only just started hanging out with Adam, like what, end of freshman year?"

"Sure."

"You don't have friends."

He coughs out a laugh. "I'm glad you think I'm so endearing."

His tone is light, but guilt washes over me. I think about what Adam said about me being too hard on him. "Sorry, I'm not trying to be mean."

"I know." He gives me a sly smile. We slow to another stop and he looks over at me, one hand on the steering wheel and the other lightly on the gearshift. "Kind of."

"What I mean," I say slowly, "is to everyone else, you seem to be an enigma, selective, and if we start suddenly hanging out..."

Ash looks over and when I don't answer, he prompts, "And...?"

I point the vents to my face as if the summer heat is the reason my cheeks are so warm. "They'll think we're involved in some capacity."

He stops at the four-way before the bridge. There are no other cars, but he lingers a little longer than needed before turning. My fingers knead my palm, waiting.

"So, tell them we're not."

I slide my gaze toward him. "You know what high school is like, right? What life is like? When I told my parents I was studying with you, they immediately asked if this was a date." I blow air over my lips. "I hate all the defending, all the attention, all the teasing. Which is what will happen if I tell my friends about you, if we talk at school, and for God's sake, if I'm seen in your car."

He runs a thumb over his bottom lip, the rhythmic sound of the car's blinker almost deafening. "I can understand not wanting the extra scrutiny," he says at last. "Would it be easier with Adam?"

"No!" I blurt, causing his brows to shoot up. "That could be disastrous."

He nods in understanding, turning onto the Beaumont bridge, one of the two that connects the Western Crescent to the rest of the island. The car dips as we hit the cobblestones of the W. C., the rhythm of the tires changing.

I knead my palm as I say, "People will think what they want. That's how rumors get started."

"I suppose."

He looks over at me with a neutral expression, but I can tell from the look in his eyes he's assessing me again. I hold his gaze until he's forced back to the road.

Ash's fingers drum his steering wheel as we stop at a four-way next to a park I am well familiar with from all the times I've gone to Meredith's. Magenta begonias smother the red brick arches on all four entrances. Black iron and honeyed wood benches surround a small playground in its center.

Before we turn, I hook my finger to the right. "Meredith lives that way."

"Northwest beach? I run there on the weekend sometimes."

"Oh?" A smile tugs at my lips, remembering all the giddy whispers when Meredith and Kat gossiped about her St. Claire sightings.

Ash heads south, where the mansions get bigger if that's possible. Between the grand houses, flashes the intracoastal on our left and the blue-green ocean on our right. We follow the curve until Ash is pulling into his light stone driveway. The gate is still sliding away as we slink through. I didn't really absorb the size of his house the only other time I was here. It's a magnificent sight of white stone and ornate windows, framed by dark gray roof tiles. Something that belongs in the English countryside than on a tropical island.

Ash veers towards the two-story garage instead of taking the circle around the front of the house, with the fountain cascading water down into the shallow basin. The garage bay door slides close behind us.

I follow close behind St. Claire as we travel up the garage staircase to the overpass. The afternoon light burns through the windows, casting harsh shadows on the tile floor. I feel different since the park; like a chasm has opened up behind my breastbone. Things would be easier if this was some short-lived curse, as weird as that sounded. What if Ash hadn't been the one to find me? What if what we're doing isn't enough, and I do hurt someone, someone I care about?

My body hums like a plucked bowstring the closer I get to really doing this. Facing what this all means. The overwhelming sense of Deja Vue and dread slow my footsteps. I remind myself that I *have* been here before, but last time I was walking away. Now I'm walking towards something that feels terrifying, and still very much unbelievable.

The weird buzzing in my veins feels like an alarm. A voice whispers, *"Turn back,"* but when I look around, it's only Ash and me in the overpass.

I press my hands to my temples. "Did you hear that?"

St. Claire glances back at me, his brows pulling down in concern. The walls narrow, the windows coming towards me. The overpass darkens. I shake my head. Not now. Not now. Not now. I grab the windowsill, taking in small breaths.

Ash's eyes widen in alarm. "Tell me what you need me to do?"

"I don't know." Everything is always fine until it's not. Things become too much. Too loud, too bright, too scratchy, too much information, too many thoughts.

I can feel it coming like a storm. Purple, angry clouds on the horizon. If I knew how to control the panic attacks, life for me and everyone else would be easier. The edges of my vision darken like static, and my heart feels like it's going to explode. I look down at my hands, my fingertips turning bright. I feel my legs buckle under me.

"Breathe, Echo, Breath." Ash's voice reverberates in my head. I open my eyes to find he's crouched in front of me, his face only a few inches from mine. I shake my head. Breathing doesn't help. "Hey, look at me," he says gently.

A burning sensation rushes through my veins. I can feel the heat coming off my fingers. It's happening again and I can't stop it. I squeeze my eyes shut.

"When I was ten, I jumped off the garage roof." I tilt my head up to see his throat move. "My father had finished lecturing me about how I would start training next summer, our legacy, and my future as a Dominus. I told him I wasn't ready, but he was insistent that I had already begun the shift. So, I jumped off the roof to prove a point."

We watch each other before I ask, "And did you?"

"I broke my leg in three places. I had to wear a cast. My mother was furious." His small smile dims, as his eyes drift off, caught in the memory. "My bones healed a week later, and I started training a summer early."

I wonder what kind of child St. Claire was to think jumping off a roof was the best course of rebellion. Instead of offering him pity, I ask, "What do you train for?"

"Everything, anything. Domini train in all disciplines, all fighting styles." He shrugs. "I'm supposed to practice every day."

"And do you?"

Another shrug.

I lean against the wall and add that piece together with the rest of the details he's shared about his unique existence. I let out a long breath. The fire has crawled back to whatever place it comes from, and the tension is slowly dissipating from my chest.

"Thank you."

Ash pushes a hand through his sun-bright hair. "For what?"

I roll my eyes and he gives me that award-winning grin as he stands. He reaches down to help me up, but I shake my head.

"It's okay, Echo, you can't hurt me."

"Not at all?" I ask, pushing off the floor.

Ash sticks his hand in his pocket, tilting his head as he meets my eyes. "Not physically."

A different type of electric current rushes through me, tingling all the way to my toes. I give him a questioning look before I can stop it.

His brows raise. "Okay. It hurt a little when you electrocuted me," he says with a lopsided grin.

I know he was trying to lighten the mood, but it reminds me why we're here. I clench my hands into fists as I ask, "So how's a bunch of ancient books going to help me, anyway?"

The corner of his mouth lifts. Another private joke. "We're quite the historians." His grin quickly flashes. "I'm sure there's something in these old books that can help you."

"Don't you know how to do that already, since that's kind of your thing?"

He pauses long enough that I think I might have said something offensive. "We're more about stopping it than bringing it out."

"Oh."

He gives me a tight smile before he asks, "Are you sure you still want to continue?"

I give a quick, certain nod.

Ash gives me the highlights as we descend further along the brightly lit hallways of the second floor, pointing out guest rooms and bathrooms and a small staircase that leads directly to the kitchen. I get a glimpse of the first floor as we pass a landing with twin staircases leading down to the stone foyer and the massive, aged wood front door.

The light from the floor-to-ceiling windows on either side of the door hit the crystal chandelier in the center of the room, casting rainbows that even reach the walls of the landing. It's like something out of a fairy tale.

We continue down the hall, making a right down a short hallway, stopping at a set of double doors. They look like the rest of the doors of the house—thick wood carved with flowers and filigree—but there's something off about them.

Ash's eyes flicker to mine, but I can't read his expression. He presses his thumb on a black square above a keypad. I turn around as he enters a code and turn back when I hear the door make a sound like it's sliding a bolt through the wall. It clicks. The light on the keypad now green.

"Top security for a library?"

He says, looking a little embarrassed, "Better than having to keep guards at the doors."

Ash flicks a light switch as he enters, illuminating the library beyond. I follow him into what appears to be the second-story entrance. Tall bookcases face us on either side, with scones illuminating the books within.

I walk to the railing, surveying the space below. The centerpiece is a brick fireplace framed with diffused glass windows stretching up to the ceiling. A collection of leather chairs and a matching couch circle a long coffee table with a small stack of books on one end. Floor-to-ceiling bookcases with ladders attached to metal railings border the room below, similar to what's up here, but triple the amount.

I make a low whistling sound and Ash shrugs his shoulders. "It's easy to accumulate when you're around for a while."

He motions for me to follow him down the staircase into the main room below. I try to soak in every detail. I skim my fingertips along the book titles, and then the soft wood of the banister. There are even more rooms branching off from the main one. It's impossible not to feel awestruck coming down the stairs into such an impressive space.

"So, does this hold all your Domini knowledge?"

"No, only a fraction," he says coyly. "Except for a few personal libraries like this, most of our archives are held in the Selah Libre." When I give him a raised eyebrow, he adds, "It means Library of Truth."

I assess the enormous library with fresh eyes. Only a fraction, huh? I drop my bag where I stand and wander over to the nearest bookcase, my fingers running over their tops, my eyes skimming titles. Some of them catch the lights overhead, some of them familiar, most of them not. I move around the stairs as my eyes snag on titles in a language I've never seen before. I pull one out, my eyes roam over the loopy and jagged scrawl.

"What language is this?" I call out.

St. Claire comes up beside me. I can feel his breath tickle my skin, raising little goosebumps, as he leans over to inspect the book in my hand. He's wearing the school uniform, but he's removed his jacket and tie since I've last seen him at school. He fiddles with the first couple of buttons he's undone.

"Seraph," he says, pulling back. "That's what we're called—what I am."

"Angels?" I squeak in surprise.

"We're not like the biblical or romanticized angels, no," he says, putting his hands in his pockets.

I snort and he looks at me quizzically. "That's funny to me," I say. At his genuine curiosity I continue, "You're immortal and beautiful. Why wouldn't you be called an angel?" As soon as the words leave my mouth, his brows lift and his head tilts to the side. Heat rushes to my face and I clear my throat. "What I mean is, your species are called angels." I avoid looking at him and stuff the book back in place, hoping he didn't notice I called him beautiful.

"No one thinks of us as angels," he says flatly.

"Right, okay." I take a few steps away, pretending to search the titles.

"I was thinking we'd start with some Siphon journals." He scans the bindings until he lands on what he's looking for, pulling it out and tucking it under his arm.

"Why do you have Siphon journals?"

"Well," he says almost sheepishly, "part of Seraph law is to protect our secrecy, that includes the knowledge of Siphons. The Domini confiscate anything that would compromise that."

"So what are you, Domini or Seraphs?"

"Both." He pulls another book from the shelf and sticks it under his other arm. "Like how you're human, but can also be a doctor, mechanic, artist, or whatever."

"Are you saying that Dominus is your profession?"

His eyes narrow on the slim binding of a well-weathered book, the title barely legible in that loopy writing. "More like a calling." He takes the book out, and tightly flips through the pages, taking care not to drop the books under his arms.

I grab the one closest to me, sliding it out from under his arm. He gives me a thankful look. I reach for the other one, and he turns, putting us inches apart. I quickly grab the book, shifting back. His eyes hang on me for a second before going back to the journal.

I clear my throat and ask, "Are all Seraph's Domini?"

"No." He closes the book and tucks it back onto the shelf. He moves around the bookcases, his eyes purposely searching for something. The titles here are a mix of Seraph and other languages.

"Do you get to choose?"

"Yes," he says as he pulls out two more books.

He tucks them under his arm, trying to keep them in place and also keep his hands free. I make a sound and he passes them into my waiting hands. I tuck my chin on top to keep them from falling.

I watch him as his eyes scan the bindings, occasionally pulling one out and reading a few pages before putting it back in. His blond brows pulled down in concentration. And I think of how bizarre it is that I find myself in St. Claire's mansion, perusing through his library. I feel a small sense of smugness that I'm here when many girls would kill to be—Kat one of them—and then instantly feel ashamed of it. The thought of keeping this grand secret from them sobers me up and I look away, but I find my eyes keep gravitating towards his.

Ash quickly looks over at me out of the corner of his eye, not for the first time, before moving back to his search once again.

"Does this make you uncomfortable?"

He straightens up, hitting a light attached to a bookcase. It makes a ringing sort of thud. He rubs the spot on the side of his head as he says, "Does what?"

"Talking about all this?"

"Ah." He seems relieved. "No. I just... don't do this." He gestures between us.

"Hang out with girls?" I ask with a sly smile.

He rolls his eyes and gives me a rueful grin. "Talk about my real life to..." he looks back at the books, concentrating a little too hard on the bindings, "to anyone."

"Except Adam?"

He nods, tucking his bottom lip under his teeth.

"I think it's fascinating," I sigh, tipping my chin towards the bookcase beside us.

Ash chews on his lip a second longer before he says, "Come over here."

He takes the stack of books from me and I follow him into a side room with bookcases end-capped in glass display cases. Ash sets the books down on a nearby table as I peek inside the metal case closest to us. Inside is a leather-bound book with designs embossed into the cover, a small dagger with a white handle, and an old necklace with the same design as on the cover of the book.

"Seraphim artifacts," he says, nodding towards the case, "there are a few of them peppered around the room."

"But what is it?"

Ash rests his hand next to mine on the metal frame. "It's a spell book to control an immortal army."

"Really?"

His mouth lifts. "No, not really. That was stolen." He's grinning now and I shake my head at him.

"You're funny," I say dryly.

"It's a collection of poems."

I flick my hand, unimpressed. "And here I thought you actually had something interesting in these cases."

Ash puts a hand on his chest. "That book is over two thousand years old," he says, heading past the cases to the corner of the room.

"Books are boring," I say, stopping beside him.

He glances at me from the corner of his eye. "I've seen you do some pleasure reading at school." He says it casually, but his eyes narrow on the bookcase in front of him.

"Yes, but those were entertaining." I gesture around us. "This feels like homework."

He hums low in his throat as he plucks a book from a shelf above my head. He smells like the ocean. It's darker back here and I can't see the title. I look up at him expectantly. Waiting.

Ash's eyes flick away from my face as he hands me the book. "You might like this," he says. "It's written in Seraph, but it's illustrated."

"Thanks." I take the book from his hands. It's bordered in an interweaving pattern stamped into the soft leather, the gilded title a Seraph word I can't read.

"The genesis of Seraphim," he tells me, voice soft.

I tear my eyes from his and land on a set of locked bookcases with diamond-paned glass doors veined with something that looks metallic. I run my fingers down the glass to feel the texture. It's smooth, and surprisingly warm.

"What's in here?"

"Cursed books."

I jerk my hand away, not sure if he's joking again. He soberly nods towards the cases, taking a step towards them. I'm acutely aware of how close he is. Like I am with anyone, I remind myself.

"The bookcases are weaved with special metals that trap the energy inside." He gestures to the room. "Most of the books in here are harmless, but there's a few that are dangerous in the wrong hands."

"Has anyone ever gotten one of your secret books?" If they're immortal like he says, how could they have kept their secret all these years?

"Some of our books have found their way into human hands, but we get them back, eventually."

Ash grabs the stack of books off the table as we make our way back to the couches. I study the security pad of the main library door as we pass. What else do the St. Claire's have to hide?

I plop down on the soft leather couch and ask, "Are there other high-security rooms?"

"The training room," he says, taking a seat next to me. He divides the stack of books into two piles. At my pointed look, he adds, "Immortality doesn't come without a cost. There's a certain amount of... energy that needs to be burned off. Exercise helps."

He holds out his hand for The Genesis of Seraphim and I pass him the heavy book. He carefully skims past some pages in the beginning. Mostly tightly packed Seraph writing until he lands on a colored illustration that reminds me of ancient paintings. There's a decorative frame around the page that catches the light as he shifts, holding it so I can see it better.

"What are you training for if you're unbreakable?"

His fingers drum on his thigh. "Our bodies heal from injuries, but we can be overpowered. Caged, tortured, or trapped for eternity."

I grimace, and he gives me a sympathetic look. "By Siphons?"

Ash flips through the pages and back again before he answers. "Mostly," he admits. "Seraphim and Siphons will always have a complicated relationship," he brushes his fingers through his hair, "people who enjoy doing evil don't want to stop."

I frown down at the coffee table covered in books. "And you think that's all Siphons?" I ask quietly.

"No," he says confidently. "No I—" he stops, recomposes his words, "the Domini were created to stop Siphons' who abuse the gift of Light. Only the ones who enjoy causing havoc and hurting people."

My shoulders slump inward. The way he talks about Siphons, it's like they're all bad, but if that was true, why is he helping me? "And you think there's a way to teach me how to control this, Light or whatever it is, in these books?"

"Yes," he says and angles the book towards me. "I thought we'd start with the beginning."

The illustration shows people in a primitive-looking village. Circular houses with walls of what looks like clay and straw, thatched roofs, some with smoke coming out of little chimneys. The people all have little glowing balls of light where their hearts should be. Some glow large enough that it surrounds them like an aura.

"Siphon abilities are as unique as human talents," Ash says, pointing to the different Siphons. "Some are better at manipulating their affinity than others." He flips the pages in the book to a scene where three Siphons sit in elaborate thrones on a dais, their Light the brightest.

"But you said they weren't powerful?"

"They're not anymore, not like they were." He turns the page as he says, "Thousands of years ago, they were cursed by one of their own, called Genevieve. A war had begun between the Siphons and humans. We call it Sul'Dae Kehda, it means devastating war."

"What started the war?"

"What starts most of them? Power, either a lack of or a desire for more."

I absorb the scene of Siphons battling Siphons, powers of different types swirling on the page. Storms, rain, great waves crashed upon houses, roots bursting from the ground to tangle around legs and throats, and beasts conjured from fire and stone to attack Siphon and people alike.

I touch my fingertips to an image of people with no lights running for their lives, only to be cut down by whips of starlight conjured from the hands of a Siphon, its heart glowing with light. Pages and pages of death. Humans didn't stand a chance against the supernatural power of Siphons.

"Why are there no other records of this?" I ask, my stomach turning sour.

"Written accounts outside of libraries like ours are rare. And any verbal history became more and more distorted and less believable through time until it morphed into some of the famous folklore we know of today."

"Where does your kind fit into all this?" I ask, afraid of what the answer will be.

Ash flips the pages as he says, "Even before the curse, there were Siphons who were more powerful than others. They call them Principalities. They usually become their leaders, even now. Genevieve was arguably the most powerful Siphon, and she fought against the coming war." He flips to a page with a young woman, with a halo around her head. She drops balls of Light, and where they fall shapes form. "She created us," he says with a sort of reverence.

"Created you?" I breathe the words.

He searches my face before his eyes drop to the book. The page shows the shapes formed into angelic-looking men and women in gold armor, some sort of star-burst crest surrounded by wings on their breastplates and shields, swords raised as they charge into battle. I give him a knowing look.

He clears his throat, the tips of his ears looking a little pink. "She called us Seraph, the Dominus of the Light."

"And you won the war?"

"Not exactly." He sadly gazes at the next page. "Back then, the Siphons outnumbered us. Genevieve could only create so many of us before it killed her." He sighs, shaking his head. "Remember when I said there were other ways to hurt us?"

A new page shows gold armor soldiers pulled tight by ropes, their arms cut off, tied to stakes, or set on fire, locked in cages, and dumped into the ocean. I press my fingers to my lips.

"Genevieve knew they wouldn't stop, so she used all the glorious Light in her, that powerful energy, to curse every Siphon and every Siphon born after from ever accessing the full power of the Light ever again."

The next page shows the young girl rising into the sky, her light getting bigger. The page opposite illustrates her floating high above everything, that searing Light casting down on all the Siphons below.

"She saved the world."

I can feel the emotion in his voice. My hand twitches to hold his, but the feeling of ice sliding down my back jolts me out of the impulse. I curl my fingers into a soft fist and shift away from him. Ash doesn't seem to notice my self-imposed turmoil as he flips to the next page. The girl, Genevieve, is lying on the ground circled by seven Seraphs, their armor more regal than the ones shown before.

"The first Dominus, her loyal Guard." His finger taps a Seraph on the page. "My grandfather," he says, moving his hand away.

I study the detailed illustration. The knightly Seraphim have their helmets in their hands, each of them different skin colors with their swords resting at their feet, each pommel different, but I'm focused on the one with bright blond hair. Ash's grandfather.

I raise my brows and log that one away. "What happened after she died?"

"The Siphons were no match for the Seraphim." He flips the page. All the Siphons wear shackles of light. The Seraphim in their shining gold armor stand proudly over them. I swallow. "It's a little embellished," he says apologetically.

"Are all your books so cheery?" I ask, only half serious.

He makes a gruff sound. "I think there's an illustrated copy of the bubonic plague around here somewhere."

I grimace, shaking my head. Ash offers me the Genesis of Seraphim and I take it politely but exchange it for another book from the pile he's made of English titles. I've had enough of the brutal illustrations for now. The images of Siphons torturing Seraphs and humans cause an unsettled feeling in my stomach I can't shake away. I shift, tucking my ankle up under me on the couch and resting the small journal on my uniform skirt.

"Do you think a Siphon killed the girl they found on the beach?"

He drapes his arm on the back of the couch as he turns to face me, bringing his thigh to press into my shin. His right hand taps the open book on his lap.

"Unlikely, but my father looked into it."

I wrinkle my nose. "Do Domini investigate regular human murders?"

"No," he says almost sadly, "they stick to Seraph or Siphon business only."

"Oh. That's a shame. With all your talents and longevity, you could do a lot of good."

Ash taps the back of the couch considering me, "There's a few Seraphim that think that too."

"And you?"

He pulls in a deep breath. "I don't know what I think," he says and sighs, his fingers brushing his hair off his forehead. It's gotten a little floppy from all the times he's run his hands through it. "The council believes it's not our place to meddle in the human world. We're created to protect humans, but nowhere in our laws does it say to protect humans from each other."

"So, if you witness a crime, you do nothing?"

"No, of course not, but it's complicated," he says and when I look at him to explain he gives me a small laugh, "the council has been alive for thousands of years, I can't even imagine what that kind of wisdom looks like."

"If you say so." I lift my shoulder as I keep my eyes fixed on his.

"Historically, humans don't do well with things that are different from them. Can you imagine what it would be like if the human world found out that immortals existed? What they would want to do to us? It could start a war and they wouldn't win."

I weigh his words along with the images in his book, and with what I know of human history. "Okay, maybe you're right."

"It's not just us. The Siphons don't meddle in human politics either."

"So we don't have to worry about being enslaved by immortal knights," I tease, but dread blooms in my gut.

"No, it's forbidden," he says, bending his head down to read.

"What else is forbidden?" I ask, remembering his tone when he talks about his Laws.

Ash's eyes flick up to mine and then quickly back to his book. "Only a few things," he mumbles. He gestures with his chin to the book in my lap, his eyes not leaving the page. "That book should be in English."

I pick up the Siphon journal and feel the smooth leather, where it's worn in places like it was well-loved. The ink bleeds together, making parts unreadable, but most is legible. I skim page after page about mundane chores and how they use the Light in small ways. But nothing about how to control the Light from randomly manifesting.

I trade one journal for another, but I find I'm mostly skimming now. I know I should be more interested in reading about Siphons, but the mundane details of their lives bores me. My gaze wanders to St. Claire's relaxed hand on his thigh, to the surrounding books and how impossible this will be if we have to get through an entire library of dusty old books.

Ash's arm bumps into my bare knee as he turns the page, alerting me to how close we're sitting. I quickly shift over into a more normal position, rubbing away the sleepiness I feel wants to overtake me.

"Find anything?" he asks, his voice practiced and cool.

I drop my eyes quickly to the journal, where my finger rests next to where the author mentions being excited to learn about her affinity.

"What are affinities, exactly?"

Ash drapes his arm on the back of the couch, his watch loose on his wrist. "The Light is a power source, and Siphons are a conduit for that energy. They draw their power from the Light, but what that power will manifest into depends on what we now know are their genetics. Their specific affinity is based on one of the four elements."

He moves his body towards me, getting more confident with the topic. I grab my leg, pulling it closer to me. "Does that make sense?" he asks.

"Yes," I say. "So can a Siphon have more than one affinity?"

Ash licks his lips, his fingers worrying the edge of the book in his lap. "Before the curse, it was possible, rare, but possible."

I stare down at the journal in my lap. "So glowing hands would be?"

"Fire, most likely."

I swallow, his tone prickles the skin along my arms. "Is that bad?"

"No." He shakes his head. "Each affinity has its own challenges to control."

I give him a weak smile in return, turning back to the journal, hoping that some long-dead girl can give me insight into what I am becoming.

Ash hasn't moved. The warmth radiating from him is a soothing sort of comfort as we read in companionable silence. My lids grow heavy and I stifle a yawn.

Ash's thigh presses into me, as he says, "Siphon abilities are instinctual, like blinking or breathing, or defensive...." He taps a finger where he holds the book. His focus shifts to me. "At school, it came out when Charity threatened you, and then later in the park when you were scared, and earlier when you had a panic attack."

"But I've had panic attacks before. Why is it happening now?"

"I'm not sure," he says slowly, trying to piece it all together. He plays with his bottom lip. I'm not even sure he knows he's doing it.

Ash closes his book with a satisfying sound. He stands up with a stretch, his blue eyes bright on me as he says, "Let's get some fresh air."

ASH PUSHES A SET of doors open on the ground floor with practiced ease as we enter what looks like an elaborate mudroom off the kitchen.

The built-in shelves hold plush towels and toiletries. Next to it is a private shower and across from it is a large basin sink with a brass towel bar almost as long as the wall. The floor is tiled in tiny white and blue mosaics with a drain in the center.

"Where are we going?"

"Somewhere a little less flammable," he says, giving me a lopsided smile. "I thought you might want to try controlling the Light. It's fairly private here, so no one will see you, and I have the resources if something went wrong."

I halt in the door frame. "Do you think that's necessary?"

He shrugs. "Probably not, but I don't want to get grounded for a hundred years for burning down the library."

"No, I mean, the practicing?" I knead my thumb into my palm. "Most of the time I'd like to pretend it never happened."

Ash takes a step closer to me. "I understand your apprehension," he says, putting his hands in his pockets. "But learning to master your new power will help keep everyone safe, keep you safe from anyone finding out what you are."

"Shouldn't I find another Siphon to help me?"

Ash's brows pull down in thought. He weighs things over before he says, "It wouldn't be safe to reach out to some unknown Siphon for help. There's a lot of them you can't trust." He spins a ring on his thumb as he says, "And what if you had another episode like at the park? Someone could get hurt."

The thought of meeting a Siphon gives me a strange little stir of excitement. Like the anticipation right before the rollercoaster drops but if they're as bad as he says, I'm not sure I'm ready for the dark side of what they are. What I am. There's a lot to learn about St. Claire, but I don't know who else can help me. It's not like I know any Siphons to go to for help, anyway.

I let out a breath and nod for him to lead the way.

I step onto the patio and raise my hand to shield my eyes from the blinding sun, giving them time to adjust. Large clay pots filled with ponytail palms, hibiscus, and miniature citrus trees decorate the large stone patio. I follow Ash down a set of steps to a flagstone path leading to a workshop made of the same stone as the house.

The sun beats down on my head and sweat beads on my hairline as he pulls open the large doors, letting the ocean breeze chase away the earthy air inside. There's a workbench on one side and a peg board filled with tools. The rafters hold pieces of wood and the corners are thick with webs. The cement floor is cracked from the sandy earth settling, and remnants of paint and spilled oil mar the floor. It's the first time I've seen anything less than immaculate about Ash's house. There's a lingering smell of oil, gasoline, metal tools, and wood that puts me strangely at ease. Reminding me of our own garage and all the summers helping my parents with their newest project.

Ash dusts off a stool and sets it down for me, grabbing a bucket and turning it upside down for himself.

"You sure you don't want to experiment in the air conditioning?" I tease.

His mouth lifts in a half smile. "My father would kill me."

"Is he here?" I ask, fingering the edge of my skirt, my knee bouncing with nerves. My face warms as he arches a brow. "I wasn't sure if this was allowed?" I quickly go on, "it doesn't sound like you guys like Siphons that much."

"It's not that we don't like them." Ash brushes his fingers through his hair. "Siphons are dangerous, Echo," he says gently. "They have done some terrible things in the world. Much more than what you saw on those pages. That's the reason we exist; to protect humanity. It makes us cautious, with good reason."

I stare at my fingers worrying my uniform skirt. I hear him take in a deep breath and let it out before he asks, "Aren't you worried about what could happen if you can't control this?"

"Yes, of course, I am," I say in a rush, remembering how I didn't even mean to, and I electrocuted him. It's always on my mind how unpredictable this thing is inside me. I motion to our surroundings. "That's why I'm here."

He gives a quick nod. "Right, so let's begin."

I listen to him walk me through connecting to the Light. It's like a muscle, as easy as closing my hand around a door handle. Ash has a pleasant voice. It lulls me into a more relaxed state, but I don't feel this pull that he speaks of. If I was born into a Siphon family, they would have prepared me for the day I felt the pull and how to call it into me, a ready vessel. The Light would become a part of me, like another extension of my body, but as a Quiescent, a latent Siphon, it's not as fluid. I can feel my body rejecting it as much as it wants to accept it.

"Feel anything yet?"

Sweat slides in places that make me feel fidgety. I close my eyes tight, willing for anything to appear in the dark behind my closed eyelids, for a spark behind my heart, but all I feel is my heartbeat and my stomach growling.

"No, nothing," I finally say, opening my eyes.

St. Claire has his elbow on his knee, his chin resting on his knuckle and his attention solely focused on me. I blink, stunned by the bright blue hue in his eyes.

I shiver, the sweat feeling cold on my skin. "Have you been staring at me the whole time?" I ask, feeling a little prickly.

He quickly collects himself, pulling on his collar. "Not the whole time," he says, a little embarrassed.

I certainly won't be able to relax if he keeps staring at me like that. What I do say is, "I can't do this. I'm defective." Searching for this mysterious energy feels like wandering around a dark, empty room the size of Canada.

"You're not defective," he says tightly. "Maybe if we go through what happened at school, it'll spark some sort of memory of how you called the light?"

"We've been over this," I say, rubbing my temples. "I didn't call anything. It came to me."

He holds up his hands. "I know. Tell me again." Ash leans forward with interest, sliding his forearms on his thighs. His hands hang loosely between his knees, waiting.

I repeat what happened with Charity with an indifferent tone. All I remember is the shock and anger at the things she said, and furious at myself for feeling powerless.

Ash's brows knit together, but when he sees me watching, he composes himself, sitting up. He clears his throat. "We need to recreate what happened in the hall."

Sorrow hits me hard like a punch to the chest at anyone else seeing deep down into my insecurities and calling me out on them as Charity did. "You want to bully me like she did just to invoke a reaction?" I say acidly.

"Of course not," he says, looking a little irritated I would suggest that. "I only meant maybe we need to try a different approach." I shake my head but Ash still tries to convince me, "But you said you felt scared, trapped, maybe if we could—"

"I said I don't want to," I say, getting to my feet.

Ash rises with me. He holds my glare. "You need to learn how to control this, Echo."

Only a few inches separate us. He's even taller in the dusty cob-filled workshop than at school. Everything in me bristles like a little rabbit being trapped by a lion. I put my hands on my hips. "Or what? You'll turn me in?"

Ash looks like I've splashed water on his face, that authoritative tone wiped clean as he says, "Of course not." He drops his hands, looking abashed. "I'm trying to help you."

I take a step back, needing to put some space between us. "Then don't push me."

He analyzes the distance between us and then gives a curt nod, checking the time on his watch. "It's getting late, anyway. I should take you home."

ASH IS QUIET IN the car as he drives me home. It's the type of silence that makes me feel like I've done something wrong, and I only get angrier knowing I haven't. I watch the houses pass by, slumped into my seat until Ash pulls his Chevelle to the curb in front of my house.

My hand is on the door handle when he asks, voice rough, yet tentative, "I'll see you tomorrow?"

An apology gets stuck in my throat and instead, I give him a small nod before I push open the car door. I hear his car rumble off behind me as I move my heavy steps toward the front door. Cicadas and katydids take up the space Ash's car has vacated, starting their twilight concert.

I dig my keys out of my backpack when the door opens. Dad narrows his eyes into the fading light. "Where's the boy?"

I eye him carefully. "On his way home."

He makes a gruff sound as he widens the door open for me to enter. He gives one last glance outside as if St. Claire hides somewhere in the shadows.

"How was studying?" Mom is sitting on the couch with a cup of tea in her hands and a blanket pulled up to her chin despite the air-conditioning working hard to compete with the summer temps outside.

I rub my arms, feeling the artificial chill. "Fine, boring," I say, heading into my room. I drop my backpack on my desk chair and dig out my phone. A knock jerks my head up towards the door.

Mom leans against the door frame. Her eyes skim the room and back to me. "Everything alright?"

"Yes." I plug my phone in and kick off my shoes, sending one flying into my closet door. "I hate studying."

"You hate studying or something happened?"

"Nothing happened," I sigh. "St. Claire is a perfect gentleman."

"Is that what's wrong?" The corner of her mouth lifts.

I wrinkle my forehead. "Gross, no."

She hums knowingly and when I purposely avoid looking at her, she says before she leaves, "Leftovers are in the fridge."

I change into my pajamas and settle in front of my desk, pulling out my textbooks to do some actual homework. The words on the page keep blurring as my mind wanders. I rub my fingers along my scalp as I try to reconcile fact with fiction, fiction now becoming fact. The illustrations from the books in Ash's library flicker through my thoughts. How am I supposed to pretend everything is normal?

I rub my fingers along the curve of my palm, down the length of my fingers, wondering how it's even possible for them to glow with fire. I glance at my door as I think about my parents. If this is happening to me, wouldn't it have had to happen to one of them? Is that why I'm so broken because of this dormant power finally showing up in my genetics? *Lucky me.*

I feel a petulant sort of pang at how bossy Ash was in the workshop, telling me what to do—but he wasn't wrong. Uncontrolled

Siphons are dangerous. I drop my head down on my textbook; the page crinkling as I slowly turn my head back and forth and let out a groan.

The air pushing through the vent rustles a picture on the corkboard above my dresser. It's a photo of Kat and Meredith I took over the summer. What if something bad happens to them, or my family, because of me? I wouldn't be able to live with that sort of guilt, not when I could have prevented it.

I lift my head, pushing the hair out of my face. I'm tired of running away, tired of feeling defeated. I need to be brave and gain control over this power inside me before it consumes me.

CHAPTER 6

DARK SILHOUETTES OF trees surround me, their branches reaching overhead. I can barely make out the stars through the limbs. There's nothing like it anywhere on the island or the mainland that I've ever seen. The trees here are too tall, too dense, their trunks thick with age. My eye catches on darker shadows through the trees and I hug myself, feeling foreboding.

It's cool, colder than any winter here. The trees groan with the frigid temperature. I lift my hands and whisper words too soft to hear, but the trees know them. They shrink back from me as fire spits out of my hands, dropping to the ground like water, climbing along the earth, chasing the cold and shadows away.

Echo

My name whispers through the trees, the shadows retreating except for one. Then I see her.

"Echo."

The dead girl is calling my name. She stands in the forest with me, water dripping off her in rivets, her pale skin luminescent in the moonlight and her face contorted into alarm.

"Echo, wake up!"

I startle awake and try to shake off the paralyzing effects of another nightmare. My hands are fisted tightly in my sheets and they are burning. I jump up and rip my comforter off the bed. I quickly put out the small fires. The room is a dusty yellow with the first touches of daylight and fills with smoke.

I curse and rush to push up my window before I set off the hallway fire alarm. My heart is pounding inside my chest as I fan some of the smoke out the window. Once I'm sure my hands are back to normal, I grab my phone. My fingers can't move fast enough as I text St. Claire, asking if he can meet me before school.

I'm getting dressed when the text comes in that he'll meet me in the darkroom.

Dad is up this early for work and it's no surprise to see him sitting at the kitchen table, staring out the French doors, watching the neighbors Pomeranian trying to dig under our fence. Its tan-colored paws flashing in and out under the fence pickets, its tiny pinched face trying to squeeze through the freshly dug hole.

Dad lifts his brows at the sight of me, making a show of checking the time.

"I want to hit the library before class. Can you drive me to school?"

He gives me a quick once over, taking a sip of his coffee before he asks, "The school is open this early?"

I nod. "They unlock the gates an hour before school starts."

He makes a gruff sound in the back of his throat as he tears his eyes away from the backyard. "Lots of studying going on."

I rock back on my heels, trying not to look too eager. I understand his hesitation about dropping me off at the mostly deserted school with a potential murderer on the island.

Dad nods before he downs the last of his coffee. The corner of his mouth twists into a frown as he says, "I'm really hating that dog." He cast one long forlorn look at the little dog, who is almost through the hole he's enthusiastically dug. "Alright, let's get you to school for some studying." He flashes me a wry grin.

The school is quiet, almost deserted, and the air is heavy with mist like it's going to rain. My footsteps on the concrete are the only sound I hear as I make my way to the library. I brush a few wet blades of grass off my shoes before I push open the back doors. The library is silent and chilly, like a morgue.

I take the same route Adam showed me, careful of the stack of chairs in the storage room. My heart jolts when I touch the handle of the old darkroom. It feels forbidden to be in this forgotten place.

I round the odd-shaped corner into the belly of the darkroom and see Ash sitting on a table, his attention focused on me. I stop, stunned by the intensity of his ocean eyes, and ask, "Super hearing?"

"The door squeaks." The corner of his mouth inches up to a smile.

"Oh. Right."

I drop my shoulder, letting my backpack slide to the floor with a resounding thud next to a set of old developing trays. Ash raises his brows and I give him a sheepish shrug before I hop onto the table across from him.

I take a deep breath before launching into a detailed account of this morning, including my nightmare. St. Claire listens, his eyes watching my shoes as they idly swing back and forth as I talk.

When I'm finished, he asks with a clinical sort of curiosity, "How long have you been having nightmares? Was it before or after your abilities started?"

"Nightmares?" I use my nail to pick at my chipped nail polish. "For a while," I answer doggedly. "My brain has a funny way of dealing with anxiety." I brush the bits of dry nail polish off my skirt. When I glance up, St. Claire is patiently watching me.

I sigh. He's already seen me at my worst. Why stop now? "Usually monsters, creepy things in the dark. Sometimes there are people trying to hurt me, pin me down, hold me underwater, sometimes they are familiar." I close my eyes for a moment as the images grip me. When I open them, I'm back in the present.

Ash has gone contemplative, but then his eyes meet mine, shifting to sympathy. I wave away his concern. He has his bottom lip between his thumb and index finger, and I wonder if he thinks I'm insane if this is what I dream of every night. Or maybe he's wondering if he's gotten too far over his head with me and wishing he could take back his vow to help me.

I wouldn't blame him. It's a mess right now. I can see it in the way he furrows his brows. And in the frustrated way he looked at me yesterday when I wouldn't try harder. Reliving that moment hits me with a wave of fresh pain. I don't want to change; I don't want to be a Siphon, but it's impossible to pretend this isn't happening. My ruined blankets further proof.

"It's getting worse," I say, my voice cracking.

Ash glances up as if I had caught him thinking the same thing. He nods solemnly. "It appears so," he says, weighing how I'll react.

"I'm afraid of what will happen."

"I know what I'm signing up for. I'll heal."

I shake my head. "I'm afraid of this thing inside me," I admit, feeling like a part of my chest is cracking. He stares at my pleading hands, then travels to my face as I confess, "I don't want to be a Siphon. I don't want one more thing that makes me feel different. I don't want to worry for the rest of my life if I'm going to hurt someone or not." And before he can tell me again, I add, "I know, I know. Control. I'm just terrified."

His throat moves, and his eyes turn sad before he looks away. I drop my hands to my skirt. My soul feels ripped out, exposed. All my fears laid plain before an unlikely confidant. The silence stretches on and with it I feel heavier and heavier, despair settling in along with it.

"Say something," I whisper.

Ash lightly sighs before crossing his broad arms over his chest, partially blocking the Shorecrest Academy crest. He's wearing a sweater today in the school's cobalt blue, that more than complements his eyes.

He tucks his bottom lip under his teeth before he says, "I know what it's like to be afraid of what you are," he narrows his eyes and tilts his head as if he's having an inner struggle, "and I had plenty of time to adjust to it." I hold his gaze at his open admission. "The control part gets easier, but I'm afraid the secrets never do."

I let out a deep breath over my lips, along with some of the tension between my shoulders. The old light bulb overhead makes a tinny sound that draws my attention before I ask, "So, why *did* you tell Adam?"

He gives me a rueful half smile as if he knew this question was coming. "Secrets isolate you," he says, looking up toward the ceiling, "maybe I was tired of it."

I can feel the weight of my cell phone in my jacket pocket. A reminder of the lies I've already told my friends, burning guilt through me. When I glance up, he is watching me with a raw and wary look, like maybe this admission cost him more than I know.

Feeling bolstered by his confessions, I ask, "Have you told anyone else?"

"I told you." He unscrews a knob on one of the antiquated machines next to him. "People don't react well to things that shatter their perception of normal," he says, tossing the small knob into the air. "They can't handle the pressure secrets demand, or they use it against you. Bribery, blackmail."

"Is this about me?"

"No," he coughs out with a laugh, snatching the knob out of the air again, meeting my eyes. "Not about you, but maybe a warning. Learn from my mistakes?"

I raise a brow. "You don't think my friends could handle this?" I ask, gesturing to myself.

He gives a half-shrug, "I think they'll fear you, be jealous even."

"Jealous," I say with a derisive snort. "I don't think so."

He casually tosses the knob up in the air, catches it. "You'd be surprised. After the skepticism and astonishment are over, then comes the envy," he says wistfully.

Ash's sure hands artfully flip the knob in the air, catching it every time. While his attentions are off me, I tentatively study his features. His beautifully sculpted profile, the long line of his neck, and his tousled hair. My eyes skimming over the way his uniform only partly disguises the true strength underneath.

I can see why people would be envious of St. Claire. I see it every day in the hallways. The way heads turn as he passes, whispers in his wake from people who want to be his friend, date him, or *be* him.

The loneliness is something I wouldn't have ever guessed, but I can see it now. How he kept himself apart all these years. In his solemn frowns towards the gossip blatantly spoken in his presence and in the frustrated clipped tones whenever someone asked him why he doesn't play sports, or come to parties. I mistook it for arrogance and entitlement.

He catches the knob just as his eyes snap to mine. I quickly look down as my face gets uncomfortably warm.

"Do you think your friends could handle it?"

I clear my throat, resisting the urge to fan my cheeks. "I don't know."

Meredith would try to find some scientific explanation for what I am. Kat would exploit it for social or monetary advantage. That's only if they could get over how much I've lied to them so far. And then would they fear me? Jealous like he says?

Ash watches me rub my arms. "What do you do if people find out?"

"Locally or globally?"

I chew my cheek. "Both."

He screws the little knob back on the old developer as he says, "We have algorithms that scan the networks for photos, videos, or anything that even hints at the existence of Seraphs or Siphons and wipes it from the servers, any device that can get a signal. That's one thing Seraphs and Siphons can agree on, is that our existence needs to stay hidden."

"And locally?"

He gives the knob a couple of unnecessary turns. "Make sure it never happens."

I tip my head back, eyes closed, before I say, "I still don't believe this is happening."

He stops worrying the knob and asks with a small smirk, "To me or you?"

"Both," I answer truthfully. "I think I'm more shocked at you."

He lets out a surprised laugh. "Really, how so?"

The warmth returns to my cheeks, and I shrug. "I don't know. Maybe it's a tie." I gently kick my shoe into his leg.

He looks at me quizzically for a moment before lifting his wrist to check the time. The bell rings before he's even dropped his arm.

I jump off the table and scoop up my bag. "Is sensing the time a Seraph thing?"

"I wish," he admits, "then I wouldn't always be late for training."

"Yeah, but that's because you hate it," I tease, but the way he looks at me makes me feel like I've read a page from his diary. I quickly add, "Sorry, I didn't mean..."

His furrowed brows lift as he says, "No, I do hate it."

I smooth the front of my skirt to break eye contact, giving my heart a break. When I look up, he has a rueful smile.

"Am I that easy to read?"

"An open book," I say wryly.

He places a hand on his chest in mock astonishment, and I playfully shoo him toward the door. I sober up in the hallway outside the storage room as my fears of being seen together come roaring back with the sudden loss of the darkroom's privacy.

"I'll go out the back," I tell him, stopping before the mouth of the hallway. "You take the front."

Ash ruefully shakes his head but gives me a two-finger salute in agreement. "Are you still coming to my house?"

I cover his mouth with my hand, his grunt of surprise drowned out by me shushing him. I glance behind me, but I can't see around the corner. My heart is hammering in my chest. "Don't say that where people can hear you," I harshly whisper.

He mumbles under my fingers and I abruptly let go, feeling heat creep up my neck and cheeks. "Sorry," he says, looking more than mildly amused. He drops his voice to a whisper. "I'll text you?"

"Give me two minutes and then head out the front."

I push the door open quickly before I can see the smirk I imagine is there. It swings eagerly, carried by my haste, and almost slams into another student who catches it just in time.

"I'm so sorry!" I say and then gasp when I realize I almost bludgeoned Alex Carter.

Alex raises his brows, his amber eyes twinkling with amusement. "In a hurry?"

He glances behind me and I shove the door closed. I clear my throat and his gaze returns to me.

"Sorry I was..." Not expecting anyone to be out here. I scan the deserted colonnade and wave my hand impatiently. "I'm running late."

A crease forms between his eyes. "That was only the starting bell."

"Well..." A tingling has begun under my skin. "I have English on the other side of the quad."

Alex tilts his head towards the Language Arts building, his lips turning up at the corners. "I have Econ near there. I'll walk you."

I open my mouth, but I can't make the words come out. Alex and I both look at the rear library door. "Okay," I drawl.

Alex chuckles to himself. He arches a brow as he asks, "Unless you're waiting for someone else?"

I shake my head and take a step forward, my movements feel disjointed. As we continue down the hallway, my body loses some tension, but the strange feeling inside me turns into an uncomfortable buzzing.

We turn towards the quad and take one of the crisscrossed walkways that cut straight through the middle. Depending on the time of day, there's quite a crowd mulling around the stone benches, and potted dwarf palms under the covered pergola.

My gaze travels over the patches of sun-burned grass between the cement walkways and longingly towards my usual path to class. The one St. Claire is taking. His eyes snag on mine and I give him a small smile, which he returns with an almost imperceptible nod.

"You're eleventh?" Alex asks, pulling my attention back to him.

I nod, clutching my bag strap.

"That's why we don't have any classes," he says. "I was wondering how I haven't seen you around before."

A weird weight in my stomach pulls my brows down. We had two classes together last year but I don't correct him. Instead, I nod along and try to ignore the curious and hungry looks as we cut through the pergola.

"I guess I'll have to settle for seeing you at lunch?" He flashes me that all-star smile of his.

I have to look away from the intensity of his hazel eyes as they wait for my answer. Before I can give him one, an arm comes around Alex's chest, pulling him back. The stocky boy with sandy hair laughs a greeting to Alex, effectively ignoring me.

Alex shrugs off Tyler's arm which only causes him to tip his head back and laugh. "Damn maybe you should bring those reflexes to the field."

Alex chuckles, sparing me a glance. "Nah, you got it under control."

"Damn right." Tyler hits his chest and glances at me as if he's only now noticing I'm there. "Hey Martin," he says with a gruff lift of his chin.

"McKee," I mumble.

I've never liked Tyler. He's loud and pushy and attractive enough that it makes some people forget his lack of personality. Kat flirted with him for a little while, but it went nowhere because he's an absolute troll. I think he blames me, or Meredith, for Kat losing interest in him, but if he'd listen to his own idiotic ramblings, he'd realize *he's* the problem.

"I see you're not covering up that freaky green eye anymore."

Annoyance creeps up my neck. "It's called heterochromia, and it's perfectly normal."

"I like it." Alex says, "It looks pretty cool."

Tyler shares a pointed glance between Alex and I. His mouth crawls up into a grin that feels like cold slime dripping down my back.

I know he's remembering the other morning when Kat pronounced my adoration with Alex.

Before Tyler can execute whatever is behind that shit-eating grin, I excuse myself, "I've got to go."

Before I leave, I allow myself one last devouring of Alex's dark hair and sharp features. Even with the look he gives Tyler, he's still gorgeous. Tyler's smile drops, but it's too late.

I hurry towards the English building and when I look back, Alex has his head bent towards Tyler's, both boys heading away. I remember what Charity said, that I was at the bottom of Alex's list. Even if she was lying, at that moment I believe her.

CHAPTER 7

THE CAFETERIA NOISE is a subtle murmur around me as I silently replay my awkward stroll with Alex this morning. That was the perfect opportunity that Kat's always talking about, to get to know him better. Isn't that what I've always wanted?

Alex prefers to sit at the picnic tables outside. Tyler and Charity are usually beside him, and today is no different. Alex's jacket is off, and his white dress shirt is taut over his back as he leans over the table, pointing to something in front of Tyler whose tie is undone. He looks a little aggrieved at whatever Alex is saying.

Charity is sipping her soda next to them and as if she senses me watching, her eyes sharpen on mine, sending cold right through me. I cast my eyes down, temporarily chastise at being caught staring. I push my spaghetti noodles around, wishing I could tell Kat or Meredith about this morning, but not wanting to get too close to anything that might make me slip up about St. Claire.

"Okay, what's up?" Mere's voice cuts through my thoughts.

"Hmm?" I take a sip of my chocolate milk and notice her expression. "What?"

"Echo, seriously," she says, her hands on the table. "You've been acting weird all week."

The chocolate milk goes down hard, and I try to stifle my cough. I set the carton on the table and shake my head. "No."

"I agree," Kat says with a swipe of her finger across her phone screen. She doesn't look up as she adds, "Weirder than normal."

"How could you *even* tell?"

Meredith's nostrils flare as I self-depreciate myself, sarcastic or not. "Is it the Alex thing?"

I cough out a guilty laugh. "What?"

Meredith's keen eyes narrow at me and I take another sip of my drink, breaking eye contact.

"You can't avoid him forever," Kat says.

My gaze moves to Alex's table reflexively. Charity is sitting next to Alex, their backs facing me. The space between them is smaller than friendly. Tyler is silently fuming at his lunch tray. Maybe Charity is right, and Alex and Tyler are messing with me.

Worthlessness and indignation make my eyes burn. "I don't know, maybe I can," I say sourly.

Kat sets her phone down. "I'm going to talk to him?"

My eyes widen in justified panic. "No, please no! Are you trying to kill me?"

Kat trills her red lacquered nails through the air. "You can't nurse this crush forever. You don't want to have regrets, Echo."

I suppress the urge to argue. We've had this conversation on multiple occasions that I don't need to confess to every boy I find attractive. Kat's biggest downfall is she doesn't understand why everyone isn't exactly like her. She can be incredibly supportive, but also frustratingly oblivious.

"I like regrets," I say, dipping a piece of French bread through the oily sauce and popping it into my mouth.

Kat gives a frustrated huff. Meredith and I exchange a sly smile. Kat levels a dangerous finger at Mere. "You're next."

Meredith gives a delicate shake of her shoulders as her nose wrinkles. "All the boys here are gross."

Kat chokes out a derisive noise, her long fingers splayed on her chest. "How can you say that? Have you not looked around?"

Meredith and I instinctively glance at a table where a group of boys are seeing who can spit the farthest into the trash cans. They're dressed in the same uniforms as everyone else, but theirs are rumpled, and their hair is a little slicker than attractive. I make a face at her assumption that because someone has rich parents that they have aesthetically pleasing genetics.

Kat doesn't even need to see where we're looking. The Garbage Table Boys are always up to something gross. Usually, it involves daring each other to digest foul concoctions from the condiment section. Kat rolls her eyes. "Okay," she admits with effort, "maybe not every boy here."

"Thank you." I stress my point as Billy Thomas the Third accidentally spits on himself, causing an eruption of laughter from his table mates.

Meredith pushes her food away from her, shaking her head. "That's so nasty."

Kat visibly reins in her disgust, her eyes lighting up on something, someone, across the cafeteria. She folds her hands under her chin and purrs, "I bet he's never disgusting."

I don't need to follow her gaze to know whom she's referencing. Ash St. Claire sits at a long table in front of the large windows overlooking the outside sitting area. A group of girls from the softball team at the other end. The girls keep casting glances to the other end of the table, followed by whispers and smiles, and the occasional conspiratorial elbow. Probably having a similar conversation as us.

Adam is beside him, his chair pointed towards his team captain Calvin Alvarez. Their heads are bent over something I assume has to do with soccer. Ash crumbles up a napkin, throws it on his empty tray, and fishes his phone out of his pants pocket. I watch his blond brows pull down as his fingers move on the screen.

Seconds later, my phone vibrates, sending a jolt of excitement and fear racing through me. Meredith and Kat's attention have already moved from St. Claire as Mere points out that Kat has only named three boys that aren't disgusting. Kat names others, ticking them off on her fingers, Meredith occasionally murmuring an agreement.

I make sure they are still preoccupied before I take out my phone.

> **ASH:** So is texting allowed? Or are you going to attack me again?

> **ME:** I heard a rumor you can take it.

After I hit send, I steal a glance at him in time to see his mouth lift into a sly smile. It awakens a fiery thrill low in my stomach.

> **ASH:** Fair. So, are you sure about today?

> **ME:** It's a ten-minute walk. I think I can handle it.

> **ASH:** I'm confident you can.

I didn't realize I was smiling until Kat's voice effectively wipes it from my face. "Who are you texting?"

I snap my head up, my veins turning to ice as I scramble with an explanation. My hands tighten around my phone, almost protectively. "My. Mom."

Kat's fingernails click on the tabletop as she taps them in a cunning rhythm. Her eyes slowly, almost purposely, drift over to the table by the window.

"How is Adam doing?" She jerks her chin to where Adam is sitting next to St. Claire.

I shift my attention to their table, letting confusion drip over my features like I haven't been sneaking glances the whole lunch period. "Uh, well, I guess."

Meredith is taking notes from her chemistry book, her steady scribbles slow as she asks, "Do you talk much in the library?"

"A little," I say warily, pocketing my phone back into my blazer.

Kat and I have avoided bringing up Adam since the breakup. And recently I have avoided all conversations involving Adam that might lead to Ash or vice versa.

Kat folds her fingers under her chin, her big green eyes curious. "What do you guys talk about?"

"Books," I say, resisting the urge to fidget. I lift a shoulder, feigning casual disinterest, keeping my voice even as I say, "You know, library stuff."

"He doesn't talk about anything else?"

Only when I probe him for information about Seraphs and Siphons. I look at the ceiling, my eyes narrowing on a stray balloon that got caught in the sprinkler system. Long since deflated, it gently sways, waiting to be freed.

"Um, nope." I shake my head.

Meredith is hyper-focused on her pen strokes. She misinterprets my caginess, as she says, "It's okay, Echo. I'm fine if he's said anything about me."

I shake my head vehemently. "No, nothing. He never talks about you."

I internally wince as Meredith's eyes widen with hurt, her face falling as she misunderstands my meaning. She looks down at her book, nervously chewing the side of her cheek to hide her torrent of feelings.

"Okay. Good," she says, but there's a heavy catch in her voice. She clears her throat, putting on an air of aloofness. "It's probably better that way."

Kat gives me a look that says *superb job, fix it,* and I try. "I didn't mean...," I tell her, "I meant we don't talk about anything."

Meredith furrows her brows, nodding as if she understands, but her throat moves tightly as she suppresses how much talking about Adam affects her.

Kat keeps her sharp gaze on me as she asks, "You don't ask him what his problem is?" Meredith fidgets with her pen as Kat continues to talk, "I know you avoid confrontation, but—"

"Does Mere want me to ask him, Katerina?" I hiss at her.

Kat makes a disbelieving sound. Her expression to Meredith is incredulous, as if she knows what Meredith really wants. "*I* want her too." She turns that unyielding stare back at me. "I want to know what his problem is."

"I really don't want to dredge it all up." Meredith shakes her head. She pushes her shiny black hair over her shoulder. "Just drop it." She closes her book with a hard thump that has Kat's mouth snap shut.

I slump in my chair, feeling helpless and partially responsible for the look on Meredith's face. She stuffs her book in her bag, putting up her hand when Kat tries to smooth things over. She heads off towards the trash cans, dropping the remains of her lunch away.

Kat tosses her hands up in the air, frustrated by Meredith's inaction over what happened with Adam and defiant in her stance on it. Kat would need answers. She'd push even if it made it worse. Meredith and I are fine with quiet goodbyes. We both want to be fought for and not wage a dying war.

Kat crosses her arms, looking a little regretful. "Why doesn't she ask him?"

"She doesn't want to go through it again," I say, picking off the last of my nail polish. Kat doesn't date anyone long enough to get emotionally attached. It's hard to reason with her about this. She is so infallibly stubborn sometimes.

Her eyes soften as she says, "I want her to be happy."

Of all the nights Meredith cried over Adam, I don't think I could handle that kind of heartbreak. I share a kinship with Kat in that aspect, though I could never stay so emotionally unattached, either. I want to tell Kat that I'm not ready to go through that kind of pain, and that's why I don't pursue anyone for myself, but I don't. Instead, I say truthfully, "Me too."

I SCRUTINIZE EVERY SHADOW and every sound the deeper I travel into the heart of the park. My skin prickles with goosebumps despite the heat and I glance behind me. I let out a breath, sharp and sudden when there's no one there.

Dry leaves crack to my right. Jerking my head toward the sound, I search through the sticky immature trees that thicken this part of the park. Everything grows quiet. The squirrels that were fighting over popcorn a moment ago are gone. Even the bees that were fluttering around the flowering weeds seem to have departed.

A black shape flashes in my peripheral, but when I turn, it's gone. Birds erupt from the trees to my left, giving me a fierce start.

The sun-dappled path darkens as gray clouds block the sun. Trees sway as the wind moves through their branches, becoming more agitated. The squirrels come out of their hiding spots only to run off toward safer places.

A summer storm is brewing.

A black shadow moves between the trees and I spin to track it, but I lose sight of it behind a large oak. It was too tall to be any animal that frequents the park. In fact, it was distinctly human-shaped. My blood vibrates, a low hum like I'm standing too close to a concert speaker.

I'm over halfway to the gate. I can do this, it's fine.

I run.

I don't get far before I'm wrenched backward into something hard. I try to shout as a hand covers my mouth and vice-like arms pin me to my sides.

The trees around me creak and crack as the wind whips up around me.

Is this what happened to her? The girl they found dead on the beach? A lifeless body caught by the sandbar. Was she snatched in the daylight and taken from her life, her family?

I kick and squirm, but my attacker is ready for it and much stronger than I am. Their grip doesn't loosen.

I am completely powerless.

I am hyper-aware of my feet planted on the cement path, of the earth beneath me, the wind in the trees, the water in the lakes and in the ocean beyond that, and the fire crackling through the clouds overhead. My body hums eagerly at all that waiting power.

Then I feel it. A small tendril of something reaches out from the deep dark void and burrows into me, pouring light into that dark place inside me. Like a flutter behind my heart, jump-starting an old car battery and then I feel the energy there, charging through my veins and into my hands.

My attacker curses, abruptly letting go. I spin around and trip over a raised crack in the pavement. I fall hard on my tailbone. The tall hooded figure, dressed similarly to my stalker, holds up a hand in surrender as he quickly pushes his hood back, revealing the strikingly handsome face of Ash St. Claire.

"I told you that was a bad idea," I snap.

"But can you feel how you called the Light?"

I reluctantly nod, then scowl at his outstretched hand. The leather gloves he wears are peeled back and melted, revealing the red and blistered skin underneath. He kneels down beside me, his eyes searching over me with concern as I do the same to him.

"Are you okay?" We say at the same time.

"Yes, but your hands." I implore him to see some sense of self-preservation. "I should have never agreed to this," I scold him.

He offers his hand a second time, and I let him pull me up. I dust off my uniform skirt as Ash scrutinizes the sky. The clouds have moved, and the sun now shines through the branches, which have gone still once again.

"I think we found your trigger," he says, looking down at me.

I punch his shoulder. "What if I really hurt you?"

He gives me that incredulous smirk. Ash stifles a hiss as I raise the evidence of his ruined hands between us. They are warm, too warm.

"I heal quickly." He gingerly removes the ruined gloves and stuffs them in his pocket.

I shake my head, dropping his hands. "But I don't want to be the *reas*on."

I search for my bag a few steps behind us. When I turn around, St. Claire is massaging his palms, trying to hide his pain. I look away, my throat feeling warm.

We continue to the rear gate, Ash falling into a reflective silence beside me. There's still a range of emotions swirling through me. I know I agreed to this, but I didn't think he'd get hurt. Sure, I thought I might have some stirrings, or maybe my hands would light up again, especially when I let myself pretend it was real, but I didn't think it would work so well.

I spot Ash's car by the curb right when we exit out the rear gate. He fishes his car keys out and unlocks the passenger door. I tilt my head up at him, my lips turning amused.

"What?" he asks, mirroring my expression.

"You opened the door for me."

"I open the door for you all the time."

"I know," I say, hiding my grin as I slide past him and into my seat.

I watch him walk around the front of the car, flipping his keys around in his hand and sliding his sunglasses down over his eyes. He starts the car as soon as he sits down. It wakes like a sleeping dragon. He turns to me with a grin. The world reflected off his sunglasses.

"Ready?"

I FEEL LIKE I'M on the edge, about to fall into something. We were pretending before. It was all theories and games, secrets and whispers. It was easy to keep a safe distance from this world St. Claire is a part of, that I am a part of, but not now. I feel a nervous whirl like you get from plummeting from a great height. That spark in my chest flares for an instant, and that warning buzz dies down as I decide.

"Ready."

St. Claire watches me with his impossibly blue eyes. Waiting. We're in the workshop behind his house again. Dust motes float in a beam of sunshine coming from the side window. I can hear the ocean waves calmly lapping on the other side of the stone privacy fence. I don't feel calm though, there's a nervous torrent in my gut that makes me squirm and it only partly has to do with summoning this power inside me.

Ash has his hands under his chin, patiently watching me as I try to bring back the energy I conjured in the park. We've been in here for half an hour now, as I struggle with magical stagefright.

"Stop staring at me," I say.

"Where else am I supposed to look?"

"I don't know, the ground?"

He tilts his head up to the wood beams of the workshop roof, exposing the bump in his throat. I feel like a little kid again, sitting cross-legged on a yoga mat in front of Ash St. Claire. He doesn't look like a little kid. His graceful fingers are loosely clasped in his lap as he obeys my request to look somewhere else. He's discarded the black hooded sweatshirt he wore in the park to reveal his uniform shirt underneath, the sleeves rolled up to his elbows. The top few buttons undone and the tan triangle of skin is almost as distracting as his eyes.

I clasp my fingers tightly together to stop this nervous feeling growing in my belly. Needing a distraction, I ask, "So, where are your parents?"

He slowly lowers his eyes to mine. "You're awfully interested in my parents."

I half roll my eyes. "How come I never see your mom?"

Ash absorbs my question. His eyes move to the wall of dusty tools as if he can see the house through it. "She's giving us space."

I give a derisive snort. "What? Why?"

He takes a breath, his arms crossing as he prepares himself for a conversation he'd rather not have. "Because, I'm training to be a Domnius," he says it like that should be explanation enough, "whose purpose is to regulate and control Siphons, and now, here I am helping a wayward Quiescent to develop her abilities, something Domini are explicatively not to do." He gestures to me, not unkindly. "It's like the police helping the criminals to be better criminals."

I wrinkle my nose at being compared to a criminal. "I could see how that's a conflict of interest," I admit, and Ash nods in agreement. "Are you going to get in trouble?"

"With my mom?" The corner of his mouth lifts in amusement.

"Yeah, well, with anyone? Your Dominus commanders?"

He barks out a laugh. "My mother... trusts, I know what I'm getting myself into."

"And your dad?" I ask, equally curious.

Ash's amused smile dims. "Isn't here," he says. I raise my brows at the hint of bitterness but before I can ask he adds, "And I don't have a commander, it's a council I answer to, and since I'm underage, cannot be punished at the same level as a sworn Domnius for my reckless pursuits."

I shift my gaze from his wicked smile to his eyes. "Hmm. Do you pursue recklessness often?"

"My father thinks so." He shrugs. "He thinks telling Adam was reckless."

"What does he think about you hanging out with a low-class Siphon like me?" I tease.

Ash rolls his eyes, giving me an incredulous smirk. "Are we going to spend all day talking about my parents?"

I tap a finger on my chin. "Do they wear shiny gold armor like in your books?"

"Echo," he groans in exasperation.

"I'm kidding." Sort of.

Ash's parents fascinate me with a guilty pleasure sort of curiosity. They are fables in a book. Ash is the only one of his kind I've met and even he doesn't seem as *Other* as he should. Dressed in the school uniform I'm accustomed to seeing him in for years, he's just another boy from the Western Crescent. *Well*, not *exactly*. Even before.

I steal a glance at his hands. How quickly the skin is healing. Will I ever get used to this? I have more questions, but I can tell he's getting impatient and my curfew is fast approaching. I take in a deep breath.

"I need to work up to it."

Ash checks his watch. "That's what we've been doing for the past thirty minutes." He leans back on his hands, looking up at the ceiling. "I wish I brought something to read."

"Like what?"

"Echo." He closes his eyes, regaining his composure.

I laugh, finding way too much amusement in messing with him, and close my eyes, my smile still in place. I take in a deep breath and concentrate on that dark black hole I've always carried with me, the place where my fears, doubts, and anxieties live.

I listen to the waves hitting the sand, over and over as they match my racing heart. That little place behind my rib cage awakens and fills with warmth. It burns away the dark, chasing back the shadows. The energy flows into me, spreading from that place in my chest, out along my nerve endings, and through my veins. It's slow at first as it wakes from hibernation. My fingers tingle, like when they've fallen asleep, but it doesn't stop, instead, they begin to burn.

My hands are glowing, but they falter. Red hot and then not. An orangish glow and then it's crawling up my hands. Images from the Seraph books, the horrible things that Siphons performed, flicker through my mind. The energy stops. I gasp, clutching my chest.

"What's wrong?" Ash asks, very alert.

"I can't, I can't do this," I say, my voice breaking. "They did horrible, awful things." I blink holding back tears. "Siphons are monsters," I cry. "Why would I want to be one of them?"

Ash's face fills with sympathy as he struggles with something to contradict me. Hurt and desperation burn through me and I stand. Ash quickly gets to his feet and takes a step toward me. "Echo—"

"You said it yourself. Siphons are dangerous."

Ash pushes his fingers through his hair. "But I also said it's not all of them."

"Look at your books, look in the mirror. It's the reason you exist, remember?" Hurt quickly flashes over his features before shifting to something close to sadness. "I didn't mean it like that," I tell him, the fight leaving me.

"I know." He sighs up to the ceiling. "It was a war, Echo. Horrible, brutal things happen in wars. Do you think humans don't do monstrous things?"

"No, I know." I give a derisive pout. "I'm not that naïve."

"I was too harsh when I was telling you about Siphons. I know we shouldn't base all Siphons on what went on in the war." He pushes his hands through his hair again. "We have to stay detached," he says, searching my eyes, pleading with me to understand. "They keep Dominus purposely separate from Siphons, so we can judge them more critically. Do I think all Siphons are bad? Of course not. Like not all people are bad." He watches me, softening as he says, "I don't think you're a monster."

"I hurt you," I plead. "How is that not dangerous?"

Ash touches my arm. It's light, but his fingers are warm on my skin. "Because you're untrained. That's what we're doing here. You need to remember that. You can control this."

I shake my head. This feels impossible. "Are all Siphons so sporadic in their abilities?"

Ash chews his lip for a moment before answering, "Imagine the Light like an electrical current. Now imagine your electrical wire is frayed and broken in parts. The connection isn't reliable, the electricity is weak and when it comes, it sputters, stronger sometimes, but never works as it should."

I shudder as the memory of that pure energy racing through me raises the hairs on my arms. If this is what a frayed and broken connection feels like, I'm not sure I want the whole thing. "What if I try... to suppress it?"

Ash looks evasive, his thoughts considering as he says, "Siphons who can't control their powers are also problematic."

"Great." I rub at my temples. "I'll always be broken."

"You're not broken," he says softly, drawing my eyes to his. I get a covetous thrill when I look at him and turn away, my thoughts feeling chaotic.

Ash comes around so we're facing each other again and I eye him warily, but not for the reason he thinks. "This is your first real training session and you're ready to quit?"

I let out an incredulous snort. "You don't understand. It's not like learning the piano," I plead with him, my voice rising as I become increasingly frustrated that he can't see why I'm so afraid.

"I do understand," he grits out, his cool exterior cracking. "I have to constantly stay in control. That limits what I can do, if I might hurt someone," he says, his blue eyes blazing. "I'm just as dangerous."

Ash picks up a spade shovel and before I can ask him what he's doing, he gracefully flips it around, taking the metal spade in his hands and folding it in half. He tosses it to the ground and searches for something else. His eyes land on a piece of rebar, bending it easily. He grabs a three-inch piece of iron railing, his biceps pulling his shirt tight as he folds that over, and drops it to the cement floor. The loud metallic clang makes me flinch.

I look around at the bent-up metal at our feet and ask, "Are you trying to be relatable or show off?"

He shakes his head. "I'm trying to show you that—" He sucks in a breath as he takes in his show of strength littering the ground. He releases out a low chuckle. "I guess I was showing off a little."

I pick up the rebar; it scraps along the floor. I give a futile pull to see if it even flexes under my grip, but the iron doesn't move. Ash takes it from me, looking a little chagrin, and sets it on the workbench.

"I understand what you're trying to say." I gesture towards the floor. "That just because there's this power inside me doesn't mean I'm out of control."

Ash picks up the thick metal railing and eyes it curiously before setting it next to the rebar. He frowns at the metal shovel. "My dad might be a little irritated about this one," he says distractedly.

He slowly bends it back into place, an obvious blemish cut vertically through the spade, the metal looking like it might not recover. Ash grimaces as he places it against the wall with the other garden tools.

"I'm sorry," he says, sticking his hands in his pocket.

I furrow my brow. "For what?"

He holds his breath, looking pained. "For being hypocritical."

I rock back on my heels, "Oh I don't know, maybe you need to lose control more often."

He breaks eye contact, his cheeks turning a hint of pink. A dimple in his cheek appears as he gives me a rueful smile.

THE LIGHT IS READY and hungry when I try again. Like turning on a fire hose to water your houseplants. I'm not trying to put out any fires, or in my case, start one.

I slowly try to siphon the smallest of energy, going painfully slow. Ash is patient, almost looking mournfully subdued after his demonstration. I've finally gotten enough energy to slowly, almost disappointedly, flow through my nerve endings. I make a noise that draws Ash's attention to the glow in my hands.

He reaches out to touch my fingers tentatively, smiling when he realizes they're cool to the touch. He turns my hands over, marveling at their sunset glow, probably relieved I'm not burning him again.

"Yay, I have glow sticks for hands."

Ash raises an eyebrow at that. "Can you cause any heat?"

A flush creeps up my neck, burning my cheeks that's unrelated to the Light coursing in my veins. Ash lets go of my hand as I try to siphon more of that bright energy. My body clenches as I try to only take a little. I can feel that bright void, feel the effervescent coalescing energy there. It dangerously brushes against the fragile control I've gained, wanting. Fear hits me cold as ice and then the Light frizzles, sparks and cuts out. I slump in frustration, shaking my head.

"Well, if you ever need a flashlight, you know who to call." I wiggle my fingers for emphasis.

Ash smirks, leaning back on his hands. "It's a start."

"A stupid start." I pout, reaching up my arms to stretch out my tight muscles.

Ash's eyes move down my body and then away. "You've heard the expression 'Rome wasn't built in a day'?"

"We're building empires now?" I say cheekily, rising to my feet.

Ash's chest moves with amusement. "You coming over tomorrow?" He's looking out the window towards the cloudless blue sky, all languid grace.

I let myself drink him in for a moment, telling myself it's to better understand his subtle nuances. "I have a test to study for."

He leans forward, rising and dusting off his hands, his face pleasantly neutral as he says, "You're welcome to study here?"

"Like actual studying?"

He gives a small nod. "We could practice after. I also set aside some books you might find helpful."

A tiny weight falls into my stomach. Dominus Stuff. A sliver of shame at wanting and then having. Hope crushed in the same heartbeat. I rub my forehead, frustrated with my own conflicted feelings. He's *Ash St. Claire*, stupid.

Unaware of my true hesitation, he says, "Am I pushing again?"

"No," I admit truthfully, pulling my phone out of my bag and checking the time. "It's been a long day."

Ash clears his throat. "Of course, I'll take you home."

We exit the workshop and take the stone path to the garage near the front of his house, passing the sparkling pool, its clear waters an invitation. In the summers, I practically lived in the water, alternating from Meredith's swimming pool to the ocean behind her house. I briefly imagine what it would look like if Ash and I were normal friends, swimming in his pool, sunning in the white lounge chairs on the patio, Meredith, Kat, and Adam with us.

A jealous snake wraps around my heart as my daydream shifts, and everyone is there except me. The dangerous Siphon locked away so she won't hurt anyone. One day, that could easily be Ash who has to arrest me, or whatever Dominus do.

We stop beside his car, and I touch his arm to get his attention. "Are we... friends?"

He searches my face before he says, "Yes."

"Or is this like some kind of duty to you? Helping me because I'm Adam's friend, because we go to school together, and you don't want to hunt me down someday?"

He cast a glance at his house, his face pained. "Yes, Echo, I'm your friend."

"Okay," I say, "just don't lie to me, whatever it is."

"I won't." He swallows, his eyes once again moving toward the house and back to me. He gets a faraway look as he whispers my name, "Echo, I—"

Tiny hairs on my arms prickle as I wait. Ash seems to snap out of whatever spell he put himself under, raising an inquiring eyebrow, he asks, "So, I'll see you after school?"

I let out a long sigh. "Yes."

He gives me a lazy smile right before he pulls open the passenger side door. I roll my eyes at his chivalry, but warmth still spreads down to my toes. I tell myself not to get too used to this, but I have a nasty habit of ignoring my advice.

CHAPTER 8

THE NEXT DAY I had to bear Charity's frosty glare through most of Latin, feeling self-conscious and a headache forming behind my eyes. After class, she bounded up to Alex and Tyler, throwing her arm easily through Alex's, giving me a satisfied, knowing smile.

I narrow my eyes back at her, competitiveness flaring before I can think better of it. I go down a different hall, heading towards the library. My mood quickly soured and I don't have the energy to pretend.

There's a comforting solitude of the old darkroom, the noise of the school drops away, and it's like a little protective bubble where I can catch my breath while at school. I slide up onto the top of a table and drop my bag beside it. I hear the door squeak and freeze as my thoughts scatter to find an excuse for why I'm here and not where I'm supposed to be. Ash rounds the corner, his book bag slung over one shoulder, as he takes in my surprised state.

"What are you doing here?" I eye him questionably.

"I saw you headed this way." He shrugs as if this explains it.

"I didn't feel like going to the cafeteria."

He raises his brows in understanding. "There seemed to be some tension with Charity in class." He drops his bookbag next to mine and casually rests on the table ledge. He's tall enough to do it comfortably.

I cough out a dry laugh. That's an understatement. "Ah, you noticed."

The look he gives says *who didn't?* We're silent for a few moments before he asks, "Would you mind if Adam comes over today?" He spins the ring on his thumb, gazing at me sidelong, apprehension in his eyes.

"No," I hesitate.

Ash misinterprets the pause. He turns to face me full-on. "I can tell him no."

I shake my head quickly. "No, it's fine."

"I would completely understand..."

I riffle through my lunch bag until I find the coconut chips. "It's not that," I say, popping a small piece into my mouth. "It's the 'him and Meredith thing'."

A line forms between his brows as he crosses his arms over his chest. He studies me while I put another coconut chip in my mouth. "Is there... something else between you and Adam?" he says it all slowly, like the words are being pulled from him against his will.

I cough out a laugh, partly choking on my food. "God, no." I give him the most sardonic look I can muster. "Adam is great, I mean, I'm sure he'd make a great boyfriend," I say, and the way his brows lift causes heat to creep over my neck. "But he's Meredith's Adam," I say pointedly.

Ash considers this in that serious way of his. Finally, he nods. I turn away, giving my cheeks a chance to cool down and notice he didn't bring a lunch tray. I offer him the coconut chips and after a small hesitation; he takes them. I break my sandwich in half, but he waves it off.

"Come on, it's honey-roasted chicken and there's probably nothing good left in the cafeteria."

When he finally accepts half, I set a container of grapes between us. Ash adds the coconut chips to our shared loot.

"I'm surprised you eat." He looks at me with an arched brow, popping the last bite of his sandwich in his mouth. "Being immortal and all, I'd think you didn't have to?"

He dusts off his hands and reaches for the grapes. "I'm not immortal yet," he says, "and we still need to feed our bodies." He suggestively raises his eyebrows while he chews.

I unscrew the cap on my water and take a long drink before I ask, "Could you die from not eating?"

He shakes his head, taking a couple more grapes. "No. Our bodies go into a dormant state, conserving energy."

"Would you stay like that forever?"

He nods. "Until we get food or water."

I pop a grape in my mouth, giving him a quick once-over. "Have you ever done that?"

Ash stares at the floor for a moment, crossing his arms over his chest. "It's a part of Domini training."

"Yikes," I say. "So what's up with that, anyway?"

Ash tilts his head. "What do you mean?"

"You don't seem like you want to be a Dominus?"

He gives me a measured look as I take a bite of my sandwich, waiting. He takes in a deep breath while he looks up at the ceiling. "It's what I was born for. It's my legacy."

"So you've said," I say around a mouthful of food. "But you also said you have a choice, that some Seraphim choose not to be Domini," I add, "like your mom."

He's still staring up at the ceiling.

"Your dad's not here, spill," I tease, hoping I'm not going too far.

Ash's shoulders move with a silent laugh. He unfolds his arms, leans on the table, and inspects the container of grapes. I nudge them over. I've seen Adam and him eat. There's no way he's full. He takes a grape, rolls it in his fingers, and sighs to himself. "My father's not happy about it, but he knows I have reservations."

"Which are?"

He glances at me, then back at the grape before he finally eats it. "Being a Dominus means for life." I watch him, waiting for him to elaborate. "My family has quite the legacy to live up to." He frowns, a little bitterly.

I see the image of Ash's knightly Seraph grandfather clad in gold armor as I ask, "What's your famous grandfather say?"

Ash laughs without humor. "He... Let's just say he's old fashion. He definitely wouldn't approve of our little rendezvous here," he says, smirking.

I feel my face heating again and take another drink to hide it. "You followed me, remember?" I say with false bravado. "You could tell him you were just making sure I wasn't causing trouble."

Ash makes a face that tells me that old granddaddy wouldn't buy it. "Truthfully, my interactions with him have been brief, but he has quite the reputation."

"Oh?"

"He came to see me before I started training." Ash stares at his hands, lost in the memory. "He didn't seem all that impressed with me." Ash makes a derisive sound, straightening up and crossing his arms over his chest again. "He's very black and white, his terms on the council are always—" Ash's eyes dart to mine, "busy."

My brows raise at his implications. The Dominus focus on dolling out punishment for both their kind and Siphons. I can only imagine what Ash's grandfather's reign on the council looked like.

There's a lump in my throat as I say, "Yikes."

Ash nods, looking lost in memory again. I stick my hand in the coconut bag. The crinkling draws him out of his thoughts and he reaches in after me.

"So he's not on the council now? How's that work?"

Ash shakes his head, swallowing before she says, "Only three originals have a seat on the council at one time. They're to bear witnesses to the Olrum Lari'el, our Laws, to offer their wisdom in those matters."

"What are the laws?"

Ash chews his cheek, his eyes moving over me. His attention has me feeling a little weird. I pick at my sandwich, pretending I'm unhappy with a piece of lettuce until he finally says, "They're a set of moral guidelines that we follow. Genevieve gave them to the first Seraphs."

His cheeks pink ever the slightest at my knowing look. He waves away my meaning, choosing to ignore the obvious comparisons his people have to the stories of angels.

"Can you break these laws?" I ask, trying to hide my smile.

He hesitates, apprehensive. "Some of them."

Cold current prickles along my spine. "That doesn't sound like free will."

He looks uncomfortably away, bending down to retrieve a stainless steel thermos from his bag. He unscrews the cap, taking a drink of water before he finally says, "We are given a choice to become a Dominus or not."

"Does that mean that once you become a Dominus, you lose your free will?" I ask, trying to hold in my alarm. "What if your laws tell you to kill someone? Do you have to do it?"

He sets his thermos down with a heavy clink that echoes in the space, reverberating in my bones. "No, it's not like that." He emphasizes his point with his hand, "The Olrum Lari'el doesn't tell us to kill anyone." Ash seems like he's conflicted with not only the conversation but with his own belief system. "They mostly pertain to Seraphs; our moral code for each other. How long someone can serve on the council, that sort of thing."

I dig around in my lunch for my yogurt and a spoon and catch the tail end of him eyeing the last of the coconut chips. I nudge them in his direction. He gladly takes them, tipping them into his mouth.

I don't hide my concern when I say, "Okay, so you mostly have free will."

His mouth turns up, amused. "I am completely in control of my actions," he says, placing a hand on his chest.

I look at him sidelong, finish scraping the last remnant of my yogurt as I say, "Until you become a Dominus."

He gives me an exasperated smile. "Even when I'm a Dominus, Echo, my thoughts and actions are my own." He crumples the chip bag and stuffs it into my empty yogurt container.

"When or if?" I look away as I pack the remnants of our lunch into my lunch bag.

He leans back, forcing me to look at him. "Worried we won't be friends anymore?"

I roll my eyes, catch sight of his watch and turn it to check the time, pretending not to notice his grin that's directed at me, or that he's so close I can smell the shampoo he uses.

"See you after school," I say as I slide off the table. It's not until I'm far from the library that my traitorous heart finally stills.

ASH AND I ARE leaning against his ostentatious muscle car in front of his garage when Adam arrives. He gives us both a languid wave as he slowly pulls up beside us, which I return. I catch Ash staring and he breaks eye contact by tucking the humidity-curled blond strands behind his ears.

Adam climbs out of his truck as I'm still eying St. Claire and his purposeful aloofness. Adam clears his throat, giving me a jolt I try to hide by bouncing on my toes and asking, a little too cheery, "How was your day?"

He gives me a funny look, the side of his mouth lifting and his eyes crinkling. "Good."

I roll my eyes, "What, no one asks you about your day?"

Adam rests his arm on the hood of his truck, considering me. Finally, he shakes his head, a bemused chuckle on his lips. "No, I mean, yes, it's—never mind." His brown eyes shoot over to Ash, almost guiltily. "Heard you had lunch in the darkroom again," he says, directing the next part to Ash, "if you told me, I'd have brought lunch."

"It was a last-minute decision," Ash says tightly, "but next time."

St. Claire pushes off the car, and we follow him to the stairs at the back of the garage. While the boys are deep in conversation, I run my fingers along the museum-like hallway walls and ogle any open doors without the fear of them noticing.

When we enter the library, I stop at the railing before the stairs, breathing in the rich smell of wood and the comforting smell of paper. Ash and I share a look before he heads down the stairs. I let out a contented sigh and follow.

"So libraries are okay, it's only studying you hate?" Ash asks over his shoulder as Adam and I follow him into the room we have claimed for our research.

There's a long mahogany table and chairs in the center, with a row of bookcases along the right wall, sparsely filled with a few titles from our other study sessions and on the opposite wall are display cases.

"I like libraries," I tell him, dropping my bag into a chair, "even if they're filled with boring research and reference books." I scrunch up my face, getting an amused smile from Ash.

I find I'm doing things more and more to invoke that smile. I turn toward the display cases to hide my smug enjoyment. The wood is cool as I run my hands along its smooth surface, appraising what's inside. Everything from ancient books, to curved swords, to rough forged jewelry, to what appears to be a dinosaur claw. I turn around when I hear a heavy book hitting the table.

"While you two are researching cool magical things, I have some actual studying to do." Adam shakes his head as he pulls out a pack of highlighters and a pad of paper.

"Yikes." My eyes widen at the sight of his textbook. "I have a test to study for too, and not some cool, magical test."

"I have an Econ test tomorrow." Ash rubs the back of his head and then sees my face. "What? Even immortals have to study."

"Almost immortal." I give him a coy grin.

"But very hard to break," he counters with a lopsided smile.

Adam lifts his eyebrows. "It's okay, keep your inside jokes." He flips open his chemistry book.

I take the seat across from him and pull out my marine biology book as Ash takes the seat at the head of the table. "Ash didn't tell you I electrocuted him?"

Adam sits up straighter in his chair. "He said you shocked him and he took you home, but I thought that was some kind of introvert flirting thing." Adam delivers the tease so deadpan it's hard to know if he's joking or not until he grins at his book.

"Funny," Ash says, his cheeks a little pink, sneaking a glance at me before taking out his textbook.

"I heard it was very entertaining," Adam says, highlighting a line in his notes.

"Oh?" I glance over at St. Claire, now very interested in his accounts of what happened.

"Accusations of kidnapping. You threatened to punch him." Adam lifts his head to meet my eyes. "That I'd like to see."

"She was very intimidating," Ash says, trying to keep a smile out of his voice.

I let out a small laugh. "This was before I knew what I was dealing with." I motion toward Ash, who raises a blond brow at me.

Adam focused on his book, a private smile in his voice, as he says, "Oh, I don't know, I bet you could take him."

The way he says it makes everything in me all squirmy. I sneak a glance at St. Claire. There's a deep line between his brows, a little too serious even for economics. That little buzzing in my belly makes me shift in my seat. I'm having trouble focusing on how dolphins communicate. I run my eyes over the stack of books on the table. A familiar gilded title catches my eye and I slide it off the stack.

I casually flip through the pages until I see one Ash skipped the first time we looked through it. Mostly he spared me more scenes of violence, Siphons on Siphons, on humans. I look through them quickly, not wanting to linger on the reminder I'm part of something with a past so brutal and violent. It's a part of my history that needs to be recognized for the horror it is, but not now that it's all so fresh. I'm still dealing with the fact I am Siphon, let alone connected to such a brutal war.

St. Claire notices the page I'm lingering on. The freshly made Seraphim in their regal armor, an aura of gold light surrounding them.

"You guys were born wearing armor?" I challenge.

He taps the page with his pencil. "Naked and confused doesn't make for such a pretty picture."

Adam snorts and I nod in agreement. The next page is another I've definitely not seen. The new Seraphs are down on one knee. Their creator, Genevieve, is placing crowns of light on their heads. It looks like it's supposed to symbolize a great honor being placed on them, Protectors of the Earth, Dominus of the Light, but to me, it looks like servitude.

The longer I stare at it, the more the noble faces of the Seraphim look angry. The benevolent face of their creator turns cunning.

The small bands of light placed on their heads remind me of the mind control devices that Mr. Levitato used in The Magnificent Seven: Volume two. I chew my lip and steal a glance at Ash. He's focused on writing his study notes, oblivious to the unease that crawls up my spine. I think about his Laws and his caginess about how much control he really has. A hard lump has formed in my throat and I swallow it down to keep my thoughts of slavery to myself.

I flip past the scenes of Siphons torturing Seraphs and stop on a page that shows Genevieve casting the last of her Light. She floats above her trusted guard, the first Domini, her hair out around her like water, and lassos of Light flow from her body out to Siphons tangling their wrists, torsos, and around their necks. Her eyes blaze white, filled with the Light within.

In the next picture, she is a bright ball of light, a little sun, that explodes out of her. Little stars rain down upon a crowd of what looks like humans. They don't have an aura like the Siphons.

I brush my fingers on Ash's arm to get his attention. "What's this mean?" I ask quietly.

I turn the book towards him as he leans over to get a better look at it. His blue eyes skim the illustration. "It's after Genevieve cursed her kind. It symbolizes how she blessed the people of earth."

"How did she bless them?"

"She believed humans were the first people of Earth, the true rulers, as we believe. It's said that when she died, her light glittered down on the humans, symbolizing her last wish for us to protect them."

I frown down at the page, thinking about the amount of energy she must have needed to curse her own kind, and what these little remnants of her light might mean for the people they touched.

He gives me a rueful half-smile. "I wasn't there. I'm only the interrupter." His voice is soft, like an autumn fire. I realize my hand is still on his arm and pull back.

Ash watches me thumb through the pages of my marine science book before he returns to writing notes. Something is nagging me about their story of creation, a dark feeling that sets goosebumps along my skin.

My phone lights up beside me, vibrating on the table. Meredith's name flashes across the screen and guilt washes over me, quick as lightning. I glance at Adam before I excuse myself. I head to the stairs out of earshot.

"Hey," I say, a little too cheery.

"We're coming to get you." Meredith's voice is mixed in with the indistinct sound of music coming from the radio, Kat's muffled voice, and then louder, telling me to "Be ready in five minutes."

Panic flares in my bones as I realize I forgot our plans to go look at homecoming dresses after school. I can see Ash and Adam bent over their books in the other room and duck further behind the stairs facing the bookcases. I lean my forehead on the dark wood, mentally calculating the odds of sneaking back to my house without getting caught.

I close my eyes tight as I say, "I, uh, I'm actually not at home."

"Oh?" Mere's voice lifts in surprise.

I clear my throat but it won't clear away that I'm an awful friend. "Yeah, I'm at the library." Not a lie. I stare at the books in front of me, mildly surprised to see some popular fiction titles. The music cuts off in the background and I close my hand into a fist. "I have this really hard test to study for. I'm sorry."

"She seriously forgot us?" Kat says, raising her voice so I'd hear her. "Tell her that homecoming is in a few short weeks."

"I know, I'm sorry, it's been a weird week," I tell Meredith, knowing it'll get back to Kat.

"Yeah, okay..." Meredith's voice trails off.

She's probably remembering how often I've skipped out on the lunchroom and how cagey I've been lately. You'd think my grades would be stellar with all the 'studying' I've been doing.

"But you're still coming to the sleepover, right?"

"Yeah, of course."

"Okay, well... Have fun studying." There's still a warble to her voice that makes me feel like a garbage friend.

I tell them to take pictures of their top picks before we hang up. Dress shopping together has been a tradition since freshman year and I hate that I've bailed.

This hollow feeling grows not only because I forgot about our plans but also because of where I am and who I'm with. I try to focus on the titles in front of me and not think about how they'll react if they found out I was at St. Claire's house. *In his massive library!* I'd have to confess that this secret friendship has been going on long enough that we're comfortable being study partners—that I'm riding in his car.

The thought of them thinking I am another doe-eyed girl from school after Ash, stoking the fire of another hopeless fantasy makes me nauseous and admittedly a little bitter. There's a part of me that doesn't want them to talk me out of it. The selfish part of me likes this secret with ocean eyes and mysteries of his own.

I squeeze my eyes shut. I should have told them, but the thought of Meredith's face, the inevitable tears when she finds out Adam is here too. Like I'm cheating on her friendship—cheating with him.

Oh, God.

More lies, and more lies to cover up lies. I rest my head against the bookcase.

"Everything okay?"

I straighten up at the sound of St. Claire's voice. He stands at the edge of this little alcove I've hidden in, his hands in his pockets and his brows pulled down at the sight of me. I look at Adam hunched over his book and I wonder how much they heard. "I forgot I had plans to go dress shopping," I tell him softly.

"Do you need me to take you home?"

I shake my head. "I told them I was at the library." Ash steps further into the alcove, his eyes lighting with understanding. "I hate lying to them, but I can't tell them the truth," I say, almost pleading. "It's not like I can invite them to our practice sessions and they'll wonder why. They'll think—" I break off, not wanting to say what they'll think.

Ash leans against the bookcase next to me, letting me reign in my torrent of emotions. I press my fingers into the wood, nervously feeling the grain.

"How do you do this?"

Ash tilts his head. A flash of sorrow crosses his features before he says, "I think your secrets are more complicated than mine at the moment." At my withering stare, he crosses his arms over his chest, accentuating his biceps. "I mean it," he says, "I've known my secrets my entire life and had plenty of time to adjust. I had a private tutor until I was old enough to know how to hide what I am, and I don't have a clique of human friends to keep secrets from."

"That only gives you the whole mysterious thing." I gently bump my hip into him.

His smile is sad. "Or the arrogant, unsociable rich kid that ignores everyone at school and doesn't play any sports—because I'm afraid of hurting someone."

I study the underside of the stairs as I say, "It sounds lonely."

"Sometimes," he confesses. "You have a family, friends, and social life that you have to navigate around." He inclines his head toward Adam and I understand why he took the risk, just to tell one person.

"So what do I do?" I look up at him, searching his eyes.

"I don't have a right answer for you," he says, his features filling with concern. "It was an enormous risk that I told Adam. It could have ended badly." He uncrosses his arms and turns to face me. We're a few inches apart and something about that feels dangerously on the edge of something. "People don't like being lied to and odds are that one of your friends will handle this badly," he says, "it'll hurt, finding out who you can trust or not."

"What would've happened if Adam handled it bad?"

His eyes drop to my lips for the briefest of moments. I could almost pretend it didn't happen. The buzzing in my stomach grows almost painful, my heart kicking up a gear. Our conversation shouldn't make my face feel as warm as it does.

"The Domini would have to intervene and they don't care about feelings or friendships, only about keeping our world hidden."

I shiver as images of Seraph warriors in golden armor descend upon my friends. I shift back, taking it all in.

Ash rests his arm on the shelf a few inches from my head, watching his words play out on my face. "You could eliminate the secrets you don't need to keep," he says cautiously, wetting his lips.

"Such as?" I arch a brow up at him, feeling bold.

He taps the shelf, watching his fingers as he does. Or maybe he's looking at how we're almost touching. "You could tell them about us."

I chew my cheek. My face is uncomfortably hot. I lower my voice to a whisper, "Meredith won't be happy I've been hanging out with her ex."

Ash glances in Adams' direction as if only now remembering he's here. I see a muscle in his jaw jump before he leans back against the bookcase, crossing his arms over his chest, creating an appropriate amount of space between us once more.

He scratches his chin. His gaze focused on something ahead. "You can't help it if I invite my friend sometimes," he says with a lift to his shoulder.

I narrow my eyes at his change in mood, wondering if maybe I imagined the way he leaned toward me, the huskiness in his voice. I swallow hard, remembering who we both are.

I take a step back, shaking my head.

Ash nods, his brows pulled low. "I understand." He pushes off the bookcase, cocks his head towards the study room. "But we are only studying?"

The cold weight in my belly drops to my toes. I push off the bookcase, giving myself a minute to gain control over the hurricane of emotions turning in me. I muster up a weak smile, "Of course."

CHAPTER 9

FRIDAY EVENING, MOM drives me to Meredith's for a sleepover. Mer's already texted me twice to confirm I'm still coming, further proof my friends now think I'm unreliable. It makes me squirm in my seat. All the lies I've told. How long must I keep this up? Ash said I can try to minimize the lies, but I don't think I can. Telling them about Ash is potentially admitting a bigger secret. How will my friends believe it's purely platonic when Ash and I will need to be alone to practice my new abilities?

I *hate* lying. I hate lying to *them*. There has to be a compromise without them getting territorial if I spend time with Ash. He's a friend, more like work really, a professional relationship. It looks scandalous on the surface. You know, the late-night texting, the secret study sessions at his house all these weeks, and the rendezvous in a deserted classroom.

I internally wince. It's all very incriminating. Maybe if I would have told them in the beginning, it wouldn't look so scandalous. Besides, I don't like St. Claire like that.

All week we've been splitting our time between actually studying and practicing in the workshop in his backyard. Ash found some books on Siphon affinities he had to translate for me, spending the evenings after I left to write notes in a green notepad he gives me the next time I see him. I was worried about the extra time he was spending on me, but he assured me it wasn't taking away from his studies. That he was using the time he'd study for Latin, since he's fluent, to translate the Seraph books for me.

Yesterday, I read how Quiescents are often riddled with depression and anxiety, and other mental illnesses. The Domini who wrote it believed that being cut off from the Light was like removing a limb and that phantom pain causes problems to the psyche. Siphons crave the Light. A forever sense of longing, even if they don't know what they're missing. It was a painful reminder of my own anxiety and struggles.

My attention travels over to mom, lightly singing along to the radio. Both my parents always seem so happy, so carefree. They have normal stresses for sure, like bills and work, and clients making last-minute changes, Pomeranians digging up their yard, but overall they're both normal.

All the books say that being a Siphon is genetic. Even before they knew what genetics were. The texts say there was always a generational connection. I've wondered not for the first time which one of my parents it comes from. Why they don't have any magic? If maybe they wrestle with a sort of anxiety or sadness from being denied the Light in their genetics. They're only better at hiding it than me.

Mom sees me staring and gives me a warm smile. "You okay? You've been quiet today." At my nod, she adds, "How's the boy?"

"Hmm?" I feign ignorance.

Her smile gets mischievous, and I prepare myself. "The boy you don't want your friends to know about?"

"My friend is just fine."

"A friend you don't want anyone to know about." She gives me a pointed look before turning her attention back to the road.

I rub my hand, my face scrunching up in displeasure at where she's going with this. "You're proving why I don't want to tell anyone." I gesture between us. "It'll be way worse with Mere and Kat."

Mom makes a face that's caught between seeing my point and not. "Well, I hope you'd say something if this friendship turns into something more." She gives me a reprimanding look. "You don't need to hide a secret boyfriend."

I slide down into my seat, cringing at this conversation. "He's only a friend," I remind her.

Mom laughs as she turns down the curvy coastal road toward Meredith's. "I know you said you didn't want the teasing and that this *particular* boy would cause some extra attention." I don't like her choice of enunciation. "But it's rather conspicuous." She gives me a loaded arch of her brow.

"I know," I say as I rub my temples. "I've got to tell them soon, but I don't want it to be a big deal."

Mom licks her lips and tightens her hands on the steering wheel, focusing too hard on the road ahead. Her universal sign she has something to say, but the other person might not like it.

Finally, she says with the tone she uses when she's asking a question she already knows the answer to, "Maybe you like having the attention of this particular boy all to yourself?"

I wrap my arms around myself, trying to contain all the squirmy feelings. "Or because after three years of relentless teasing over Alex, I don't want to get it for Ash, too?"

"I could see that point." She slows as she pulls into Meredith's driveway, rolling down the window once she gets to the gate box. She enters the code, and it slides open. "But think of how hurt they'll be if they find out on their own. You've been lying to them, and sneaking around with a boy, that I think a few of them have crushes on."

These are things I've said to myself, many times over and she's not wrong, but she also doesn't have all the facts. Ash and I are not simply friends. He's a Seraph helping her Siphon daughter gain control over her Light powers before she hurts someone. Telling Meredith and Kat will only eliminate one secret and create more animosity when they're never invited to our secret training sessions.

I give mom a withering look because I can't tell her the truth and let out a sigh, grabbing my middle tighter. "I want a friendship without strings, just for a little while."

"That's fair. And maybe you should tell them that too." She gives me a sympathetic smile, her hand comes out automatically to touch mine. I grab her fingers, giving her an appreciative squeeze. She looks at our hands, her eyes glassy when she realizes I didn't flinch away.

Meredith's three Yorkies come barreling out her front door, barking like they've seen the devil himself, Mere and Kat trailing after them. Meredith waves hello as Katerina curses down at the dogs as they circle their legs. Mom gives them both a wave hello.

"Yay, you're here!" Meredith pulls open the car door, her springy hair bounces as she leans in, "Hello, Mrs. Martin."

The dogs are barking too loud for us to catch what mom says. Meredith tries to shoo them away but eventually, mom waves a never-mind, tossing me a look that says *good luck* as I close the door.

As soon as we head towards the house, the herd of dogs runs past us, their little legs bounding up the steps and through the door. Kat slips her arm through mine, telling me all about how much fun we're going to have tonight.

It's not until later while Meredith, Kat, and I are eating popcorn snuggled up on the big puffy couch cushions in the theater room watching a movie that I realize I don't feel the usual aversion, the uncomfortable feeling in my gut when someone is too close. This revelation feels a little like I've left something behind, but I also feel something else.

I feel free.

MEREDITH'S BEDROOM IS CHILLY as we walk in, ready to settle into our sleeping arrangements. The room smells faintly of cotton candy and her hibiscus hair gel. I head straight to my trundle bed as Meredith and Kat continue their deep analysis of the romantic comedy we just watched, clearly unhappy with the protagonist's choice of love interests, as we get ready for bed.

"She was better off with Grayson."

Kat brushes out her long curls on the twin bed opposite the room, and adds, "But Jay was hotter."

Meredith waves a dismissive hand. "But if she hadn't forgotten her phone in the art room, it would have been a completely different movie," Meredith huffs.

"Exactly," Kat croons, "that's why it was fate."

"It wasn't fate," Meredith's nose scrunches up in displeasure. "It was poor plot devices."

She reaches for her book. The conversation stalled for now. Kat fluffs the thick pink pillows up behind her, her heart-shaped face lit up by her phone screen as she checks her social media before bed. Meredith settles further into her book, pulling up her down comforter around her while I slip under my own blankets on the trundle bed below her.

I reach for my phone to make sure my school alarm is off when I see Ash's name on my screen. My stomach does a nervous sort of flip, soon replaced with guilty fear. I quickly glance up at Meredith, but she has her back to me, engrossed in her book.

Since they're both preoccupied, I burrow under the comforter, hiding my phone screen. I bite my bottom lip as I send him a message, wondering if he's still awake.

ME: Hey, you still up?

ASH: Yeah, training ran late, icing my shoulder and trying to get some homework done.

ME: Ouch.

ASH: How's the sleepover?

ME: Winding down.

ASH: No raging parties then?

ME: Not this time.

ASH: What do girls do at sleepovers, anyway?

ME: Probably the same as boys, except we're going dress shopping tomorrow.

ASH: Same.

ME: That will be interesting to see.

ASH: It's not pretty, actually.

ME: I doubt that.

ASH: It's true.

ME: You'll have to prove it. I don't believe you.

ASH: Haha, we'll see.

ME: I'll bring my camera.

ASH: Better not.

We spend the next hour texting back and forth about movies, video games, photography, books, and vacations we've taken with our parents. Neither of us brings up Seraphs or Siphons and I find I like this bit of normal.

Meredith lets out a loud snore, bringing my attention back to my surroundings. Even though I'm bundled up under this thick blanket, my fingers and toes are cold, but my face is warm. I'm playing a dangerous game that I keep telling myself is harmless, but my heart hammers in my chest and I want to keep typing, but ultimately I decided I should go to bed.

ME: Goodnight.

ASH: Goodnight, Echo.

I cradle my phone in my hand, my eyes drift toward Meredith and Kat's sleeping forms. I need to tell them and soon, the longer I keep this secret, the further into its dark depths I go. Soon. I hide my phone in my overnight bag, along with the urge to read more into it than there is.

THE FOLLOWING AFTERNOON IS a blur of colorful fabrics, sequins, and tulle as we go from shop to shop looking for a home-coming dress. As Kat heads to the dressing room with an armful of evening wear, Meredith and I decide to take a break and head over to the Sandbar Cafe next door.

We carry our cold drinks to an outside table, the large saltwater taffy-colored umbrella providing much-needed shade. A seagull hops eagerly on the ground under the table next to us as a toddler drops her french fries while her parents look over apartment brochures.

"You okay?" Meredith asks, sipping her pineapple orange drink. "You seem off."

"*Good* off or *bad* off?"

Meredith studies me for a moment, humming in her throat. "You're less tense, but also.... preoccupied."

I sip too much of my hibiscus peach ice freeze and get brain freeze. It gives me a moment to recover. "I *do* feel less anxious," I say truthfully.

"That's good, right?"

"It is," I say with a relieved sigh, happy to be on a topic I can handle. "Strange. But it feels so good not to be emotionally heavy all the time." I take in a breath and let it out.

"What has changed you think?" Her eyes are bright with curiosity. Everything.

I take the lid off my cup and use the straw to poke at some frozen bits. I haven't fully accepted that this anxiety and the overwhelming cascade of emotions have all been because I couldn't access my genetic birthright. The Light that Siphons, I, am connected to. So simple and yet so terribly complicated. Because I do feel lighter. I'm not so worried that any minute my heart will race for no apparent cause and threaten to suffocate me.

I haven't mastered control—but with the little energy I've been able to play with; I feel better. What would happen if I used it more? Would all my anxiety and fears go away? Would this constant weight on my soul lift?

"I don't know," I lie, my brows pulled down. "I've been trying some new breathing techniques." A smile tugs at my lips as I think of practicing in the St. Claire's workshop.

Meredith smiles along with me. A lump forms in my throat at how good a friend she's been to me over the years and I've repaid that with lies. Tell her. It'll be easier if I break it to Meredith first, so she can help me with Kat.

"Meredith," I start, taking in a deep breath to steel myself for what I'm about to say.

Her eyes cut to my left, and her hand shoots out to grab my arm, startling me, and kicking up a nest of bees under my skin.

"Look who I found," Kat purrs from behind me.

Meredith's gaze on me is apologetic and encouraging at the same time. "Oh hi," she says, tucking her hair behind one ear, as she stares behind me.

The sweat from the balmy afternoon becomes ice on my skin as I turn around and see Alex Carter on Katerina's arm. Even in heels Alex stands about a foot taller than Kat, who has her hand on her hip, grinning from ear to ear. Alex flashes me a shy smile.

I have an out-of-body experience as my hand lifts, my wave disjointed. "Hi."

Kat grins like a cat that's brought home dinner. "Alex's invited us to lunch." She smiles, bouncing on her heels.

Meredith's gaze fixes on me, waiting for something. Kat's smile dims as her eyes dart to Alex at her side, urgent. Meredith kicks me under the table.

"Oh, cool." It is definitely not *cool*.

"Hope it's alright?" Alex says, cheerfully oblivious.

Can he see how hard my friends are giving me the go-for-it-eye? When I realize everyone is waiting for me, I say, "Yeah. Yes."

Kat practically radiates. She gives her biggest, most satisfied grin as she says, "I know the perfect place for lunch."

PARADISE PIZZA HAS THE best breadsticks on the island, but it's hard to enjoy the sweet savory garlic yumminess when I'm squished in a booth with Kat elbowing me in the ribs every five minutes. Alex sits across from me, looking like a group of girls he barely knows has taken him hostage. He smiles a little tightly down at Meredith, who looks up at him like a kitten, and he's the ball of yarn.

"So Alex, were you shopping for homecoming?" Kat asks, subtle as ever.

Her sharp elbow hits my ribs again, but this time she adds a pointed look. I ball my hands into fists under the table. My anxiety may be less, but Kat's definitely testing the limits.

"That's what we were doing," Mere adds, trying to keep the conversation from lagging. "Dress shopping."

Alex plays with the end of his straw, and one shoulder lifts. "I was running errands." His hazel eyes lift to mine, and the nest of bees in my stomach ratchets up.

I feel Kat tense beside me, another elbow jab coming my way, so I quickly ask, "Oh, like what?"

Kat cringes a little at the robotic sound of my voice, but Meredith gives me an encouraging nod. I wish my ability was to turn invisible so I could flee.

Alex licks his lips before answering. "I was running errands for my father and stopped into Divine's." He hooks his thumb towards the antique shop across the plaza.

"That weird store with the stuffed armadillos in the window?" Kat scoffs.

"Ash says they have some neat stuff in there." I would have regretted my sentence even before they all turned to look at me.

"St. Claire?" Alex asks, picking the skin on his thumb. "I didn't know you were friends?"

"No. I mean, we're not."

Kat angles her body toward mine, her razor sharp brow lifts. "When did you talk to Ash St. Claire?"

I wipe my clammy palms on my shorts under the table. My eyes flicking towards Alex and Meredith. I wave my hand airily. "It wasn't anything, just one of those get to know you assignment in English." I take a sip of my water to wash down the burn of my lies.

"You didn't tell us that?" Meredith says, her excitement palatable. Her eyes flick to Alex and she reins it in.

"It was nothing." I shake my head, unable to look at anyone. "I don't really know Ash at all."

"No?" Alex shrugs his shoulders carelessly and leans towards Meredith with a conspiratorial smirk. "St. Claire is right," he says, "Divines has some hidden treasures. My father loves that stuff. He's particularly interested in objects with a story. One of a kind."

"Did you find anything?" Mer asks.

Alex takes a long sip of his water. "One. An old metal casket."

Kat winkles her nose. "Like, for a body?"

Alex hold his hands apart about twelve inches. "No, it's small, more like a vessel." He checks his phone. "I'm working on getting it verified now."

The bell over the door chimes. I don't give it much attention until I see Meredith suddenly very interested in the wrapper of her straw. I look over my shoulder, already guessing who I'll see. Adam stands at the pickup counter. His sunglasses perched on his head and dressed in basketball shorts. A light sheen of sweat on his skin and a flush in his cheeks as if he just came from playing. My stomach clenches with nerves at the sight of him. Alex does a quick assessment of the table and leans back into the bench seat. Oblivious to the tension brewing around the table, he calls Adam over.

Adam looks surprised, and his expression only turns more com-plicated when he sees the rest of us at the table. He does this half-turn where I think he might leave, but walks over to our table instead.

"Hey man," Alex says cordially.

"Hey." Adam nods to Alex, and then his eyes land on me. "Hey, Echo."

I can feel the eyes of everyone at the table on me as I give him a small wave. Kat scrutinizes the gesture, probably reading too much into it. I slide my hands back under the table, squeezing my clammy fists tight.

"We're you playing at the park?" Alex says with a feral grin that has me furrow my brow.

Adam glances down at his clothes. "No, I was running on West beach."

Meredith's brows perk up at the mention of Adam so close to her house.

"Much better views." Alex's laugh doesn't sound like he's talking about the ocean. Adam steals a quick glance at Meredith as Alex adds, "You know, I saw your boy St. Claire out there this morning, too. A little far from his house, huh?"

"Not really." Adam shifts his weight from one foot to the other. "What were you doing on the W. C.? It's a little far from you, right?"

Adam doesn't live on the crescent either, and even if he did, he isn't the type to be an elitist. There's a meaningful sort of silence that follows. It has me wondering if maybe they're not that friendly after all.

Alex's jaw tightens, and his throat moves. "Not as far as you think."

An awkward silence falls on the table. If I hadn't been watching Alex, I would have missed the bitter look in his eyes before he quickly blinks it away, grinning. "I thought it was funny, is all." He waves away the tension as if it's that easy, and leans back into his seat, one arm draped loosely on the table. "I've seen St. Claire in a lot of funny places lately."

Adam sticks his hands in his pockets. His friendly expression shifts before Kat blurts, "What, do all boys go running on Saturdays? Is that like a thing?" She smirks at Alex.

Meredith sighs in relief at the topic change. "Coach has the soccer team run the sand to build terrain endurance," she says as she twirls a strand of hair around her finger, "or that's what she claims."

"It's a good workout." Adam glances behind him toward the pickup counter. "Well, looks like my order is ready." He gives me a tight-lipped nod before he turns away.

He couldn't have known what that small amount of attention would do, unaware of the complexity of girl friendships, of Meredith's ongoing heartbreak, and Kat's armchair detective work. Katerina knows I'm hiding something. She's just on the wrong trail. I work to keep my face blank under Kat's scrutiny as Meredith shreds every straw wrapper on the table. Kat gives her a sympathetic look that Meredith waves off.

Alex waits until Adam pushes out the door before he leans forward and says to Meredith, "Didn't the two of you have a rough breakup or something?"

"Or something," Meredith mumbles, the straw wrappers now confetti.

Kat narrows her eyes. It's the first time she hasn't looked smitten. "What was that all about with Woo about St. Claire?" She asks, tucking her hands under her chin.

Alex shrugs, tapping his fingers on the side of his glass. "Nothing."

"Oh, come on," Kat purrs, her big brown eyes sultry and inviting, "you can tell me."

Alex smiles down at his water before he answers, "He puts on a good show, you know?" He smirks down at Meredith, chuckling to himself before he adds, "The perfect golden boy, but deep down he's just another asshole."

"I wasn't aware you were friends?" I say before I can think better at keeping my incriminating mouth shut.

"I know him pretty well," Alex says, voice honey smooth.

Kat uncurls her fingers from under her chin, and the look she's giving me is like I've grown two heads. She says something to change the subject, her flirty laugh echoing in my ears, but all I can think of is my defensive behavior.

When the server returns with our food, I excuse myself, pretending I don't notice Meredith watching me. I'm not surprised when Kat follows me to the restroom.

As soon as the door closes she asks, "What's going on?"

I turn on the faucet, cupping my hands and splashing water on my face. What *is* going on? I grab a fistful of paper towels and dab at my cheeks. "Nothing."

"You finally get some time with Alex and you're acting weird."

"I *am* weird," I tell her.

She huffs. "Not like this." Kat puts a hand on her hip. "He specifically asked for you, Echo. He's into you." When I say nothing, she shakes her head. "So what, you're into Ash now?"

A tension headache has formed behind my eyes. I pinch the bridge of my nose as I say, "No."

Kat searches my face, her jaw goes tight. "Then stop acting like it." She opens her purse, pulls out her lip gloss, and meets my eyes in the mirror. "I thought you'd be happy Alex's here."

"I am," I say. Because isn't that how I'm supposed to feel?

"Did you notice how he was looking at you?" Kat's eyes soften. "I knew once Alex got to talking to you, he'd see how amazing you are." She closes the gap between us and picks up a strand of my hair affectionately.

Her intentions are coming from a good place. I only wish it wasn't the Kat-way. I know she wants me to be happy like I want all good things for her. It gives me hope that she'll understand when I tell her the truth.

"Alex's a good fit for you," she tells me, giving my hair a little tug before she drops it. "St. Claire isn't," she warns. She turns to the mirror and checks her makeup one last time. "Guys like Ash St. Claire will break your heart."

"But I won't push you with Alex anymore," she says, turning back around. "Okay?"

"Okay," I say, throat tight.

Kat fans her face. "The air conditioning must be broken in here," she says, pulling the door open. "Come on, I'm starving."

I'm used to wearing a happy mask when inside I feel like I'm drowning. I put it on through the rest of lunch. Smiling and laughing when I needed to. It wasn't until I was home alone in my room that I let the emotions wash over me.

The glimmer of hope that I could be honest about who I really am and who I want to spend my time with had completely dissolved.

CHAPTER 10

I T'S A HUMID September day. Ash's air-conditioning is on high, blowing the artificial air over my arms and face as I buckle into the seat. The low growl of the engine, a steady, familiar sound, masking the torrent of emotions waging war in my body. I bite at my nails as Kat's and I's conversation plays on repeat in my thoughts. The heavy reality that I'll never truly be honest with another person again continues to drag me down.

I'm forced to focus on my surroundings when Ash's car pulls into the little garden park a couple streets from his house.

"What are we doing here?"

His face is unreadable as he turns in his seat to face me. "You've been quiet the whole drive."

"It's a short drive."

"And you usually have a lot to say."

I slump back in my seat. The last few days, weeks maybe, have put me on a roller-coaster of sour moods and the worst is it's mostly my doing. The secrets, the lies, the sneaking around, the creepy stalker whose identity is still unknown, and something about the oddly familiar way Alex was talking about Ash; has wiggled its way under my skin.

I settle on asking, "How well do you know Alex Carter?"

He arches one blond eyebrow. "Why?"

I chew on my lip before I add, "I had lunch with him yesterday."

Ash's expression is guarded as he says, "Okay."

I pick at my nail polish. "He said some *things* about you."

Ash's hand tightens on the bottom of the steering wheel. "That doesn't surprise me." When he looks over and sees that I am waiting for an explanation, he sighs. "Everyone at Shorecrest has *something* to say about me." He gives me a pointed look.

"It seemed personal."

Ash furrows his brow in thought. "Probably him asserting the social hierarchy." He shrugs. "I'm familiar with the type."

"I guess," I say, thinking about Tyler. Who is *exactly* the type. I shake my head, feeling slightly frustrated my words aren't conveying right.

Ash taps his hands on the steering wheel, staring out the windshield. He asks, "So, was it like a *date?*"

"Oh," I say, my face heating. I stick my hands under my thighs. "Not *really.*" And then because he's too quiet, I add, "Kat and Meredith were there too."

"Ah." We listen to the tick, tick, hiss of the engine.

I watch him in my peripheral. He's looking out at an empty swing set, doing that thing again where he plays with his bottom lip. I narrow my eyes at him, not sure how to take him.

He's still not looking at me when he asks, "Do you like ice cream?"

"Yes," I answer, still suspicious.

Ash drives to a little ice cream shop shaped like a giant ice cream cone on the east side of the island near the pier. I'm licking the chocolate sprinkles off before they melt to the ground as Ash stuffs the leftover bills and coins into the tip jar.

We head towards the boardwalk that overhangs the water. The breeze has that fresh, sharp sting of the sea in it. A mix of brine and ocean foam that's in my bones. I take in a deep breath, letting it clear away all the darkness in my thoughts, breathing in the island's scent. When I was little, my parents and I would come here to the floating bait shop to get shrimp and go fishing off the pier, but we haven't done that in a while.

The smell of cooked food floats on the breeze and I glance down at the row of touristy shops, towards a couple of restaurants on the end. I lean into the railing, watching the water lap as a charter boat goes out.

"So why the island?" I ask.

"Hmm?" he says around a mouthful of chocolate chip ice cream.

"Your parents could live anywhere. Why the island?"

"Oh." He catches a few stray drips running down his cone with his tongue. "Well, look at it." He nods towards the channel leading out to the ocean.

The water is swaying in gentle peaks; the sun glinting off the crests like diamonds twinkling in the sea. A pod of dolphins slices through the wake of incoming fishing boats. An outgoing charter cuts through the water like a knife through whipped cream. People are fishing further down along the jetty. Waves spray up between the rocks, making a couple of kids giggle.

"Okay, yes," I concede, "but seriously, you could live anywhere in the world."

"My father says there are only a few places in the world he feels at peace, and the island is one of them."

Ash and I are thoughtful as we watch the water. He takes another bite from his cone, but mine continues to melt as I ask, "Are there any other Siphons on the island?"

Ash continues to watch the water as he says, "I don't know. Siphons tend to stay away from the St. Claire name."

A pelican lands on the dock, hopping around looking for food. It hobbles further down towards the people fishing. It feels so good with the sea breeze blowing away the day's growing heat. We stroll away from the shops towards the fishing pier. The boardwalk ends at a cement path and a set of steps through the sea wall where there's a little sandy beach before the channel.

During low tide, you can have a picnic under the shade of the boardwalk on the white sand. I hop onto the seawall and crunch into my waffle cone. Ash leans his elbows on the wall next to me. His cotton shirt brushes my arm as we finish our cones.

We watch the channel and the people fishing further down. An old man with a bandanna tied around his neck has a cast net in his teeth. He spins and throws it into the water a few feet from us. It balloons out like a parachute and then ripples with tiny fish as he pulls it to shore. A pelican hops anxiously nearby, hoping for a handout.

"What about your parents?" he asks, breaking the silence. "Were they born here?"

"My mom was," I say. "Her parents died when I was little. My dad's parents are from Colorado. They seem pretty normal whenever they visit."

He nods thoughtfully, "And what about your family? Do they have heterochromia, like you?"

I shake my head. "No. Just me." I let out a long sigh. When I look up, Ash is watching me.

He looks so miserably apologetic as he says, "I'm sorry. I know you hate talking about it."

"No, it's fine." And I mean it. "I just don't like the attention."

He nods, his eyes fixed on the channel. And then because he doesn't ask me more, I confess, "When I was little, people would just come up to me and touch me. My arms, my hair, my hands, once someone picked me up." I repress a shiver, remembering.

Mom's back was turned, so she didn't see right away. I'll never forget the way her soft face turned feral as she snatched me back, yelling at the woman that you don't just go around picking up people's kids. I feel bad for the woman now, but back then I just remember feeling afraid.

"I would have worn an eye-patch, but then *more* people would stare."

"I see why contacts were easier." He gives me a sideway glance, his mouth lifting, "But I like the pirate look too."

I sway my shoulder into his. "And what about you? Where were you born?"

"I was born here," he says, keeping his shoulder pressed to mine. "My parents moved back to the island when my mom was pregnant with me."

"How's that work?" I wonder, asking gently, "since she's immortal, can she keep having babies forever?"

"No." He watches a couple of bold sandpipers who haven't noticed us yet. They flit around picking at the sand. "The older we get, the least likely we are to have children."

"That's sad," I say, watching the birds with him. One of them finally notices us and they all scamper off down the waterline, chirping little sounds of alarm.

"Multiple births are incredibly rare." A soft ringing sound comes from his pocket, but he ignores it. "They are highly reverend with my kind."

"Oh?"

He gives me a private smile. "Yes, Seraphim even have a special name for them. Glyth'ian. They're believed to be quite exceptional among our kind."

"And are they?"

He shrugs, pushing off the seawall, and offers me his hand. I take it without thinking as I slide off the wall. I quickly drop it, climbing the stairs back up to the dock. We trace our steps along the boardwalk, past the ice cream shop, and towards where we parked.

My gaze travels along the row of cars parked in front of the boutique shops, snagging on a familiar red car. I reach for Ash, grabbing a fistful of his shirt, and pull him towards a skinny alley between the Salty Siren restaurant and the Glittering Jewel.

I push him further into the shadows of the two buildings. His back hits the wooden planks as he blinks at me. "This is... different."

I cover his mouth with my hand. "Kat's here. I saw her car." I whisper, my heart hammering in my chest. "If she sees us, I'm dead. Deader than dead." Ash's lips tickle my palm as he tries to talk, and I whip my hand away.

"I thought you were going to tell them?" he asks, his amused gaze wandering to my hand still clutched in his shirt.

I drop the soft fabric and dig my fingers into my scalp, messing up my ponytail. "I was, but obviously... I haven't."

Sounds of conversation draw our attention to the mouth of the alley. We are far enough in that the passersby don't notice us. I hold my hand up for St. Claire to stay put, which only amuses him more. I carefully poke my head out of the alley and scan the boardwalk. I don't see Kat anywhere. She's probably in one of the dress shops.

Ash asks, "Are we going to stay here all day?"

"No. She can't shop here all day."

"Right. Of course," he says, his eyes glittering with amusement.

I pace the alley. Ash says my name, not for the first time, but I need to think. When he calls it again, I ask, in a harsh whisper, "What *is* it?"

"You're glowing."

I jerk, startled at the sight of my fingertips. The glow intensified in the shadows between the two businesses. It reflects on Ash's features, accentuating his face, giving him an ethereal appearance.

I stuff my hands into my pockets and take a deep breath, pulling my nerves back into place. "What kind of stupid power is this, anyway?"

"You will always have a light in the dark." His lopsided smile shows the little dimple in his cheek.

I make a derisive noise in the back of my throat at how lame that is. "Okay, listen, we double back towards the fishing pier, through the bait shop, and behind the apartments, and then cut through the arcade and sneak through the parking lot back to your car."

"That's exuberant," he says, his brows disappearing into his hair. "Or I could leave first and pick you up behind the ice cream shop." He points in the opposite direction of the boutiques. "It's right there."

"Yeah, or we could do that."

The plan decided, Ash leaves to retrieve his car. I wait a full three minutes before I exit the alley. I see Charity with a group of people waiting for a table outside of the Salty Siren. She grimaces like I've got an infectious plague when she sees me. Her look is reproachful as she purses out her lips, and then she spins around, ignoring me.

Ash's car pulls up as planned behind the ice cream parlor, far from Charity's line of sight. "That was close," I say, clicking my seatbelt into place. "Did you see Kat?"

"No."

Seeing Charity makes me a little nervous, but I doubt she'd think Ash and I were here together. She's more focused on keeping me away from Alex right now. Kat is keener, however, and I'm thankful she didn't see us.

"I completely support your decision in keeping our... *friendship* a secret, but this seems... worse?"

I wrinkle my nose. "You make it sound illicit."

Ash arches a brow. "You pushed me down a dark alleyway," he says with amusement, enjoying this a little too much.

I make a frustrated sound because he's right. It was different when we were only hanging out in his private library, practicing in his walled backyard. It's getting harder to keep this a secret, especially if we're going to be going out in public together. And especially since I don't want to stop.

His blue t-shirt makes his ocean eyes sparkle. His hands are loose on the steering wheel, and the way he looks over at me with that lazy smile makes my heart ache with something dangerously close to longing.

When he stops at the red light, he asks, "You still want to come over?"

"Yes." I blow out a breath, my heartbeat chaotic. "If my Siphon powers are connected to my emotions, it's probably a good time to get a handle on it?"

ASH'S PHONE BUZZES AS we pull into his long driveway, Adam's name displayed on the screen. "You sure you're alright doing this with Adam around?"

I shrug. "Yes, I'm not really *doing* anything, anyway."

Fifteen minutes later, Adam appears in the workshop doorway, still dressed in his church best, one eye closed and the other cracked enough to see where he's going.

Ash and I watch him curiously, before Ash finally asks, "What are you doing?"

Adam cautiously opens his eyes. "I didn't want to see anything traumatizing."

"I'm new to this, but is that something I have to worry about?" I ask Ash.

"He's joking," Ash says, looking exasperated. There's a little pink to his cheeks that causes me to scrutinize both boys.

Adam is still grinning as he sits down on an old bench seat, the wood creaking as he settles in. Ash and I are sitting across from each other on the yoga mat. Adam leans forward on the bench, his hands on his knees, expectant.

"I've never seen real magic. Unless you count when Ash cut his arm to prove how fast he heals?"

"Really?" I say, eyeing Ash's tanned forearms. "I want to see."

Ash pushes my knees down, keeping me rooted in place. "Let's work on you first and then I'll stab myself for everyone's entertainment, okay?"

I flash Ash a smile. He shakes his head and I close my eyes, settling into the thick foam mat. I breathe in, focus on that warm presence behind my heart, and hold up my fingers.

The tips glow like ten tiny orbs. Adam raises his brows. At least he is impressed, but I give Ash a withering look because I still think it's the stupidest power ever.

I twirl my fingers in the air. Ash's gaze moves away from mine as he rolls his shoulders. I hold out my hands, pushing a little more of that energy into them.

Ash floats his hands above mine. Our fingers brush, sending a different type of warmth through me. I can tell by the way his eyes flash to mine that he can feel the heat now coming from my hands.

"Now, a little more," he says, his voice low.

This is the part where I always get nervous. With every practice now, it's getting easier and easier, but I'm still apprehensive. I don't want to hurt anyone, no matter how many times Ash tells me not to worry.

I flex that invisible muscle inside me, and Light pours through my veins. I can feel the featherlight touch of his fingers and it makes me shiver, despite the warmth filling the room. The glow has spread up my wrists. I watch the sparks from my fingertips dance in Ash's eyes.

"Start pulling it back now," he says, sliding his hands away before he can get burned.

I close my hands into fists, like turning off a valve the Light stops. Only today it flares out, unwilling to go to sleep now that it's tasted freedom. Fire travels up my veins, like cracks in my skin, they glow orange.

The power flares making me flinch, but in its place is pure euphoria. No anxiety, no stress. I wonder what would happen if I opened the door and let all the Light out.

There's a sharp smell, like burning plastic. Ash and I both come to the same conclusion and quickly stand. We're staring down at the melted yoga mat when he says, "Don't panic."

But that's exactly what I do. I try to stop it. I open and close my hands several times, but all it does is throw sparks onto the floor.

Adam stands, taking a step back. He casts a wary look at Ash. I catch sight of myself in the workshop's warped glass window. My entire body glows.

"I can't stop it!" The workshop fills with the scent of burning things.

"Yes, you can, focus."

I glance down at my clothes, which are smoking. The hem of my shorts burns like the edges of a piece of paper, the flame traveling up the threads. Part of my shirt breaks out in flames and I reflexively smack the small fires, trying to put them out, but it only makes it worse.

"*Ash*," Adam warns, backing towards the doorway.

Ash grabs my wrists but recoils back with a hiss. "The pool," he says, grabbing my shirt and pulling me out of the workshop.

We run to the pool and crash ungracefully into it. The shock of cool water breaks whatever hold the Light had on me. I sputter to the surface, pushing wet hair out of my eyes as I tread water. Ash breaks the surface beside me, pushing his wet hair off his forehead. He runs a hand down his face, looking strained as steam fogs all around us.

I swim to the edge and look up to see Adam slowly approach, looking equally terrified and relieved.

"Does that usually happen?" he asks.

Ash swims up beside me. "No."

"I'm so sorry," I say to Ash, then to Adam, "I don't know what happened."

"It's fine," Ash says, wincing as he lifts onto the edge of the pool, swiftly climbing out of the water.

Adam reaches down to pull me out, but Ash shakes his head and offers me his hands instead. I let him pull me up, knowing it won't hurt him like it would Adam. My waterlogged clothes threaten to drag me back into the pool, but Ash is strong. I fall into him, his hand resting on my lower back before I step back, pushing the hair out of my face.

Ash's mouth is tight, so I gently grab his hands, turning them over to see the blistering skin.

"I'm so sorry," I cry, keeping my touch soft. "This was a bad idea."

"It'll heal."

"I didn't want to hurt you," I tell him, wrapping my arms around myself.

"You're getting better."

"Better?" I scoff. I jerk my hand out angrily. "I almost burned down your garage."

"That's why we jumped in the pool," he says with a lopsided smile.

He's as drenched as I am. His wet clothes hug his body. Water drips from his shorts onto the patio stones. I glance down at myself, surprised to see the tattered remains of my shirt. I quickly cross my arms to cover myself.

Ash spins around, heading towards the house. He clears his throat, and calls over his shoulder, "There are towels in the mudroom."

Adam, his eyes already respectively averted, follows behind him. I drag behind, feeling deflated. How bad would it have been if the pool wasn't there? I join them in the mudroom as Ash opens a closet and grabs us towels.

Adam says, "That was the coolest thing I've ever seen."

I give Adam a weak smile and take the offered towel from Ash. He toes off his wet shoes and socks as I wrap myself up in the thick towel. I follow his lead, not wanting to leave wet shoe prints all over the St. Claire mansion.

"I might have some clothes you can wear," Ash says, nodding his chin for us to follow him into the house.

We take an almost hidden staircase up to the second floor and to Ash's bedroom. Adam makes himself comfortable the way someone does when they're acquainted with a space. He lounges on the soft leather sofa and grabs the remote, turning on the television.

"Don't look so sad Echo, you'll get better at this Siphon thing." He winks at me and though I shake my head, I feel a little better.

Ash touches my elbow, showing that I should follow him into his bedroom. It feels weird being in this private space that's all his own. I feast on the details with fresh interest. There's a stack of books on the nightstand with a half-empty glass of water next to them. A t-shirt and jeans tossed carelessly on the bed, and a pair of running shoes half out of the closet.

He grabs the clothes and tosses them into a laundry basket inside his closet and kicks the shoes inside before shutting the door. I arch a brow behind his back as he rummages through his dresser. He digs out a forest green t-shirt and running shorts.

"See if these will work." He meets my eyes briefly and then quickly steps out of the room.

I change out of my wet clothes in his bathroom. Sunlight from the window above the tub shines on the white and silver tile that covers almost the entire room, even the enormous shower in the corner.

I drop my clothes in the tub as I exchange them for the borrowed ones. I cinch the drawstring on the shorts so they're snug before I check out how I look in the gilded mirror above the sinks.

My hair hangs in wavy clumps, and my face looks drenched in despair, but the clothes will do even if they are a little frumpy. I lean against the marble counter, my palms digging into the cool surface as I stare at my reflection.

When I come out of the bedroom, Ash is sitting at his desk in a fresh pair of clothes, wrapping a bandage around his hand. Adam says something low that I can't hear, causing a grunt from St. Claire. They glance up at me when I come into the room. Whatever conversation they were having stops.

"Nice outfit." Adam grins.

I stick my tongue out, which only makes him grin wider. Ash ducks his head as he checks his wrap job with his brows pulled down so low I think he's angry at it.

"These are awfully short," I direct my comment to St. Claire.

"They prevent drag," he says and then changes the subject, "so practice today... was unexpected."

I give him an incredulous look before flopping down on the couch. "A huge disaster is what you mean."

Adam rolls his head toward me. "I was impressed."

"It wasn't a complete failure." Ash rubs his unburned hand on his neck. "We discovered how hot you can get."

Adam throws Ash a bemused smirk before he tries to hide it with a cough. St. Claire studies his bandage again. "What I *mean* is, now we know what you are capable of and can prevent it from getting out of control again."

I blow a strand of wet hair out of my face. "How did that even happen?" I ask. "I thought Siphons couldn't do anything because of the curse?"

"Siphons aren't as *powerful* because of the curse." Ash rubs a hand over his head, "but they can still be dangerous."

Dangerous.

I chew my thumbnail. "What good is this if every time I try to use the Light, I catch fire?" I gesture to myself. "No one will ever be able to touch me."

"Except Ash," Adam says, his mouth curving up, even though his eyes never leave the television screen.

Ash clears his throat, giving Adam a look out of the corner of his eye. "Well, *any* Seraph, technically," he says. "But we should definitely stay close to the water."

That I can agree on.

Ash absently runs a thumb over his bottom lip. His bandage stands out stark white against his tanned skin and I feel a stab of guilt that I'm the cause. My gaze snaps to Adam, who's staring at me. "What?" I whisper.

"Nothing," he says with a surreptitious smile.

I pinch him below his ribs, causing him to yelp. Our heads turn as Ash stands suddenly, heading towards the door, mumbling something about *Magellan's manifestos.*

"Are we supposed to follow him?"

"He'll be back," Adam says, picking up a game controller.

I reach for my phone, realizing I've left it downstairs. Though I'm familiar with the library, I'm apprehensive about wandering around the St. Claire mansion by myself. Since Adam knows his way around, I ask him if he can come with me.

"Have you been to the theater room?" he asks along the way, and when I shake my head he says, "you should ask Ash to show you."

"Do you want me to pinch you again?"

Adam holds up his hands in surrender, but his smile says something else.

Once outside, Adam slows down to soak up the sunshine as I head inside the workshop to grab my phone off the workbench, where I left it next to Ash's. I grab his phone for him. The screen flashes with a text from someone named Charlotte. I feel like a weight has dropped to my toes, along with a wave of possessiveness. I have to work to push the feelings away. It's foolish to think he doesn't have a life outside of school, outside of these obligatory training sessions.

Adam catches me staring at St. Claire's phone and I quickly stuff it into my pocket, busing myself with my own messages. There's a text from Meredith saying to call her. Guilt replaces whatever else I was feeling and I reflexively glance at Adam.

He clears his throat. "How is Meredith?"

"Good."

He nods, his dark brows pulled low, and turns to study the tools hanging on the wall behind the workbench. He picks up a hammer and sets it back down.

"So, is that why you broke up?" I blurt before I can think better of it, "because of Ash's secret?"

Adam carefully turns his head towards me, a pained expression as if he knew this was coming. "Not like you think," he says with some reservation. "I know you girls think he had something to do with it, but it wasn't Ash's fault *at all*."

I chew my lip, and Adam runs a hand down his face. He makes a derisive sound, lost in some memory. "That's what she said towards the end, *'he turned me into a snob'*. That I thought I was 'too good for her now'."

"I hadn't heard that," I say, softly.

Adam's frown turns bitter. "What's worse is I *know* I'm not better than her. It was never like that." He turns and leans against the bench. "She knew I was hiding something and kept prying, and I was handling it badly and things snowballed."

My eyes sting. Was that me? Was I following in Adam's footsteps?

"But you didn't have to break up with her," I say carefully.

"No," he agrees. "But you know Mere, she doesn't give up. I kept telling her it was nothing, but I'm a terrible liar." His voice is a little thick and I feel bad for opening old wounds. "It was soon after Ash told me. I was still awestruck by everything. He took me to some places. It was crazy. I couldn't tell Mere where I was, or what I was doing. I didn't realize how far I had alienated her until it was too late."

"Why didn't you stick it out?" I ask. "Once the excitement of Ash St. Claire's secret life was over, you could have gone back to normal. Meredith would have forgiven you."

"*Would she?*" he says it with so much doubt that it makes my heart heavy. He lifts his shoulder as if he'll never know the answer to that one. "She said, *'just tell me the truth'* but I couldn't, and she didn't accept anything I told her. She was convinced I was cheating on her and it tore me up to see her looking at me heartbroken all the time." He grabs a fistful of his shirt, right where his heart is.

My eyes burn with the threat of tears. For Adam and Meredith, and for myself.

I watch him swallow hard, and compose himself. "I've thought of a million things I should have said to her..." he lifts out his hand as if it's too late.

I want to tell him she still thinks about him, that she still loves him, but what if Meredith doesn't want me to tell him these things? Don't I despise how much they've meddled with my minuscule love life? All my secrets are becoming too intertwined for me to pick out the good from the bad. What if I do more damage than good? Adam searches my face as if he can tell I'm holding back.

"I think I've found it."

We turn as Ash walks through the doorway. He assesses the small space between Adam and me, and whatever he sees when he looks at our faces pulls him up short, his expression guarded.

"Found what?" Adam asks, stepping away from the workbench, his hands sliding into his pockets.

"Magellan's dairy," Ash says reserved, searching my face. I slide his phone out of my pocket and hold it out for him to take. He stares at the screen as it lights up, his eyes hooded as he slides it into his pocket.

"Who's Magellan?" I ask.

Ash taps the side of the book. His expression conflicted before he runs his hand through his hair to clear it. "Magellan was a Watcher. His writings are some of the most detailed I've read of Siphon culture."

"What's a Watcher?" I look over at Adam, who's as puzzled as I am.

"Watchers were a sect of Domini who studied Siphons," Ash says, a little sheepishly. "It was a failed experiment rallied by a former council member. Siphons don't let Seraphim in their communities anymore. Most Watchers are retired now, but there's a few that still observe under more creative ways."

"You mean spying," I say.

"Technically," he says, looking a little chagrin. "But recording history is important."

"Depends who's doing the recording." I grin at Adam, getting a smile in return.

I startle at the appearance of a man stepping through the workshop doors. "Are you suggesting that one party is being less than honest?" he says.

He's dressed in a crisp white dress shirt and navy slacks that fit him in a way that clothes from the big box department store never will. A smartwatch slides in and out of focus from under the sleeve of his shirt as he moves. He's as tall as Ash, with the same chiseled features, looking only about ten years older—and there's a terrible sense of Deja Vue as I look at him.

"Hello dad," Ash gives him a curt nod.

Ash's father studies the book in his son's hands, inclining his head and raising his palm. Ash reluctantly hands over the journal. He wears an expression that I've only ever seen at school. I've gotten so used to seeing the unguarded version of him, it surprises me how indifferent he can look.

Ash slides his hands into his pockets as his dad subtly studies him. The corner of his father's mouth lifts surreptitiously. He casually opens the book, his fingers ruffling a few pages, eyes skimming it over before he closes it with a significant snap.

"Magellan," he says, his eyes coolly meeting Ash's, "was overly involved, and look what it cost him. Hmm?" The statement makes Ash's jaw jump.

"Adam." Ash's dad nods a greeting.

Then his eyes slide over to me, taking in my appearance. From my baggy t-shirt hastily tied at my side to look less like I'm drowning in it, to the rolled waistband of Ash's shorts that exposes an abundance of my thighs. I swallow under his gaze.

"And this must be the Siphon."

"Echo," Ash supplies.

Ash's dad smiles at the ground. "An interesting name," he says, his striking blue eyes flicking up to mine. "A girl who talked too much punished for distracting a god from her task."

"Of catching her cheating husband," Ash retorts. "But you know the story," he says pointedly.

"My parents just liked the name," I say, feeling a little small in the presence of the two Seraphim.

"And it is a beautiful name, for a very unique girl, I'm told," he says, extending his hand. "I'm Henrik."

I hesitate before I take it. My stomach is buzzing with nerves, but I manage to shake his hand, quickly taking it back when he lets go.

I twine my fingers behind me and pray that I don't go all fireball in the presence of Ash's Dominus father.

Ash's brows furrow as he says, "You're home early."

Henrik flashes an easy smile, sticking his hand in his pocket in a gesture that mirrors Ash. "Yes," he sighs, looking momentarily tired, "a temporary reprieve." Henrik puts a hand on Ash's shoulder. "I'm hoping to get a much longer break in a few weeks."

He gently steers Ash out of the workshop and Adam and I follow like little kids who got caught breaking the rules.

"Since I'm only going to be home for less than a week, I'd like to spend time with my youngest son."

Ash nods, all serious. "Of course, I'll take Echo home."

Henrik still has his hand on his son's shoulder. It flexes slightly as he says, "Adam, I'm sure you wouldn't mind taking Echo home?" It's not really a question.

"Yeah, no problem," Adam says.

"See you at school?" I ask Ash and he nods, flashing me an apologetic look.

Henrik guides him towards the back door as Adam and I take the flagstone path to the garage. Once we're inside Adam's truck, the doors firmly closed, I say, "He's kind of intense."

Adam blows out a breath, starting the engine. "Just for the first thirty or so times you see him."

I can't tell if he's joking or not.

CHAPTER 11

KAT IS ANIMATEDLY telling me about a video that Jerrod Osmond posted online and seamlessly launching into how a girl from her first period is now dating Grant Richards, which is totally crazy because she was going to ask Grant to homecoming but *'who cares whatever'*.

Meredith is filling in the blanks of her weekend and I'm nodding along to it all, trying to find the right time to interject with 'Hey, I've been secretly hanging out with Ash St. Claire for weeks'.

My conversation with Adam yesterday made me realize I didn't want my friendship with Meredith and Katerina to end like his relationship did. I'm worried how Meredith will take the news that I've also, by proxy, been sneaking around with Adam, too. I'm so torn that it feels like I might rip in half.

Kat, who's been multitasking between our conversation and liking posts, pauses with her phone a few inches away and asks, "Echo, you okay?"

My knee stops bouncing as I blink at her. *Now, tell her, now.* Snippets of conversation float to my ears and I'm gripped with cold feet. They are going to be angry at me for lying. What if we cause a scene in the middle of the lunchroom?

Kat tilts her head at the same time Meredith looks up at me. There's a cold sweat covering my skin, and a hornet's nest in my stomach. What if I start glowing right here in the cafeteria, or worse?

I excuse myself, complaining of a stomachache. It's savory omelet day, and that's always a little risky. I grab my stuff and mumble out a few excuses for why they should stay and finish their lunches.

I leave out the side exit, heading to the library and my new favorite place to hide.

"Hey Echo." Alex pushes off the picnic tables and falls into step with me.

I stop short, exasperated. A few weeks ago, I would have been giddy to have his attention. Analyzing every detail of our interactions with Meredith and Kat, but now I want to leave before I catch fire.

The hum under my skin gets more insistent and I wrap a hand around my middle to keep all the emotions in.

"I, uh, wanted to see if you'd like to hang out this weekend?" He sticks his hands in his pockets, looking a little unsure. He flashes a smile, the smile I used to dream about.

My mouth pops open, and I quickly close it. There's a stirring of something other than bees in my stomach, it flutters hopefully. "Oh."

Alex adds quickly, "Pizza or a movie, or whatever?"

I stare at his hazel eyes, rimmed with dark lashes that I wished for so long would look at me like he is now. Why *are* they looking at me now? It took overhearing that I liked him for him to ask me out. He had two years. I can feel someone staring and when I tear my eyes from Alex's, I expect to see Charity glaring, but my eyes lock on Ash's.

I feel something in my chest clench and look away. The surrounding tables are sneaking glances. I see Tyler first wearing those too-big sunglasses with the rainbow tint he loves so much. Charity is beside him with her hair in a high ponytail, her face pinched as she whispers to Tyler, whose expression remains blank.

Alex is still waiting for an answer. His smile slipping.

"I can't," I hear myself say. "I'm spending the night at Kat's." It's the truth, but I still feel my heartbeat pounding in my ears.

Alex presses his lips together. "Maybe another time, then?"

I give a non-committal nod before I leave. The further I get from the cafeteria, the better I feel. The electricity in my veins slows, along with my heart. It's not a long-term fix, but it must do for now until I can work up the nerve to tell my friends the truth without losing control. I'll deal with the Alex thing after I tell them.

I tense up at the sound of footsteps behind me, expecting to defend myself against Charity marking her territory again, but it's Ash who jogs up beside me.

He touches my arm. "Hey, you alright?"

That small amount of contact has me nervously glancing around. Ash makes a frustrated sound and nods for me to follow him between two of the buildings. He stops at a little alcove blocked from prying eyes by overgrown cypress. Cigarette butts litter the ground, along with other suspicious paraphernalia. I wrinkle my nose in distaste. There's a curving cement wall here that looks like it was once a flower bed, but now it's a trash can with one sparse holly bush still clinging to life.

I lean back against the wall, closing my eyes. "This is getting ridiculous," I sigh. I feel St. Claire beside me, his shoulder barely touching mine. "I'm going to tell them Friday at the sleepover."

When he doesn't comment, I open my eyes. He's staring at the ground, the detritus of cigarettes and some fancy-looking skinny cigars. I can picture a few of my peers sneaking back here for a midday smoke, teachers too, but St. Claire isn't one of them.

Finally, he says, "Sorry about my dad the other day."

"He is a little intense." I give him a half smile, but his expression is still so serious.

"I'd understand if you wanted to take a break from training."

The question takes me a little by surprise. "Am I still *allowed* at your house?"

"Yes, of course," he says roughly, looking at me. He clears his throat, his attention on the ground again. He furrows his brows, and then he asks, trying to keep his tone even, "So what did Alex want?"

I study him for a moment, the way he's not looking at me. "He wanted to hang out this weekend."

His eyebrows turn even more brooding as his heel smashes a cigar end into the sandy dirt. "And what did you say?"

"I told him I couldn't."

I watch his brows lift a fraction. "Oh?"

"I've got the sleepover at Kat's on Friday."

His expression goes stormy again. "That's right." He chews on his cheek before he asks, "If you were free, would you have gone out with him?"

His ocean eyes lift to meet mine, causing lightning to strike and thunder in my stomach, sending little tingles along my spine. I hold my breath for a moment before I let it out in a rush.

Ash shakes his head and brushes away the question. "Never mind, it's none of my business."

I press my lips together, feeling a little unmoored. The bell rings too loud in the deafening silence, making us both flinch.

"You go first, don't want to start any rumors," he says, nodding to the way we came. His tone aloof in the way I hate.

"Right," I say, but don't move to leave.

The backs of my knuckles brush against his, sending warmth all over. The sounds of people walking drift down towards us. We're secluded in this little spot, but any minute, someone could come down looking for a different type of privacy. I push off the wall. Ash watches me leave, and I turn back.

"No," I tell him, "I would have told him no."

CHAPTER 12

THE LAST BELL rings, releasing the enthusiasm for the weekend. Katerina and I make our way to the student parking lot where she's parked her shiny red car, my overnight bag retrieve from my locker minutes ago.

Kat goes through tonight's movie options when we spot Meredith's dark hair up ahead. Kat whistles out to her, making her blush. Car horns blast to our right, causing Meredith to clutch at her chest. Jerrod Osmund is obnoxiously showing off for a couple of his teammates. They return his horn with cheers.

Kat yells something to Jerrod I miss, but whatever he says back has her roll her eyes. My gaze drifts to St. Claire's car parked a few spaces down. His fingers drum affectionately on the hood. His eyes lift to mine, giving me a small nod before he ducks into his car.

He's been more formal since our conversation in the smoker's corner, or maybe since his dad's been home. I'm not sure what to make of our conversation. Was he only concerned because of the things I told him Alex said about him, or is there something else?

I got the impression his dad wasn't thrilled to find us in the workshop, and from what I've gathered from their books, the Domini have a decidedly prejudice view of Siphons. The thought of Ash's parents not liking me sets a squirmy feeling in my stomach. What if they forbade him from being friends with me?

Kat, Meredith, and I climb into Kat's car and I drop all thoughts of boys and focus on the much-needed time with my friends.

WE'VE CHANGED OUR UNIFORMS for pajamas and camped out in the living room, testing out the new surround sound system Ms. Montez's new boyfriend installed. Meredith digs into a plate of Kat's mom's amazing empanadas, as Kat and I play rock paper scissors to decide on the first movie.

Meredith breaks apart one of the meat pies and blows on one half. Her lips turn coy before she says, "So I heard Alex asked you out."

"Where did you hear that?" I sputter.

"Francesca."

"*Francesca*," I mumble, wondering how she always knows what everyone's doing.

I glance at Kat, who picks at her plate. Francesca and she are good friends. I wonder why she didn't tell me. I'd think she'd be the first person to interrogate and lecture me on why I turned down one of the most desirable guys at school.

I chew my nail. The food in my stomach feels like an anchor. "I told him I was busy," I mumble. I wait for the 'why did you turn him down' lectures, but they never come.

Meredith waves a hand, giving me an empathetic smile. "Well, I'm certainly happy you choose us over him," she flashes me a grin, "but whatever you decide, Alex or not, we support you." She reaches over and gives my arm a comforting squeeze.

"Thanks," I say, returning her warm smile.

She doesn't know how happy that makes me. It pushes away the dark cloud that's been looming over me since I made the choice to keep Ash and I's friendship a secret. However professional it started, I'm not sure if it still is.

"People change," Kat mumbles with a delicate arch of her brow before she presses play on the DVD player.

She fiddles with the surround sound volume as my phone vibrates. I discreetly check the screen, expecting to see Ash's name, but frown when I see Charity's.

> Secrets out

I hold my breath as I read her message again. She *can't* know. There's no way she'd keep this quiet for so long, if she saw what happened to my hands at school. And except for maybe twice in the privacy of my room, I only practice at Ash's.

Then I remember the frosty way she watched Alex and me when he asked me out and realize this is about him. Well, I don't care who knows that I used to have a crush on him. Feeling bolstered, knowing I have my friends' support, I message her back.

> Alex's all yours. Don't text me anymore, I'm blocking you.

Before I can talk myself out of it, I hit send. I will not let Charity ruin my night. I head into the kitchen to make popcorn when our phones go off. Kat and Meredith share puzzled expressions, but it's as if someone has dumped cold water over my head.

I hurry back to my phone. *Please, Charity, don't.* An anonymous account has tagged me in several pictures, along with most of the school. I open it to a picture of Ash and I in the alley between the Salty Siren and the Glittering Jewel.

We're only inches apart, and Ash holds my hands up between us. But I think it's his lopsided smile and my disheveled hair that really does it. To anyone not knowing the context, we look almost scandalous. Charity was there that day. She must have seen us go down the alley. Must have been *watching*. The next picture is of me in his car. From the angle the photo was taken, it looks like we're about to kiss.

Charity was waiting for the most opportune time to use these pictures against me. *She's evil.* The comments have already started coming in and they're not nice, full of speculation and assumptions about my ulterior motives. The gossip is already like wildfire, destroying everything in its path. My stomach turns sour, dinner threatening to come up.

"What is this?" Kat asks accusingly.

I try to explain, but no words come out as I take in their expressions of shock, confusion, and hurt. Finally, I blurt out, "I can explain."

"I knew you were hiding something," Meredith says, closing her eyes to compose herself. "But you and St. Claire?" Her big brown eyes blink in disbelief. She shakes her head as she asks, "How long has this been going on?"

"It's Charity," I say. "She's messing with me."

"Are you seriously trying to say it's photoshopped?" Kat crosses her arms, her words hard enough to cut through steel.

I wring my hands, seeing the situation spiraling. "No, but they look way worse than they are."

Kat scoffs bitterly. "It looks like you're having a secret alley hookup with Ash freaking St. Claire." I cringe, but before I can clarify, Kat adds, "I thought you agreed that St. Claire isn't a good fit for you."

"No, you said that. I just didn't correct you."

"So you've been secretly seeing him?" Kat's mouth twists into something that sets my temper flaring.

I rub my forehead as I say, "No, it's not like that."

I look to Meredith for some support in this. Surely she sees Charity is manipulating the facts, but Kat isn't done yet. "So you dropped Alex, because you found someone *better*?"

Kat's inflection is clear. She means *richer*. Everything I feared comes crashing down on me. I stare at her aghast, and she has the decency to look regretful for half a second before it's gone.

Meredith's voice cut through the charged silence, "Tell us the truth."

The truth. Such an easy word to say, but much harder to execute, especially when you're buried so deep. I scoff bitterly. All the words I rehearsed for my confession tonight feel weak and insignificant when Charity provided photographic proof of a narrative they're choosing to believe. I shake my head. The truth caught in my throat, wanting to choke me.

My silence is enough.

Kat makes a derisive cough, looking away from me. Meredith squeezes the pillow she clutches to her chest, and implores me with glassy eyes. I can't fix this, it's too late, but I try anyway.

"It started a couple of months ago—"

"Months!" Kat mumbles something under her breath. She arches her frigged brow. "Of all the girls in school, he's dating *you*?"

I jerk in surprise at her vehemence. "What's *that* supposed to mean?"

"Kat," Meredith hisses.

"Nothing." Kat purses her lips, looking slightly chastised.

"We're not dating." I try again to explain, but Kat shakes her head like I'm a stupid little girl who fell for some Internet catfish.

"Even worse," she says.

I rub my temples, feeling like the situation keeps veering further and further off course. There's a fire in my veins that's threatening to spill over. I stand jerkily to my feet. "It's so ridiculous, isn't it Katerina that Ash would like me?"

"That's not what she means," Meredith says, her eyes slanting toward Kat, whose only response is to cross her arms.

Tears sting my eyes. "It was so easy for you to keep pushing me on Alex because you didn't want him...," I say, mimicking her harsh tone. "If you were meeting Ash in secret, it'd be no problem, right?"

"That's not what this is. I'm not *jealous*." Kat swallows, and her cold armor falters. "He's using you, Echo."

"He gets *nothing* out of this," I hiss at her, clenching my hands into fists. The tips of my fingers tingle. "You don't even know him."

"I know he ignores you at school," Meredith says, her brows drawn in concern. "What kind of *friendship* is that?"

They both tense at my bitter laugh. "It was *my* idea because I knew you guys would act like this." My words fall like stones in the silence.

Kat says with a pitying frown, "I'm sure he let you think it was your idea."

I look to Meredith, my last lifeline in this shipwreck, but she says, "I can't believe you kept this from us."

I push my palms into my eyes, feeling the crushing sensation of my hope dying. "You didn't even take my side. You just started accusing me over some stupid pictures."

"It's not just some stupid pictures," Kat says resolutely, making us turn in her direction. "I saw you two at the pier getting ice cream." At my stunned expression she goes on, her chin lifting, "And when you skip lunch, you're with him, aren't you?"

When I say nothing, she shakes her head at me. "I wanted to see how long you'd lie to *me*—to *us*." She licks her lips. "If we never saw these pictures, you'd still be lying to us."

Meredith's eyes are shining with betrayal. "I was going to tell you tonight," I plead.

Kat makes a disbelieving sound low in her throat and turns away from me. Meredith won't meet my eyes. The movie keeps playing in the background as tears choke my throat.

"Forget it," I tell them, storming off to grab my bag out of Kat's bedroom. I don't even look at them as I walk out of the house.

No one stops me.

MY ANGER CARRIES ME a couple of blocks away without a destination in mind. Things got screwed up so quickly and everything I was trying to prevent came crashing down. I needed to get out of there.

The sun has almost disappeared into the horizon. Cicadas have started their song, mosquitoes buzz near my ears and I swat them between my hands. The street is empty save for a couple of cars parked along the curb.

A shameful part of me hoped they'd come after me. When the sidewalk behind me stays empty, I realize I'd officially ruined things. The view blurs in front of me and I roughly swipe at my eyes. A wave of grief hits me so hard my knees buckle and I sit on the curb and cry into my hands.

Everything hurts, and it's all my fault.

I rest my head on my knees, feeling hollow, and scooped out. Would they really have reacted any differently if I told them first? My thoughts flit through all the things I should have said, but it's too late to fix it now.

The street light above pulses with an electric sound. Little bugs fly around it, hitting their tiny bodies against the light cover. The sun has now completely disappeared and in its wake is an eerie feeling. I think about the dead girl on the beach, and the mystery of the hooded figure following me in the park. The intense quiet now that the sun has gone down prickles down my spine, like ghostly fingers.

I pull out my phone and dial Ash's number.

"Hey," he sounds surprised, but not bothered. The television in the background cuts off.

"Can you come get me?"

"Of course." There's a rustling sound on his end. "I thought you had the sleepover. Is everything alright?"

"Yes. No." A sob catches in my throat. "I need you to pick me up," my voice wavers, tears spring to my eyes, and I bite my lip to hold it in.

I tell him my location and tuck my legs under me on the sidewalk as I wait, feeling exhausted and weary as if I haven't slept. My eyes burn from all the crying and I want to crawl into bed and sleep away the pain.

I press my palms into my eyes. How am I going to fix this? It feels like I've been sitting here forever, but in reality, it's only been minutes. The dark thickens, adding to the feeling that time has slipped deep into the night. Even the cicadas have stopped chirping.

A weird sort of shimmer cuts across the road. The houses across the road appear distorted, like I'm looking through a glass or the windows in the St. Claire's library. A person in black clothes steps through the shimmer, and then another. They wear masks over their faces and everything about them screams a warning. I get to my feet and run.

I don't get far as arms come around me, their grip tight enough to hurt. I scream for help, but my voice echoes back to me all wrong. A masked man lifts my hands and cinches them together tight at the wrist. I dig my heels into the sidewalk as they pull me towards a van parked right inside the shimmering wall. *Magic.* I scream and kick, connecting with one of their legs.

A breeze tosses my hair in my face, temporarily blinding me as they half drag me. I wriggle and shout, trying to make it difficult for them. The wall follows us, but I can't tell which one of them is conjuring it. They look too focused on getting me into the van, which we're now horribly close to. I flail harder, bucking against them, but I'm not strong enough. My screams bounce back at me as if this bubble holds all the sound inside.

I brace my feet against the car frame and push back, surprising them enough that they lose their grip. I fall hard on my shoulder; the air pushed from my lungs. There's an unmistakable popping of the joint.

One of them curses, sounding male. "She burned me."

I try to suck in air—I'm suffocating—but it's hard, my chest squeezes and I'm gasping. I try to stand, give my lungs more room to get air in them, but the pain in my shoulder has me collapsing back to the ground.

"Help," I yell again, but it's useless. My cries don't leave the bubble.

I reach for the Light, but the pain in my shoulder breaks my concentration and I cry out.

The driver calls out, "Let's go, hurry."

"Get the gloves," someone yells.

A man wearing thick rubber gloves lifts me up. They drag me backward into the van. My hips hit the door frame. I plead with them to let me go but they ignore me, turning their faces away. I feel the Light flutter behind my rib cage and I pull. It answers with a roar, filling me with a power.

I do not bother with being subtle, like when we are in the workshop. I flex my hands and the plastic ties snap under the heat. Veins of light trail up my arms, over my skin.

The men curse and shout. They drop me again, but this time I am half in and half out of the van. There's a strong smell of burning leather and hair in the air. I squirm to my feet, prepared to run, but one of them grabs me again. He quickly lets go. The skin on his hands is peeling back as he screams.

I run.

Everything happens at once. There's a sound like a mortar shooting into the sky on the fourth of July. It echoes in the bubble, ringing in my ears and then I hit the ground. There's a horrible ache in my shoulder. I think I've broken something.

I gasp as one of them presses me down into the road, tearing up my skin. There's a knee in my back and thigh pinning me down, but I still claw to get away. He grabs my arms, and I scream from the pain in my shoulder. I reach for the Light but I can feel only agony.

"Stupid little witch," he snarls, his weight no longer pressing me down.

154

I roll to my side, catch sight of blood on the road. My blood. I look up to see a gun pointed at me.

"No more tricks," he says, waving the one with the gloves over. "Time to get your hands dirty."

They know what I am. Are they Domini that decided I was too dangerous to live? Or maybe Siphons? I look at the shimmering bubble around us, knowing that some Siphon magic is definitely at work.

The gloved man hesitates before he reaches down and pulls me up. I cry out, the pain much worse. Warmth soaks my shirt and I look down to see the red, gory wound in my shoulder.

I'm pulled toward the open van door. It looms like a doorway to hell, gaping dark and whispering promises of a slow and painful death. I try to use the Light, but I can't focus through the dizziness.

"Hurry," one says, hoisting himself into the driver's seat.

My eyes blur from pain and visceral sadness. My parents won't even know what happened to me. I will never see them again, or my friends, or Ash. Exactly like the girl on the beach.

A barrier crumbles inside me and power spills out. Cracks of light spread along my body, like lava pouring out of the earth. I can see the blinding Being I have become reflected in my captor's eyes.

Burn them.

I grab the gloved man with my newly freed hands.

"What's happening?" he cries, his voice suddenly sounding boyish and young. "Stop," he pleads, unable to pull his hands free.

The gloves have melted, trapping him in place. The others try to pull him free, but they give up quickly as the heat becomes too much. Light pours from my hands, enveloping the man in its glory. His screams die off as he turns charcoal black. His body cracking, turning to ashes.

The light spreads hungrily towards the others, like bright galloping horses. I see the gun lifting, its barrel turning red. I feel the pain this time. A punch to my side and then I am on the ground again.

All sound comes back in a whoosh. Tires squealing on the road, the roar of an engine, and then it fading away. Embers float down around me, catching in my hair and clinging to my sweaty skin. I touch where my side throbs, and my fingers come away bright red.

The wind has calmed, but now rain falls from the sky, making me shiver as I die on the street.

CHAPTER 13

I FEEL THE VIBRATIONS of the road under my broken body and I whimper. I want to cry, but it feels like the life is bleeding out of me. Metaphorically and literally. There's a strange wrapping around my body and shoulder, making me feel stiff and trapped. The Light inside me sputters and flickers. I'm afraid I've used it all up. A tear streaks down my skin and I feel myself sinking into the darkness again.

I broke the rules; I killed someone, and now I'm dying.

Ash's voice pierces through the darkness. "Echo, you're going to be alright."

The engine revs higher. I close my eyes and don't open them again until warm night air blows through the open car door. Voices whisper urgently out of view. Ash warns me that this might hurt before he lifts me out of the car. I try to prepare myself for the pain, but it comes fresh and urgent. He carries me to the house. A car door closes behind us, making me flinch.

A woman with a light accent directs Ash to take me into the dining room. We move swiftly down the hall into a formal dining room. The crystal chandelier sparkles above me as he lays me on the table. Someone has placed a thick blanket under me.

"So much blood," the woman says, coming into view, her delicate hand pressed over her mouth. "Who did this?"

She appears to be in her late twenties, but I know that's deceiving.

"I don't know. I found her like this."

Henrik comes into view with a bent pair of shears and starts cutting my shirt. I push his arm away and he backs off instantly, his expression remaining calm.

"It's okay. We need to make sure the bullet is out," Ash says.

I concede, and his dad moves back into place. A practiced movement as he runs the scissors down my shirt, moving it aside. The woman slips in with a sheet to preserve my modesty, but the pain has me not caring who sees me like this.

"I'm Helen, Ash's mom," she says, grabbing my hand.

I open my mouth to answer, but a hiss comes out as Henrik's warm fingers press on my skin. He instructs Ash to turn me over, and they both firmly take hold and move me to my side. I clench my teeth and brace myself against Helen.

"She needs a hospital," Henrik says.

"Just make sure the bullets are out." Ash says, his voice oddly commanding.

"It went through," Henrik says, his fingers still probing my wound. "It's... healing," he says, his voice strained.

Helen's worried gaze travels from Henrik to Ash, and then to my face, my mouth. Her eyes widen at what she sees. "Ash," she breathes, her fingers skittering over her full lips nervously. "You *didn't*."

Henrik nods for Ash to lay me back down. He fingers on my jaw are gentle as he turns my head, focused on my mouth, and then my pupils. His jaw clenches.

Ash stops chewing the side of his thumb. "She was dying."

Henrik shakes his head. "You know what this will mean?"

"I know," Ash says, crossing his arms. "What was I supposed to do?"

"What," I ask, "what is it?"

They share worried glances amongst themselves. Henrik looks like he wants to say something to his son, but Helen puts a hand on his arm, drawing his attention to her.

His face softens, and he says, "I need to work fast, then." His eyes flick to Ash. "And we should get that shoulder in place."

"I'll get started cleaning her wounds," Helen says, taking off her gold bangles and setting them down on a dining room chair.

She disappears from view as Ash grabs my hand. Henrik takes my arm, bending it at the elbow, and gently starts rotating my arm. There's a horrible pressure, a building ache and then he pushes on my elbow, towards my head. I cry out and feel a sickening pop as my shoulder slides back into place. The dull ache is still there, but the stabbing pain is gone.

Helen sets a pitcher of hot water and a bowl full of washcloths down on the cherry buffet along the wall. She fills the bowl with water, wrings out a cloth, and hands it to Ash, taking one for herself.

"Get to cleaning out those wounds. We don't want any debris left in them," she says, and then to me, "this is going to hurt."

My tender flesh is pulled and scrubbed as tears leak down my cheeks. I even beg them to stop before it's all over. When Henrik sews up the largest of my wounds, I faint, catching snippets of conversation as I flit in and out of consciousness.

"Why was she alone on the road..."

"... no sign of anyone."

"Blood everywhere..."

"... severity of what you've done..."

"... she's healing fast."

"Healing?" I ask, coming to as Henrik is finishing my shoulder. "Is that a Siphon thing?"

His blue eyes lift to mine briefly to say, "No." In his palm is a metal tool that he twists elegantly in a way that reminds me of when my mother ties off a sewing project. He holds the needle up with another tool, cutting the thread with a small pair of scissors. "Did you see who did this?" he asks as he packs away his medical kit.

"They wore masks," I say, "but I think one of them was a Siphon."

Henrik's eyes flash to mine. "Why do you think that?"

My throat tingles when I swallow. "There was a shimmery dome around us, and it did something odd to my screams."

Henrik rubs his knuckles against the stubble on his cheek. "A Siphon could create something like that, but not alone."

"Why would they go after her? Echo had broken no laws," Ash says, his mom putting a hand on his shoulder.

I close my eyes, trying to push the sight of that man burning from my thoughts. I'm not so innocent now.

"If there was a sanction to bring her in, I would have heard about it," Henrik musses to himself. He brushes a hand down his neck, feeling the stubble there as well.

The smell of burning flesh is a scent I won't soon forget, nor is the fear on all their faces; palpable even through the masks. Terror clear as day as he begged me for his life. I curl up on my side. Ash's mom puts a hand on my forehead.

Ash says, "Maybe she needs more—"

"No." Henrik shakes his head. "We don't know what it'll do."

Helen rubs my back to comfort me, but it makes me wish my mom was here. "It'll take a few days before your wounds heal completely," she says, her voice soft. She helps me to sit up, her eyes searching mine. "The emotional pain will take longer."

I shift my gaze away from her and pull the sheet tighter around my body.

Helen puts a hand on Ash's arm, drawing his attention to her. "Will you take her upstairs to get cleaned up? I'll bring something she can bathe in."

"What about my parents?" I ask at no one in particular, my voice high and panicked. "I can't go home like this. They'll freak out."

"You can stay here tonight. We'll deal with the fallout tomorrow," Helen says, purposely ignoring the look her husband gives her. "You need to rest."

Henrik's eyes pierce mine. "You can answer my questions in the morning."

I REST MY HEAD on the side of Ash's enormous bathtub as he tests the water. The thunderous sound of the water reverberating through the porcelain helps to drown out my thoughts. I'm wearing another one of his shirts and the pajama shorts I wore to the sleepover, now covered in blood and ash.

I rest a hand on the bandage Henrik said might be closed by morning. I ache all over and things sting when they're pulled, but I feel surprisingly good for being shot.

"What did you give me?" I ask, "to heal me?"

"My blood."

The water sloshes as I slip. It only gets worse as I try to push myself back up one-handed, my shoulder still aching. Ash helps steady me.

"Seriously?" I ask, and he nods. "That's kind of disgusting."

He shrugs in agreement, a sad smile on his lips. "I didn't think I could get you to a hospital in time."

"So Seraph blood..."

"Can heal humans," he finishes for me, "and Siphons."

I brush my fingers over my lips, trying not to grimace. "Thank you," I tell him, and mean it. I might be dead if it wasn't for him.

Ash nods, his brows pulled together. He sets a washcloth and a bar of lavender-scented soap on the side of the tub and gets up to leave. There's a chill in my bones and I close my eyes and soak up the warmth of the water, even if it only comes to my hips.

"I can get my mom to help you?"

"No. I just need to warm up a little," I say as a shiver hits me.

Ash kneels beside the tub, picking up the washcloth and submerging it in the water. He lathers it with soap and gently takes my arm. He carefully starts scrubbing away the dried blood and road debris.

When he sees me watching, a little pink comes to his cheeks. "I didn't save you just so you could drown."

"I guess not, but I can wash myself."

He hums in disbelief. "You can barely stay awake," he says, but hands me the washcloth so I can scrub the stickiness and grime off my face. "So what happened at Katerina's?"

I splash water on my face before I answer. "We had a fight," I say, handing him back the washcloth. "About you."

"Me?" He raises his brows, gingerly cleaning the road rash on my knees.

I lean back against the tub. "I planned to tell them tonight, but they found out before I could. Charity posted pictures of us together..." I sneak a look at him, his eyes so impossibly blue are waiting. "... and they weren't happy to find out that way. Things got heated, and I left."

I tell him all the details I can remember about what happened after the fight, leaving out only one.

"They acted like they knew what I was," I say after he's drained the tub and refilled it with clean water. He has his elbow on the rim so he can worry his lip. I bring my knees up to my chest and rest my chin on them.

I watch him pick apart all the pieces, trying to make sense of what happened. Once he finds out I'm a monster, it's all over. Either he'll hate me forever or he'll lock me up or whatever they do to dangerous Siphons like me. Guilt strangles at my throat, threatening to steal my voice. This is how I got into this mess. Lies.

"Ash," I say his name softly, a part of me wishing he doesn't hear.

His eyes lift to mine. "Hmm?"

I grip my legs tighter, my fingers digging in. "I did something horrible."

His thumb stills on his lip. "What you said in the car?"

I nod. My eyes burn but I push on, even if he hates me. "I thought they were going to kill me," I tell him. "Then something snapped, and it was like that day in the workshop, but way worse."

"You had to defend yourself. No one's going to blame you for that."

I shake my head. "I tried to run away but they were stronger." Ash's face is unreadable, but I still feel like my heart is ripping open. "Then the Light was pouring out of me and then he was dust in my hands," I tell him, tears snaking down my cheeks, hot where my skin feels cold. "I couldn't stop it."

Ash looks away and my chest heaves. I clutch at it, trying to hold in all the pieces. After everything that's happened tonight, I can't lose him, too.

"It was self-defense," he finally says, meeting my eyes.

"It feels like murder."

His eyes are hard. "It's not. I know the difference."

I search his blue eyes, afraid to ask what I really want to know— *Am I dangerous?*

"What are they going to do to me? I broke the rules."

"Nothing." He says, standing. "We're not going to tell anyone."

He grabs a towel off the counter next to my overnight bag and a pile of clothes his mom provided. He helps me out of the tub, wrapping a towel around me in a way that would have me blushing if I wasn't consumed with his willingness to lie for me.

Ash leaves so I can get dressed. I feel weighed down, and it has little to do with my wet clothes and everything to do with my soul. I change into clean underwear, my tank top, and the soft night pants his mom lent me. She's taller than me, so the fabric pools at my feet.

I find my phone in my bag and check for messages. None. My parents probably think I am still at Kat's. There are no messages or calls from my friends either. I push the heels of my hands into my eyes to stop the pressure building there.

I find Ash in the living room outside his bedroom, leaning against the back of the couch. He's changed into a clean set of clothes and comes to attention when he sees me.

"Thank you," I say, walking up to him. "For everything." I wrap my arms around my middle, suddenly feeling vulnerable.

A look flashes across his face, and he takes a step toward me. He pushes his hair off his forehead, his voice thick when he says, "of course."

There's a horrible heartbreak in my center that doesn't all stem from the fight with my friends. My heart aches for what those men forced me to do, what that means I'm capable of, and lastly, what Ash must think of me now.

I want to sleep for ten thousand years. I never want to sleep again. The loneliness makes me stupid; makes me bold.

I wrap my arms around him, catching him off guard. His hands tentatively rest on my back, but then they wrap tighter around me. I inhale into his chest, soaking up the warmth and comfort even if it's fleeting. I don't know if this is allowed, but I don't care.

He rests his chin on my head. "You're safe here," he says, and I bury my face into him. "We'll find out who did this, I promise."

Rain pelts the sliding glass door leading out to his patio. Another late summer storm. I frown at the darkness outside his balcony windows, remembering the feel of the sudden rain on my skin before I passed out.

It's as if the storm is telling me something; lightning streaks across the sky. A shiver moves through me. I bury my face in his chest and clutch him a little tighter.

CHAPTER 14

M Y BODY IS stiff and sore. There's a sterile feeling to the room, like waking up in a hotel room. It has all the parts of a bedroom, but it's not mine.

Ash's bedroom.

My parents are going to kill me.

When I see the time, I groan. I have barely slept, but if I stay here any longer, my parents might realize I'm not at Kats, though it is very tempting to crawl back under the plush comforter.

I head into the other room, looking for Ash. The curtains look hastily drawn over the balcony doors, with a small crack letting in enough light to cast the room in soft blues. St. Claire is asleep on the couch, a blanket hanging halfway off his body as if he got hot in the night. His arm draped above his head, accentuating the muscles in his arm as the other rests on his chest.

The light coming from the window shows off the facets of gold in his hair. He has a small dusting of bronzed freckles over the bridge of his nose. Sun-kissed, my mom would say. Most of Ash is sun-kissed as if he was born from the rays of the sun, his skin the warm glow of the beach. Behind his sleeping lids are eyes the color of a tropical ocean blue. It's like he's made of the island.

His eyes open, catching me staring. "Hey," he says, suspiciously.

"Hey." I step back, my neck guiltily warm.

Ash sits up with a yawn, rubbing a hand down his face. His eyes roam my face and bare arms. I feel self-conscious and wrap an arm over my chest.

"How are you feeling?"

I make a noncommittal noise. "Sore, but not dead."

Ash stands, stretches languidly, and sighs. He tells me he needs to change my bandage and disappears into his room; the door closing behind him. When he comes back, he's carrying a first aid kit. I sit down as directed and lift my shirt so he can peel off the old bandage and replace it with a fresh one.

"It's healing, but not fast enough." His eyes flick up to mine. "You'll have to hide your wounds for a few more days."

Ash presses the new bandage to my side, frowning at the angry scab on my shoulder. "This one will scar, unfortunately."

"Do you get scars?"

He finishes covering the wound on my shoulder, gathering up the wrappers and crushing them in his fist. "Even the worst of our wounds will repair itself with enough time." He snaps the locks on the medical kit closed and turns to me with a concerned expression. "Echo, about last night..."

Dread fills the pit of my stomach, along with hot embarrassment. I shouldn't have stepped over the careful lines we've drawn. I was feeling so afraid and alone last night. Ash has been a good friend to me, but better for both of us if we keep it that way. I swallow, bracing myself for the awkward conversation because he misread my affections, where he tells me he doesn't think of me that way, how we should keep things professional, platonic.

He searches my face. His hand flexes on the med kit, looking unsure. "My father's going to want to know what happened and it would be best if we didn't tell him the fourth man is dead."

"How I killed him?" I say flatly.

Ash winces. "How you defended yourself." He holds my stare. "But yes."

I blow out a weary breath. "Okay."

I broke the law; I killed someone. Even though Ash says it was self-defense; I don't think the Domini upholds human legal practices. There would be no fair trial, only punishment.

I wrap my arms around myself, and close my eyes, pushing my emotions down, down, where I can't reach them.

Ash puts a hand on my arm, causing me to look up at him. Something swells up and I try to push that back down, too. He's going to be a Dominus whose sole creation is to protect humanity from dangerous Siphons, like me. It was foolish to imagine that this was anything other than duty. Bitterness and self-loathing erase whatever warmth I was feeling toward him.

I step away from his touch. "Better get it over with then."

YOU CAN SMELL THE food cooking from the hall as we head to the kitchen. His mom is at the stove, pushing sausage around in a pan. When she sees us, her eyes light with a smile as she greets us.

It makes me homesick in a way I haven't felt since I was little. Once the excitement of a new place wears off and you get a terrible longing for home. I miss my mom. I wish I could tell her everything that's happened and cry in her arms. Confess how the chasm that has always seemed to separate me from everyone has opened even further. That there is an uncertain power in my veins and I fear what that'll mean for the rest of my life. The terribleness of what happened last night and how it feels like a storm is coming and I'm going to be punished horribly for it.

Henrik sits at a round table in the breakfast nook, sipping from a steaming coffee cup. Late morning light fills the kitchen. I glance nervously toward Ash. He's made his way over to the cabinet, grabbing two cups. His mom whispers something in his ear that causes him to give her a face before he moves to the fridge.

"Please have a seat." Henrik waves to the chair next to him.

He closes his laptop as I take the seat across from him. He looks pristine as ever in his tailored button-down and tan slacks. His stubble only adds to the intimidating demeanor. I get that sense of déjà vu again as I sneak a glance at him. He has a similar dusting of freckles on his nose. But if Ash was born from the rays of the sun, then Henrik St. Claire came from its center.

Ash sets a glass of water in front of me and Henrik comments, "She should have orange juice, after what happened," and then asks, "have you checked her wounds?"

"Yes." Ash sets the glasses down on the table and takes a seat. "They're healing well."

His father makes an indirect sound in his throat that could translate as *'of course they are, you gave her freaking angel blood'* but what he says is, "Do I have to talk to her parents?"

The glass stops at my lips, as I cast a worried glance at Ash.

He sighs, "No, sir."

Henrik sets his hands on the table, crossing them together as if he's going to negotiate the terms of a hostile business transaction. "I just like a little warning before I have to do damage control with the parents."

I stare into my glass, taking a small sip, hoping the cold liquid will do something for the heat creeping up my face.

Ash's mother tsks as she sets down our plates. "And how *often* have you had to do that?" she pointedly directs this to her husband.

Henrik mumbles something before he takes a sip of his coffee, his eyes on his wife.

"They think I'm at a sleepover," I say. Or I hope they do. My hand flexes with the urge to check my phone again.

"That's where you were last night?" Helen asks as she sets out a large plate of pancakes, and another loaded with sausages.

"Um yes." I duck my head, feeling shy.

It's strange to be meeting his parents under these circumstances. It's also strange to see them in a domestic situation, as I've dreamed them up to resemble something straight out of a gladiator war.

"I looked over the crime scene," his dad says, plucking three pancakes from the stake. I cringe at his choice of words. "Besides one burnout tire track and faded blood on the street, there wasn't much else to go on." He reaches for the maple syrup. "I'll check the surrounding houses for security cams, but I'm guessing that cloaking bubble was keeping everything inside undetectable."

"Siphons can do that?" I ask.

"Oh, they can do all kinds of things," Henrik says. "Air affinities are good at cloaking and manipulating shadows. Damn squirrely most of the time." Ash's mom gives him a look, and he adds, looking a little cajoled, "but not all of them." Henrik clears his throat. "Does anyone other than Ash know what you are?"

I don't even know what I am. "Only Adam."

"And he wouldn't tell anyone," Ash adds.

Henrik decides not to argue that point as he pushes a piece of sausage into his syrup. "Have you used your abilities outside of this house?"

Henrik's blue eyes seem to bore into me, and I push my food around. Surely alone in my room with the door firmly locked doesn't count? I sneak a glance at his authoritative gaze, feeling conflicted.

"A few times in my room," I say, stealing a glance at Ash, bracing for his disappointment.

Ash is impassive as he asks, "When was this?"

"In the beginning. It was late at night. No one saw me," I say. "I haven't done it since."

Henrik nods, not looking happy about my late-night experimenting, but at least I don't get chastised for it.

Ash takes a sip of his water, watching his dad over the glass. "You're going to investigate Adam, aren't you?"

Henrik sighs, setting his fork down. "I wouldn't be thorough if I didn't." When Ash shakes his head, Henrik adds, "If you want to keep her safe, I need to follow all leads. That's why I need to know everything, any detail, any enemies."

"I don't have any enemies."

"What about Charity?" Ash says, ducking his head to look at me.

I wouldn't have considered Charity an enemy even after the confrontation in the hall, but after she sent out the pictures, well, maybe that's what she is. I shrug in answer.

"What happened?" Helen asks.

Ash says, "There was an altercation with another student at school."

Henrik leans forward on his elbows. I imagine him going to Charity's house and questioning her like some gruff detective. "It was nothing, only a misunderstanding," I say. "Besides, you don't really think a girl from school would try to kidnap me?"

Henrik drifts his attention to his son, raising a brow. Ash says, "Charity is vindictive but otherwise seems harmless."

"I'll look into her as well," Henrik sighs.

I must make a noise because the three of them turn to me. I rub at my knuckles, feeling like I've tattled, sending a mercenary to fight my school bullies for me.

"I'll be discrete," he says, his voice softening, "It won't come back on you, I promise."

Henrik's fingers scratch against the beginnings of a beard. "They may try again," he says, and then to Ash, "you'll need to be on guard."

"I'm always on guard," Ash says, tapping the side of his glass.

"Is this something we can ask the Primes about?" Helen asks Henrik.

"No," Ash blurts, getting his father's attention. "We don't know if they were behind this."

"True," his dad agrees. "We need to keep this quiet as long as we can. Once the Domini and Siphon Primes find out you're involved, it'll complicate things."

"Why is that?" I ask.

Ash has been worrying his bottom lip, and his eyes shift uneasily in my direction. Henrik clears his throat. "There's a bit of history there."

I raise my brow, and Ash says, "We're going to need backup."

Henrik levels a look at his son. "One fledging Dominus over-reaching is one thing, but if we involve others?" He shakes his head. "We will have both councils down on us."

"I thought you guys were in charge?" I ask, their attention now on me.

Henrik waves an insouciant hand. "We've brokered a fragile trust over the years. We don't interfere with Siphons unless they are terrorizing or killing humans. So far, what we're doing borders on treason."

"Because of me?"

Henrik leans forward. "Because on the surface it looks like the St. Claire family is harboring a Siphon for whatever purpose I'm sure the Domini and Principalities will let their minds run rampant with." He throws up his hands. "For all they know, I could try to start a coup d'état, or worse." His eyes cut to Ash's briefly.

I feel breakfast threatening to come back up. "I don't understand how that's fair."

"It's not about fair, it's about laws and appearances." Henrik pinches the bridge of his nose. "Our duty for now is to figure out who tried to kidnap you. The rest will fall into place."

"Callum and Charlotte are still fledglings," his mom musses, breaking the silence, "they won't be breaking any laws."

Henrik considers this. "Will they fight for your Siphon?"

"Maybe," Ash says, looking less than sure. "Callum will."

"I suspect Charlotte will as well." His mother gives him a lopsided smile very similar to her sons.

I go rod straight at the mention of a Charlotte, not happy with the feeling of jealousy that creeps over me. I scowl down at my glass, breakfast turning to lead in my stomach.

Henrik nods once. "Out of the fire and into hell," he sighs as he stands. "I better get to work. There was an attack on my island, and I mean to find out who's behind it."

Helen nods proudly up at her husband before she clears away the table. I rise to help her, anything to distract myself from the previous conversation.

"Oh, I'll take care of this. You need your rest," she says, taking the plate from my hands and placing it in the sink.

"Thank you for everything."

"Of course." She gives me a warm smile as her eyes travel over my face. They don't match her smile. "It'll take a few days for your body to feel whole again."

I thank her again; the word doesn't quite feel large enough for the gratitude I feel. It's coalescing into a tremendous deal that they're helping me, putting them at a monumental risk, and though I'm grateful, I also feel guilty about putting them in this place.

Again, like the first time I met Ash in the darkroom, I feel like I've no place to go and no one to turn to except him. This realization is both comforting and confining.

"Who are Callum and Charlotte?" I ask, trying to keep my voice even as we take the servant's stairs back up to his bedroom suite.

Ash turns in the narrow space and leans against the wall. "Friends," he says. "Seraphim, about my age."

I chew my lip. "Are you going to get in trouble?"

He smiles as he looks heavenward. "I have done nothing wrong." He continues up the stairs. I almost don't catch him mumbling, "technically."

I check my phone once we get back to his room. Ash leans against the doorjamb, watching me. "You've been checking that a lot."

My lips pull tight and I toss it on the comforter. No messages. "I'm such an awful friend." I run both hands over my head and sit heavily on his bed.

Ash pushes off the doorway to sit beside me. He leans back on the bed, looking like it's a regular lazy Sunday. "You're not an awful friend."

I give him an incredulous look. "I didn't want to tell anyone *we're* friends. That sounds like a pretty crappy friend."

"You had valid reasons," he says in that scholarly way of his.

I roll my eyes in disbelief, but I don't argue the point further. We both know the truth. I was a coward. I pick at the corner of my phone case. "Should we talk about the pictures?"

He tilts his head. "What about them?"

"Did you see them?" I ask softly.

He slowly nods. "Adam sent them to me," he says, wary.

I don't know why I thought Adam wouldn't have seen. He's in the school directory. He was probably tagged or someone on the team told him. I swallow a lump as I think about how quickly it has rotated around the school. There were more comments on the picture than students at Shorecrest. My shoulders slump at the possibility of it getting around outside of school. Not like those opinions matter, unless it got around to my parents.

I groan, rubbing my eyes. *"And?"*

"And what?" he asks, watching me. "I was there. I know what happened."

"You're not mad about what people might say?"

He shrugs. "I can't control what people say."

I flop back onto the bed, covering my eyes with my arm. "It's horrible, what they're saying."

"You shouldn't read it."

I peek out from under my arm to look at him. He's so beautiful it hurts. "It's going to be hell on Monday."

He hums in agreement, low in his throat. "It'll be strange to actually speak to you at school." He gives me a sly look. "I was getting used to being pushed down dark alleys and shushed in class." His eyes twinkle mischievously. "It's a real confidence booster when a girl is completely embarrassed by your existence." He gives me a wicked smile.

"You know it wasn't like that." I go to hit him and he catches my wrist, his face sobering up as he turns my hand around to look at the healing road rash on my palms.

"Someone tried to kill you," he says, studying my hand. "I'm not as concerned about a little high school gossip."

My heart races, but too soon, he's letting go. "I should take you home."

I nod, pressing my fingers into my eyes. I feel the bed move, the sound of him in the other room. So much has changed in a day. So very, very much.

THE HOUSE IS EMPTY when I walk through the doors. The kitchen still smells of breakfast, a coffee cup on the counter next to a stack of my dad's work papers. I had half expected them to be standing in the living room, arms crossed and fuming, having known I wasn't at Kats' where I was supposed to be. A pang of horrible guilt rises as I add more lies to the pile.

I hear laughter on the back porch and make my way out the sliding glass doors. Mom is in the middle of telling dad where to hang some outdoor curtains on the patio as dad is balancing on a ladder, holding them up and down as she tries to decide where she wants them.

They haven't seen me yet, and I stand there trying to decide if I should go to my room or not. I rub the bullet wound on my shoulder, seeing the man's coal-white eyes. I must make a noise because mom turns around.

"Oh good, you can help me," she says, waving me to her side. "Up," she directs this order to dad, who obediently obliges, giving me a weary look as he does. "How's that look?" she asks me.

The curtains are about an inch off the patio. I tilt my head. Dad lowers them. "Or there," he asks. The fabric now gently sweeps the cement.

"They'll get wet if they touch the concrete," I say.

Mom puts a hand on her hip. "See," she says, and dad moves them up with an exasperated expression.

He marks where to install the screws as Mom asks, "How was the sleepover?"

"Good," I lie.

She smiles, and then something in my face makes hers falter. "Did you get to talk to them?"

"Yeah, it didn't go well."

"Do you want to talk about it?"

The truth hovers on my lips. All of it; my fight with Kat and Meredith, what happened with Charity, and awakening some dormant lineage, even the masked men who tried to abduct me. It all wants to come pouring out, Siphons and Seraphims, and how the world, my world, is off its axis and spiraling towards doom. Pressure builds behind my eyes as mom waits. Dad cast a concerned look my way.

Will they fear me, especially once they know what I did? My parents are not Siphons. They won't understand.

I shake my head and rub my eyes. "No, I just want to go to my room."

"Okay." She searches my face. "I saved you some apple cinnamon strudel if you're hungry."

I flick the light on in my room, jumping at my reflection in the mirror above my dresser. For a second, I thought there was someone behind me. I turn, eyes searching the room, my heart thudding at the memory of being held down, pushed and pulled, and shouted at to move. I put my hands over my ears as if that'll block out the noise, but it's in my head.

"Stop it."

When I open my eyes, I'm still alone. Just my reflection staring back at me. I hold up my hands, little sparks flicker from my fingertips. I watch transfixed as I dance the energy along my fingers. It's not a secret space behind my heart anymore, the Light is everywhere within me. Woken up like a sleeping dragon and I think it has something to do with the Seraph blood moving through me, repairing my damaged cells.

When I look back at the mirror, I see a faint ring of Light around my eyes.

CHAPTER 15

WHISPERS FOLLOW ME down the halls, and heads turn as I make my way to class. Everyone is talking about the pictures. A girl I recognize but don't know asks if I'm really dating Ash St. Claire. There's a giddy sort of excitement as she waits for my answer and when I tell her no, her eyes light up. She pops the gum in her mouth and turns on her heel.

Marybeth, who was my elementary school best friend, pulls me aside to probe me for some rather embarrassing details about Ash and frowns when I don't have the answers.

I get asked so many times about the private workings of our relationship that by lunch my throat is sore from saying, *'We're just friends'*.

All morning I try to explain the pictures, how they're taken out of context, but no one cares. I've gotten a couple of hopeful nods at my vehemence that it's not romantic but mostly narrowed-eyed doubt, like I'm keeping the last cup of water from a bunch of thirsty individuals.

There are so many haughty opinions at Shorecrest Academy and only one of me. It's the most exciting thing to happen this year. Ash St. Claire is already a cryptic puzzle everyone wants to crack, and the fact it includes me is mere happenstance.

Well, it's a little about me.

Apparently, I wasn't as secretive about my distaste for some of the more entitled boys at our school. Tandy Demonte thought it pertinent to remind me how I said Ash St. Claire was overrated. And Lawson Christensen reminded me how I said I'd rather tattoo my face than date anyone who lived on the Western Crescent.

While I'm at my locker before lunch, I overhead Brandy Anderson's distinctively nasal voice questioning why Ash would ever date me when she's available. She's huddled around her locker with her best friend Jasmine and her younger brother who sees me and gives me a wink before he says, "Hey Echo, why don't you dump St. Claire and go out with me?"

I shut my locker door with a heavy clang, cutting off whatever else they had to say, and head towards the darkroom.

I'M PREPARED TO BE alone and miserable all lunch period when Ash and Adam enter the darkroom surprising me. Adam carries a cafeteria tray full of food that has me admiring his balance and his metabolism. Ash carries two slices of pizza on a paper plate and a massive amount of crinkle fries and sets it down on the table beside me. He pulls two drinks from each of his pockets. I watch them while I chomp on salted pretzels.

"Thought you'd be in here," Ash says. "Hiding." He folds his pizza in half and takes a big bite.

"Has it been as bad for you as it has for me?"

He lifts his shoulder. "Probably not."

"My popularity has risen," Adam says, setting his drink down to spoon a heaping portion of cornbread casserole. "*Ash. Echo.* Tell me *more*," he says in a much higher octave.

Ash coughs on his soda and glances at Adam sidelong, who grins around a bite of food.

"What do you tell them?" I ask, staring at my peanut-butter sandwich.

Adam finishes chewing, mostly, before he answers, "That I don't get what's so scandalous about two people standing next to each other and that everyone needs to stop feeding the gossip."

I give him a big grateful smile, which only makes him shrug his shoulders like—*of course, it's no big deal, don't even worry about it.* It feels nice to have people backing me. The thought sobers me up and I pick at my sandwich. My hand twitches to check my phone, but I already know they haven't messaged me.

I can see Ash watching me from my peripheral. "It'll all blow over," he says.

I shrug and busy myself looking for something in my lunch bag. "The darkroom is a lot quieter than the cafeteria, anyway."

Adam nods. "I can't get seconds, though."

"How many lunch credits do you have?" I ask, eyeing his already half-empty plate.

"*Lots,*" Ash says, his brows lifting.

"It's easier than bringing a cooler to school," Adam says, scooping up the last of his chili-con-queso.

I glance at Ash's meager in comparison plate of pizza and fries. "Where's the rest of your lunch?"

"I don't think anyone eats as much as Adam."

"Seraphs drink blood anyway," Adam says, popping a grape into his mouth.

I spit out my water. It sprays all over the darkroom floor, even hitting some of the old dusty machines on the back wall.

Ash's face has gone red. "He's joking."

Adam is laughing, unaware of how timed his joke could be. I feel my cheeks heat as well, wondering how much St. Claire has told him of Friday night. Adam is still chuckling as he leaves to take his tray back to the lunchroom.

"He really is joking," Ash says again, rubbing the spot above his eyes.

"Did you tell him?" I ask, "how you healed me?"

"No," Ash says tentatively, shifting so his body angles towards mine. "I wasn't sure how much you'd like to share about that night. I told him the pictures caused a fight with your friends and I picked you up."

I breathe out a relieved, "Okay, good."

I assumed he would have told Adam and mostly I don't mind, but the thought of Adam thinking any differently of me twists my insides. Ash and I agreed to keep what I did to the kidnapper a secret, but I'm still processing the blood thing.

"We can't tell *anyone* how I healed you," he says, picking at his plate. "It's against the Olrum Lari'el for a Seraph to give any human or Siphon, especially a Siphon, their blood."

"What will happen if they find out?"

Ash's crystal blue eyes stare at me for long enough that I want to squirm. "I'll be imprisoned."

"For how long?"

"There will be a tribunal before the council to determine the length, a couple hundred years or more."

My eyebrows hit my hairline. "A couple hundred years! That's ridiculous."

"It's the Law," he says so matter of fact.

"It's a stupid law."

He stares at the remains of my lunch. "If we used our blood to heal everyone, we'd change the course of the world."

"But aren't Domini meant to protect people?" I shake my head, thinking of all the good they could do.

"Protect them from Siphons," he nods. "The council believes Siphons are a stain on humanity, which is why it's even more of a sin to give our blood to one." His eyes lift to mine.

I look away from him. He knew what the punishment was and still risked everything to save me. My heart is thumping too fast inside my chest at the thought of Ash being imprisoned for hundreds of years because of me. I'd be long dead when he's finally released.

I anxiously gesture with my hands. "Can't your dad do something? Isn't he some big deal in your world?"

Ash smiles sadly at his soda. "He's on the council," he says, and my mouth pops open. "He's sworn to uphold the Laws even with his son."

I'm shaking my head. The image of Ash before a group of rigid immortals sentencing him to prison for centuries, all because he didn't want to see someone die, sounds archaic and unfair.

"It'll be fine," he says, touching my elbow. "We just can't let anyone find out."

I nod, but I don't quite believe him. "But what about your dad, though?" I ask. "Won't he tell?"

"No," Ash says confidently. "Despite clashing over my future, he will keep this secret."

"Until he can't."

Ash reluctantly nods. "Until he can't."

My lunch has soured in my belly at the guilt and grief of possibly sentencing a friend to centuries of imprisonment.

"And I think we should put a pause in training for a little while."

My heart jumps with relief, grateful at least for this thing. I can feel the Light hungry within me like a starved wild beast. I'm worried there's not enough water in St. Claire's pool to stop me. Disappointment follows it, as I've gotten quite comfortable with the company.

I stare at my hands on my uniform skirt, gripping my icy fingers tighter. "Okay."

He searches my face but doesn't ask why I'm not protesting. Maybe he knows. He tosses a napkin down on his plate. "But you shouldn't be alone." He's looking at the old machines on the other table. "In case they make another attempt for you."

I raise an eyebrow, trying to mimic his incredulous look. "Are you going to watch me day and night?"

"Are you going on any late-night walks?"

I shake my head, suppressing a shiver. My stomach feels weightless as I roll the words over in my thoughts before I say them. "Do you want to come over to my house?"

"Your house?"

My stomach drops to my toes. "Or whatever," I say with a flippant toss of my hand.

"Yeah, sure," he says, clearing his throat. "We could actually study." He bumps his shoulder into mine, lingering.

We get too quiet and I feel St. Claire tense beside me. He pushes a hand through his hair, casually creating some space between us. I pack up my lunch as my phone beeps, telling me the lunch period is almost over.

"Do you want to go out first?"

I slide off the table. "It's pointless now."

He catches my arm, a light touch of his knuckles. My body wants to sway towards it like a plant to the sun, but I keep myself still. "It's not pointless if it's important to you."

I shake my head. "I don't want to hide anymore." My insides do a little flip and I break eye contact to look at my shoes.

"I don't want you to hide either," he says and turns away before I can see his expression. He holds the door open for me as we slip out of the darkroom together.

THE LATE BELL RINGS right before I reach Marine Science, halting me before the door. I hate walking in late with all eyes on me and today of all days, there are so many eyes. I peer down the hall in the library's direction, but I can't hide in the darkroom forever.

Several pairs of eyes swivel in my direction as I cross the threshold and head to my seat. Ms. Walker is at her desk, her laptop open, and projecting today's lesson on the whiteboard. She is busy preparing while the rest of the class is watching me.

My seat is usually in the back row behind Meredith and Kat. Today Chandler Hastings is sitting in my seat and my group of friends are the only eyes not on me. There's an open seat in front of Ms. Walker's desk. I hear whispers as I make my way to it.

"Did you see the pictures?"

"I heard they snuck off to the drama loft during lunch."

"She was practically throwing herself at him."

"I heard it was the other way around."

"She was crying in the bathroom because he dumped her."

"She's only with him for his money."

"I heard it was a bet."

"I give it a week."

I pull out my notebook and try to ignore the regurgitated gossip from the comment section beneath the pictures. It seems there's a double standard between the sexes. The classes I share with St. Claire have been quiet. No one wants to say these things around him but feels comfortable voicing these things to me. It's unfair. I don't want Ash to have to bear the gossiping lies as well. I only wish they would all shut up.

Ms. Walker turns back to the lesson and I focus on writing what she's saying when Victor DeSantos leans over and asks, "Hey, Echo, when you're done with St. Claire, call me." He waggles his brows at me.

Someone giggles to my right. I stare at Victor like the idiot he is. He swallows, looking uncomfortable, and leans back into his seat. I clench my fists under the desk. Everything I was afraid of is now my reality. I lied to keep the gossip and questions at bay and avoid drama with my friends, and it caused the same problems I was trying to avoid.

Like the strength I used to clench my hand, I'm calling forth my power as easily. Too easily.

I stop short. What am I doing? I look down at my desk and take in some deep breaths. I want to flee from the classroom, from the whispers and eyes I feel boring into my back, but that's what they want. To humiliate me. I'm painfully aware of my friends a few seats back and yearn for their support in all this, but all I'm met with is silence. A flash of anger rears up. They didn't even give me a chance to explain before the accusations came in.

But you lied to them.

Hurt, anger, guilt, it all swirls around like a hurricane as I keep my eyes focused on the board and what Ms. Walker is teaching. I want to run, but I don't. I'm tired of feeling weak, of giving in. How I felt when Charity accosted me, the stalker in the park, and the men with masks.

I won't let anyone make me feel small, not when I've so much power flowing through me, filling up all the dark places. For the first time in a long time, I feel like I have control over my life and I will not let the rumors break me.

WHEN THE LAST BELL rings for the day, I walk with purpose to the senior parking lot and towards a familiar black car. I step onto the black tarmac right as Ash is unlocking his car. His head lifts in my direction, a brow raises in question.

He taps his fingers on the hood. "Are we breaking all the rules now?" he says, not hiding his amusement.

"Might as well give them something to talk about," I say, ignoring all the looks in our direction.

I open the passenger side door and toss my backpack into the back seat. I catch his lopsided grin before he starts the car. The engine growls in anticipation of speed. "Ready?"

I feel the pull to see all the faces that are watching us, to add them to the collection that already exists in my mind. Instead, I take a deep breath, focus instead on the warmth behind my breastbone, surrounding my heart. "Yes."

ASH ST. CLAIRE HAS his hands in his crisp uniform pockets, standing under the awning of my front porch, looking a little lost. He's removed his sweater vest with the Shorecrest Academy emblem on it but curiously kept his tie. He's rolled his dress shirt sleeves to his elbows to stave off the afternoon heat, but sweat is already beading at his temples.

"You alright?" I ask, giving him a sidelong glance.

"Yeah," his voice is rough around the word. "I've never been inside your house."

"It's not as impressive as yours." I unlock the door and motion for him to follow me.

"Oh, I don't know."

He's looking around the living room at the much-loved couches, a faded crocheted blanket draped over one corner, and dad's favorite recliner with the cushions broken in. The television that's pushed into the corner to make the room look bigger and the white walls decorated with framed fonts that say things like, *Family, Gratitude,* and *Home is Where you Grow.* There's only a sprinkling of mom's real talent here, as much as our meager budget allows.

I fidget in the space between the living room and dining room, suddenly self-conscious.

St. Claire walks up to a colored pencil drawing of the North Beach jetty at sunset. My mom had it framed with my middle school's first-place ribbon next to it.

"You can see life here. It's loved. My house is a museum."

"It's a pretty nice museum," I add, getting a disapproving look in return.

He doesn't like when I remind him how much money he has, even less when I'm self-deprecating.

I continue to my room. Ash follows, his hands in his pocket and his posture slightly stooped. I've never seen him look so uncomfortable with his surroundings. If I didn't know any better, I'd think he was feeling a little self-conscious as well.

Ash stops at a row of family pictures in the hallway. Some candid shots and some posed and stiff photos in a studio. He taps on one of my dad and me. I'm six years old and we're fishing over by South beach. I'm holding a little fishing pole with flowers on it and a big smile where you can see I'm missing one of my front teeth.

"You had chubby cheeks," he says with a coy smile.

I direct him away from the shrine of my childhood and call over my shoulder, "You have any pictures from when you were little?" I turn on the light in my room and drop my bag on the floor by my desk.

"Yes, lots."

"Really?"

He looks amused. "Yes. When you're a miracle birth, your parents memorialize your youth. There's even a painting or ten."

I roll my eyes but stop short at his expression. "You're not kidding, are you?"

He doesn't confirm or deny, but his mouth lifts in that sharing a secret way of his. He stands at the threshold, his eyes roaming the space with focused interest. I'm too aware of how utilitarian his room is compared to the carelessness of mine. I tossed aside the blankets on my bed from my rushed departure this morning. My pajamas are in a heap in front of my closet door, hangers poking at odd ends. My trashcan by my desk is nearly overflowing, with an empty pudding cup precariously on top.

I kick a pair of jeans under my bed and grab the trashcan to dump out in the kitchen, forcing St. Claire into the room. When I come back, he's studying a corkboard on the wall. It's filled with photos of family and friends, quotes that I thought were inspiring, and a couple of sketches I had every intention of coloring one day.

With his back turned, I straighten my sheets and close my closet door.

"Do you ever leave the island?" he asks.

"Not really," I say, sitting on the edge of my bed. "Everything I need is here."

His eyes linger on a picture of Kat, Meredith, and me during the first cold front of winter break. Winters here are quick but chilly. We're bundled up like it's forty degrees out when it was probably closer to sixty. The icy breeze off the ocean gives a flushed look to our faces. We're happy and smiling, and it fills my heart with a deep ache every time I look at it.

Ash turns around and sees me massaging my shoulder. "Does it hurt?" he asks.

"It aches sometimes."

I pull my shirt aside so we both can get a look at the star-shaped scar. I smooth my thumb over it, feeling the change in texture. He presses his lips into a hard line and I shift my shirt back in place.

"Has your dad found anything?" I scoot back on the bed and pick at the corner of my fingernail.

"A bullet casing that washed down the street, but no prints." His eyes roam over a stack of books and movies on a small bookcase by my closet. "The rain did a number on the crime scene."

"You went back there?"

"After you left," he says, pulling out a post-apocalyptic book and flipping it over to the back. "Father retrieved video from two neighbors who had cameras." He shakes his head at the hopeful look I give him, then slides the book back between a Greek mythology retelling. "The cloaking bubble made it impossible to see what was happening. There's only one frame where you're there and then gone again."

"That's terrifying," I say.

Ash's eyes are unfocused as he says, "I've been analyzing everything we know, and it's very possible that someone other than Adam saw you that day at school."

"Those kidnappers *definitely* weren't high school students."

Ash hums in agreement. "Maybe someone intentionally or unintentionally told someone..."

I worry at the hem of my skirt, pulling the fabric tight, loose, tight again with my hands. "Could your dad have told another Domini?"

"No," Ash says confidently, finally sitting on the bed next to me. "He wasn't happy about it, but he didn't forbid me from helping you."

"And now?"

Ash levels me with his gaze. "He wants to know who did this. He wouldn't tell anyone. You can trust him."

Can I trust you? I can't force the question from my lips, so instead, I wave a dismissive hand in the air. "Are you sure he's not mad you're spending all your time with an abhorrent Siphon?"

Ash looks at me apologetically. "No, he's not *mad* I'm spending time with you." He lays back on my bed, putting his arms under his head. "He wishes I'd put this much effort into other areas." His eyes dart away from me. "But he likes that I'm getting involved, that I'm hunting for some rogue Siphons, like a good little Dominus." He blows a breath over his lips.

"Is that who you think tried to kidnap me, rouge Siphons?"

"It's one theory," he says cagily.

"What would they want with me?"

Ash stares up at the ceiling. He focuses on that lone star on my ceiling. "I don't know."

We're both quiet. I don't know what has him lost in his thoughts exactly, but mine keeps pinwheeling over everything that happened over the weekend, trying to settle on any one thing. The weight of it makes me want to cry.

His eyes soften as he looks at me. "Echo," he says my name like it's meant to be whispered softly in the dark. He slowly sits up and I slide from the bed. His arm drops heavily on the comforter where my hand was.

I run my finger over my collection of movies, to give myself a minute to collect myself. "How about we watch The Adventures of the Magnificent?"

"Sure," he says. "What's it about?"

My eyes widen. "You've never seen it?" When he shakes his head, I go on, "Mr. Levitato's Revenge? The Adventures of the Magnificent: The Rise of Blue Comet? Magnificent Defeat: the Final Showdown, everyone has seen that one."

When he shakes his head again, I give him an incredulous push. A bemused smile lights up his face. "It sounds *interesting.*"

I insert the disc into my computer, turning the screen towards my bed as I do at night. I fluff the pillows by my headboard and settle in to watch one of my favorite movies. Ash is giving me a funny look, a mix of amusement and something else. I push on his arm again and focus on the opening credits. He leans back, his shoulder and arm pressed into mine, taking up so much room on my small twin bed, but I don't dare move.

CHAPTER 16

THE LIBRARIAN TASKED Adam and me with cataloging and labeling the new books that came in. We have brokered a steady routine that's both comforting and therapeutic. There's no judgment from these sleeping pages, no expectations or anticipation, and definitely no confusing signals.

"Can you believe he's never seen The Adventures of the Magnificent?" I say, securing a plastic book cover. I run my finger over the seal and lay it on top of Adam's pile to be entered into the database.

"Yes," Adam says confidently, his fingers tapping on the keyboard. "His entire life is like the plot of some movie, so why would he watch fake superheroes saving the world when he could just go be one?"

I purse my lips as I carefully place a bar code on the back right corner of a book about consumerism and environmentalism.

"That's true, I guess," I say, my sails temporarily deflated. "We finished The Magnificent Chronicles and I'm debating about showing him the spinoffs."

Adam gives me a sly smile as he grabs a book off the stack. "At your house *again* last night?"

"Yes," I say cautiously, narrowing my eyes.

There's a suspicious inflection to his question that gives my middle a nervous sort of squeeze. I try to ignore it as I tuck another book inside its new protective covering. I catch the tail end of Adam's knowing look that makes me want to punch him.

"Stop it," I warn.

He feigns innocence, typing out the call number and setting the book aside, and grabbing another. "Only stating the obvious." He shrugs one shoulder like he's observing something as mundane as the weather.

We both know better.

"It's not like that," I say, feeling my cheeks bloom with heat. "Those men are still out there, he's..." I flap my hand, trying to make a point that doesn't lead back to more smirks from Adam. "Keeping watch."

"Uh huh," Adam says, his face intent on the computer screen.

Henrik strongly suggested we keep the kidnap attempt from Adam, lest he becomes a target for information, but then Ash argued that he's already a target by association, and having Adam informed made him safer. He'd be more aware of the possibility of danger, Ash pointed out. The more eyes on our side, the better. Ash's dad looked dubious but also impressed.

I pick up a copy of The Power of Myth and flip open the pages, suddenly very curious about the hero's myth and how it translates through time and culture, shaping our own existence. It also covers the flush of my face.

"Don't be weird," I say. "Well, I'm spending a lot more time with *you* too, so it's whatever."

"Uh-huh." Adam concentrates a little too hard on the back of the book, his eyes squinting on the numbers, fighting a smile.

"He's going to be a *Dominus*," I hiss. "We're just friends."

Adam looks at me, his brows lifted in an understanding that makes me feel more raw and exposed than any of the teasings so far. Mortification swells for the nanosecond I allowed myself to think of it as *Ash and I*, and for Adam to have discovered it so deftly. I catch his gaze, my look daring him to correct me.

He looks away.

He grabs another book and types the numbers into the catalog, his fingers slow and deliberate. Click, click, click the keys. Loud in the sudden anticipatory pause.

Finally, he says, "How's Meredith?"

I shift in my seat, not sure if this is a better topic change. "Still not talking to me."

"Have you tried talking to her?"

I chew the inside of my cheek before I say, "Well, no."

"Maybe they're waiting on you?" I cut him a sharp look, and he holds up his hands. "You did lie to them first. Don't look at me like that. I know it was justified. I'm only saying that maybe they're waiting for you to apologize first."

"I did apologize," I say, trying not to sound petulant. "That night." I inhale deeply through my nose, feeling the pain afresh. I want to toss all these books on the floor as I remember how they threw accusations at me. "You don't think I deserve an apology, too?"

"Yes," he chides, giving me a look. "I don't know everyone's inner motivations, but I assume things were heated that night and maybe no one was thinking straight. Now that everything's out in the open, why don't you tell them the truth? What you can, anyway?"

My expression tells him how impossible that is. "It all feels like more lies."

He presses his mouth together, folding his hands on the table in front of him. "I can see that." He nods his head in thought. "You'll have to compromise, since there are parts you can't tell them, you can't escape that. Unless you want to give up on your friendship?"

"Is this a pep talk?"

Adam gives me a patient look. "Kind of."

I rub my temples feeling a stress headache coming on. "You know how it goes though," I tell him. "They'll always think I'm lying to them. Because I *am*." My heart gives a sharp retch to speak the truth aloud.

Adam ducks his head in thought, and finally, he says, "Do you know any of their secrets that the others don't?"

I cut him a sharp look. "Maybe."

Adam leans forward, his hands sliding along with him, as his posture dictates he's onto something. He licks his lips. "Sometimes we have things about ourselves or knowledge about other people that aren't meant to be shared and you don't have to be guilty about that."

As a group, Kat, Meredith, and I share a lot together, but there are a few secrets we keep because it might hurt the others' feelings or something happened that was so embarrassing we never want to relive it. I think of the conversations whispered late at night and how I wouldn't have dreamed of sharing them without my friend's permission.

I sit back in my chair and cross my arms. "Since when did you get to be so smart?"

Adam laughs. "I've always been this awesome, Martin. You've just been a little preoccupied with a certain mutual acquaintance of ours."

I roll my eyes with a mutinous shake of my head. Okay, two can play this game. I jut out my chin towards him. "Is that what you're going to do with Meredith, then?"

He had gone back to typing, satisfied with his own wisdom, but now his eyes squint on the screen, concentrating on an info box he's spent the last twenty minutes well accustomed to.

He sighs when he sees my face. "It's my turn, huh?"

I lift my brows, waiting. Adam's fingers slide softly away from the keyboard. "You think she'd forgive me?" he asks, with no hint of a teasing tone, only a heart filled with hope.

His question catches me by surprise, forcing me to call my bluff. There was a time when I wouldn't have mettled—choosing to let them figure it out by themselves, seeing how much I didn't like it in my own life—but if I lose Meredith, at least I can give her this last thing.

"Yes, I think she wants to," I tell him honestly. "She misses you."

Adam looks away from me. "I miss her too."

He sinks into an intimate sort of reflection, so I go back to adding bar codes and wrapping protective covers on. After a moment, the sound of typing resumes beside me.

"Don't tell her, okay?"

"Of course," I say.

CHAPTER 17

THE SKY IS painted with the pink and cream clouds of sunrise and the early morning ocean is calm; the waves are a gentle caress on the shore, slow and languid like they too are having trouble waking up. Seawater coats the air with a salty, sterile smell that will forever remind me of home. I take it all into my lungs, purifying the cells, comforting me deep in my soul.

"Why did I agree to this?" I say with a yawn.

Ash pulls his leg back to stretch out his calf muscle, balancing effortlessly. He's dressed in his running clothes, his shorts—I note—not as short as the ones I borrowed. Adam is beside him with his arm behind his back, stretching out who knows what.

"Fresh air is good for you," Ash says with a big grin on his too-perky-for-this-early-in-the-morning face.

They go running every Saturday, weather and schedules permitting. I wouldn't admit to either of them, especially this early, that I find it very boyish and endearing.

"It's not the fresh air that I have a problem with. It's six a.m. on a Saturday. That's sick."

Adam gives a rueful shake of his head as he switches to the other arm, but keeps out of our debate on the insanity of sunrise runs.

"There are fewer people this early," Ash says.

"You don't like all the eyes ogling you?"

I look over at an elderly woman dressed head to toe in a windbreaker jogging suit and a sun visor hat that says Best Grandma. She has two water bottles clicked to her fanny pack and a mesh sack for collecting shells. In another four hours, a much younger crowd will claim the beach.

"I don't actually," he says, turning his head to stretch out the other leg.

I lift my brows in a gesture he doesn't see. "Well, you're going to have to go slow with me," I say.

Adam is standing a few feet away, out of St. Claire's peripheral, so he doesn't catch Adam's amused smile.

"Because I'm not a fast *runner*." The emphasis directed at Adam.

Adam tries to hide his grin by bending down to stretch, but I can still see his cheeks pulled tight, the laugh on his lips. Ash finishes his stretch and I can finally look over at him without feeling an uncomfortable blush on my face.

"Go slow," he nods, oblivious to Adam's barely hidden mirth. "I can do that."

The heat returns to my cheeks, but I'm saved by Adam punching Ash in the shoulder. Ash turns, brows raised with camaraderie. "Kiss my dust then." Adam grins, jogging away.

Ash gives an encouraging nod in Adam's direction. "Come on," he says while jogging backward, "it'll be fun."

I wouldn't call it fun, but their energy is infectious. Even though I'm not a fast runner, it gave me an inclusive thrill to be invited along. I roll my eyes, which only makes his grin bigger as I jog up beside him.

Ash is a wild mustang, bridled, and forced into a slow canter beside me. He looks as if he could keep this pace forever, but all that raw power that flexes as he moves is just waiting to be released. It's almost cruel to keep him tethered to my much slower stride.

Adam has a nice lead on us and occasionally I've sensed Ash coiled to strike after him, only to glance back at me.

"Go ahead," I tell him, jutting my chin towards Adam, who is steadily getting further and further away. He shakes his head, but his expression looks conflicted. "If someone tries to kidnap me, I'll scream."

"Okay. I'll be right back," he says, "three minutes."

When I nod, he takes off after him. I laugh, dropping into a slower jog. He wasn't the only one trying to keep pace. They'll get to the rock pier before me anyway, even if I push my muscles to the max.

The beach is quiet on this side, with no real public access. Mostly private homes line the whole western side, with an occasional pricey rental. There are only a few chairs set out in the sand, steaming tumblers or books in hand, as they ignore everything but the sounds of the waves.

Not all the houses on the beach have privacy walls like the St. Claire's. Some estates have white sand right until it meets their heavily tended lawns. This close to the sea, more care needs to be done to keep the grass looking green and the plants from wilting under the high level of salt in the air. Except for the palm trees, they seem to thrive no matter if it's seawater, drought, or hurricane.

The eastern beaches are busy. Full of tourists and locals who know that the further you go into the thick mangroves the more likely you are to get away with coolers full of alcohol and loud music.

I give up on pretending I can keep up with the boys and jog over to the edge where the fluffy meets the hard-packed sand. I toe off my running shoes and socks and flex my toes on the hard wet sand, padding to the edge to let the ocean flow over my feet. Over and over. Little coquina clams tickle under my toes if I stand still too long.

The wind changes and a smell I can't name tickles my nose. It brings up a sensory memory of a girl lying half in the sea; her eyes no longer blinking. I wrap my arms around myself, feeling a chill though the sun is now higher, blazing down on me.

I hear the boys' voices, teasing each other as they push themselves in a race toward me, casually competitive. Adam was gaining on Ash until St. Claire pushes forward in a sprint. I move out of the way as they rush past. Adam playfully pushes St. Claire as they both collapse, their chest heaving on the sand.

"You're such a cheat," Adam says, breathing hard, the back of his head resting on the sand.

Ash leans up on his forearm, white sand coating his sweaty skin, to say, "You said don't hold back."

"I lied. Hold back!" Adam's gasping. "Hold back."

Ash falls back onto the sand with a grin.

I stare down at them. "Is this what you do every Saturday?"

"Pretty much," Adam says at the same time Ash says, "Yes."

"It's good for me," Adam says as he closes his eyes. "Makes me stronger."

I toe his thigh. "Don't die," I tell him.

Adam waves me off and lazily rolls his head over to Ash. "Ready for round two?"

Ash glances over and a second after they make eye contact, Adam takes off toward the jetty. Ash scrambles up after him, kicking sand into the air. They race towards the outcropping of rocks. Adam veers towards the ocean, his legs gaining better traction on the hard sand. Water sprays from their shoes as they've gotten too close to the lower part of the beach face.

Ash is winning until Adam pushes him into the sea. You can hear their laughter carried on the gentle breeze. They splash and wrestle in the waves, turning their landrace into a front stroke towards the hazard buoys warning the boats of the shallow shore.

They may look like men, but they play like little boys. I shake my head and walk along where the sea break hits the soft sand, looking for shark's teeth and sea glass.

I glance up to make sure the boys haven't swum all the way around to the other side of the island when I see her. Our eyes lock. Meredith looks as surprised to see me as I am. She looks away, trying to find a way out, but there's no place to hide on the open beach. Her face falls and with it, my heart sinks.

Meredith looks better dressed for an early morning run than I am. She's in form-fitting lycra with a colorful stripe down the side and a sleek tank. For the first time in a long time, I feel frumpy and awkward standing next to my best friend.

She fidgets with her earbuds, and then finally pulls them free. Her eyes flit everywhere but at me as she asks, "What are you doing here?"

I hate her indifferent tone. How quickly we have become strangers.

"Running."

"*Running*," she repeats, indignant. The silence stretches as neither one of us wants to call a draw. Finally, she says, "Well, I better let you get back to it." She puts in her earbuds, dismissing me.

"I'm sorry," I blurt before anxiety can seal my lips. Meredith removes her earbuds. "I'm sorry I lied to you."

Her eyes narrow on me, making my palms sweat. "I don't understand why you had to lie at all?"

I rock back on my heels. "My reasons were stupid. They don't matter anymore," I say and her eyes turn to slits.

"They do," she says. "Why lie to us if you're only friends? The entire school is saying—"

I scoff. "You're believing the school gossip now?"

A guilty look changes her features before she hardens again. "You had the chance to explain, and you ran out."

"You also had the chance to follow me and you didn't," I implore.

Her face pinches with either guilt or resolve, maybe both. "We could go round and round on this," she says with a tired sigh.

"You hurt me too, you know," I say, feeling a little unfairly judged. "I left because it didn't look like you two wanted to hear my side."

Meredith bristles, both of us feeling justified. "What were we to think?"

"Maybe not the worse?"

My voice has risen slightly, getting the attention of a beachcomber. She scrutinizes us, her eyes finally narrowing on me, deciding I'm the troublemaker. I pinch the bridge of my nose. I'm ruining this apology fast.

"I lied to avoid this. I was afraid you would react this way. "

Meredith worries her fingers, watching the old woman until she's out of earshot. "I thought you hated St. Claire?"

"I didn't hate him," I say truthfully. "I didn't even know him."

"And now you do?" She raises a perfectly sculpted black brow, insinuating.

"As *friends*," I say, clearly.

"Why wouldn't you tell us then?"

I touch the tips of my fingers together, feeling like I'm wading into liar's territory, but Adam's advice whispers back at me. Sometimes we have things about ourselves or knowledge about other people that are okay to be secrets. There were a few reasons I lied about Ash St. Claire, and I don't have to feel guilty about hiding the supernatural stuff.

I tell her my truth and hope for the best. "I was worried you guys would tease me about it, like with Alex, and I didn't want that." She opens her mouth to argue and I quickly rush on, "I didn't want anyone jumping to conclusions, like what the entire school is doing now," I say. "And maybe a part of me enjoyed keeping it a secret." I swallow, waiting.

Meredith crosses her arms, but she doesn't look hostel, only sad. "You knew Kat liked him."

"Everyone likes him," I say, throwing up my hands. "Kat has crushes on everyone. Does she want me to stop talking to every boy at school?"

Meredith tilts her head in agreement and I feel hope seeping into the small crack in the stone casing of my heart. Familiar laughter draws Meredith's gaze to their source. Her softening posture hardens so abruptly I'd know why, even if I hadn't looked.

Adam and Ash are dripping wet as they jog towards me, heads turned in conversation, laughter on their lips. When they get close, Ash elbows Adam and both boys stop, pretending to look for shells on the surf's edge. Ash shoots me an apologetic look, silently asking if I need saving. I shake my head.

Meredith's brown skin is flushed. "You're here with Ash and *Adam?*" she says tightly, not really a question. "How long have you been hanging out with Adam?" she asks, an accusation.

"Adam is Ash's friend," I bristle.

"How *long?*"

I search her face, her eyes looking glassy. This time guilt does slam into my chest, warranted or not. "Since school started."

Meredith turns, then quickly levels her gaze at me. "You know how I feel about him, Echo, and you lied to me about it. *Me.* After everything I've confessed to you?"

Meredith jogs off down the beach, not giving me time to explain.

"Meredith, wait!" I call, but she doesn't slow down.

I am frozen on the shore but I could even catch her even if I tried.

IT WAS OBVIOUS THINGS went badly with Meredith, but neither Ash nor Adam ask about it. As I somberly make my way over to them, Adam declares that it's slushie time. Another Saturday tradition.

Ash drives to the corner gas station right outside the bridge to the Western Crescent. It's also the closest one before South beach so the floors are perpetually covered in a thin layer of sand. Adam shakes out his dark brown hair as we get out of the car. Salt and sand still cling to their arms and legs as we make our way to the giant ice slushie machine.

As they stick their giant cups under the spout, I ask, "Isn't this counterproductive?" I eye their cups meaningfully.

Adam shakes his head, his mouth on his straw as the blue liquid travels upward. "No, see, because I just burned like a thousand calories and this drink is only four hundred."

"I don't think that's right," I tell him and he laughs.

"Sounds good to me," Ash says right before he takes a pull of his icy drink.

He watches me watching and then tips his cup in my direction, straw pointing in invitation. I resist the urge to look at Adam, sure I'll find something there on his exuberant face as I take a drink. It's cola flavored.

I grab a much smaller cup and fill it as they wander over to the snack aisle. The syrupy ice drinks and rotating corn dog machine, obviously the biggest draw, are located right when you walk into the store, so I have an unobstructed view when the door pings and Alex Carter walks in. He lifts his dark sunglasses up, his eyes light up when he sees me.

"Hey Echo," he says, all smiles and charm as he joins me.

"Hello."

Alex leans in, brushing his arm against mine as he reaches for a cup. It sends a little electric hum through me, like plucking a guitar string. I shift on my feet, unsure of the little flutter that's started in my stomach.

He nods at my drink. "Banana? I thought you'd be a blue raspberry girl."

I tilt my head. "Why is that?"

"Because everyone loves blue raspberry." He flashes me his movie-star grin.

He drops his cup under a dispenser and fills it with thick, frosty blue liquid. I scan the store to find Adam and Ash over by a rack of surfing and fishing magazines, engrossed by whatever is on the pages of Anglers Adventures. I turn back in time to see a muscle in Alex's jaw tense.

"So the rumors are true?" He shifts his gaze back to me, all smiles again. "You and St. Claire, huh?"

The cold drink is leaching into my fingertips through the cup, making them numb. "We're just friends."

Alex rakes his teeth over his bottom lip. He is deliberate about snapping the lid on his drink.

"How'd that happen, anyway?" he asks, taking a sip. He leans his elbow on the napkin dispenser, bringing him closer to me.

"How did Ash and I become friends?" I frown, shifting back.

"Yeah, I mean, Golden Boy likes to keep to his own kind," he chuckles. "Except for Woo, I mean, what's up with that, anyway?" His straw makes a loud slurping sound despite the 80's music softly playing in the store.

My spine stiffens. "I suppose it's like you and Tyler."

The straw rests lazily on Alex's bottom lip, looking like he's modeling for the company. His shoulder lifts. "Yeah, I guess it is like that." He leans down like he's going to tell me a secret. I lean in a little despite myself. "Since you guys are only friends, maybe this weekend..."

I get that heart-racing feeling right before presenting in front of the class. I shift my hands on my cup. Their warmth melting the frozen drink. It cracks and shifts in my cup.

Alex's movie star smile falters, and his eyes darken as he mumbles something I can't make out. He straightens up to his full height as his mouth shifts to a smile I haven't seen before.

"Hey," he says, pushing a hand through his hair as Ash walks up beside me.

"Hey Alec, right? You're hogging the straws," Ash says, reaching over and forcing Alex to step back.

"Alex," he corrects, looking mildly affronted. He watches Ash hand me a straw and lid. His eyebrows raise in a way that makes my face feel warm.

Adam appears on my right side, a bag of chips in his hand. "Hey, Carter."

"Woo," Alex acknowledges, taking a leisurely sip of his drink. "You guys enjoying the surf?"

"No surf today, you?"

"Nah." Alex leans over to inspect the hot rack. "Just came in for a snack." He uses the tongs and grabs a corn dog, sliding it into a small paper bag. He eyes Ash and Adam's attire and says, "Running the W.C. again?"

"W.C., South Beach, East." Ash crosses his arms over his chest. "I like to change it up."

"I'm sure you do," Alex mumbles. "I'm a little less Mercurial," he says, meeting my eyes. "I don't run around." He takes a sip of his drink.

Ash's eyes flick to mine. Alex's gaze moves meaningfully over to St. Claire before he turns that grin back on for me. He puts his hand on my bare shoulder, stirring up a school of fish in my stomach.

"I'll talk to you later?"

I'm painfully aware of Ash and Adam standing beside me. I tuck a stray strand of hair behind my ear. "Um, okay."

Adam refills his drink as Ash watches Alex pay at the cash register. "I don't like that guy," he says, getting a raised brow from Adam.

As we walk to the car, a line forms between Ash's brows and only deepens when Alex honks his horn, a grin on his face before he turns onto Bayou drive. He sticks his hand out the window, giving a little two-finger wave goodbye as if he knows we're still watching.

Ash closes the driver's side door with a little more force than necessary and I raise my brows at him. "Why are you being so weird?" I ask him, watching as he struggles to buckle his seat belt.

"I'm not."

I put my hand on the back of the seat and turn towards Adam, looking for him to back me up. St. Claire looks at him in the mirror as he adjusts it. Adam holds up his hands, one still clutching his drink, staying out of it.

Ash says, "He's got some kind of problem with me."

"Other than that weird misunderstanding you guys had a few years back? Why would he still have a problem with you?" I ask.

Ash shifts in his seat, his eyes flick over to mine before he puts the car in gear, and backs out of the parking space. "I don't know. Maybe it has something to do with you? Maybe he's jealous?"

Adam coughs on his drink and we both glance back at him. "Brain freeze," he says.

"Jealous?"

The car stops at the red light, the engine a soft rumble. Ash clicks the blinker to turn right onto Bayshore, away from the Western Crescent and towards Adam's home. He gives me a sidelong look as I'm still waiting for an answer.

He presses his lips together before he says, "I don't know." He sighs, looking everywhere but at me. "Because you're hanging out with me?" The light turns green, forcing him to glance at me. "Didn't he try to ask you out back there? Again."

I narrow my eyes at him for eavesdropping. He gives me a knowing look, his hands tightening on the wheel. I've never seen him so focused on driving before.

"I don't know."

"It's obvious he likes you." His eyes flick up to the rear-view mirror, and he runs a hand through his hair.

"I didn't say yes."

The slurping sound from the backseat reminds us we're not alone. Ash and I relax our tense posture, an awkward silence settling inside the cab. The only sound is Adam's drinking through his straw, the car's engine, and my heartbeat.

"You can do whatever you want," Ash says, lifting one shoulder. "I was only concerned with what happened and all."

"Right. You think someone will abduct me while I'm on a date with Alex Carter?"

A pained expression washes over his face. "They have ways of concealing their actions," he says, turning off the main road into the adorable historic district filled with restored houses from the early nineteen hundreds. "As you know."

"Okay," I say slowly, a smile spreading across my face. "So is it hanging out with other people that's the problem, or Alex Carter?"

Ash's frown deepens, and he declines to give me an answer. I catch Adam's amused expression in the side mirror, his lips tinted blue.

"I don't think you're safe with him," he finally says.

"I'm safe with you," I tell him without question.

He turns towards me. "Yes."

Ash pulls in front of Adam's house, the silence feeling less awkward and more on the cusp of some great thing. It feels private and meaningful, though it could be my imagination. Adam clears his throat from the backseat, breaking the moment and bringing warmth through my body that he heard this entire exchange.

Ash gets out of the car with as much need to let Adam out of the backseat as his need for movement.

"See you in class," Adam says, giving me a look meant only for me before he climbs out of the car.

Adam pats Ash on the shoulder before he bounds up the stairs to his door.

Ash takes a deep breath once he's back behind the driver's seat. "Do you still want to come over?"

"Yes," I say. And wait until after Ash starts the car to add, "I kind of like it when you act weird."

His mouth lifts in an uneven smile as he pulls away from the two-story storybook house and heads toward the ocean.

CHAPTER 18

I STARE AT MY phone screen with an odd detachment. The longer I stare at Ash's message, the more disappointed I get. Though I shouldn't be. I remind people at least daily that we're only friends, and I tell myself that with the same regularity. So why do I still feel rejected? *You know why.*

I turn my phone face down on my desk, but the conversation is burned on my eyelids.

> **ASH:** Something came up. Adam will watch you today after church.

> **ME:** Everything alright?

> **ASH:** It's fine. I'll see you at school.

Watch, like it's part of his job. A soft knock at the door proceeds mom popping her head in. "Adam is here." A crease forms between her brows as she sees my face. "Still no word?"

My thoughts sputter until I remember she's talking about my friends. "Oh. No," I give a lofty wave of my hand.

Her frown turns sympathetic. "They just need time."

It feels like there's been plenty of time. I follow her out into the hallway to find Adam sitting at the breakfast table in his dress slacks and pale yellow button-down and tie. The curtains are open, making the dining room bright and cheery, a contrast to my mood.

My parents have decided to feed him. Dad sets a glass of orange juice down as mom places a full stack of pancakes in front of him. Adam hasn't been inside these walls without Meredith and though he's spent a few nights watching movies with us on my living room sofa, he looks nervous.

He gives me a shy smile when he sees me. A small patch of red up high on his cheekbones. I take my seat across from him as mom sets a plate down for me. Adam's back is Sunday school straight, his hands clasped neatly in front of him until the delicious smell of mom's cooking perseveres over his nerves. He digs into his thick pancakes, thanking them for breakfast.

"Anytime." Mom smiles, happy to be feeding someone. Since the fight with my friends, it's been a lot quieter around the house.

The table murmurers with pleasantries; how's school, how's baseball, mom says she saw Adam's mom at the grocery store last Thursday, tell her she said hi. Dad asks about college plans and there's a brief animated conversation where they compare who has the better team to play for. Mom looks amused by the interest my father is taking in Adam.

She dabs her mouth with her napkin and directs her question to either Adam or me. "Where's Ash?"

I shrug my shoulders, looking at Adam for answers. Maybe Ash gave him more than two sentences.

"He had a family obligation," Adam says before he shovels in a huge mouthful of pancake.

"Oh?" Dad sits up with interest. "What kind of family obligation?"

Adam's gaze flits guiltily to me as he finishes chewing. "His brother is in town."

"His brother?" I gasp.

Mom lifts her brows at me. "I didn't know he had a brother."

"What's his brother doing here?" I try to keep my voice level, a contrast to my pulse.

Adam either doesn't register my surprise or he's ignoring it. He keeps his head down, stabbing the remaining pieces on his plate.

"To help his dad with some work." At this, Adam meets my eyes, and understanding washes over me. He's here because of me. Or for me.

I feel numb as we finish breakfast. I move through the motions, helping mom clean up. When it's less conspicuous that I'm trying to get Adam alone, I pull him into my room.

"Door open," Dad yells from down the hall. I would feel embarrassed if I wasn't preoccupied.

"What's Ash's brother really doing here?" I whisper harshly to Adam.

"To help his dad, you know, with *work*." He points at me.

"Yeah, but why?"

Adam shrugs. "They don't tell us mere mortals the details."

"Well, Ash obviously told *you*," I snap back.

Adam runs a hand over the back of his neck, looking like we're wading into waters he doesn't want to swim in.

"Is that *really* the reason? Or is it something else?"

A line appears between Adam's brows. "What else could it be?" Something in my face makes him raise his brows. "*Ah.*"

"What's *'ah'* for?"

"Nothing," he says with a smirk that says it's definitely something.

Feeling irritated for all the wrong reasons, I say, "He didn't need to send you over here to babysit me. I'm not a little kid."

A dark desire to call Alex Carter rises from a petty part of my soul, but I'd only be creating my own metaphorical dragon, hoping a knight will come to slay it—and that's not fair to anyone. Still, I can't shake this petulant mood.

Adam scratches his chin and turns away from me, studying the pictures and memories on my corkboard. "He thought you wouldn't want to be alone today after what was on the news," he says, his back to me. "He'd have come himself if he could."

The hairs raise on the back of my neck. "What was on the news?"

"You haven't—," he half turns, sees my face, "never mind."

"Adam. What is it?"

"It'll upset you. Forget I said anything."

"I can't now, just tell me."

Adam looks pained. He rubs his neck, looking at the door. I get up and close it. He says, "The mainland police found some bodies in the city."

I cross my arms. "Why would that bother me?"

Adam chews his bottom lip. His fingers fidget with his tie. "Because it was the men who attacked you."

"Show me," I whisper.

"Echo..."

"Please."

Adam reluctantly fishes out his phone from his pants pocket and pulls up a news site, handing me his phone. I watch the sixty-second clip, my blood turning to ice. Three bodies were discovered behind an old train station in the city. One of the deceased nephew is still missing, last seen with his uncle.

A high school yearbook photo appears on the screen of a boy about eighteen, though when I last saw him, he looked older, a little scruffier. The reporter is saying; that the police are looking for any information. They don't suspect him of the murders at present; the family hopes he's still alive.

But I know he's not.

"He's only a few years older than us." I hand Adam his phone before I drop to the floor and pull my knees up to my chest.

Adam kneels down beside me. "Echo..."

His face is watery as I say, "They're all dead?"

Adam put his hand on my knee, his eyes slanted in sympathy. "They weren't doing anything good. You need to remember that."

But I can't. All I see is his face. I rest my head on my knees and wrap my arms tighter around myself. "I can't stop the nightmares, can't stop feeling like I'm one of the bad ones."

"You're not one of the bad ones, Echo, you're not."

I lift my head to look at him. "What would you have done?"

Adam searches my face. "I would have survived."

ADAM DRIVES NORTH TO the Mangrove Island Preserve. We pass the recreation complex with the huge soccer fields and public pool and full parking lot. Behind that is Kat's neighborhood, and I wonder briefly if she's home.

Adam continues along the long curved road, passing the last bridge to the western Crescent and far away from anyone. The North end of the island doesn't really have a beach as much as it has sandy banks and is host to an interesting ecosystem where the freshwater lakes and canals of the island trickle into the salty sea. It's booming with a variety of flora and fauna, and a great place to paddle board down the snaking channels of the preserve, all the way to the inter-coastal between the W.C. and the main island.

I have spent many school field trips in the preserves education building listening to talks about sea turtle conservation, manatee zones, tortoise dens, the different mangroves on the island, and iguana sightings.

Adam has spent his fair share of school days too doing animal scavenger hunts and collecting water samples and dissecting mangrove pods and then having lunch on the picnic tables under the large oak trees heavy with moss. It's almost a rite of passage.

Adam pulls into the parking lot in front of the closed visitor center and museum of local Native American artifacts. There are a couple of vehicles near the small canoe and paddleboard ramp, but other than that, it's empty.

The scent of seawater is stronger here than on the beach because of the high concentration of mangroves. We enter one of the boardwalk trails, the one that leads up to an observation tower in the middle of the park. We walk side by side, the worn planks making a steady rhythm of soft thumps as we walk. Adam's arms move casually at his side. My fingers trail over the railing, looking through the bush for signs of animal life.

Once we reach the tower, we climb to the top; the view is mostly the tops of mangroves, but you can see the brackish canals weaving through all the bright green in the preserve. And beyond that, they lead to an estuary before the sea. A cormorant perched on the railing flies off once it sees us.

Adam leans over the railing. He closes his eyes, his face up towards the sun. "I love the smell of this place," he says, and we both take in a deep breath, filling our lungs with the fresh air.

I stare at my hands on the railing and wonder at the power building inside me. My cheeks still feel salty from mourning what I've done. I rub a palm over my face, trying to clear not only the residue but the ache in my soul. If this is what it's like to be a Siphon, I don't think I want it.

I turn my back on the treetops, leaning against the railing. It's not that I don't like the view or the preserve, or being here with Adam, it's just... I wish Ash was here.

"So," I say, digging my nail into the grain of the wooden railing, "did he say if he's going to be busy all day?"

Adam smiles out at the preserve, his shoulders moving with a silent laugh. "Am I that boring?"

"No," I blurt. "Not at all."

I ramble out more of an apology, but he waves a hand, cutting me off. "No, I get it." He looks down at the water with that big toothy grin of his. "I'm not as dazzling or exciting as Ash, but I've got better jokes," he says, bumping his arm into mine.

"I enjoy hanging out with both of you," I say truthfully, but right now I want to talk to someone who understands this world I'm becoming a part of.

"I'm only teasing," he says, his face sobering up. "No one's forcing me to be here, you know, you're my friend. I've got your back."

"Thanks," I say, "and same." I bump my arm into his.

We both gaze out over the greenery and watch a blue heron slowly wade through the shallow water under the tower.

I chew my cheek. "Does he…" Adam looks over at me, waiting. "Never mind." I turn away from him.

"Oh," Adam says, looking mildly uncomfortable. "We're going to talk about that."

"I know you're mostly teasing, but…" I bite my lip and rock back on my heels.

"But does he like you?"

I nod as my face becomes horribly warm. Adam's throat moves, his eyes cut away from me, and I feel a weight drop to my toes.

I shake my head. "Forget it. I don't want to put you in the middle of this."

Adam coughs out a dry laugh. "I think…," he says, "that you should ask him."

"That's a no." I turn back toward the view, putting my elbows on the railing.

"It's a *'ask him'*."

"I told you about Meredith," I grumble.

"And I told you about Ash," he says, the corner of his mouth looking devious.

There's a little chirp from his pocket, and my brows raise. He checks the screen and mouths *'ask him'* before taking a seat under the covered roof of the observation tower. There's a happy sort of smile in his eyes as he writes the sender back.

"So, new girl or ex-girl?"

He grunts at my teasing, his eyes on the screen. He slides his phone back into his pocket and leans back on the bench. "You're awfully nosy, you know."

"Yes." I push off the railing. "So, when did that happen?"

Adam sighs noisily, before he says, "Saturday, after you guys dropped me off."

"*Oh?*"

"See, that's why I was keeping my mouth shut. That face right there." I hold up my hands in surrender and he blows out a breath. "You said Meredith was upset because we were hanging out. I didn't want her to think..." A bloom of color spreads on his face.

"Oh!"

"I mean, you're great and all."

I hold up a hand. "It's fine. We don't need to go there."

He runs a hand over his face, looking as uncomfortable as I feel. "I didn't think she'd even answer." He shakes his head, lost in the memory. "But we talked..." He lifts a shoulder, both of us knowing what he means.

"*And?*"

"And we're just talking." He smiles. "But it's a start."

"That's great," I smile with him, a catch in my throat. I'm happy, I am, but it's hard not to feel sorry for myself. "I'm thrilled for you."

His phone chirps again, and I wander back over to the railing to give him some privacy. My purse feels heavy on my shoulder, but I leave my phone inside. A breeze moves over the tops of the trees, making them sway in a somber dance. I lean over the side, my hands gripping the railing as tightly as it feels inside my chest. I watch a small school of fish dart out of the shadows in the water.

The breeze picks up and blows my hair in my face. The sky darkens with the threat of an afternoon shower.

Adam touches my arm, his head tilted up to the sky. "That came on fast," he says. "Come on, before we get electrocuted."

I follow him under the shade of the roof and down the stairs as thunder booms above us.

CHAPTER 19

A SH ISN'T AT school on Monday.
    The events of the following weekend tumble through my thoughts until they reach avalanche proportions. I don't like this feeling. It's the type of possession that I don't have a right to, and I wish my heart could understand that. I enjoy being in the secret Ash St. Claire Club, even as only friends. The fact he didn't call or tell me about his brother bothered me more than it should.

Latin derivatives and grammar concepts blur together, and the day only gets worse after my solitary lunch in the darkroom, alone with my thoughts. For my last class, Remedial Arts, I was a hurricane of emotions that I was losing the battle of hiding.

I share the class with Meredith, which used to be a lot of fun, but lately is a constant reminder of my mistakes and regrets. She's booked the pottery wheel for most of our falling out, but today she got here late and lost her spot to Kenna Juarez.

I keep my head down, focusing on my landscape, the sound of the colored pencil scraping over the paper a soundtrack to my thoughts.

I see Meredith fidget beside me. She twirls her carving tool in her red clay-stained fingers. She opens her mouth, closes it, and finally, she says, "I talked to Adam."

"I know." Her eyes widen, and I rush to clarify, but she beats me to it.

"I know there's nothing going on with you and Adam..."

"I would *never* do that to you," I plead.

Her features shift. "It's Kat...," she says, shaking away whatever she almost admitted. "She's still mad you lied. You know how she gets." Meredith chews her cheek. "She's hurt."

"I'm hurt too," I tell her, pushing aside my annoyance that Kat gets to have feelings, but I don't. "I'm sorry I lied, but I had my reasons and look, some of them came true."

She looks away and I inwardly cringe. I didn't plan on unpacking it all over again in the middle of art class, but I feel like I need closure.

"How do I fix this? How can we go back to normal?"

She shrugs, looking a little uncomfortable. "I forgive you, Echo," she says, but I can sense the caveat coming. "Everything is a mess. You know Kat takes the longest to swallow her pride, but it'll get there."

"You could have told us about Ash. We would have kept your secrets."

"We're just friends," I say, exhausted from how many times I have to repeat that.

After a moment, her mouth lifts at the corners. "I bet that's an interesting story." Her smile turns reflective. "I hope you tell me someday."

I hope so too.

We don't talk the rest of the class period, but the silence doesn't feel as permeable. All I have to do next is talk to Kat, a conversation I knew was going to be the hardest and the one requiring the most emotional armor. If she can't forgive me and we both can't move past this, then that's it, and hopefully, I haven't lost Meredith either. The possibility that I might, hurts more than they'll ever know because sometimes it feels like I need them more than they need me.

If I'm going to lose my friends, at least it's going to be on my terms facing it head on and not hiding like I've been doing. I need to swallow down my fears and talk to Katerina.

I SEARCH FOR KAT in the parking lot, but I didn't have time to talk to her even if I found her. Adam insisted on taking me home, and he only had thirty minutes until soccer practice.

"Sorry to rush, but if I'm late, coach will make me run laps. And I really don't want to run laps."

"No worries," I tell him. "Thanks for the ride."

"Yeah, boss's orders," he says, starting the car.

His innocent comment puts me in a foul mood. I haven't heard from Ash, but he obviously has no problem texting Adam. I slide my phone out of my bag to turn the ringer on. My heart goes into overdrive when I see Kat's tagged me in a post from her account.

Adam pulls behind an obnoxiously loud yellow sports car as we join the queue to leave. I open the picture, my eyes soaking in the details as Adam's truck slowly pulls forward. Kat's sitting on the picnic table, her lips pouty in her usual way. I frown, not sure why she sent it to me when I see there's more.

Adam's truck moves up as I flick through the pictures. Kat has her arm draped over Tyler's shoulders, Hannah Bardi is making a face to the camera beside them and Meredith is laughing at something funny off camera. The last picture is of Kat with Alex beside her all white-teeth, and smiles.

Jealously hot and hurtful blazes through me. They have replaced me so quickly, and Kat is flaunting it in my face. Trying to hurt me on *purpose.* It's cruel.

I drop my phone on the seat. Adam glances at it and then at me. He does a double-take. "What's wrong?"

"Nothing." I cross my arms over my chest.

He looks unsure, but someone honks, and he's forced to turn onto the road.

"Was it Ash?" he asks, looking anguished.

That brings up another storm of emotions, but I've only got enough anger for one at the moment. So I tell him all about Katerina tagging me in her pictures, gloating in their happiness without me, trying to bait me with her arm seductively around Alex.

"Oh." Adam studies my slumped posture and crossed arms. "But you don't like that douchebag, right?"

I don't answer right away, and Adam arches a brow. "No," I say quickly, but Adam's gone reflective. "Did you know they were hanging out?" I ask, wondering where he was at lunch.

"No." He shakes his head and then sees my face. "I wasn't there. I had a makeup test."

Adam pulls into my empty driveway, putting the car in park. He looks cautiously over at me and then at the clock on his dash. "I hate to bail but... *coach*," he says, pained.

"It's okay, I'm fine." Though my body feels coiled too tightly.

He taps his fingers on the steering wheel. I grab my bag and open the door.

"You're not going over to Kat's as soon as I leave and get me in trouble, are you?"

"I promise you I'm not going to Kat's," I tell him with more vehemence than Adam deserves—I feel bad instantly. I let out a long, frustrated sigh. "I don't mean to take it out on you, sorry."

Adam looks relieved that some of my anger has dissipated. "I get it," he says. "I'll see you tomorrow?"

"Sure," I say, shutting the door.

I watch his truck pull out of the driveway as I close the front door. Is Ash having him babysit me because he's worried or thinks

I'll do something reckless? Well, if I'm so dangerous, then he should babysit me himself.

I let out a frustrated noise, dropping my backpack on the couch. All my anger is bouncing around at different people. At Kat's obvious jab, at Meredith for not automatically taking my side after all these years of friendship, at St. Claire for ghosting me.

My fingers twitch to comment on Kat's post, but I don't. I want to tell Adam I don't need to be supervised, but I don't. I want to text Ash that if he's so worried about me, then he should be here and not pawning it off on poor Adam, but I do nothing because I never do anything. I keep my feelings bottled up inside and it's killing me.

I push my fingers into my hair, my heart racing, and the pressure building behind my eyes. When I lower my hands, little sparks dance from my fingertips. The astonishing sight of it temporarily makes me forget my anger. The sparks quickly stop, leaving only my chest thudding as any proof it happened at all. I back up into the wall, making the keys on the hooks jangle.

I stare at them, still swinging. I told Adam I wouldn't go rushing over to Katerina's, but I didn't say I wouldn't go to Ash's.

I grab the keys to the shed and head into the backyard. The rusty padlock opens easily and I pull the metal door aside. It grinds on the tracks, making me push harder to get it to open. My bike is past the lawn mower, a sun-cracked hose draped over the handlebars. I toss the old hose aside and use one of dad's shop rags to brush spider webs and grass off the seat and spokes.

I walk it around to the front gate, passing the holly bushes and rose beds planted along this side of the house. It looks like the neighbor's dog has been doing more than using our backyard as his bathroom. The holly bushes under my window look slightly trampled, a wilted rose blossom pressed into the dirt. Dad is already unhappy with the little Pomeranian and now mom will be after Mr. Tingles for what he's done to her plants.

I get the sense I'm being watched as I climb onto my bike, but I think it's only my conscious trying to tell me that this is probably a stupid idea. I block that part of my brain and head down Greenlee Avenue and towards Belleair Street, the same way I go to school in the mornings, but instead of turning left at the light, I make a right and head towards the WC. It doesn't take long before my bike's tires are vibrating on the cobblestone roads.

I lose my nerve on the other side of the bridge. This was a stupid idea. I stare down the palm tree-lined road and then turn my bike around. If I hurry, I can pretend I wasn't about to bike uninvited over to St. Claire's house.

I hear the rumble of the car before I see it. The familiar sight of it makes my heart drop out of my chest. I cringe as the car slows down and stops beside me. I avoid making eye contact with the driver as I regret my life choices.

"Echo, what are you doing here?"

"Out for a bike ride?"

A frown turns his handsome face pensive. The heat from his car warms my calves. Ash puts the car in park, taking his keys out of the ignition as he climbs out. I look away as he leans against his door, his arms crossed over his chest. He's dressed in dark gray workout pants and a faded surfing brand tee. Not something he usually wears when he leaves the house.

I finally break the silence. "So, what are you doing?"

"Looking for you."

My eyes narrow with suspicion. "You coincidently are looking for me right here?"

He runs a hand down his face, looking tired. "I felt you were close."

"That's… weird." I give him a side-eye. "Is that like a Seraph thing?"

"It's *I-healed-you-with-my-blood-thing.*"

"Oh." Super weird then.

"You remember someone tried to kidnap you, right?"

"Yes," I say, exasperated.

"Then why aren't you taking it seriously?"

I toss up my hands. "I am taking it seriously."

"Then why are you out here alone?"

I pull my braid over my shoulder, worrying the end. "You weren't at school," I tell him.

He uncrosses his arms, glancing toward his house. "My brother is here," he says, as if that explains it.

"Yes, I had to hear from Adam."

"I'm sorry, I've been busy." His aloofness stings. "We were working on your case, and then some friends came into town."

"Friends? Other Seraphim?"

He nods as he sticks his hands in his pockets, looking at me in that detached way I haven't seen in a while. We stare at each other long enough that I feel like such a fool. Of course he has friends and a life well before me and a well after me. An eternity.

My throat feels tight with embarrassment. "I should go."

"Echo," he says as I mount my bike.

I wait.

He pushes a hand through his hair and then sighs. "I'm coming back to school tomorrow."

"I'll see you there, I guess."

He worries his bottom lip with his teeth, a little harder than normal, as if he wants to tell me something, but the moment has dragged on and I can't wait forever. I raise the kickstand and he pushes off the car.

"Wait," he says. "I'll give you a ride home."

I walk my bike over to the back of his car, feeling more morose than when I left my house. The metal whines as Ash opens the trunk, the space smelling like gasoline and rubber. He moves a jump kit out of the way right as a black SUV slowly pulls up behind us. Ash glances over his shoulder, his body rigid when he sees the driver.

A harder version of Henrik steps out of the car. His features are obviously similar, but everything about him looks cunning. Ash's dad is intimidating, yes, but he's also a king to command armies.

Ash's brother is the sharp tip of a sword, the fire in the dragon's mouth. Beautiful and deadly.

"You're going to scratch your paint." He nods at my bike.

"I'll be careful," Ash says, his posture tight.

The older boy laughs, an amused chuckle to himself. "Take my car," he says.

I touch Ash's arm, wondering if I should be worried. He glances from my hand to my face. "Echo, this is my brother Sebastian," he says and closes his trunk.

Sebastian opens the back hatch of his SUV and I eye him curiously. He looks about twenty, but I know that's not a measure of his true age.

"Nice to meet you."

Ash takes my bike around to be loaded into the back.

"What's the girl doing here, anyway?" Sebastian asks.

"We're friends," Ash says, his eyes lidded, careless but defiant. His entire posture and demeanor are deliberate and guarded around his brother.

Sebastian smiles to himself, and then low enough that I can still hear, says, "I thought we agreed a little distance was good."

Ash rolls his shoulders, making him appear a little taller than his brother. Sebastian switches to Seraph, the words a harsh song with the vitriol in his brother's tone.

Ash's jaw is tight as he says, "I get the point."

Sebastian tosses Ash his keys. He catches them with a frown. I step back as his brother opens the Chevelle car door. He turns the engine over and an almost boyish smile touches his lips. "I liked the old muffler," he tells Ash.

Ash lifts a shoulder. "I was tired of getting pulled over for noise violations."

"I was looking forward to having some fun with it."

"You can take the Nova then," Ash says dryly.

Sebastian laughs, and says to Ash, "Eternaili et D'urial."

As we watch Sebastian drive off, I ask, "What does that mean?"

"Duty over everything."

Tension radiates off him as we climb into the car. I feel like I've caused more trouble than I meant to.

"I'm sorry."

"You did nothing wrong," he says, his knuckles white on the steering wheel. "I should have told you what was going on." He steadies his emotions before he turns the key.

"Your brother's a little intense."

Ash grunts in agreement. "That's Sebastian." He drives over the bridge, the light still green, and he smoothly turns onto Belleair. "He doesn't exactly like that I'm helping a Siphon."

"I picked up on that," I say. "I'm sorry I'm making your life difficult."

Ash looks over at me apologetically. "You're not making my life difficult." He turns his focus back to the road as he shakes his head. "I'm making my life difficult. Sebastian is making my life difficult."

"How are you making your life difficult?" I ask, my fingers gripping the seat belt strap.

His eyes travel over to me before he focuses back on the road. He says, "It would make things *less* difficult if I didn't have to worry about you getting hurt."

"Fair point," I say, shifting in my seat. "So, tell me more about this magical GPS you have on me?"

He rubs his forehead, looking like he might not tell me. His eyes squint as if it's too bright outside. "It's a side effect of the Siphon magic that was used to create us," he says, turning down my road. He parks in front of my house and turns in his seat to face me, his hands dropping into his lap. Butterflies dance in my stomach. "It's probably a good idea if you don't come over to my house for a while."

"Okay," I say, squeezing my hands in my lap.

"Not because I don't want you to," he says.

I drop my eyes. "I'm making things complicated for you."

"Things were tense with Sebastian and I before I met you." He sighs. "He's got a God complex, probably from being the only child for so long, and then I came along and he likes to act like my father." I raise my brow and Ash runs a hand over his face. There's a slight darkening under his eyes. "Sometimes Sebastian is all Dominus and nothing else, like our grandfather."

Electricity sparkles along my skin, giving me goosebumps. "Do you think he'll tell on us?"

Ash watches me rub my arms. "No," he says.

"Would he turn you in?"

Ash sits up straighter in his chair. "No," he says, less confident. "Sebastian does a lot of posturing, but family is first."

I look away from him. I'm not so sure I trust Sebastian as much as Ash does. "But he told you to stay away from me?"

He digs a fingernail into the soft leather of the steering wheel. "He tells me to do all kinds of things."

"Is that what your whole family wants?" I ask, kneading my palms. "For you to stay away from me?"

A complicated look crosses his face. "No," he says, but it's an open sentence with much left unsaid in that tiny word. Ash frowns at the steering wheel. "They are cautious. What we're doing is very unusual for a Seraph and a Siphon."

"What is it we're doing?" I ask. The question feels dangerous. The butterflies rise and twirl, a wicked dance, my heart thumping out their rhythm.

His blue eyes lift to mine, so bright even in the shade inside the car. I see his throat move, his eyes turn pained, and then everything shudders back up again. He turns away from me to look out the windshield, bringing his fingertips to his mouth. The warmth leaches out of me.

"You could have called me," he says softly. "You *can* call me."

"I didn't want to bother you."

He rests his head on the seat. "You're not." He holds my eyes again and some of that frost thaws.

I lean my head back, mirroring him. "You've already done a lot."

"Not enough," he says and closes his eyes. "We couldn't find those men before they turned up dead. Now we're back to square one."

How could he say that? He's helped me when I had no one, even at a personal sacrifice. I know it was a hard decision to heal me. His father, brother, and possibly other Seraphim are here trying to figure out who's responsible for my attack. He's even protecting me from other Siphons, and I know that's complicated for him. Plus, he's keeping my secret about that night.

It feels like I owe him more than he owes me.

I open my mouth to tell him when his phone goes off. He pulls it out of his pocket, tossing it on the dash after he checks the screen.

He lets out a breath, long and slow. "I need to get back."

He turns to me and I'm struck with a longing so great it hurts. I take in a deep breath and push it back down. I went years learning to push the greater parts of my anxiety into hidden little cracks inside me, and now the Light has burned it away so I can shove my heartache back into them. It'll probably come back blazing to the surface horribly—like my panic attacks—but for now, it gives me the strength to put my hand on the door handle and say goodbye.

CHAPTER 20

ASH IS BACK in school the next day; with light circles under his eyes, and his tie slightly off-center. No one appears to notice his less-than-pristine appearance and I wonder, as I chew on my thumbnail, if I would have noticed before either.

He's doodling in the margins of his notebook, not paying attention to the lecture. Ash told me one lazy afternoon in his library that he was fluent in Latin and every language they teach at Shorecrest, but he still needed to pad his transcripts for college if that's the route he takes. Seraphs, he said, still lead relatively human lives, and usually take positions in society that best serve their race. It's only in the shadows of their secret world that the truth lies.

Mr. Hammond is having a hard time getting many of us to focus because any minute the bell will ring for the pep rally. I watch the clock feeling morose because usually, I'd be meeting my friends by the entrance to the bleachers so we could sit together. Kat doing commentary; making Meredith and I laugh.

Ash leans over the aisle, his voice pitched low, "What's wrong?"

My eyes flit around the room out of habit. "The pep rally."

"The crowds?"

"A little," I say truthfully. "I usually sit with Kat, and Mere."

The intercom clicks on, dismissing classes to the football field. The classroom erupts in noise and excitement about the rally and the free period. Ash and I make our way into the crowded halls. There's an energy among the surrounding bodies. The students around us have dressed up their uniforms for the event. Boys wear bands around their arms or wrists in the school's colors, neon socks flash in the crowd, and curled ribbons bounce in high ponytails. Laughter and hoots follow us toward the football field.

Ash leans down, his breath tickling my ear. "We could slip off to the library?"

Mr. Hammond walks on our left, his eyes scanning the traffic, making sure we're all being good little lambs following the lane. I nod towards another teacher with his arms crossed over his chest, blocking one of our escape routes.

"I guess not," he mumbles.

Once through the gate, I head for the top bleachers. A couple of heads turn as we pass. I hear someone call out Ash's name, but he doesn't acknowledge them. It's early enough that the aluminum benches aren't on fire, but they're still warm on the back of my thighs as I take a seat. We watch the bleachers fill while the band plays far down below and the cheerleaders warm up on the sidelines.

Everyone gives us a respectful amount of space that has less to do about me, since most of the sneaky glances are for him. I reap the benefits, propping my shoes up on the seat in front of me and leaning my elbows on my knees to watch the newspaper and yearbook photographers compete for the best shots. St. Claire leans back and props his legs out on the bench in front of him like we're sunning on the beach.

"What are we celebrating, exactly?"

I give him a curious look and when it's clear he's serious, I say, "Homecoming pep rally, you know, homecoming is in two weeks?"

"The dance?"

I laugh. "Yes, where have you been? There're posters everywhere and the cheesy invites have already begun."

A line forms between his brows. I bump his ribs right as the band changes to the school fight song. No, he probably wouldn't have noticed. I don't remember seeing him at any of the previous year's dances.

The cheerleaders move to the field and start their routine. I watch them flip and chant along with the music. My eyes scan the crowd with a purpose, as I am a glutton for punishment. I spot Kat's dark wavy hair first, finding Meredith beside her, and my heart sinks. It still stings to see them moving on without me; that I need them more than they need me. If our roles were reversed, I know I would have heard them out before I passed judgment.

I tell this to Ash, who follows my gaze to where they sit huddled together.

"Hindsight is always clearer." When I make a face, he bumps an arm into mine. "You still haven't talked to Katerina?"

I shake my head. "I feel like I shouldn't have to," I say. "She should apologize to me."

The taunting pictures she posted still stings, and I'm feeling less remorseful about my part in all this. A line appears between his eyebrows and I let out a weary sigh. I tell him about what happened yesterday. The pictures Kat tagged me in documenting them all hanging out without me.

He arches a brow. "Is that why you were so upset yesterday?"

I can't truthfully answer that without having to admit he made me feel left out. I turn my gaze back to the football field. "Mostly."

I can see him in my peripheral, waiting for an explanation, but thankfully the real pep rally has begun. The cheerleaders run onto the field holding a long banner with the school's name. The football players burst through it, and the crowd hoots and cheers.

Brody Bradshaw, the quarterback, dressed in his jersey of gold and gray, runs up to the podium as his team gathers on either side. Brody waits for the crowd to quiet before he leans into the microphone, thanking us all for being here—how this is going to be the best year; they're going to crush it this season. He finishes his speech with Shorecrest's motto; Excellence, Integrity, Commitment, and Courage.

The crowd claps and cheers.

The football players take their seats on the sidelines while the principal takes the podium. He congratulates the teams for making Shorecrest proud and thanks the cheerleaders on their routine, including wishing them good luck on their cheer completion at Disney World next week. Then he introduces Margo Bradshaw, the student body president, to announce the homecoming court.

I perk up when I hear Meredith's name called for the Junior court, elbowing Ash in case he missed it. He looks over at me with a funny twist to his mouth and I realize I'm smiling. I still feel the joy and excitement for her, even though I can't be right beside her cheering her on.

I hear Kat hoot and watch as she leans in to whisper something that makes Meredith smile. That loneliness in my heart gets a little bigger. I feel myself deflate back against the seat, shoulders slumped.

Ash leans into me, his shoulder pressed to mine. "Why don't we take small steps?"

Goosebumps pepper my skin despite the heat. "Hmm?"

He nods toward Kat and Meredith. "We should have lunch in the cafeteria today?"

My heart thuds for a different reason. "Sit with them?"

"No, but stop hiding." I squirm in my seat and he adds, "You should show them you have nothing to be ashamed of." I make a pathetic noise to show how I feel about all that, holding his eye. "Adam and I'll be there. You won't be alone."

"Promise?"

"Of course."

I've missed whatever the closing speech was. The crowd cheers again. I lean away from St. Claire, my body humming with nerves. I get that feeling of being watched again and scan the crowd, but bodies rise like a wave as we're dismissed.

The feeling passes anyway.

I TOLD ST. CLAIRE it'd be a big deal if we walked into lunch together but even though I'm prepared I still don't like the glances, the smirks, and the downright jaw-dropping as we walk through the open doors into the cafeteria. It's noisy like always, but I can't help but feel like some of the chatter is for us.

Ash already informed Adam of our change in lunch plans. I find him sitting at a table by the window, and leave Ash in the lunch line to join him. Adam grunts out a greeting around a mouthful when I sit down. I pull out the packed lunch I prepared for eating in the darkroom.

"I love the darkroom and all, but I'm so glad we're eating back in the cafe," Adam says before he takes a big bite of his hamburger. Ketchup and mustard ooze out the sides.

"I'm kind of missing it," I confess, giving a discreet peek at the table beside us.

I can't hear what they're whispering about, but the way their heads keep turning back, stealing glances, I can guess.

Adam waves his hand, dismissive. "They're not looking at you, they're looking at me."

I roll my eyes. "Yes, if you keep chewing with your mouth open like that."

"Dude, manners," Ash teases as he slides his tray onto the table. Adam grins a messy mouthful in response.

I've been watching the lunch line, so I see when Meredith and Kat walk out. Meredith sees us first, but Kat loops her arm through Meredith's and steers her towards the outdoor picnic tables, pretending she doesn't see me.

"It'll get easier," Ash tries to make me feel better, but my mood is tanking quickly.

The cacophony of the cafeteria changes, there's an exciting vibration to the talking and I look up to see a sophomore dressed as a present wearing a sign that says, *Jasmine Please Say Yes*. Jasmine Harvey squeals, a blush covering her face as she tells him yes three times. They awkwardly hug, with the big box between them. The nearby tables clap, and her date to homecoming gives a flourishing bow. I can't help but smile, even though Jasmine has been one of my more negative gossipers.

Charity walks out of the lunch line behind them, looking disgusted with their show. She heads towards the outdoor tables but stops when she sees Alex leave his usual table and slide into a seat in front of Meredith. I can't see what he says, but it makes Meredith duck her head. Charity sits at her table, her narrowed gaze lingering on Alex until they lift venomously to mine as if it's all my fault.

"What was that about?" I mumble.

Adam glances out the window. "Charity asked Alex to homecoming, and he said no."

"How do you know that?"

He shrugs. "I know all the hot gossip," and then he laughs, amused with himself. "I have second period with Alex when she stopped him before class. He wasn't very nice about it."

"Poor Charity," I say.

Ash's feelings for Alex are clear in the complicated look he gives me. I hide my smile with the back of my hand as Adam raises a brow.

"Are you going to homecoming?" I ask Adam, folding my hands under my chin.

He licks the ketchup off his thumb and says, "I see how we're playing it."

Ash shifts his confusion between Adam and me, and I tell him, "I'm wondering if he's thinking about asking Meredith."

Ash's face relaxes. "I heard it's going well."

Adam's cheeks are officially pink as he tries to give a careless shrug. "I mean, I'd love to, but I don't know if we're there yet."

I look over and catch Meredith watching us; her head ducks down as she moves her food around on her plate. Kat is talking to Alex, and something about it squeezes my middle. It's not envy, or not the way it would have been months ago. I'm envious of Alex. I'd be envious of anyone sitting in my place.

Darkly, I wonder if he's doing it to hurt me for turning him down, though I know that can't be right.

I pick at the rest of my food, stealing glances at the outside picnic tables for the entire lunch period. The irony is that once I got what I wanted; it helped me to realize that it wasn't what I wanted after all. I steal a glance at Ash. His phone has been vibrating in his pocket for the past five seconds and he fishes it out to silence it.

What if what I thought I didn't want was what I needed, after all?

CHAPTER 21

I RUSH OUT OF my last class and head toward the back of the
school. I catch up to Kat under the colonnade right before the
student parking lot. Her black hair swishes as she walks, her purse
hanging off her elbow. She smiles as she talks to Bianca as they both
head toward their cars.

I call her name and she turns. Her smile dies on her lips as she
sees me. Her bright eyes turn suspicious, but she tells Bianca she'll
see her tomorrow and waits for me.

"Now you want to talk?" She brushes her hair out of her eyes,
looking bored as she watches the people moving past.

Hurt crashes over me at her cold and aloof attitude, having never
been on the receiving end before. "Forget it." I start to turn away.

"Wait," she says, catching my arm.

We both move out of the main walkway onto the patchy grass
between the covered sidewalk and the gymnasium.

I press my hand into my chest, right where my heart is. "You
believed the gossip over me."

Kat's face hardens again. She doesn't enjoy being reminded of her faults or mistakes. "You lied to us."

"*Because* I knew you'd react like this," I tell her. "That's why I kept it a secret."

Kat's argument gets caught in her throat. Finally, she huffs, "I think we would have done better if you'd told us the truth." She wraps one of her curls around her finger, watching the track team warm up. I'd think she was checking them out, except her eyes have a reflective look to them. "Do you like Ash?"

The question takes me by surprise, despite being asked so many times. I open my mouth and close it. "Yes," I admit, surprising us both.

She nods. "Ash freaking St. Claire." She laughs. "I never saw that one coming."

"Neither did I."

Kat looks over at me. "I've seen you two together." She shrugs. "It makes sense."

I scan the parking lot until I find Ash and Adam leaning against Ash's black car, waiting for me. They probably assume what Kat and I are talking about. It's the other part that makes my face warm.

"We really are only friends."

Kat follows my gaze. "Sure." She smirks. There's an awkwardness to us now that wasn't there before. I wish I could fix it. Kat sighs. "I would have been jealous, sure, but I would have gotten over it," she says. "I want you to be happy."

"I miss you guys." To admit that aloud feels like my heart has cracked open, but after everything I've been through, it can't get any worse.

Her eyes are as glassy as mine. "I miss you too."

"Can we fix this?"

Kat's expression turns pained, and it kicks me right in the gut. "I don't know." She sighs, twirling her hair around her finger. Her big brown eyes are sad. She tips her gaze my way, her mouth lifting at the corners. "But I hope so."

I push my instinctual need to hide in the darkroom way down as I brave the cafeteria the next day.

I'm stuffing my mouth with pasta salad when Meredith's tray slides onto my table, followed by Kat's. Meredith shyly takes a seat next to Adam, who straightens up, giving her an equally shy smile in greeting.

"Hey," Kat greets with a red-lipped smirk.

"Hey," I say, trying to keep the emotion out of my voice.

Ash pauses with a bite of food at his mouth when he realizes Meredith is staring at him. "Hello," he says, flicking a quick look around the table. He sits up a little straighter, glancing at me for help—but he'll have to endure their curiosity and get it over with.

Kat thrusts her fork in Ash's direction. "So the mysterious Ash St. Claire. Tell us everything about you." Kat flutters her big brown eyes at him. "We know all about Woo, of course, but we know nothing of you."

Ash's gaze flits from me to Adam, but he gets no life preserver from him, either. "Hmm?" He takes a sip of his water. "What do you want to know?"

"Everything," Kat purrs. "But we'll start with pets, siblings, favorite color, and life's ambitions."

Ash smiles down at his food before he answers. "No pets, brother, Phthalo blue, and the freedom to always pursue happiness?"

Kat's brows lift and she hums with interest. "Brother? Younger or older?"

Ash flicks a glance my way, his lips twitching in a small smirk. "A few years older than me," he says.

Sebastian *looks* only a couple of years older, but it's not like Ash can tell them the truth.

Kat leans back in her chair. "Single?"

Ash scratches his chin. "As far as I know."

Kat nods her approval. "I'd like to meet this brother."

"Sebastian's not really a people person," I say.

"He can when he chooses," Ash adds, and I wrinkle my nose in disagreement.

"Oh, so you've met this brother?" Meredith asks, her eyes dancing between Ash and I. Something about her tone makes my neck heat.

"So Ash St. Claire," Kat says with a detective's authority. She trills her long fingers in the air. "What do you do for fun?"

"Pardon?"

"Movies, sports, what do you do after school, weekends?" Meredith adds, looking like she's surprised she spoke.

Ash rolls his shoulders and glances down at me. He can't really say that for the past couple of months that most of his free time has been researching Siphons and working with me to control my wonky abilities.

He says, "I spend most of my downtime reading, or helping my father with work."

"Ah, the collector," Kat says. "Do you collect things like your father?"

The question pulls Ash's brows down. "Occasionally," he says, his eyes narrowed.

"Have you picked out a dress?" Meredith asks me.

"My dress is red, of course," Kat grins.

Meredith shoots a smirk Kat's way. "It only took her forever to decide and about three hundred dresses."

Kat flicks her hand in the air. "You're so dramatic."

I've been busy training or researching with Ash, but truthfully, I haven't made time for it because I haven't felt like going to the dance. It doesn't feel the same this year. I reach up and rub the scar on my shoulder. I can feel the weight of it, the constant reminder of why I have it. What I did.

"I don't think I'm going this year."

Kat pauses with her fork over her salad as if this is the silliest thing she's heard all day. She turns her incredulity to St. Claire. "You haven't asked her yet?"

Ash startles at her question. He sets his water down carefully as Kat waits for an answer. "I, um... haven't?"

I try to kick Kat under the table but miss and get Adam. He shoots me an alarmed arch of his brow.

"On, no, we aren't—" but I can't seem to finish.

Adam's eyebrows are practically touching the ceiling as he stares down at his plate with a look that says he is thanking the heavens he's not in Ash's place. I can't tell if Ash is so unsure because of Kat's scrutiny, which can make even an immortal squirm, or because he hasn't given the dance or taking me to it a single thought.

It's clear we're only friends, but most of the school doesn't understand that. Ash doesn't seem to care if people think we're dating, but I wonder what he thinks about my friends thinking he should take me to the dance. People go as friends, *we* could go as friends, but maybe he doesn't want to lead me on.

Ash looks at me. "I guess with everything going on..." he searches my face as I stare at him, biting my tongue to keep my face void of what I'm feeling. "We never really talked about the dance?" He lifts a hand, his expression asks 'am I saying the right thing?'

An epiphany crosses his face, and he turns in his chair to face me. He asks softly, "Do you want to go to the dance?"

I'm aware of everyone at the table. Adam has the decency to eye whatever mystery substance is at the bottom of his chocolate milk. Meredith picks at her food. Kat is the only one openly observing our exchange.

"Are you asking *me* to the dance or asking if I *want* to go to the dance?" I shift in my seat, purposely avoiding making eye contact with anyone else at the table for fear my face might glow.

"*Both?*"

"*Okay?*"

"Is it always like this?" Meredith asks Adam.

"Yes. Always," Adam says, taking the last bite of his second hamburger.

My embarrassment at having this conversation in front of the others intensifies, but I don't look away. Ash wears a mix of startling realization that is hard to interrupt. He looks like he's about to say something, but Meredith clears her throat, cutting him off.

"You'll need a dress then." Meredith perks up in her seat. "We could go Saturday?"

Kat claps her hands joyfully. "Perfect. We'll all go into the city." She grins mischievously. "Ash can tag along so we can get to know him better."

Ash and I both tense. We have discussed that leaving the island could be dangerous for me. I try to find answers in his face about what I should say. Is it safe or not? But he's as still as a statue. Finally, he clears his throat into his fist and asks Adam, "You're free Saturday, right?"

"*Me?*" Adam looks around the table, his eyes landing on Meredith, and the expectant look on her face brightens him up. He grins. "Yeah, dress shopping. Sounds fun."

"Fun?" she says, her laugh a little flirty. "Thankfully, they have a food court."

Adam smiles. "Oh, you know me so well."

They share an affectionate look and I am certain that if Adam asked her to the dance, she'd say yes. I tuck that smile towards my plate and when I look up, Kat has her eyes on the boys like a shark who's found fresh meat. "Excellent then, it's a date."

I WAIT FOR ASH in my living room, my hand on my knee to keep it from bouncing. Dad idly flips through the channels, trying not to be obvious that he's waiting for Ash, too. I know there will be a conversation eventually. I can see it brewing on his face, but I'd rather it not be today.

Mom walks into the living room with a basket of laundry on her hip. "Don't wander around downtown," she says, "that's where those men were murdered."

We don't actually know where they died, only where they were dumped. I keep that fact a secret and how I am more than capable of protecting myself.

I hear an engine and pull the curtains aside to see Sebastian's black Suburban pull into my driveway. Ash behind the wheel.

"Stay in a group," Mom calls as I rush to the door.

"But not too close," Dad adds.

Ash is halfway to the porch when I intercept him and pull him into the shade cast by the garage. He lifts his glasses in a question, a curious look crosses his face as we move further away from my parent's view.

"Sorry you got dragged into this?" I say. The smell of fresh-cut grass is strong in the air and you can hear the neighbor's lawnmower.

"I don't mind." He leans back against my dad's truck, watching the neighbor's dog bark as it runs along the chain-link fence between our properties. "Whoever sent those men are still out there. Of course I'd come."

I rock back on my heels. "So this is Domini duty then?"

"No, it's not like that."

"Isn't it?" I tilt my head.

Ash frowns, a line forming between his eyes. "That's not the only reason." I look up at him incredulously and he continues, "I'm here because I want to."

"Because it's the perfect training for a future *Dominus?*"

He removes his sunglasses, tossing them on the hood of the truck, and runs a hand through his hair. "Would you stop? It's not like that."

I rub my hands on my jeans. "What's it like then?" He gives me a frustrated look at my tone. I hold up my hands as I lean against the truck door beside him. "It's -," I start, blowing out a frustrated breath. He waits with his brows raised for me to finish. "You don't have to feel obligated to take me to the dance."

Ash flips his car keys around his finger. His expression goes broody. "I don't feel obligated."

"I don't mind going alone."

"Do you *want* to go alone?"

"I didn't say that."

His blue eyes meet mine. "I was surprised you wanted to go with me."

"Why?"

He glances up, squinting at a lone cloud. "Because of Alex Carter." He flattens his lips. "Maybe you'd rather go with him."

"Well, that's stupid."

He rests his arm on the roof of the car, angling his body towards mine. "I'm pretty stupid sometimes."

I snort. He's half right.

I'm very aware of the little space that separates us and the way my body leans towards his, my heart racing behind my breastbone. He's stopped playing with his keys, and the silence is deafening.

"Doesn't this complicate things?"

"I've already complicated things," his voice is low and rough. A small smile tugs his lips up. "You're not wearing your contacts?"

I press my hip into the car door. "Yeah, well, maybe I'm tired of hiding?" I say pointedly, referencing an early conversation.

Ash glances down at the concrete driveway. His expression goes contemplative before he looks back at me. "Yeah, well, I like seeing the real you," he says with a lopsided smile. He licks his lips as I hold his gaze.

It feels like I'm jumping into oblivion, knowingly throwing myself into a Blackhole not knowing if I'll survive to reach the end.

This is going to hurt.

It's going to be painful and heart-aching, probably more for me, because I'm on a time limit and Ash will have thousands of years to get over me, and yet I can't stop myself. I've already stepped off into the void and I can't stop falling.

Ash tears his gaze away from me, taking a step back as we hear the roar of an engine on the road. Adam honks the horn as he pulls his truck to the curb. Meredith in the passenger seat waves.

Adam slowly walks around Ash's borrowed ride, giving a low whistle. "Nice, Sebastian has the Chevelle?"

Ash shakes his head. "He thinks I turned it into a kitten. He took the Nova."

Adam inclines his head. "Nice trade-off."

"Sebastian only likes to dabble. He loves modern luxuries more than classic beauty."

Adam tilts his head. "I might agree with him. Heated seats?"

Meredith laughs. "For those two miserable weeks it's cold?"

Adam rubs his hands down his shoulders and arms with an invisible chill, "Those brutal two weeks."

She fans herself as she walks into the shade with Ash and me. "We definitely don't need them today."

Kat pulls up, parking her red car behind Adams. She slams the car door, a testament to her personality more than any malfunction on the car's behalf. She's all teeth as she joins us. Ash raps his knuckles on the roof two times, signaling that it's time to go and we all pile into his borrowed ride.

I watch the sun sparkle on the ocean's surface like diamonds as we race away from St. Sierra. It hits me there on the long bridge to the mainland that I am sitting next to Ash St. Claire and Adam and Meredith are talking again. I have my friends back and we are all together.

Elation fills my chest and spreads like the Light all over my body. I steal a glance at Ash. The sun hits his hair like a halo. He smiles at the road and drops his hand on the seat between us. Casually resting it in invitation. I slide mine over until I can feel the warmth of his skin. He doesn't take his eyes off the road as he hooks his little finger around mine.

CHAPTER 22

AFTER TWO HOURS of browsing the smaller boutiques, we head to one of the big chain stores to peruse their inventory at the far end of the mall. Meredith and I stand amongst a cluster of racks hung with everything from spring dresses to evening dresses. Frills spill out of the rows of fabrics and tulle sticks up sporadically. Sequins sparkle as I push the hangers aside, studying each dress.

Kat is trying on shoes. Adam and Ash slouch on a low-backed couch over by the dressing rooms. Adam leans his head back on the couch cushions, maybe sleeping. Ash appears to be engrossed in a game on his phone, but at regular intervals, his eyes lift and scan the room for threats.

It's a chilling reminder of what's still out there.

The longer we are in the city, the more I feel the island's absence. Like peeling off a wetsuit. You don't feel the weight of it until you are out of the water. I miss the island's sense of protection and also feel the echo of its shackles.

I can feel energy pulse inside my chest, tingle along my skin, the Light wanting to play. It's been noticeably more present since that night I was almost abducted, ever since I had Seraph blood. The Light is a dangerous thing and joyously addictive.

I sneak a glance at Ash and find him watching me. If I tell him how close it feels to the surface, he'll worry, maybe even suggest we leave. He gives me a shy smile that I can't help but return.

I grab a short yellow dress and hold it up to my body in front of the mirror next to us as Meredith asks, "What exactly is the thing with you and Ash?"

I wrinkle my nose at the dress, but to Meredith, I mumble, "That's the million-dollar question."

Meredith holds a pretty purple dress with a shimmering bodice, her fingers move nervously on the hanger. "The way you are around each other... and now he's taking you to the dance..." A vertical line forms between her brows and I'm right there with her.

I sigh and she asks, "But you *do* like him?"

I itch the back of my leg with my shoe. I make sure no one is listening before I admit the truth, "Yes."

Meredith bits her lip. "Has he said anything?"

I think about our conversation earlier, my eyes drifting over to where the two boys wait patiently. "He's very... *shy*," I tell her.

Meredith's soft features turn thoughtful as she unabashedly studies St. Claire. He has sensed my gaze on him most of the day, but now he's distractedly listening to Adam, occasionally nodding along. We assumed he was a snob, but I know the truth, the secrets he was protecting. I have them now too and can see it's easier to alienate everyone than suffocate under the lies.

Meredith gives me a telling look. "You're not exactly forward, either."

I make a noncommittal noise and move the dresses aside, not really seeing them. "We're... different." Meredith tilts her head and I reach for the words to explain. "We come from different... worlds."

Her face contorts into a chiding look. "The money thing?" she chides. "I'm surprised that would bother you?"

"It doesn't," I blurt.

Meredith moves a row of black dresses aside and idly fingers a strapless gold dress. "Some might say Adam and I come from different worlds, too."

"That's not what I meant," I say desperately.

"I know." She smiles sadly. "I'm trying to make a point. Unless there's something else?"

I look away, pretending to consider a white halter dress. "Nope."

Meredith grins mischievously right before she holds up a blue dress that shimmers with the colors of a frosted sea. "You should try this on."

Meredith disappears into the dressing room next to mine. I can hear fabric rustling next to me as I struggle out of my jeans and into my dress. The skirt shimmers in blues from navy to sky, the aquamarine bodice reminds me of Ash's eyes and I know why Meredith told me to try it on.

The star-shaped scar from a bullet to my shoulder stares back at me from the mirror. A constant reminder of what I've done, of what I am. My fingers reach up to trace its outline and it's like I'm there the night it happened.

The small changing room fills with the smells of car exhaust and asphalt, blood, and roasting human flesh. It's a horrific combination that makes me gag. The room begins to feel smaller, the walls closing in. I close my eyes but it only makes it worse. I see the man's face stuck in a silent scream.

You murdered him.

It's whispered from behind me, but when I spin, I am still alone in the stall. My heart thuds in my ears, and my vision darkens around the corners before it clears.

You're dangerous.

I shake my head, putting my hands over my ears, but the voice is inside me.

You're a monster.

My skin tingles; warms. The lights overhead start to buzz and flicker. I can't lose control. *I can't.* My friends will see, they'll know what I am. And then the Siphons of Seraphs will take me away from everything I love. Like those men tried to do.

I need out of this room.

I try to keep my panic at bay as I quickly change out of the dress. Flames lick up my arms. I reach for the knob, but strange blue flames cover my hands. I'm losing control.

I can feel Ash several feet away, but he's too far to save anyone. There is no pool to jump into. I'm going to burn down the dressing room.

Meredith.

No. Not again. I grab hold of that invisible tether and concentrate with everything I have in me. The fire along my skin snuffs out, the power going dormant once again.

My relieved breath is short-lived. *I could have killed my best friend.*

I burst out of the dressing room and heave into the nearest trashcan. Meredith is quickly by my side, Ash a step behind her with Adam three steps behind. Meredith is talking to Ash, but all I can hear is my pounding heartbeat.

Meredith finds me some scratchy paper towels, calm, even though she does not know how close she was to death. Kat shoos the boys out of the dressing room as I finish wiping my mouth.

"I'm fine," I tell them, waving off their worry.

One of the dressing room doors cracks open, and Kat wraps her arms around my shoulders and steers me out.

"Who was that?" I ask. Kat shares a look with Meredith. I ask again, "who was that?"

"Some girl," Kat says, "don't worry, she didn't see a thing."

Adam and Ash are relieved to see us when we exit the dressing room. Ash takes a step towards me, searching my face. He asks, voice low, "Are you okay?"

"Yes, upset stomach," I say, but hold his searching gaze.

He gives a quick nod, his eyes shifting to Meredith as she holds out my purse for me.

"Oh, thank you."

I reach to take it from Kat's outstretched hand but Ash grabs it, holding up a key chain dangling off the zipper tab. His voice is eerily calm as he asks, "Where did you get this?"

I stare at the unfamiliar dolphin-shaped rock. No crystal. I hold my breath as Meredith inspects it with her fingers. "They sell these at the pier." Her narrowed eyes move between Ash and me.

"I don't know where it came from." It's becoming obvious that Ash is holding my bag hostage, so I say, "It's not mine. Throw it away."

"You sure?" Kat asks. "I'm not into dolphins, but it's pretty."

"Yes, I'm sure."

Ash smoothly unclips the keychain before handing over my purse.

"Let's get some food," Adam declares, and then to me, "sorry, too soon?"

I shake my head.

"Come on," Kat rolls her eyes, pulling us toward the exit.

Ash and I share a meaningful look after he mimes throwing it away, smoothly pocketing it like a proper thief.

ADAM DOES A GOOD job of distracting Kat and Meredith. He's also great at pretending nothing is wrong, all smiles and jokes as he steers them over to Pretzel Palace, distracting them with stories of him and his brothers' pranks while Ash and I step aside into the mouth of a hallway. Away from foot traffic or prying ears.

"What happened in there?"

I lean back against the pastel-tiled walls and tell him what happened in the dressing room. "Do you think it had anything to do with that strange keychain?"

Ash lowers his hand to where the dolphin is inside his pocket. "It didn't feel like a panic attack."

"Feel? You can sense my feelings now, too?" I ask, crossing my arms over my chest. "More weird blood magic?"

He pushes his fingers through his hair, stealing a glance behind him. "It's not magic," he says firmly.

I roll my eyes, not convinced. I think Seraphim have more in common with Siphons than they like to admit. "It's really annoying how cryptic you're being about the whole..." I gesture between us, "... thing."

"I can't exactly talk about this *here*," he says voice pitched low, his eyes darting to our friends over by the food stand. He pushes a hand through his hair at my pursed lips and finally says, "I can feel when your emotions spike. And they were very intense in there."

"I wish I had a link to your emotions," I mumble.

He sighs. "Ask me."

I bite my lip and shake my head. Only one stressful thing at a time. Ash slides his hand into his pocket, the same one with the crystal. "If it was a curse, it's empty now."

"You can tell that?"

He nods. "They're warm or cool. Some vibrate, but most humans can't tell."

I rest my head on the back of the wall. "It was horrible. It was like I was back there that night."

Ash's hand cover mine where I rub at my scar. I didn't even realize I was doing it. "Do you remember seeing it on you before we left?" He asks softly.

I shake my head.

Ash is worrying his lip in that way when he's thinking something over. His back is straight, making him tower over me. I don't think he realizes he's doing it, slipping into Dominus mode. It's easy to be deceived that he's only a normal human boy until then; he's not.

Finally, he shifts on his feet, his eyes meeting mine. "If there's someone here slipping you cursed stones, we should go home."

Adam is handing a man in a pretzel hat money while Meredith grabs the food bags. I find Kat at a table a few feet away, watching us.

"I can't leave now. They'll think I'm hiding things again," I plead. "Things are finally back to normal." He arches his brow but doesn't point out that I *am* hiding things. "I still haven't found a dress." It's a frivolous thing to pout about, but I want to cling to these last bits of normal for as long as I can.

Ash crosses his arms over his chest. "I'll buy you a dress."

"I want to pick out my *own* dress." I try to mirror his domineering posture, but I feel like a kitten mimicking a lion.

"Are you mad at me?" he asks suddenly.

My face flushes, and I uncross my arms, wrapping them around my middle. "Not at *you*, I'm mad at... *things.*"

Ash watches me rub the scar on my shoulder. "You can tell me."

I want to tell him I'm afraid of what I am becoming. That it took nothing to burn that man down to dust and it frightens me. What if the reason someone is after me in the first place is because they know that there is something dark and twisted inside me? That I am a monster.

And I fear what will happen to Ash when the Seraphim discover he's been protecting me.

A strange little static has started in my bones. I glance down the hall as I get that feeling of being watched. I rub my arms and turn back to Ash. "Maybe you're right, we should leave."

Ash rubs the bridge of his nose. "No, if you want to stay," he says, "we'll make it work."

I shake my head and rub away the pressure there. It was naïve of me to think there wasn't still a threat out there. It was also too soon after what happened to test my control.

We join our friends at the table. They mostly do a good job of pretending they weren't spying on us. I can only imagine what it looked like from the outside, more strange behavior I can't explain.

Adam shakes a bag in front of me. "Saved you some in case you were hungry."

I pull out a soft pretzel and leave the two pretzel dogs for Ash. While Adam and Ash go to refill their lemonades, Kat leans forward to ask me if everything's alright. She nods towards Ash as if I didn't catch her meaning.

"Of course," I tell her, waving off her concern with a smile. "I wasn't feeling well."

"And that required a private conversation?"

I frown down at my pretzel. "He was worried."

"That's sweet." Meredith gives Kat a look, taking a meaningful pull of her drink.

Kat leans back in her chair, her maroon fingers clicking a rhythm on the table in obvious rebellion, but she doesn't press anymore.

NO ONE COMPLAINED OR protested when I said I wanted to leave. My throwing up was a good enough excuse, but there was still a polite tension in the car on the drive home.

Adam climbs out of the car as soon as we stop at my house, stretching his arms up over his head. Meredith helps Kat transfer her bags over to her car and they both thank Ash for driving.

"Next time, bring that brother of yours." Kat flashes him a grin before she pulls Meredith and me in for a hug goodbye.

Meredith and Adam had worked out between them for him to give her a ride home. I waggle my brows at her as she climbs into his truck. She casts a nervous glance in Adam's direction behind the driver's seat, but he's busy talking to Ash. She mouths that she'll call me later and I give her a thumbs up.

When Ash and I pull away from my house, he says, "We need to keep what happened between us?"

I shift on the seat, the leather warm from sitting in the sun. "I thought you wanted to tell your father about the crystal?"

"I do," he says, "I will, but not about what happened in the dressing room."

"More secrets?"

He gives me a pained expression, his blue eyes dark. "My father and Sebastian are toeing the line between duty and loyalty, and I don't want to break it. The less they know, the better for them."

"So they don't get in trouble?"

He nods. "My father would agree if I could tell him, but I don't want to even tempt his curiosity."

My lips press together. I am new to this world, and these rules, but Henrik and Sebastian frighten me a little, and what their well-established Domini ranks mean for me. Even if they are Ash's family. The little hairs on my neck tingle. Ash wants to keep secrets from them too. Is there something he's not telling me?

The nerves in my stomach intensify when Ash pulls into his garage. He cuts the engine with a yawn.

"Up early?"

"Up late, up early." He yawns again, causing me to yawn with him.

"Dominus stuff or other stuff?" I shift to face him.

"Both." He gives me a small smile. His fingers trace the back of my hand. I turn it over and he sinks his fingers between mine, lacing them together. We listen to the engine tick, not in a hurry to leave. Ash presses the clock on the stereo. "Sebastian is out running intel. Do you want to search through the Dominus archives or maybe go to the workshop...?"

I wipe my free hand on my thigh. "We could do something normal?"

Ash's hand flexes in mine. "Watching movies is normal. I hear there's a spin-off series I have yet to see." I flash him a grin before he says, "After we practice."

Ash slips his hand out of mine as he exits the car. I slowly slide out, carefully shutting the heavy door. I can hear the water fountain near the front door bubbling in the distance as we take the path to the backyard. Bees hover around the flower bushes by the side gate. A brown Anole struts on top of a boxwood, waving his dewlap, flashing orange and red as we pass.

A shadow passes overhead as a cloud covers the sun and a rogue breeze blows my hair back. Dark clouds are gathering off the water. "Looks like rain."

Ash inclines his head towards the workshop. "Perfect weather to practice in."

I slow my steps. "Maybe I need to repress it?"

Ash stops a few feet from the doors, a half smile on his lips. "Isn't that what you're doing now?"

"Maybe that's the trick. *Repression.*"

He laughs. "Sounds like *denial.*"

He's teasing, but he's not wrong. I flick my hand towards the stone privacy wall, to the ocean beyond it. "I'll just stay here where nothing bad will happen."

"You won't always have my pool to jump into." He gives me an incredulous arch of his perfect brow. "And there's still the matter that someone tried to *kidnap* you." He crosses his arms over his chest.

I roll my eyes. "Don't cross your arms at me like that."

"Why?" he asks, his mouth lifting.

"You look too serious." I grab his forearms and he lets me pull them free.

"Better?" He says, holding in a smile.

I give a serious nod and turn to march into the workshop, but his gentle hand on my wrist stops me.

"Maybe I should do this instead?" He pulls me towards him, closing the distance between us, wrapping his free hand around my waist as his other weaves with mine. He holds me like a dance. We've never been this close and my heart knows this, thudding erratically between us. Blood rushes to my cheeks.

"I think sleep deprivation is getting to you," I tease, trying to ease some of the nervous tension building in my belly.

I glance towards the house, the many windows of the St. Claire estate, a mirror's reflection. He gives me a mischievous grin that starts my heart back up. The clouds shift and the sun shines on us once again, accentuating his golden hair, his skin warm where our hands touch.

"Maybe," he grins down at me. He brings our hands up to his mouth, his lips soft on my knuckles. I suck in my breath.

The bang of a door breaks us apart. Sebastian stands at the top of the porch steps that lead straight to us. His arm rests on the railing.

"Back from the *mall?*" he says, as Ash should have better things to do than an inconsequential shopping trip with some silly girl from school.

Behind Sebastian is a boy with coppery hair who looks absolutely delighted, and a tall girl with an expression like she caught Ash about to kiss a two-headed sloth monster.

The impish boy pushes past Ash's brother and down the steps. "So this must be your Siphon," he says, giving me a wide grin.

"Echo, this is Callum."

Callum looks younger than Ash, lithe but strong. A pattern of freckles on his cheeks makes his amber eyes seem to sparkle. Callum rubs his hands together in delight. "I wasn't sure if I was ever going to meet you. Ash has been keeping you to himself."

Ash's cheeks turn more ruddy as he gives me an apologetic look. Sebastian takes his time descending the steps with leisurely grace. He watches me as he does.

The girl follows behind him with her lips pursed, looking like she either wants to toss me into the sea or turn back into the house.

Ash gives a polite nod to her when she joins us. "This is Charlotte."

Callum and Charlotte, Ash's friends, and more Seraphs. Charlotte is fair-haired and fair skin, with blue eyes as bright as the St. Claire's. She doesn't look much like a warrior, but neither did Ash back when he was just the aloof boy in class. All of them are beautiful, and I'm doubting Ash's insistence they're not in any way connected to angels.

"Hi," I say.

She doesn't bother with pleasantries. Her eyes move over me from head to toe, and then she says something in Seraph that makes

Ash a little redder. He runs a hand over his face and answers her back in their native tongue. I don't like that I can't understand them. I put my hands on my hips and try to keep the annoyance off my face.

Callum is watching me. He winks. "It's amazing you're here."

"Why?"

He furrows his brows. "Because Domini are forbidden to—"

Sebastian puts his hand on the younger Seraphim's shoulder, causing Callum to wince under his touch. "I thought you were out dress shopping?" Sebastian asks, looking at the sky like it'll tell him the time.

Charlotte gapes at Ash. "Dress shopping?" She pulls her braid forward, her fingers worrying the end as she rattles on in Seraph, looking at Sebastian.

Ash shakes his head. "For the homecoming dance."

Callum gives Ash a once over, his smirk turns rakish. "Didn't figure you at a dance."

Ash ignores Callum, tipping his head towards his brother. "I didn't see the cars in the garage. Where is everyone?"

I don't like the way Charlotte watches Ash, or really the way she purposely ignores me.

Sebastian crosses his arms over his chest, reminding me of Ash. "Mom is at her women's club thing and Dad is at the coroner's office." Sebastian glances down at me, his eyes narrowing on my face. "To get the autopsy report for your kidnappers." He says to Ash, unaware or unconcerned with my alarm, "He'll want to speak to you later."

A line forms between Ash's brows, but he nods. I touch Ash's arm, silently asking him to explain what's going on. Charlotte zeros in on my fingers on his skin. The way her body has gone ridged has drawn Sebastian's attention.

He says, "You should take Echo home. We could use your help."

Ash makes a show of checking his watch. "I think I have a couple more hours of yard time," he says tightly.

NICOLE LIGHTWOOD

Sebastian rolls his eyes. "Fine."

Callum, who enjoys this more than socially polite, puts his arm around Sebastian. "Come on, old man, let the kids have some fun. You remember fun?" Then he winks at me.

Sebastian shrugs off Callum's touch as Charlotte drops her braid in a huff.

"We're running around chasing ghosts and dead leads for a *Siphon*," she says like she's spitting out poison. "While Ash gets to—" She finishes the rest in Seraph, meaning she deliberately wanted me to hear the first part.

Whatever she says makes Ash's jaw go tight, but Callum grin. Sebastian pinches the bridge of his nose and waves his other hand insouciantly in the air. Whatever he says back to her in Seraph makes her turn on her heel and head into the house.

"What did she say?"

"Oh trust me, you didn't want to hear that one," Callum mock whispers to me.

Ash and Sebastian glance over at him with mirroring expressions of exasperation. I feel like a third wheel, and a little outmatched. They're all taller than me, even Charlotte, with different hues of tanned skin, looking like something descended from Heaven. Only Callum is lanky enough to seem vulnerable, but his feline eyes stare inhumanly at me.

"I'll go home. No need to start a war over me being here."

Callum puts a hand on his hip. "It's funny you say that—"

"Callum," Ash groans at the same time Sebastian says, "go in the house."

The younger boy raises his hands in surrender as he walks backward to the house. "Nice to meet you Siphon girl," he says before he spins around.

Sebastian watches him take the steps two at a time before he sighs.

"He's... cheerful," I say.

Sebastian looks like it's an inferior quality, but Ash smiles. "He doesn't think before he speaks, but he's loyal."

254

I kick the patio stone with my shoe. "I don't think your friend Charlotte likes me very much."

Sebastian tilts his head curiously but directs his comment to his brother. "You should have told Charlotte how involved this went."

"She knew," Ash says simply.

Sebastian casts a glance down at me. "I guess it's different once you see it."

I put my hands on my hips again and am surprised when I see Sebastian's lip twitch in an almost smile.

"What has father found out?"

Sebastian replies in Seraph but Ash cuts him off, "I'm going to tell her anyway."

"Fine," he says, jaw tight. "Three human bodies with burn marks consistent with her story, all shot execution style."

"Then that's all of them," I say.

"Except the Siphon helping them," Sebastian says, "and whoever hired them."

I furrow my brow. "Do you think that's who shot them?"

"A possibility," he says. "You've gotten yourself into quite a mess." I'm unsure if he means Ash or me, maybe both. "If the body count continues to rise, we'll have to file an official investigation."

I ask, "What does that mean?"

"It means that if there's a Siphon out there killing people, it needs to be stopped," Sebastian says matter of fact. "And you'll have to hope no one finds out you're involved or we'll all be facing the councils."

I see an image of the island crawling with Domini, dressed in their amour of gold, shackles of light on my wrists like in their paintings. Or will they serve me up to the Siphons and their brand of magical torture? And what of Ash, imprisoned for a hundred years?

I take a step back, my fingers numb and my legs boneless. "They'll punish you because of me."

"No, they'll punish me because of my actions," he says, taking a step toward me. "It wouldn't be the first time."

Sebastian glances between us. He clears his throat into his fist. "We're not calling in the Domini yet. We have Charlotte and Callum, and things are contained, for now."

I soften at the sympathetic look from Sebastian. "Thank you for helping me," I tell him.

His brows lift, and he flicks a look toward his brother before he gets his composure back. "Of course."

SEBASTIAN LEAVES, REMINDING ASH that he'll see him tonight for training. Ash and I continue into the workshop, but my mind is even further from wanting to train. I think Ash can tell. His eyes wander to the rows of tools hanging in front of him on a pegboard behind the workbench where he sits. I lay back on the yoga mat with my hands under my neck, feeling the heat seep into my bones.

There's a soft noise behind me and I lift my eyes to stare into disappointed amber ones.

"Is this what you two do in here," he says, "sulking. How *boring*."

"Callum," Ash says, sounding exhausted.

I sit up as the younger Seraph sits down, crossed-legged on the mat across from me, in Ash's usual place. I hold his gaze until he breaks eye contact.

"You have beautiful eyes," I tell him.

Red creeps up his neck and touches his ears. "It's because I'm a half-breed."

He grins at my surprise and looks over his shoulder at Ash. "What? You've never told her about us, Halfies?" he says. Before Ash can answer, Callum tells me, "My mum died when I was born and I assume my dad was a Seraph, since," he gestures to himself, "well, it wasn't my mum who passed on the Seraph genes."

My mouth is still a little open, so I close it. "Oh. Wow."

Callum laughs down at his lap. He calls over his shoulder again, "What do you guys talk about?" He rolls his eyes, "or is there not much talking?"

My face warms, and I bring my knees up to my chest.

Ash sighs. "Do you have to be so crass?"

"My sarcasm masks my pain," he clutches a hand to his chest. "Besides, it's the truth. About me, anyway." He winks, making me go even redder. "Did Ashy tell you about him at least?" Callum hooks a thumb in Ash's direction and asks, "The Golden Boy?"

I furrow my brow at the word.

"I hate when you call me that?" Ash rubs a hand down his face. "Golden boy?"

"Ashy."

Callum scrunches up his face in disgust. "Well, it's better than what Charlotte's in there calling you. Rhythms with—"

"Callum," Ash groans.

"I wasn't going to say it in English!" Callum looks chastised. "I have *some* manners."

Callum leans back on his hands, his legs crossed at the ankles in front of him. He chews his cheek as he fidgets, slightly swaying. There's a springy and energetic quality to him, and words seem to pop out of his mouth before he can stop them. He doesn't seem like the stiff and statuesque Seraph I've met so far. Despite his brashness, there's something likable about him.

"Are you training to be a Dominus?"

Callum sits forward, picking at the corner of the yoga mat. "For now, as long as I don't die." I tilt my head and he clarifies, "Sometimes the genetics get a little muddy in Half-Breeds, as genes do, and we age like mortals, and live normal boring mortal lives." He flaps a hand at me. "No offense."

I smirk. "None taken."

Callum watches me with his head tilted. He appears to like that I don't look away and that I haven't asked him to leave yet. Finally, he asks me, "Can I see it?"

"See what?" I look at Ash, who is shaking his head behind Callum's back.

"Your Siphon magic?" Callum says.

I pick at a rip in my jeans. "I'm still learning how to use it."

Callum leans back again, not taking his eyes off mine, but then he blinks, tipping his head upside down to say to Ash, "So let's talk about this dance."

"I swear you just like making things uncomfortable," Ash says, flipping a screwdriver in his hands. Callum doesn't deny the accusation. "You should visit Sebastian then. You know he's good at being uncomfortable."

Callum straightens up. "No way. He takes it out on me during training." He rubs his ribs on a memory.

The corner of Ash's mouth lifts. "We all do. You think you'd learn your lesson."

Callum looks wounded but recovers quickly. His eyes roam the workshop, flitting from item to item as if he's categorizing everything. He snags on a bent piece of rebar and says almost idly, "Have you taught your fragile Siphon any real self-defense? Might be a good idea, given her current circumstances." When he notices he's got Ash's attention, he glances back at me, raising an eyebrow. "You know, since there's a murderous kidnapper on the loose."

Ash's gaze scans over my body, probably seeing all the ways I am mortal. "He's right."

"I know." Callum purses his lips.

Ash stop stops in front of me and offers his hand. I let him pull me up. "You up for a different type of training?"

"Maybe?" I say suspiciously.

Callum stands, practically bouncing on his toes. "Please say yes." His amber eyes light up. "It'll be fun."

I'm not sure 'fun' is the right word if it's anything like running on the beach, but I'm curious, and it's hard to say no with the way they are looking at me.

I bite my lip. "Okay, yes."

CHAPTER 23

M Y NAME IS called as I'm getting ready to go to Ash's. I search for the source, finding my parents in their bedroom. I knock on the wood frame even though the doors open.

"You called?"

Dad's standing on a kitchen chair in their closet searching the back shelf. Boxes, duffel bags, a translucent box of craft supplies I haven't used since elementary school, and all other detritus of forgotten dusty things clutter their closet.

"I was thinking we could go fishing today," he calls over his shoulder. "Carl Woodford says the snapper are biting on the flats."

"I'm going swimming at Ash's," I say, chewing my lip.

A shoe box falls to the floor and old baseball cards come spilling out onto the carpet. "You spend too much time there," he says, his voice muffled by the thick blanket that's fallen on his face.

I rock back on my heels. "Yesterday was the first time in weeks."

Dad mumbles something into an old hatbox which makes mom smile to herself. "He's taking you to the dance?" She asks.

"Yes," I say, even though she already knows the answer. I feel a point coming on, and it makes my stomach feel weightless.

"Yay," dad says sarcastically. More boxes fall and he curses that he ever kept this junk.

"What are Meredith and Katrina doing today?" she asks, dropping another folded towel on the pile.

I shrug, picking up a washcloth and folding it neatly. Mom raises a brow as she continues, "You just patched things up. Don't push them away."

I sigh, grabbing another washcloth. "Things were weird at the mall." I don't elaborate on how I was part of the weirdness.

"It'll take time," she says.

I fold another washcloth as I mumble how I shouldn't be the only one to put in all the work and mom raises her brows. I can feel her staring even as she efficiently folds and stacks the towels into a neat, fluffy tower.

"Don't throw your friendships away for a boy. After the stars and hearts settle, you might miss them and it'll be too late, feelings will be hurt."

"*My* feelings are hurt," Dad says as he walks out of the closet, a hand pressed to his heart. "He hasn't even asked for my permission to take you to the dance. What kind of man is he?"

Mom hits him with a dishrag. "Stop it," she chides him, but she's laughing.

"You guys are... *weird*." I back out of the room before they can tell me I can't go.

"Don't run away yet," Dad says, and I freeze.

He grabs a towel out of the basket and takes his time folding it. They share a look that makes me internally cringe. "I think it's time we meet this boy. Like really meet him, not this hiding out in your room watching movies stuff. Dinner, face to face, more of your butt here and not alone in that boy's castle."

I resist groaning, my hands digging into the door frame. "We're not *alone*. His parents are there, his brother, his friends Charlotte and Callum," I say.

Dad huffs and shares another look with mom. "Why don't you invite Meredith and Kat over as well?" She drops the last towel on the pile.

I take a moment to imagine what it would look like mixing the antagonistic Charlotte and verbal roulette Callum with my very normal human friends. The clashing personalities would either be entertaining or disastrous. I don't see alpha personalities like Kat and Charlotte getting along very well, and I'm not sure Callum wouldn't slip up and share too much.

Then there's the fact that we're not really going swimming and it would be hard to explain why the St. Claire's have a high-security training room in their home and why Ash is teaching me self-defense.

"Maybe," I say, my throat thick with lies.

"And you can invite Ash to dinner tonight," Mom adds.

"Sure," I drawl. "If he's free."

"We could always go over there?" Dad rubs his chin, considering it. "Have a friendly chat with his parents?"

I try to keep my face blank as they watch me. "Got it, dinner tonight. Can I go now?"

Dad rubs his hands together, looking mischievously. "I'll start planning the interrogation questions now."

I shake my head, try to hide my smile, and back fully out of their room. "Please don't embarrass me."

His laugh follows me down the hall.

I STARE DOWN AT my shoes, at the line of sunlight cutting across the tips from under the St. Claire garage awning, my hand gripping the strap of my messenger bag with my change of clothes inside.

"My parents want you to come to dinner tonight."

Ash twirls his keys around his finger on the way to the back stairs. "Okay."

"You're fine with coming to dinner?"

"Why wouldn't I be?" His voice echoes in the stairwell.

"Because now we're moving from friends to..."

Ash stops in the doorway to the overpass, his arm braced on the doorjamb above my head. "To?" He asks with his smile full of secrets.

I can feel the heat creep over my skin. "... to dance partner," I finished weakly.

He laughs to himself. "It's funny you say that." He slinks off the wall and heads down the hallway toward his room. "Because fighting is a lot like dancing."

"Punch dancing. Got it."

He laughs. "We'll work on basic self-defense first."

We pass his room, continuing down the hallway to the main landing. "You think I can't protect myself?" I tease.

His smile dims. "I think you shouldn't rely on just your affinity."

We take the stairs down to the main floor. My hands glide on the polished banister as I watch the crystal chandelier dance little rainbows along the walls. There's a table in the center of the foyer at the bottom of the stairs with a flowery centerpiece of autumn colors hoping to bring the feeling of fall despite the ninety-degree temperatures.

The flowery scent trails after us as we pass under the double staircase, through an arched doorway, and down another hallway. Ornate white wood paneling covers half the walls of the downstairs hallways, the top half a warm gray. Oil-rubbed bronze sconces light the way toward the training room.

Ash enters first, flipping light switches as he moves further into the room, illuminating the two-story space. I give an appreciative whistle as I survey the room. There's a small set of lockers along the wall near the door, with bench seats in front of them overlooking a large padded space. There's a collection of weight-lifting equipment over by the door to a bathroom and a large rack on the wall filled with various weapons.

Ash walks onto the thick mats, bouncing on his toes. "You ready?"

"Not at all," I say, eying the impressive space.

I drop my bag and join him on the mat. It's soft but firm under my feet. I mimic his stance, giving him a hard look that I can't hold for long before I'm laughing.

"Look at us," I say, gesturing between our bodies, "you'd crush me easily."

He makes a face. "That's why I'm teaching you to fight."

"I thought the best defense was to run away?"

He tilts his head with a grin. "We've both seen you run."

I put my hands on my hips. "Okay *Dominus*, show me the way."

He flattens his lips when I refer to him as his future legacy. "First, I'll show you how to escape if someone grabs your wrist."

"That seems easy."

"Don't be so cocky. It's the first thing an attacker usually tries." He grabs my wrist and I try to pull out of his grip and can't. "See?"

"Raise your hand up to your face, like this, and then grab my wrist with your other hand and turn, see." I go through the steps. "Keep that elbow down, turn a little like this." He shows me how he moves his hips a little. I copy him and break his grip.

We try it again, this time his grip on me serious. When he lets me overpower him, I say, "You're holding back."

"Of course," he says. "But you're not fighting me."

"Look who's cocky now?"

He shows how to break free if someone uses the other hand "The trick will be to catch them off guard, with your size that should be easy."

"Are you calling me weak?" I tease.

"I'm calling you short." He flashes a grin. "Okay, now what if someone grabs you from behind?"

He wraps his arms around me, pushing my back snugly into his chest. "Is this okay?" he asks, his voice soft. I nod. "You want to keep your head turned towards me, so I can't choke you, and then grab my arm with both your hands."

I do what he says, my hands on his skin, his breath tickling my neck. I glance back at him, waiting for the next command.

He averts his eyes. "Right. So pull my arm down, bend your legs and move behind me, use your knee to push out mine, like this."

My movements are clumsy and slow, so we try again and again.

"I'm going to show you another way." He grabs me again. My heartbeat is thudding in my chest, and it's only partly because of the workout. "You're going to want to pull down again, but this time elbow me in the ribs, turn and kick me here." He gestures between his legs.

"I'm not kicking you there."

"*Obviously.*"

He wraps his arms around me, and I thrust my elbow into him. "You can hit me harder than that," he says, a laugh in his voice.

I grit my teeth and use my other hand to give extra strength as I hit him with my elbow and turn, miming kneeing him below the waist.

He rubs his side as he says, "That was better."

"What if it's a girl?"

"That'll still hurt." I wrinkle my nose and he chuckles.

We run through a few different scenarios, if they get my hair, or if they have a gun. Even though most of the moves are slow, demonstrative, I'm still sweaty and out of breath.

I wipe my arm over my forehead. "How do you know all this stuff? Is it written into your DNA? Is there like a secret summer camp for future Domini?"

"It's not really a summer camp."

"Get out." I push on his chest. He's circling around me to grab me and it's my job to avoid him. "There's really a training camp?"

"It's more like a retreat," he says, looking a little embarrassed. "I've been going to it since I was twelve."

"Wow."

He lunges for me, grabbing my wrist. I slip out like he taught me. "Good," he says.

I shake my head. Little wisps of hair have come out of my ponytail and I take a moment to redo my hair. "I would be no match for a Seraph if this was for real."

"Hopefully you won't be going up against any," he says. "But don't be afraid to fight dirty. Kick, pull hair, throw sand in their eyes, whatever it takes to survive."

I tighten my ponytail and drop my hands to my side. I'm momentarily taken back to that night again and I shiver. "Even if that means killing someone?"

Ash lets out a long sigh. "They weren't good people, Echo."

"And that makes it *right?*"

"What was right then?" He says, heading over to the bench seats. "Sparing his life so they could take *yours?*" He doesn't wait for me to answer. "No, of course not." He picks up his water bottle and takes a long drink.

I sit down on the bench in front of him, holding my water bottle in my hands. "What am I, Ash?"

He meets my eyes briefly before screwing the cap back on his bottle. "What do you mean?"

"You said Siphons aren't powerful anymore, but I incinerated him like he was a piece of paper." I snap my fingers for emphasis. "Either you're lying to me or to yourself."

"Siphons aren't powerful anymore."

"Then *how* was I able to do that?"

"I don't know, but I'm trying to find out." He reaches out and takes my hands, his fingers tracing from my palm to my fingertips, now glowing with the colors of flames. "There hasn't been a Siphon like this since—"

The door beeps, and Callum's voice follows him into the room. Ash grabs my hand, dropping them between us, out of sight. Henrik, Sebastian, and Charlotte are right behind Callum. Henrik's eyes the small space separating us on the bench, but it's Sebastian that looks disapproving.

I slip my hand out from Ash's and whisper, "I didn't know they were going to be here?"

"Me either," he mumbles, getting up from the bench as his father waves him over.

Callum takes Ash's seat next to me on the bench. He drums his fingers on his thigh. He's wearing loose cloth pants similar to what Ash wears. Charlotte looks petulant that she's not included in the St. Claire's conversation. She refuses to sit down or look at me. She plays with the end of her braid. Her tight yoga pants and blue tank top flatter her toned features.

"Lesson over already?" Callum asks. "I was hoping to see you in action."

"I'm not very impressive," I say.

Charlotte snorts.

Callum raises his brows expectantly. Excitement lights up his face. "Hey Char, isn't that why you raced down here when I said Ash was training with Echo? Or was there another reason?" He lowers his brows, dramatically concerned.

Charlotte's face goes pale. She lunges forward, pushing Callum off the bench. "You wonder why you're always getting beat up," she tells him.

Callum laughs, pulling himself up. "I'm always getting *beat* because you guys have an unfair *advantage*." He adds to me, "Halfies are stronger than regular humans but not nearly as buff as full-bloods."

"And some of us are stronger than others." Charlotte nods to the amber-eyed boy, a challenge in her eyes.

Callum doesn't rise to the bait. Instead, he agrees. "That's why I'm so funny," he says, "so I can disarm my opponents with humor."

"You're not funny," Charlotte says, watching the St. Claire's.

I follow her gaze. Ash and Sebastian have their arms crossed as they listen intently to their dad. I wonder if the brothers know how similar their postures are. I also wonder exactly how many years or centuries separate them.

Callum clutches his heart. "That hurt, Char," he says. "You're just in a pissy mood because—"

Charlotte's eyes blaze. Callum closes his mouth, keeping his thoughts to himself for once. Charlotte lifts her chin, walking over to the weapons rack. She picks up a long staff and twirls it around in what looks like a complicated move with a challenging look at Callum.

He watches her, his face shifting into a grimace. "I'm going to pay for that later."

"You two are good friends?" I ask, pulling my legs up and crossing them on the bench.

"Like siblings," he says. "Most pregnancies between humans and Seraphim don't survive. It's hard on their mortal bodies, or maybe it's the chromosomes mixes or something," he lifts a shoulder, "and since my father didn't stick around, I went into the foster system."

"I'm sorry," I say. Callum waves my sympathy away. "How did you know you're part Seraph?"

He nods toward the Seraphs. "They check the orphanages, search the foster homes. We all have Amber eyes and dead mothers, usually. And we're stronger and faster than humans. We never get sick." He picks at a callous on his hand. "A Watcher found me and then I was placed in Charlotte's family."

Callum deflates as he watches Henrik leave the training room. He groans. "Henrik's easier on me than Bastion."

Charlotte twirls the long baton around, prompting a coy smile from Sebastian. He calls to Ash, who hesitates a moment before turning towards the weapons rack. Callum sits up straighter as he rubs his palms on his pants. Anticipation radiates off him. Charlotte tosses her weapon to Sebastian as Ash claims another from the weapons rack. Callum and Charlotte start to hoot and cheer.

"How old are all of you?" I ask.

Callum brushes a strand of rusty hair off his forehead. "I'm fifteen, a real fifteen," he looks pointedly at me. "And Charlotte's seventeen, same as Ash. They were even born during the same Qur'iel."

"What's a Qur'iel?"

"When you live forever, they don't do individual birth dates, so they do Qur'iel years. It's like a season of births."

"Have you ever met Ash's grandfather?"

"No, but there's a gigantic statue of him at E'llythuian, where they hold the council meetings, trials, and things. Scary dude." Callum claps his hands as Ash and Sebastian take up fighting stances. "This is going to be brutal," he looks back at me. "Especially because you're here." His grin could light up a room.

"Why because of me?"

"Because they both have something to prove," Callum smirks.

Sebastian twirls the staff in a graceful arch, the wood moving as if it's light as air. Ash mimics him as they circle each other. Sebastian lunges first; Ash defends. The wood thuds in my bones as it hits. They dance around each other.

Sebastian is more intimidating. He comes closer as they circle. Ash swings and Sebastian defends, their sticks clash quickly as both try to gain an advantage. Ash fakes a swipe at Sebastian's legs and gets one on his brother's side.

Sebastian grunts and flashes him a glorious grin before launching his counterattack. It's harder, faster, fiercer. He strikes him hard in the stomach, making Ash buckle.

I lift off the seat, getting a curious look from Callum. I tuck my hands under my thighs. "This *is* brutal."

"It's only getting started."

Henrik enters the room, maybe drawn from the sounds of clashing wood. He stops at the edge of the mat next to Charlotte and watches his sons. Ash ducks under the swing, but Sebastian uses the momentum to guide the staff into his waiting hand. Sebastian hits him hard. Ash manages not to fall and swings up, slamming the staff down on his brother's back, making him pitch forward into a roll that brings him back on his feet. He swings the stick up into his other hand and sweeps Ash's feet out from under him.

Ash is back on his feet and they move so fast it's hard to track. Sebastian tries his sly hand tricks again, but Ash is ready. He spins out of the way and swings up, knocking Sebastian's weapon from his hands.

Frustration flashes in Sebastian's eyes. He picks up a sword from the weapons rack, moving it in a taunting flourish.

"Is that in the rules?" I whisper.

"No rules," Callum replies distantly.

Ash ruefully shakes his head. "Always showing off."

"When you're as good as me." His brother grins.

I snort, and Callum gives me a smile.

Ash switches out the wooden staff for a sword in a similar style as his brothers, only slightly thinner. Sebastian taunts him in Seraph, the words unfamiliar, but the wicked smile tells it well enough.

They don't waste time. Metal clashes together as they strike and dodge, circling each other. The sound is brutal enough to make me flinch.

Sebastian watches him closely and flashes a knowing grin when Ash adjusts his grip on the hilt. "You need to practice your sword fighting," he calls.

"Swords are obsolete, old man."

Ash swings. Sebastian gives a small flick of his wrist to deflect him easily and gives a counterstrike that causes Ash to stumble back.

"Bullets are finite, but a blade lives on."

Blood seeps from small nicks in their clothes from strikes that were too fast for me to see. They circle each other, then Sebastian moves deadly fast, his sword cutting into Ash's shoulder. I think they're done, but then Ash pushes forward, spearing the sword through his body, surprising his brother. Ash brings his sword up, forcing Sebastian to raise his chin or get cut.

"Break!" Henrik calls and his sons break apart, chest heaving.

"It's always the quiet ones that are completely savage," Callum grins at me, oblivious to my unease.

"That's why no one wants to challenge you at Calldy'mir. You'll do anything to win."

"Isn't winning the point?" Ash grins, looking rakish.

"Not always." His brother pulls the sword free.

Ash hisses through the pain, giving a final grunt when it's finally out. Blood blooms fresh from the wound, making my stomach turn. The front of Ash's shirt is filling with red, but I seem to be the only one concerned with the casual blood loss and brutality. I shift, trying to keep my breathing even.

Charlotte hands him a towel that he presses into the wound. Sebastian cleans Ash's blood off the sword. My skin feels clammy and I press my fingers into my cool skin. Henrik, Charlotte, and Ash are all speaking their language. Henrik has on a tilted smile and Ash is grinning. He nods his head back toward Sebastian, who calls out something that makes them laugh.

Their camaraderie; their familiarity makes me feel like an intruder. It reminds me of how different I am from them. Even before my abilities manifested, I was still worlds apart. Ash catches my eye, his face sobering.

I stand as he walks over, my stomach doing nervous flips. "That was interesting."

He tilts his head in agreement. "It always is."

Henrik looks at Sebastian appraisingly. "You were overconfident," he says, "Your biggest weakness."

Sebastian acquiesces and gives his brother an appreciative once-over. "You've gotten better." He puts a hand on Ash's good shoulder. "But that move won't work on me again."

Ash gives him a coy smile. "We'll see."

Sebastian scoffs. "You're not immortal yet. If a Siphon tried that, I wouldn't be so concerned. "

The separation between us widens. I see Callum give me a sympathetic look in my peripheral. He clears his throat and the four of them look over. Henrik checks the time on his watch. Sebastian glances down at his black tank top, flicking a piece of lint away. Even Charlotte looks abash.

Ash takes a step towards me, the others falling back into busing themselves around the room. Sebastian barks out drills for Charlotte and Callum; who complains loudly, getting a few snarky remarks about his behavior. Henrik holds up his hand and mouths, *"five minutes,"* to which Ash nods.

Ash's eyes tilt down, his mouth serious. "We shouldn't have talked like that. It's easy to forget."

"That I don't belong here?"

"That you're not used to all this," he says, his frown deepening.

Charlotte has her staff back, twirling it and switching hands effortlessly despite its long, awkward size. Callum calls out that she's wasting her time showing off, which causes her pale cheeks to pinken. Her face twists into a scowl just for him.

I can tell Ash wants to say something, but he holds it back. Finally, he sighs, pulling back the towel and checking to see if the bleeding stopped.

"Come on, my dad wants to see us in his office."

I don't know what's made my face whiter, Ash getting stabbed or having to go talk to his dad.

HENRIK'S OFFICE IS LOCATED down the hall from the library. Dark wood paneling covers the lower half of the room with filigree wallpaper covering the rest. Tall bookcases take up every corner and a long saltwater fish tank sits to the right of his desk.

Henrik drops a folder on his desk as we enter the room. Golden light filters through gauzy curtains behind him, backlighting his form and making his expression hard to see. Ash sets a medical kit he snagged along the way on the corner of his father's desk and plops down in a chair in front of it. I take the matching chair beside him.

Bright blue, orange, and yellow tropical fish swim idly around the tank to a background of sea rock and coral as Ash pours antiseptic on his shoulder. He hisses, spilling some of it on his lap.

I stand, grabbing the bottle from him and fishing out some gauze. "That was a stupid thing you did." I match his incredulity and raise it. "Was getting yourself stabbed necessary?"

Ash rips a larger hole in his shirt so we can see the three-inch wound better. It was clotting, but the antiseptic aggravated the wound.

"He was going to win."

"So?" I pour more antiseptic on the wound, giving Ash an evil smile when he sucks in a breath.

Henrik, who has been quietly watching, adds, "Domini fight without the fear of death." He splays out his hands', palm up, letting the obvious speak for itself.

I make a derisive sound as I press fresh bandages onto his injury. "But *you're* not immortal yet, correct?"

Ash nods. "It wasn't going to hit anything vital."

My heart feels like someone is squeezing it. His wound probably didn't need to be cleaned this well, but it covers the sting in my eyes as I try to settle down my thoughts. The way they fight, like soldiers, warriors, what if he's made to fight alongside them when his body can still be broken?

Ash's hand softly wraps around my wrist. "Look, it's already healing." He's right. I move the rag aside, the bleedings stop and the gash is not as deep. "A couple of days and it'll be a memory."

I know he meant to make me feel better, but there's this piercing pain in my heart now for another reason. A couple of decades and I'll be a memory.

I press a large bandage onto Ash's cut as Henrik asks, "You heard about the murders on the mainland? The coroner's report?" I nod, taking my seat. "The bodies had burn marks consistent with your story, and a van matching your description was registered to one assailant."

He hands me a set of dossiers, pictures clipped to the inside corner of each file. I flip through them, my eyes searching their faces for recognition and finding none.

"It could be them." I lift my shoulder. "The masks hid their faces."

"There are charges for possession, car theft, a couple of assault charges that resulted in a few months in jail, but nothing like kidnapping or murder. This man here," he points to a sour-faced man with a small beard and crinkles around his eyes from age or too much time in the sun, "reports say he went out that night with his nephew, he's still missing."

My fingers go white on the edge of my seat. It takes a minute to free my stiff fingers to take the file he offers me. The young man who I sentenced to death stares back at me. It's not the school picture on the news, but a booking photo.

Ash takes the file from me, his eyes skimming over the paper. "He's been in and out of the system before he was an adult."

Henrik makes a sound of agreement. I can feel his eyes on me. "This was probably initiation into bigger things."

The room feels heavy and cloying and Henrik's eyes on me feel probing. I wonder if he suspects we're being less than honest with him. I watch the fish tank as Ash asks him something about the murder, about getting the surveillance video near one of the kidnapper's apartments.

"I recognize him," I blurt out.

Henrik slowly nods. I can tell he already figured out that much from my face. He looks pleased I told the truth. What would he do if he knew what really happened that night?

Henrik leans back in his chair, drumming his fingers on the desktop. "We know the men found dead were human and that the nephew is still missing, so are the Siphon or Siphons, who aided them. I'm checking their bank accounts now, their families, seeing if there were any large deposits, follow the money trail to who hired them."

"How do you know they were human?" I tap on the kidnapper's files.

"Their blood results didn't show any Siphon markers."

"You can test for that?" I glance at Ash.

Henrik folds his hands under his chin, leaning his elbows on the desk. "We can," he says levelly. "Human scientists have yet to understand the mutation they see pop up in certain strains in the population. It helps that the council independently owns several genetics research laboratories all over the world. Our research is the foundation for which all genetic programs are calibrated. "

"Could you test me?" I ask, chewing my lip.

"We wouldn't find anything we don't already know," he says, keeping his eyes trained on me. I sit back in my chair, my eyes finding the thick folder on his desk. Henrik speaks carefully, "I assumed you already knew what affinity you were?"

Ash shifts beside me. His thumb worries his bottom lip.

"Fire," I say.

Henrik is uncharacteristically wary of his next words. "Fire Siphons are strong-willed compared to the other affinities, they get a reputation for being unpredictable, wild, and rash," he says and I feel everything in me stiffen preparing for a warning, "but they're also unyielding in principle and fiercely protective."

I think of all the times I am afraid, of the times when my mind overthinks itself into indecision, and all the times I wanted to be invisible. "I don't think that describes me at all."

"No?" His brow lifts curiously as he steals a glance at his son.

Henrik gathers all the files into a neat stack. "I'll do my best to keep you informed." He opens a drawer, a familiar book catches my eye. "If you can think of anything useful?"

"I'll tell you," I say, my eyes lifting from the book. "Thank you for all your help."

Henrik's cobalt eyes are sympathetic; fatherly as he says, "Of course."

He sets the folders on top of Magellan's journal, closing it without leaving my gaze. "I promise, Echo, I will find out who is responsible."

WE TAKE A SMALL set of stairs to the second floor so Ash can change his clothes. Once in his room, I ask, "Why does your dad have Magellan's diary?"

"Hmm?" He is messing with his bandage, rolling his shoulder as if it hurts.

"He had it in his desk drawer."

"Oh?" Ash stops in front of a tall mirror next to his desk, pulling the ruined shirt out of the way to inspect his healing wound. "He probably doesn't want me reading it."

"Why is that?"

Ash's gaze cuts to my reflection in the mirror and then back to inspecting his injury. "Because some Seraphim think Magellan was a Siphon sympathizer." He clears his throat.

I put a hand on my hip. "I wonder what your dad makes of us?"

Ash's neck has gone red. It spreads up his cheeks. He makes a low hum in his throat but doesn't break focus on his injury. He pushes away from the mirror and heads into his room, coming out in a clean, faded green shirt.

"You want something to eat?" he asks, patting his stomach. "Regenerating makes me hungry."

The kitchen is bright and pristine and thankfully empty when we walk inside. I can see the pool outside the glass doors, calm and sparkling in the midday sun.

Ash opens the fridge as I take a seat at the breakfast bar, pulling at my running shorts where they ride up. He loads the counter up with bread, lunch meat, lettuce, tomato, condiments, and two bottles of lemonade. I make my sandwich and watch in fascination as he prepares himself three; double the meat. I wrinkle my nose when he asks if I want pickles.

He leans back into the kitchen counter, one leg crossed over the other, and takes a satisfying bite of his handiwork. It's hard to reconcile this image of him with the one who was just wielding a sword and letting his brother stab him to win a practice fight. The boy in the training room looked like a warrior, comfortable with fighting and violence. They fought as if they lived forever. This one in the kitchen looks like a mortal boy who's concerned with schoolwork and lazy summer days.

It's easy to forget they're the same.

Ash is scratching his shoulder. He pulls the shirt aside. He's removed the bandage, and there's already a scab.

"That's incredible," I tell him. "What happens if you lose a body part?"

His eyes meet mine briefly before he says, "It grows back."

"Seriously?"

He slowly nods. "It takes a while, but yeah."

I give him a once over. "Have you ever?"

His mouth twitches into a smile. "No. I've not lost any limbs yet."

The yet hangs in the air between us. I pinch the corner of my sandwich, flattening the bread. "Will I heal like you now?"

"Like me? No." He pushes a hand through his hair, "but faster than before."

"Does seraph blood create other Seraphim?"

Ash laughs, catching him by surprise. "No, we're not vampires."

"Can it give me superhuman strength?"

"Definitely no." He gives me a pointed look, probably recalling my poor performance in self-defense training.

I raise an eyebrow in agreement. Athletic I am not. I use the moisture from my glass to draw shapes on the counter. "Am I connected to you?"

Ash coughs, looking away from me until he's recovered. He takes a gulp of lemonade. "What?"

"You said you could sense my emotions," I remind him. "Can I do the same? Does it work both ways?"

Ash sets his sandwich on his plate. "It might be possible." He wipes his mouth and glances down the hall. He tips his head in a way that looks like he's listening. Satisfied we're alone, he rests his arms on the breakfast bar, picking at his sandwich.

"There's not much information on the effects it has on Siphons, since it's forbidden. Any Seraph that might have knowledge on the subject is either imprisoned or wouldn't admit to knowing about it." He takes a sip of his lemonade, his eyes not leaving mine.

I'm thoughtful as I chew. "Can your blood do anything else?"

Ash picks at the tomato that's slid free. "Like what?"

"I don't know. But you could do so much good with it."

"And be bonded to every person I healed?" He shakes his head. "It would drive a person insane. You'd never know what's your emotions or theirs. It might not be so bad to heal one or two people, but how could you draw the line? How do you decide who to save and who has to die?" he asks, not waiting for an answer. "Go into any children's hospital. How could you pick only a couple to save?" His gaze shifts out the glass doors towards the yard behind it, but I don't think he's really seeing it.

He sounds as if he's thought about it before. All the good they could do with their blood, but all the torment they would feel being connected to everyone that consumed it.

"You're right, I didn't think about it like that," I tell him. "Will you always have this link to my emotions?" I ask. He nods absently, biting into his last sandwich. "Can you feel them right now?"

His mouth twitches. He's enjoying my distress a little too much. "No."

He watches me as he takes a sip of lemonade and it makes my face uncomfortably hot. I look down at my glass and catch a few drops of condensation as it rolls down the side. "What's the use then of your magical healing blood if you're immortal?"

Ash studies my face as he chews. He dusts his fingers off on his empty plate. "Not everything has to have a point," he says, but answers me, "our blood being able to heal others is only a byproduct of the energy it contains to heal us, to bond Seraph to Seraph. I don't know what the point is. I was never curious because," he says, "because I never thought I'd apply to me."

"Aren't you tortured by my emotions?"

"Not yet." He grins.

I chew my lip. "Why did you decide to heal me?"

His expression tells me I should know why, but I wait for him to answer. "Because I didn't want you to die."

I point at his shoulder. "I don't want you to die, either."

"You don't have to worry about that," he says, eyes serious.

I give him a sly look. "I don't know. We'll see what my dad has planned for tonight."

He lets out a low whistle, leaning back on the kitchen counter. "Should I bring Sebastian for backup?"

I toss a piece of lettuce at him. "Please no," I say, causing him to laugh.

I help him clean up the remnants of lunch. Ash sets our dishes in the sink and then checks his watch. "I better take you home, so I have enough time to shower off the blood."

I wrinkle my nose and say, "Yeah, that might be a good idea."

He taps a finger on his lips. "So the gold ceremonial armor or the battle armor?"

I roll my eyes. "Seriously," I say, but then see his face, "wait, do you really wear armor?"

He grins mischievously. "Only for special occasions."

I punch him in his good shoulder as we make our way to the garage, but I don't think he's joking.

CHAPTER 24

ASH DROPPED ME off with plenty of time to shower and remind dad that if he embarrassed me, I'll rebel in a fit of teenage rage and find a boy from the mainland with a motorcycle and low ambitions. We both had a good laugh after I said it, but he agreed to ease up.

Dad must have forgotten my threats from earlier as he stares at Ash St. Claire sitting on our sofa, my grandmother's summer quilt draped behind him. Ash wears dark jeans with a dusty blue button down, rolled up at his elbows, freshly shaven, with his hair in that sloppy way he wears at school. His expression is well-mannered, the kind grannies want to pinch and mummer, *you're a fine young man* as they press a hard candy into your hand. His fingers drum on his thigh, the only hint that he's nervous.

Dad's drilled him from current events to questions I think he picked off some aptitude test. While mom elegantly steers the conversation to safer topics, occasionally pinching dad when he gets too fired up. Ash doesn't seem phased and answers them all in a very neutral and practiced way that makes me wonder if it's part of his training. *How to Deal with Humans 101.*

The house is filling with the divine smells of what is cooking in the kitchen just as the oven timer goes off. Dad looks like he's not done with the interrogations but mom squeezes his knee and says she needs his help in the kitchen, telling us we can move into the dining room.

"Sorry for the integration?" I tell Ash as we stand.

"I'm used to it."

I put that in the jar of things to ask him about later as we head to the dinning room. I take a seat across from him, giving him a look that says hang in there for round two.

Bowls of mashed potatoes, asparagus, and candied carrots get passed around while mom and I fill glasses with sweat tea or water, and dad cuts into the honey-roasted chicken.

After everyone's plates are full, Mom asks, "How are you doing in Latin? It's a hard language to learn."

"Fair," Ash answers modestly.

"Echo says your dad sells antiques? I didn't realize that was legal," Dad says taking a sip of his sweet tea. "I thought they shut antiquity trading down since determining validity was difficult."

"Dad," I warn, flashing my eyes at mom for help.

"The St. Claire's have a long history in antiquities, though my father has moved towards investment properties. We've always obtain all the necessary documents, and permits to prove all artifacts were acquired by honest means," Ash says with a coy smile. "A large part of our work is returning artifacts to the countries of origins."

Dad grunts out an agreement. "Setting the wrongs of the past?"

"Just doing our small part."

"I'm sure at a sizable write-off."

Ash looks at him curiously. "That I wouldn't know." He takes another sip of water, waiting for the next probe.

"Well, it seems to be very lucrative," Dad adds.

I give dad a warning look. I don't see him ever drilling Meredith or Kat on their parents' professions or finances. And he's never scrunched up his nose at the mention of Meredeth's father, the surgeon, like he did when I mentioned Henrik's profession.

Dad puts asparagus in his mouth, giving Ash time to eat some of his meal. He stabs a carrot and motions with it on his fork as he asks, "Is that what you'll do after college? Join the family business?"

It's the first time tonight that Ash looks uncomfortable. "Yes, possibly."

It's not until his eyes cut over to me that I understand what he means. The real family business of being a Dominus. Is he admitting that he's decided?

"Is that what you want to do?" I ask.

His mouth turns down as he says, "It's what I've been training most of my life to do?"

"Yeah, but you could do something else."

Mom cast a worried look my way, hearing the odd way my voice sounded. She asks, "And your mother? She does the annual Christmas Lights stroll in the park, correct?"

Ash nods. "Yes, with the Women's Club."

"We go to that every year. Echo loves their hot chocolate."

"And the fake snow," I add.

"I heard from the Carmichael's, they're across from you, do you know them?" When Ash shakes his head mom continues, "Well Mindy said for Christmas your mom turns your house into its own winter wonderland."

"It's my mother's favorite holiday." He smiles that conspiratorial smile and I make a note to ask him about it later.

We spend the rest of dinner circling questions around Ash's family, and why he doesn't take part in any sports.

"Adam Woo," Dad says, "now he has what it takes to go big, whatever he wants, he's a triple threat." Dad adds, watching Ash's reaction, "He's been around here a lot lately too."

Ash takes the last bite on his plate, unfazed. "Adam is great."

I roll my eyes at my father. "You know they're best friends and that Adam is seeing Meredith."

"Is he?" He feigns innocence. "Well, it's hard to tell who's seeing who, high school relationships are so fleeting."

Mom coughs to cover up her laugh, giving me an apologetic look but giving dad a conspiratorial one. Traitor.

I help clean up the table when dinner is over. Taking the dishes into the kitchen while dad takes Ash into the living room. I catch snippets of conversation, the tail end of him telling Ash that in college he was on the marksmen team.

I groan and Mom says, "Go rescue him," and then she calls my dad into the kitchen.

I lead Ash to the front porch, afraid that even though we've been in my room a dozen times dad might decide to come in and continue his interrogations. He's been rather weird since I told them I was going to the dance with St. Claire as if that changes things. It's only a dance.

"You handled yourself very well," I say, taking a seat on the wicker bench.

Ash leans against the porch support in front of me a smile on his lips. "All the times I had to be around judgmental immortals prepared me for invasive questions."

"Do you get that often?"

"Oh, yeah." He lowers his voice, adding an unfamiliar accent, "are you going to follow in your father's footsteps or be *worthless* like your mother."

I cringe, kicking my shoe into his. "Do they really say that?"

"Occasionally," he says, his mouth pressed. "If you're not a Dominus, you're not doing your lineage proud."

"Wow, talk about pressure," I say, picking at the nail polish on my thumb. "Is that why you decided to join them?"

He gives me a pained look, his hand gripping the cedar support post. "I only told your dad that—"

I hold up my hands. "I get it, it's what you've been training for."

Seraphs are the perfect weapons, Gods in their own rights. Made to be warriors. The way Ash moved when he sparred with Sebastian, was so fluid and practiced, and lethal. The elation on his face to be using the gifts born to him. I saw a different side of him, one that seemed to juxtapose the soft-tempered one I'm used to. Further proof that everyone has a dark side lurking underneath, secrets that aren't seen just by looking at them. *Like me.*

Ash sits on the bench next to me. I look up at him as he slides his hand in mine. "I've not decided yet."

"Will we have to stop talking to each other?" I ask, gripping his hand harder. "Will we have to stop doing this?" I look away from him, into the inky night sky. "Will you have to turn me in?"

He makes a pained sound. "You know I wouldn't," he says, searching my eyes. "I've already broken so many rules for you."

My stomach is a ball of nerves, it flips and spins making my insides feel empty and weightless.

"Is this something then?"

He raises his brows. "Something?"

I push my shoulder into his. "Are you going to repeat everything I say?"

The porch lights flicker, making us sway back from each other. Ash stands, putting his hands in his pockets. He pulls out his keys, twirling them on his finger.

I glance towards the house and stand. "You better go," I reluctantly tell him.

He softy nods, his eyes traveling to my living room window. I wrap my arm around the porch post, leaning into it for my own kind of support, and watch him walk to his car.

He carefully opens the driver's side door and stops. "Hey, Echo?" When I raise my brows expectantly, he says, "The answer to your question?" He gestures between us. "This is something."

He taps his knuckles on the roof before sliding into the car. I watch him drive away, and even then my heart is still fluttering. There's a cool breeze that brushes my legs and my bare arms. I hold on to the post and stare up at the stars. Tiny pinpricks of light glitter in the black and I can't stop smiling at them.

CHAPTER 25

POSTERS LITTER THE halls in bright orange and neon green with big black bubble letters, reminding everyone that tonight is the homecoming dance. Carnations were delivered during the first class as part of the annual cheerleader fundraiser. I get three dropped on my desk this morning, happy to see that despite how tumultuous our friendship has been these past few weeks, they haven't forgotten me. I smile at the tags from Kat and Meredith and give St. Claire a suspicious side-eye for the one unmarked flower.

I brush the flowers under my chin as Meredith and I stand in the lunch line. She holds her own bundle of flowers to her chest, taking extra care of the one Adam sent her.

I reach out and touch my fingers gently to the red petals. "Took him long enough."

Meredith's cheeks warm as she ducks her nose to smell the flower. "You're one to talk." She playfully bumps her hip into mine. "Adam said you encouraged him to talk to me?"

She doesn't seem angry, but I still feel like taking the subject softly. I nod as I take a tray, grabbing a side of fries as we shuffle down the line.

"I'm not mad," she says quickly, tucking a strand of hair behind her ears. "Truthfully, I was a little hard on him and I really regret that."

"It's worked out now, though?"

"Thanks to you."

I hand over my student card to be scanned and hang back, waiting for Meredith. While we're walking to our table, she pauses, putting a hand on my arm to stop me. "I'm sorry about how I handled things."

"We all made mistakes that night."

She shakes her head. "We weren't fair to you after, though." Her brown eyes look glassy under the fluorescent lights. "I'm really sorry."

Her sincerity makes my eyes prickle with the threat of tears. If we both weren't awkwardly holding our lunch trays, I'd hug her, something I haven't felt comfortable doing with anyone in a long time. The thought makes me smile.

"I'm sorry too."

Meredith returns my apology with a shy smile. "Come on, before we get too sappy."

Kat is already at the table with a half-eaten yogurt in front of her. She has her phone out but sets it down on the table when we join her. Adam and Ash are almost finished in line. It makes me grin into my chicken salad at how we're all getting along, all my favorite things in one place.

Kat's phone buzzes on the table, but she and Meredith are too busy finalizing our plans for the evening to notice. After the dance, we're sleeping over at Meredith's.

The mood in the cafeteria shifts. It's subtle at first. Phones around the room beep, chime and vibrate around us. Meredith and Kat stop talking to listen to the noise or lack of noise as confusion sets in. There's a horrible ball of dread that has bloomed behind my rib cage. Kat picks up her phone, her brows pull down at what she sees.

A hush comes over the room. Whispers and murmurs replace the loud competing sounds of conversation. It sends a chill down my spine, chasing a cold weight into my stomach. I dig my phone out, but I didn't receive the same message that has captivated the school.

A ringing starts in my ears. Kat sucks in a breath and I hiss, "What is it?"

Meredith's hand goes to her mouth at what she sees. I slide over and she angles her phone so I can see the screen, then lets me take it from her.

It's a grainy photo of me getting sick into the trashcan of the ladies' dressing room. Then Ash and I are in the mall corridor, his arms are crossed and I'm looking miserable with my head down. The third picture makes it seem like he's leaving me behind.

The post tells a convincing story of how I'm trying to steal a piece of the St. Claire fortune. It paints me as a scheming gold digger who got herself pregnant and how St. Claire doesn't believe the baby is his. That our secret relationship wasn't my only one and accuses a few other boys from school, Tyler and Alex included. There's even a picture of Adam leaving my house, insinuating that he's part of this made-up love quadrangle.

I hand Meredith back her phone as if it has burned me. My name travels around the room in hushed gasps, heads turned towards our table, and snickers from the table next to us. I can't meet Meredith's eyes. If she thinks I would betray her like this, then I'll die right here, my heart breaking into a million pieces.

Ash and Adam slowly set their trays on the table, noticing the change in the room.

"Is any of this true?" Kat asks.

Everything in me feels like it's burning. My face, my hands, my body, all from shame, and something worse than hurt. After everything we've been through these past few months, after how our pride handled the last conflict, I can't believe she'd accuse me. That she wouldn't take my side. *Again.*

"Of course it's not true," I say acidly. "I can't believe you'd doubt me. A*gain.*"

Kat clutches a hand to her chest, but I'm too furious and embarrassed to take anything back. Why do I always have to explain myself? To say sorry first.

Adam cast a wary look toward Meredith, but it's Ash who asks, "What is going on?"

I search for Charity in the crowd, my eyes skimming the faces turned toward our table, sure that she must be gloating somewhere. Phones raise, recording the drama unfolding, everyone hoping to cash in on a couple of thousand likes from my pain. I hate all of them at that moment. Some boys from the basketball team make jokes that burn my face. I can't find Charity anywhere.

Meredith's eyes dance between Adam and me and that's when everything gets watery. I can't take her thinking that I would try to take Adam away from her after everything else that's happened.

I burn, but not with fire, with heartbreak. I can't do it again. I stand suddenly, heading out the back exit.

Kat grabs my arm, pulling me to a stop. All the wrong Katerina's ever done to me comes raging to the surface, all the tiny slights over the years, all the times she pushed me out of my comfort zone when I asked her not to, and how she handled my secret about Ash. The pictures she rubbed in my face of how easily they could replace me, how quickly she could cozy up to the boy I liked. It all rages inside me, fire and ice with the Light in my veins.

"It was you, wasn't it?" I ask. "You saw Ash and I at the pier and you were jealous, so you set out to humiliate me. I thought it was Charity, but you were at the mall too. It was all you." I bunch my hands up, feeling the power there.

Her head jerks back like I've slapped her. "You think I'd do this to *you?*"

"I don't know what you're capable of," I tell her. "You started hanging out with Alex and Charity as soon as you got rid of me. You tagged me in those pictures of you two to be mean."

For the first time, she falters. "I didn't tag you in any pictures."

I slowly shake my head, my mouth cruel when I say, "Whatever, Kat, who else would tag me in those pictures? Who's the liar now?"

I leave her standing there but only make it to the end of the picnic tables when Ash jogs up to me. There are still several students out here. Heads turned to watch us after getting a good show of Kat and me. I try to ignore all the stares, but my heart is racing with anger and adrenaline.

I stuff my shaking hands into my skirt pockets. "This was what I was afraid of."

"Let's go to the darkroom. We can talk there."

The large cafeteria windows give me a good view of the faces focused on us, watching the drama continue to unfold. What must everyone think as I showdown with my friends? I am being crushed under the weight of all this unwanted attention.

"I can't be here right now. I want to go home."

"I'll drive you."

"Don't," I snap. "Please, leave me alone right now." I turn away from him, but the hurt on his face stays with me.

I head to the front gate when someone calls my name. I turn to see a girl I vaguely recognize from around school. She's a little taller than me, with hair as dark as Meredith's, but skin the color of summer. She has a phone clutched to her chest and the sight of it makes my jaw clench.

"Those posts are all lies," I tell her, backing towards the gate.

She furrows her brows and glances at her phone. "Oh. No," she says, shaking her head. "That's not what I—I need to talk to you."

I hold up my hands, walking backward. "I can't do this right now," I tell her, almost pleading.

I push open the gates, and don't stop until I'm home.

THE LIGHTS ARE OFF and the house is empty. I call out for my mom, hoping that maybe she's here even though the driveway is empty. My heart feels like it's going to burst out of my chest from the pain. I drop my backpack by the door and crush the carnations in my hands, letting the petals scatter to the floor. I fist my hands into my hair, letting out a broken sound. My phone vibrates.

The words get blurry as I stare at Ash's message. I shouldn't have snapped at him. It's not his fault. There were too many people staring, watching me fall apart. I tell him he can come over and toss my phone on the couch, letting myself cry.

Huge, warm tears slide down my cheeks. I'm usually a quiet crier, but the last few months all come crashing together and I sob loud and ugly. Everything pours out of me. Discovering I'm a Siphon, the fights with my friends, the rumors at school, the kidnapping, and the man my uncontrollable destroyed.

A noise in the kitchen stops my sobs. I wipe my tears on my shirtsleeve.

"Mom," I call as I get to my feet, the flower petals get crushed under my shoes. When I hear no reply, I call out for Ash.

The kitchen is empty. The curtain covering the back door flutters. I tilt my head at it, trying to figure out why it looks wrong, and then I realize it's because someone left the door open.

I wipe the rest of my tears off my cheeks and slide the door closed. The lock makes a weird sound, the familiar click sounds hollow. I pull the door open, staring at the broken handle when everything dissolves into darkness.

CHAPTER 26

FAINT VOICES COMPETE with the raw ache in my head until a groan, my groan, cuts through them all.

"Wake up," says a muffled voice. The second time is louder, making me flinch. "Wake up."

My eyes flutter open to see blurry fingers snapping in front of my face. Snap. Snap. Snap. I blink, focusing on the hand in front of me.

"There's my girl," the voice is smooth; familiar.

I groan as I sit up. My head feels like I've left it back on the ground. I put my hands on my ears to stop my brain from pounding against my skull. There's a groggy mental weight that pulls my eyes down, begging me to go back to sleep.

"I always forget how fragile mortals are," the familiar voice says flippantly.

"My head," I groan again, touching the raised and puffy spot on the back of my skull. I try to open my eyes, but a wave of vertigo takes me and I drop my head into my hands. There's something heavy around my neck. When the dizziness stops, I probe my fingers along the warm metal, looking for a way to take it off.

Someone lifts my chin as the person in front of me slowly materializes into focus. "You," I gasp.

"Yes," he says with a slow grin.

Alex is sitting in front of me on a bare concrete floor, his arm draped casually over his bent knee as if we're sitting on my bedroom floor having a friendly conversation. But it's all wrong, the place all wrong. We're in a metal cage inside a gutted warehouse.

The warehouse walls are metal and brick. Chipped blue paint flakes off onto the floor. The ceilings are over twenty-five feet high; the unreachable windows show the orange glow of the afternoon sun.

There are men pacing the building in matching dark blue shirts and cargo pants and they wear chunky belts heavy with weapons. Two bearded men guard the doors.

Alex tilts his head at me as if I am an exotic creature. His smile turns feral. I feel the heavy weight of the collar on my neck, the pounding in the back of my head, boom, boom, boom, with my heartbeat.

The boy I've had a crush on forever watches me as I take in my nightmare.

"What am I doing here?" I ask.

"I need you."

"For *what?*"

"Oh, that's the million-dollar question," he says with that carefree smile of his. It makes bile rise in my throat.

"Please, let me go." I spin the collar around, my fingers hunting for a clasp, a break in the smooth metal.

Alex taps a finger to his lips. "How about no?"

I push down my rising panic. When Ash finds out I'm missing, he'll come for me. Something in Alex's eyes flash as if he can read my thoughts.

"Counting on someone to rescue you?" he asks and when I say nothing, he leans forward. "Golden Boy wanted the Key all to himself, but I found you first. Finders keepers."

Alex leans back, crossing his legs in front of him like we're about to tell ghost stories at summer camp. He rests his hands on his chin, watching me. An ominous feeling has been building in my soul, something terrible is going to happen.

His words flutter back to me. A memory resurfaces like driftwood after a storm. My eyes skate over the cracked floor as the pieces slide into place. Multiple Seraph births are rare and they have a special name for them, Golden Children. But how would he know that? All the strange things over the past month align themselves together.

"Have you figured it out yet?" he asks, drawing my attention back to him. His mouth tips into a cruel smile.

"You were behind it all?" I ask, whispering.

He dips his head in a mock bow. "Indeed," he says with a cruel smile.

My hands ball into fists. "I'm not what you think I am."

"You are exactly what I think you are," he growls, hands fisting on his knees. "The amplifier I gave charity brought your power to the surface but I needed to test you. I went after you in the park and you used another affinity. Then St. Claire showed up." His mouth twists into a sneer. "I was supposed to be your savior that day. Then you would have been loyal to me, not him."

My head feels foggy, but I try to put it all together piece by agonizing piece. "Charity is a part of this?" I ask, my eyes dancing around the room expecting to find her.

Alex waves his hand dismissively. "It was easy to turn her crush into jealously, a few carefully placed words and she was eager to prove herself to me."

His smugness makes me grimace. He manipulated people into humiliating me and turned my own friends against me. All for what? I yank at the collar around my neck; I need it off, *now.*

"The Domini's dirty little secret," he gestures to the metal ring around my neck, "a slave collar. It renders Siphons powerless."

My heartbeat roars in my ears. The ache in my head temporally distracted me from my hollow soul. The power that I've welcomed as a part of me is unreachable. Tossed down a black abyss. I could go stumbling in the dark, but I'll never find it.

I fruitlessly try to pry the collar off and Alex chides me. "The first collars had locks," he says, "but the sneaky Siphons could pick them with their Light tricks. Only a Seraph can take them off now. They're linked to our blood, and hard as hell to pry open."

Our blood, not *their* blood.

"You can't be Seraph," I say.

His smile drops and something dark replaces it. "Why? Because I'm not as distinguished as the St. Claire's?" He stands and pulls me up by the collar with him. I scramble to get my feet under me, the metal digs into my neck. "Because I'm not your precious *Ash St. Claire*," he hisses, too close to my face.

"You're nothing like the St. Claire's," I snarl right back.

He lets go, and I stumble. "My father is just as powerful as Henrik," his voice rises. I take a step back and Alex searches my face. "It didn't have to go like this," he says softly, almost like the boy from school. "If you stayed away from St. Claire and said yes to me—things could have been different."

"You talk like Ash put me under a spell." I shake my head. "He was *helping me* after what you *did* to me."

"Was he?" he cocks his brow condescendingly. "It was only a coincidence Ash was at the park?" He gives me a disgusted look. "He was *following* you."

"You're lying," I say, but I can't meet his eyes. I have wondered why Ash would help a Siphon.

Alex laughs, it's cruel and pitying. "You have no idea what the St. Claire's are capable of." I shake my head, closing my eyes to his lies. "You're stupider than I thought if you think Ash didn't know exactly what you are. His dad is on the *council*, and his grandfather—an original. Do you think he'd throw all that away for a defected Siphon?" He shakes his head. "Ash saw your eyes the same as I did," he says, "every Seraph knows Ash has a black mark. He was going to use you to clear his record."

"I don't believe you," I tell him, but my eyes fill with water. "Ash didn't play elaborate mind games and kidnap me. He's my friend."

Alex's smile widens. "Didn't he?" he says coyly. "He collared you differently. Made you think he *cared.*" He rolls his eyes. "It's what he does and you're a fool if you don't see it."

I turn away from him, wrapping my arms around my middle. How often have I felt that this is too good to be true? I had doubts about why he was helping me and why he would risk breaking his rules when Domini and Siphons are practically enemies. I dig my fingers into my skin to stop myself from crying.

"Think about it, Echo," Alex says, his voice soothing behind me. He walks around until he's facing me and ducks his head to meet me at eye level. "He kept you isolated so he could keep feeding you his lies," he says. "It's brilliant actually, if I didn't despise him so much I'd congratulate him."

Tears slide down my cheeks. Alex cups my face tenderly, my heart hurts too much to move. He watches the tears fall from my eyes. "I tried to get you away from him. Save you all this pain." My brows pull down as he continues, "that's why I spread the rumors."

I jerk away from him as rage surges to the surface. "You're delusional," I spit at him. "Even if you did *'get to me first'*," I say, "I would have seen how awful you are."

He smirks. "I doubt that. I'm actually a really nice guy."

"You think setting up a fake kidnapping to play the hero is *nice*, spreading lies to ruin me?" My voice is sarcastic and cruel, "you think I owe you something and I don't."

Alex's hands clench into fists before he exits the cage. His eyes light up on mine. "But you do owe me something, and I'm going to get it from you whether I'm being nice or not." He shuts the cage door.

Fury burns inside me, and I scream loud enough that Alex flinches. Some of the guards look over, hands on their sidearms. I let all the anger and rage I've felt over the past few weeks pour out, all the guilt and fear and doubt burns my throat as my screams echo in the cavernous space. I pull at the collar, hard enough that my arms shake. Alex's frown tips up as he watches me struggle.

"When this collar is off, I'm going to burn this whole place to the ground."

"Ambitious, but maybe someday," Alex says amused.

The last thread of my heart breaks, the boy I used to dream about is the monster in my nightmares. My muscles ache with my efforts to free myself. The old wound in my shoulder burns, a constant reminder of what they forced me to do, of what I've become.

With my last roar of frustration, I feel it, a tiny flicker in the center of my chest. Like that old dusty light bulb in the darkroom. My fingers crackle with energy, and then the collar sends a current through me, dropping me to my knees. I didn't think it could get worse. It was Alex the whole time. What else is he capable of? I believe I will find out.

"Everything you're saying is a lie," I say to him feeling the fight drain out of me as I float further and further away from my power. "Ash will come for me."

Alex stares down at me, his face impassive, a cat staring at a wounded fly. "Who's lying now?"

He turns on his heel, heading towards the door. The guards move out of his way like water parting a ship. The guards tap their fingers on their guns, letting me know how impossible escape is. I curl into myself and weep.

CHAPTER 27

I WATCH THE SUNLIGHT through the skylights move from the starkness of late afternoon to the golden haze of late evening. After I wept, I tried to reason and beg the guards, but they stayed emotionless to my pleading, eventually turning away from me.

Alex has yet to return, leaving me with my thoughts. I replay moment by moment over the last few months and see Alex's presence everywhere, even in places he might not have been. All the times I felt watched, shadows moving in the dark. How long has he been watching me? Did it start that day at school when he overheard us talking about him, or did it begin sooner than that? Am I still on the island and does anyone know I'm missing yet?

And then, I think about Ash.

Nothing Alex has done has earned my trust, but I've let a sliver of doubt creep into my heart and it sits there, becoming agitated as I shuffle through my memories. How quickly Ash got to the darkroom, how he was conveniently at the park that day, how he steered me from seeking other Siphons, how his family so easily broke with thousands of years of tradition to help me. I think about the library and all those Seraphs books and how easily I trusted Ash to translate them to me truthfully. He could have told me anything, hiding the truth in plain sight, I'd never know.

The cement floor is cool despite the humid temperatures of the room. I curl into a ball, feeling hollow and exhausted. The next time I open my eyes, the cavernous warehouse is lit by large industrial pendant lighting hanging from the rafters. The skylights above are black. There's the sound of paper rustling behind me, and I turn to see Alex bent over a fast food bag on a folding table, digging through its contents. The sight of him gives me a start, I scramble to sit up, feeling a pounding in my head from the effort.

He looks up and pops a fry in his mouth. His expression tells me nothing. "Good, you're up."

"Please," I beg. "Let me go."

He grabs a brown container, its corners stained with grease, and a tall plain cup with a straw. "Eat something." He sets the container down in front of me, crouching gracefully that doesn't exactly look human.

His hazel eyes stare at me. His face is smooth and ruggedly boyish, the mischievous smile that I used to like so much. Such a pretty face hides something dark and rotten. I don't know why I was so fooled before, but it's all I see now.

"Please," I say again. "I'm not who you think I am."

"You are exactly what I think you are. And soon I'll have everything I need to prove it," he says confidently. He taps the top of the container between us. "Now eat. I can't have you starving to death."

I scoot back, shaking my head. Alex sighs dramatically. "Poisoning is so trite, don't you think?" His nostrils flare. "If I wanted to kill you, I would have put a bullet in your head." He makes a gun with his fingers and aims it at me. "Now eat the damn sandwich."

I watch him as he strolls back to the table. My stomach growls at the smell of cooked meat and cheese. I tentatively open it and take a bite of the still-warm cheeseburger. When half is gone, I drink the water he's brought me, wetting my dry and sore throat.

A sound beeps from inside Alex's pocket. I watch as he fishes it out. His mouth gets thinner and thinner and his jaw tight at whatever he reads. He pockets his phone with a frown as stalks over to me.

"Come here."

When I don't move, he nods to someone behind me. I quickly turn to see one of his cronies reaching inside my cage. I scramble back instinctively only to be caught by Alex. He grabs my collar, yanking me to him, my hands grab the cage bars to steady myself.

Something flashes in his eyes, but then his mouth turns mean. He gets in my face like I'm a little kid getting scolded for throwing a fit. I try to turn my head from the cruelty there, but he follows me. "If you don't do what I say, I'm going to make you, and I'm going to break you." He holds my eyes for a meaningful moment. "Understand?"

I nod as a tear leaks down my face. "Why are you doing this to me?"

Alex straightens. "I told you." His eyes cut away from me as he pushes a hand through his hair. "You're the Key and this is how he wants it."

"I don't know why you keep calling me that." I try to plead with him, my voice cracking. My chest hiccups as I try to hold back my sobs. "You have the wrong person."

"Don't lie to me," he snarls. He grabs my wrist, his fingers tight on my skin. I gasp, the sob temporarily silenced by the glare he gives me. "I know St. Claire was training you at his house, strengthening you, conditioning you to their cause."

"You got it wrong," I tell him through my clenched teeth. I try to yank my hand back but his grip is unyielding.

"I've seen you use air and water affinities," he says, making me frown. "I watched your power growing."

I feel slimy and exposed at the confirmation he's been spying on me. Alex lifts my hand between us. I curl my fingers into a fist. His eyes narrow on me and his mouth twists. He drops my wrists so suddenly it feels cold where his fingers were.

"What about the boy you incinerated? No low-tier Siphon can do that. Was that a freak coincidence as well?"

Surprise and shame make me gasp. I rub my wrists as I say, "That was an accident, it was self-defense." Alex rolls his eyes making my blood boil. "Ash was helping me to control my powers, which I wouldn't have needed to do if it wasn't for *you*."

"Either you're lying to me or yourself." He straightens his spine, brushing a hand over his head, the calm back on his features. "It's kind of ironic what the St. Claire's are planning," he says and purses his lips when I don't rise to the bait. "Getting a Siphon to destroy Siphons." He smiles when he sees the shock on my face.

He moves in close, like a whisper. I purposely try not to flinch. "They want to eradicate all you aberrations. Everyone knows St. Claire Original hates Siphons. That's why Ash kept you close, following in Granddad's footsteps. They're tired of being babysitters, tired of having to protect the world from the Siphon plague. They want to erase them from the universe. And they will use you to do it."

I shake my head, my palms pressing into the bars of the cage. "I don't *believe* you."

He gives me a pitying look. "Just because my methods are not as gentle doesn't mean Ash and I weren't after the same things." He smirks. "You have to give him credit though. What more loyal a servant than one who loves his master? He could have had you do anything for him." Alex's face darkens. "I would have tried that too, but who can compete with someone so *experienced?*" He relishes in the way my face pales, my own insecurities rising to the surface. "He even brought in his loyal friends to watch over you during the day while he continued his farce."

My words get caught in my throat. Ash wouldn't, he wouldn't. "Shut up," I whisper.

Alex's lips turn into a pout of mock sympathy. "Everything I'm saying makes sense, but your lovesick crush blinds you."

I vehemently shake my head. Alex's mouth opens to pour more cruelty into me when the warehouse door opens and in strolls a woman dressed in a sharp, dark blue pantsuit, her curls too perfect to be real. She looks between us, standing as close as lovers but further from it, and frowns.

Alex breaks away from the cage to speak to this new person. Her heels click on the cement floor as she joins him. Their heads close in conversation.

I bang on the cage door, giving it a shake. Alex strides back to me, his eyes crinkle at the corners. "Don't worry, you won't be in there much longer."

The woman crosses her arms. "Are you sure she's a Key?"

A muscle in Alex's jaw jumps. "Yes," he says blandly. "I've seen what she's capable of, and besides, why would the St. Claire's waste time with her if she wasn't?"

The woman appraises me but doesn't look impressed. "Don't be so cocky," she says to Alex, "What about the last one? The one whose body you let wash up on shore."

"That wasn't my fault. It was those stupid humans you hired who dumped the body in the bay."

She purses her lips. "Well, you took care of them, didn't you?"

My fingers have gone cold. "The girl on the beach? That was you?"

Alex waves his hand as if murder is nothing. An inconvenience, really. I bang my hands on the bars of the cage, getting their attention. "Why, why would you kill her?"

Alex hesitates and I think he will not answer, but he says, "Because her body was weak." He steps closer to the cage. "Don't be scared," he says in what he thinks is a placating tone.

I move to step back, but I remember how fast he is, how tight his grip can be. I freeze as he reaches through the strange shiny gray bars. He grabs my uniform shirt, pulling me forward. His other hand quickly grabs the collar and pulls me towards him. I try to grab the bars for leverage, but my fingers slip.

There's a small click from the collar and then he's removing it from my neck, sliding it through the bars.

I immediately feel lighter from the weight and whatever magic makes me void of power. My chest moves with the first full breath since I woke up here. I rub along my neck, massaging where the metal bruised my skin. My eyes flick up to Alex. He licks his lips and cracks his knuckles expectantly. The woman has a phone out and aimed at me.

"Go on." He spreads his hands out like he's introducing a circus act. I even have the cage to match. "Show us what you can do."

I cross my arms over my chest, which only brings out the cruel smile on Alex's mouth. His eyes flash. The woman cast him a knowing glance and his nostril flare in annoyance. He's been wrong before and now he has something to prove. I think about what happened to the last girl and my legs shake.

The woman says to Alex, "we don't have time for this."

Alex squeezes his eyes tight, losing patience. "Show me your powers," he shifts on his feet, "or I'll show you what happened to the last Siphon who was in that cage."

I lick my dry lips. My eyes flick from the woman to Alex. "What powers?"

The woman lowers her phone. Alex's jaw only gets tighter when the woman says, "your father is going to be very disappointed if you're wrong again."

Alex bristles. "She's playing us." He gives a guard by the door a hand signal. "Fine, Echo. Let's play."

A moment later, two men drag an unconscious body into the room. Dark hair peeks out from under the black hood covering their face. Their red converse shoes drag along the floor until they drop the body down into a chair Alex has pulled in front of my cage. My blood runs cold when I see the Shorecrest Academy uniform. I study the features more carefully, the willowy arms, the long brown legs.

My legs go out from under me and I sag into the cage.

"Show us what you can do or I'll shoot your friend." Alex fluidly grabs the closest guard's sidearm and points it at an unconscious Meredith.

"Don't, please." My hands grip the bars. "Meredith," I call, reaching through the cage, my fingers clawing out to touch her because maybe then I'll wake up, maybe if I can touch my fingers to her I can do something useful and get us out of this nightmare.

Alex presses the barrel to her head.

"Don't!" I call, my voice desperate, "Fine, whatever you want just, *please.*"

Alex tips the gun away, waiting.

I take in a deep breath and try to focus past my rising panic. I flex the invisible muscles that control this foreign energy inside me. Light tickles along my fingertips, and spreads up my arms as my hands glow brighter and brighter. I lock eyes with Alex, my expression saying *'see'*.

Alex shakes his head. "Liar."

He cocks the trigger and presses the gun back to her head. I all but scream at him to stop.

He doesn't remove the gun this time. I feel nauseous, but I try to concentrate. Meredith's life is at stake. I wipe a tear away and pull more power. It floods through my veins like water over the rocks. My arms and legs are glowing with fire and I can see my orange-white eyes reflected in theirs.

A mist has formed along the bottom of my cage, heat leaks out along the floor. It curls up the cardboard fast-food container and melts the plastic straw. The cage's metal turns colors, but it doesn't melt as I would expect. Like I hoped. Whatever it's made of keeps me and all my power contained like some magical Faraday cage.

Alex turns a gleeful grin at the woman, but my heartbeat is thumping too loud in my ears for me to hear what they say. She still has her phone out, ginning at the screen, at my show. Alex's gun points to the floor. His excitement at being right has let it drop from Meredith's head. It bolsters me into thinking that maybe I have a chance.

While they're talking, grinning over what they see, I pull a little more of the Light. Whatever vessel is inside of me that holds this energy becomes endless when it should have a stop.

Little sparks dance along my skin, like lightning in a summer sky. They spill on the floor of my cage like Fourth of July sparklers.

Alex grins in absolution, having finally found what he's been looking for. Seeing the manic look on his face makes me falter. Maybe I'm not strong enough. Maybe there are too many of them. Then I see Meredith's body slumped in the chair and all my resolve comes roaring back, like my fire.

The guards are watching now. All curious about the Siphon in the cage. I wrap my hands around the bars, the metal cool under my fiery touch. Tiny bolts of electricity leak out of the fiery cracks in my skin. Alex's eyes narrow. His smile goes slack as he realizes what's happening. The metal bars soften.

Alex shares a nervous look with the woman. The phone dips in her hand. Alex raises the gun up and presses it into Meredith's head. He's shouting, "Shut it down or I kill her!"

Time slows as I see his finger on the trigger. The guards have their guns unsheathed and pointed at me, at Meredith.

The fire leaves me so suddenly that you would have never known I was capable of it. The absence of all that power leaves me shaky. I fall back into the cage and that's when Alex moves, deadly quick he has the collar around my neck. He flinches back with a hiss, long black burns tattooing his arms from touching the hot metal.

"That was close," the business suit lady remarks, her fingers tapping on her phone. "I have what we need."

A groan comes muffled from under the hood, snapping my attention to Meredith. I feel dizzy with the relief that washes over me. Then she laughs.

It's such an odd reaction against all that's happened that it takes a few torturous moments for me to realize that the girl who's pulling off the hood, standing and stretching, is not my friend.

The face staring back at me is an impostor.

It's not Meredith.

"That was perfect," the fake Meredith says, her voice carrying an accent. Alex gives her a fraction of regard, his mouth pinched in disdain.

I feel sick.

It's not Meredith. It's not Meredith.

"Well, Evelyn?" Alex asks, inspecting the red marks on his arms. "Was that performance satisfying?"

Business suit lady, Evelyn, is typing fast on her phone, a small smile on her face. "I am sending the video now," she says, glancing up at Alex with a grin. "I think it will satisfy him."

Alex rubs his hands together. "Great, let's get going then." He shifts on his feet.

Evelyn shakes her head. She presses one last button on her phone and then slides it into her pocket. "Your father was very clear not to move the girl until he saw proof."

Alex frowns. "After that, you really think she's not the Key?" Evelyn makes a flippant gesture with her hand. Alex makes a fist as he adds, "I already tested her. She's from Genevieve's line." His impatience is growing again.

"That's what you said about the last girl." Evelyn sticks her hands in her pockets and gives Alex a level stare. She doesn't seem to be afraid of him, and I wonder if that means she's another Seraph. "We'll move when he gives the order."

The fake Meredith moves towards the door, looking bored. When she sees me watching her, she blows me a kiss that makes me want to burn this whole place to the ground with her in it. They're psychopaths, all of them.

"Let me go," I tell them, my hands tight on the bars.

Alex gives me a moody glance before nodding to Evelyn. "Better get transport ready because she's the one." He winks at her, all traces of his anger gone.

The two of them head towards the door. Fake Meredith already has her hand on the handle. They're leaving. Leaving me in this cage. Treating me as if I am insignificant until they need me to perform.

I bang my hands on the bars, getting their attention. "That little trick will not work on me again," I spit, jerking my chin towards the impostor. "I won't help you. I won't do anything for you."

Fake Meredith laughs and mimes shooting herself in the head. She opens her mouth to say something, but Evelyn raises a hand to quell her. Alex's eyes narrow on me as he takes a step toward my cage, his charming smile turns cruel. "Then I'll have to get the real one," he says.

"You wouldn't," I gasp.

"Of course I would, little songbird, if it meant I could get you to sing," he laughs, joining Evelyn and the impostor as they stroll out the doors. The black void of night taunts me before the doors clang shut.

I slump to the floor, letting the metal bars dig into my back. My mind goes blank, my body and soul feeling bruised over the events of the last twelve hours. I feel like if I close my eyes, I'll slip into nothingness.

I LOOK UP WHEN Alex walks through the doors; he casts a disinterested look at the guards patrolling the room. He saunters up to my cage. His steps are a little more confident now that he feels vindicated. "Hello, my pet."

"Piss off."

He laughs, clutching a hand to his chest. "Don't worry Echo, I have a bigger cage for you, it even has Egyptian cotton. You'll love it."

"I won't help you."

His grin slips into a sigh. "You will," he levels his gaze back at me, "or I'll take Katerina or Meredith, or your parents. I'll even grab that annoying dog next door, if that's what it takes."

I brush a tear off my cheek. "I hate you."

"They say there's a fine line between love and hate," he claps his hands and rubs them together. "I knew all the signs were pointing to something big on that island and who knew that the key was hiding right under my nose?" He chuckles and then leans against the bars, his hazel eyes lingering on me that would have stopped my heart once upon a time. Now it only makes my blood burn.

"Ash will come for me."

"This bleeding heart again." Alex rolls his eyes. "Enough." He pushes away from the bars, done with this conversation.

"You're wrong about him. The night your men shot me, Ash *saved me*." I say, "he saved me when *your* men left me bleeding to death on the street."

Alex shakes his head with that arrogant smirk on his face, but then he stops, frozen. "What did you say?"

"Your men underestimated me and look what happened," I say, anger burning through my blood. "I will never stop—"

"No," Alex's voice is sharp. He holds up a hand. His face has paled. "They shot you?"

I pull my shirt aside, chin raised. I want him to see the star-shaped scar, proof that Ash gave his blood to save a Siphon.

Alex's expression goes blank at the sight of my scar. And then almost too fast for my eyes to track; he has the cage unlocked and a hand around my collar.

"You're hurting me," I say, as he yanks me out and slams me into the cage.

"You lying witch," he snarls. "Where did you get this mark?" he sounds desperate, his chest rising and falling.

I search his wild eyes, not feeling as confident as I was before. I swallow and say, "I told you. They shot me, Ash healed me—"

Alex drops me as if I have burned him. Disgust and shock flick over his features. He looks around the warehouse as if any minute the room will flood with Domini.

"He wouldn't," he whispers, emotion washing over his features. Confusion pulls his brows down, and disbelief floods his face. He shakes his head. "No. Ash wouldn't give his blood to a Siphon. It's forbidden."

We have gotten the attention of some guards; they have moved closer, confusion flickering between them.

Alex fists his hands in his hair, "*No. No. No. No.*" he chants it as if the more he says it, it will make it true. "We have less time than I thought."

Alex yells orders to the men, telling them to pack it up; we need to leave—*right now.* He orders some outside, tells them we're on full alert, that they're coming for me. My heart lifts in hope. He's so busy barking orders to pay attention to me. My heart is thumping out of my chest. I'm out of the cage.

And no one is guarding the door.

I bolt towards the door, but Alex is too fast. I twist around, trying to claw his face. He traps my wrists, so I bring my knee up between his legs. He lets out a grunt, his body bowing on the pain. I bring my knee up as hard as I can right into his face. I hear a horrible sort of crunch that makes my stomach roll.

I continue running towards the door when a gunshot echoes behind me. The memory of the night I was shot sends me scrambling to the ground, curling into a ball.

Alex is over me in seconds with the gun pointed at my stomach. "I can heal you too," he says, wiping blood off his face. "Now get up."

He grabs my arm, pulling me up while keeping the gun on me. He spits blood on the cement floor before he nudges me toward the door. Alex opens his mouth, but the sounds of gunshots coming from outside cut off his words.

One guard asks into a hand radio, "What's happening?" While another says, "They're here."

Alex curses.

He pulls me towards the back exit right before the front doors get kicked in. The remaining guards in the room form a circle around us, guns aimed at Henrik and a man and women I don't recognize. I call out to Ash's dad and Alex pulls me tight to him, cutting off my voice.

The guard in front fires at the small group of Domini. I scream as bullets hit their bodies. It makes them jerk with the impact, but it doesn't kill them. Henrik takes one in the chest, but it doesn't slow him.

Shots fire behind me and I half turn to see Sebastian disarm a guard, then use the man's gun to take him out and another beside him. I cry in relief as Ash comes into view behind him. The two remaining guards fire on the brothers. Sebastian moves in front of Ash, using his body to take the bullets meant for his brother. I scream and pull away from Alex, the urge to run to their aid stronger than the knowledge that he has a gun pointed at me.

The Dominus woman points a gun at the remaining guards. She's shouting at them to surrender, but they keep firing until their guns click empty. They run towards the door, but it's Alex who shoots them.

The horror of it leaves me speechless.

"Touch me and I'll shoot her," he says, pushing the barrel into my head.

The Seraphim in the room still. I glance at the bodies around the room, blood marring the floor, brighter than I thought. My stomach lurches.

Ash is staring at Alex in a predatory way I've never seen on him. His body poised and ready to strike at the smallest opportunity. Every bit the Dominus he was made to be.

Ash says, "Your chances are better if she lives."

Alex laughs. It's a humorless sound. "As soon as I let Echo go, you'll all descend on me like avenging Angels," he says pursing his lips. "Let us both leave or I can shoot her now and while you're scrapping her brains off the floor, maybe I get away," he shrugs. "Either way, you've got another dead girl on your hands."

Ash flinches at the colorful picture Alex paints, his eyes flick over to his father's.

"What do you want with the girl?" Henrik asks.

"Nothing really, she's my insurance policy."

"He's lying," I say.

Alex presses his mouth to my ear. He says low so only I can hear, "Remember they're not on your side, Siphon, so let's not give them all our secrets, yes? Unless you want them to put you in their own cage."

"Echo," Ash calls, drawing my attention back to him.

Alex hisses in my ear, "Remember what I told you? You can't trust him."

I glance at Ash. Alex's twisted words and my own blurry thoughts toss and turn like a boat in a storm. I don't trust Alex, but do I trust the St. Claires?

Alex edges toward the front doors, away from the Seraphim gathered around the back exit, tugging me along with him. They don't look like they want him to leave. Their hands flex and release. The Domini woman shares a glance with Henrik, a silent question.

"They know what you are," I whisper.

Alex casts a narrowed look toward the Domini. I incline my head to the trail of blood he's left behind. He's been shot. A flicker of panic crosses his face before he clenches it shut. "What's your father going to think if you get me killed because you're trying to save yourself?"

Real worry flashes in his eyes, and he lowers the gun from my head. I drive my knee up between his legs.

"Quit doing that," he snarls.

The room explodes with action. Charlotte swings in from the doorway, her booted feet connecting with Alex's head, pitching him forward and knocking the gun from his hands. Sebastian lunges for Alex, Henrik for the gun, Ash for me, and Alex for Charlotte, who quickly rolls out of his grasp.

Ash pulls me out of imminent danger. I cling to him fiercely, but it's not over yet. The sound of fighting pulls my attention right in time to see Sebastian's fist connect with Alex's face.

Alex fakes like he's going to punch Sebastian, but starts running toward the unguarded door. His body is a blur as it races toward the night. The other Domini lunges, but Alex slides under their outstretched arms like he's stealing second base.

Henrik raises up a gun in each hand and fires it into Alex's back until the clips are empty. Though it may not kill him, he still feels the pain and suffers the lethargy of blood loss and shattered bones, enough that Sebastian and the woman tackle him, pinning his arms behind his back.

I hide my face in Ash's chest as Alex's cries of pain echo in the cavernous space. Ash runs a hand down my hair, saying soothing things, but my body still trembles. Alex shouts, making us both turn toward him. He spits red on the ground as he struggles in the Seraph's grip.

He looks up and says to Ash, "You don't know what you've done. You're all going to burn. Burn!" he shouts.

One of the unfamiliar Domini carries some type of shackle. The fierce way Alex struggles as they chain him makes bile rise in my throat. I wonder if it's magicked like mine. I pull on my collar frantically, not wanting it on for another second. Ash quiets me down and trades my hands for his as he pulls it open. He tosses it to the floor as I smooth my hand over my neck, feeling relief immediately.

I throw myself into his arms, burrowing my face into him.

"It's over," he says, smoothing a hand down my back. "You're safe. I have you now."

CHAPTER 28

ASH AND I watch as they haul Alex fully shackled toward the
open warehouse doors. Sebastian stands beside us, rubbing his
jaw. "I'm going to be picking bullets out of me for weeks."

"Thank you for that, by the way."

"Any time, baby brother." Sebastian's grin is too grand for the
situation.

My eyes travel along the bodies littering the floor. Charlotte
catches me staring at the human guards.

Her face softens. "You alright?" she asks. I nod and she moves
to give Ash a reassuring squeeze on the arm.

Jealousy creeps along my spine, making a small nest in my heart.
It's interrupted by Alex shouting.

"I told her everything. *Everything St. Claire.*" He's glaring at Ash.
"How you lied to her." Alex tries to lurch towards us, but the metal
chains clang against each other. I flinch back. "The glorious Golden
Boy and his plot to—"

Quicker than Sebastian can stop, Ash punches Alex, knocking
his head back and cutting off his words. The crack of bone on bone

makes me gasp. The impact knocks Alex from the Domini's grip and he drops to the floor. I press my hand over my mouth, not sure how much blood and violence I can handle tonight—sharing a look with Sebastian.

The Domini recovers quickly, lifting Alex up by his arms. His smile is bloody. He lets it drip out of his mouth like melted ice cream on a hot summer day.

"Don't get baited so easily," Sebastian murmurs, his grip still firm on Ash's forearm.

Henrik puts his hand on Ash's shoulder. He nods at whatever Henrik whispers. Alex watches me watching them and winks right before they escort him out of the warehouse. I let out a huge lungful of air through my lips. The entire night has been one big nightmare. I still don't feel like I'm completely out of it. The last time anything felt real was this morning before school, and that feels like a lifetime ago.

Someone makes a low whistle as they walk up beside me. "Wowzers. It has been a *night*," Callum says beside me.

My heart jumps in my throat at Callum's appearance. I grab him up in a hug, surprising him. "Have you been here the whole time?" I ask, releasing him.

His cheeks turn ruddy like his hair. "Um, yeah. They made me wait outside, *'away from danger'.*" He nervously flits his gaze to the Dominus around the room. He watches Ash and Sebastian with their backs to us, and Henrik talking on the phone.

"Cal," Charlotte tries to bring his attention back to her, "what did Sebastian say?"

"He said to let me drive," he says, then his amber eyes land on me. "Glad you're not dead, girly."

Charlotte rolls her eyes. "There's no way he said that. You barely have a learner's permit."

Callum scratches his chin. "I'm pretty sure that's what he said," and then, tossing his hands up in exasperation, adds, "how am I ever going to learn if you never let me drive?"

"You need an adult present," she reminds him.

"Oh right, and you're far from an adult."

She purses her lips and crosses her arms over her chest as they bicker a little more about driving privileges and who works harder at home. Their exchange should be a welcome normalcy, but I can't help noticing how I'm the only one affected by the dead bodies surrounding us.

Is this what it's like to be a Domini? To become numb to the sight of death? What have they been through to make tonight seem like a regular Dominus exercise? Are Siphons usually littering the floors?

Ash touches my arm, bringing me out of my thoughts, and signally that it's time to go.

Callum and Charlotte jog down the steps ahead of us towards what looks like Sebastian's Suburban. The parking lot in front of the warehouse is overgrown. Grass has sprouted out of the cracks, mostly brown and starved for water. There's a weedy-looking greenery trying to overtake a dumpster that looks long forgotten. Callum and Charlotte have a brief discussion over the driver's seat, where unsurprisingly, Charlotte wins.

Ash opens the back door and climbs in after me. Callum sulks for a minute in the passenger seat before he fidgets with the radio, flicking from one song to the next. The headlights illuminate the abandoned road and a string of aging empty warehouses around us. The car bumps slowly along the potholed-ridden streets until Charlotte turns out of the industrial district into a neighborhood that's seen better days.

Close-packed row houses and older duplexes cover the next few blocks. Most of the houses are dark, like ghost ships on the water, their windows black, the porches sagging, but occasionally they'll be the bright red tip of a cigarette or the headlight will catch on someone on the front steps. Their yellowed eyes follow us as we pass.

Ash lets out a breath, his head dropping to the back of the seat. He hasn't bothered to put a seatbelt on. Mine irritates a sore spot on my neck where the collar rubbed me raw. He watches my fingers worry the spot and I drop my hand, feeling self-conscious.

Charlotte cuts straight through downtown. The neon signs of the remaining open bars reflect on Ash's face. I can hear music and people talking behind me, and then it fades as the car drives along.

I ask, "How did you know it was Alex who took me?"

Ash moves his gaze over to the Seraphs in the front. Charlotte has one hand on the steering wheel with her head angled subtle towards our conversation. Callum leans forward and turns the radio up. A soulful song about disappointment fills the awkward quiet.

Ash shifts closer to me, his voice pitched low, "I didn't. When there was no answer at your house, I called your phone and heard it ringing through the door." He laughs without humor, "then I felt you getting farther and farther away from the island." At my confused look, he slides his hand into mine, threading our fingers. "Like how I found you that day near my house."

"Oh," I say, the memory bringing embarrassment to my cheeks.

"And then I felt nothing." He sucks in a breath, tightening his fingers with mine.

I fill in the blanks after that. How Alex was at my house, how I woke up in the warehouse wearing a collar, the cage, the decoy Meredith. Ash listens quietly. His jaw gets tight in places, but he doesn't interrupt.

When I'm done, he gently cups my face so I'm looking at him. "You don't have to be afraid of Alex anymore."

Ash searches me with those ocean eyes, and I wish more than anything I could get Alex's words out of my head. *What more loyal a servant than one who loves him?* I search for any cracks in Ash's facade, any clues that he's been using me, but my heart is blind, and my mind only wants to believe he cares for me.

Even if Alex is right about the St. Claire's, I won't ever help him. There's something twisted about him, and whatever he wants me for is as evil as he is.

The cadence of the car changes as we cross into the Western Crescent. Charlotte calls over her shoulder that we're almost there, reminding me there are other people in the car. I pull away from

Ash, my face uncomfortably hot. He clears his throat, casting a quick glance toward the front.

"Meredith's safe," he tells me. "I told Adam you were missing. He was with everyone at the dance and then sat outside Meredith's house for their sleepover." Ash checks the time on his phone. "He's probably still there."

I let out a relieved breath. Meredith's safe. They're all safe. The dance. I sit up in my seat. "What day is it?"

"Technically Saturday."

The disappointment at missing the dance gets quickly replaced by fear. "Oh no, my parents."

"They're safe," Ash says. "My mom is keeping watch over them."

"They're going to kill me," I groan. "What am I going to tell them?"

"We'll figure it out," he says. "First, we need to talk to my father."

I slump into the soft leather seat. Somehow, I doubt Henrik will know of a smooth enough story to appease my dad.

THE ST. CLAIRE MANSION is quiet as the grave as the Suburban pulls around the circle driveway, stopping at the front door. Callum exits the car with us as Charlotte leaves to trade places with Helen in keeping watch over my parents. I thank her fiercely before she drives off.

Ash and I step into the downstairs bathroom where he treats my wounds. I wrinkle my nose at the harsh chemical smell as Ash tips over a bottle of antiseptic onto a cotton ball. He's quiet as he works, his eyebrows drawn.

"What is it?"

He looks up at me, aware now that he was projecting his emotions. "I want to kill him."

"I thought that was impossible?"

"He'll wish he was dead," he says matter of fact.

I ball my hands into fists. "Alex said a lot about you." I watch as Ash lifts his eyebrow. "That you had people following me."

He tosses a cotton ball stained with my blood into the trash can. "That's why Callum and Charlotte were here. I told you that." He frowns. "My brother and father agreed that someone might try to kidnap you again, and we were right."

"You didn't tell me they were secretly following me."

"I didn't want you to feel uncomfortable."

"You need to tell me, especially if it's about me."

"I will," he touches my arm. "I'm sorry."

He motions for me to turn around. I watch him in the mirror as he cleans the back of my head. I press my hands into the counter-top as I ask, "What's going to happen to him?"

There's something broken and wrong about Alex, but I don't want him to spend the rest of eternity wishing he was dead either.

The gentle consistency of the gauze on my scalp slows for a moment before Ash says, "He'll be interrogated and judged before the council."

"What do you think the council will do?"

Ash drops the last of the bloody gauze into the trash with a heavy release of breath. He leans into the counter, crossing his arms over his chest, and I turn to face him. His eyes roam over my face. "His father is a person of interest. They'll want to use Alex to find him."

"What if he doesn't tell them?"

A grimace flashes before he says, "They can be very persuasive."

A knock sounds on the other side of the door, followed by Sebastian telling us to join them in the den.

I help Ash put the supplies away, but he stops me with a serious look. "They're going to want to know what happened," he tells me. "We still need to keep the man you burned a secret, and..." he swallows, "and whatever power you showed Alex."

We meet up in a family room off the kitchen. The room glows with a warmth that's more homey compared to the other parts of the house. There's a pool table with a TV hung on the wall, books and knickknacks clutter the built-in shelves, and a scattering of family photos hang on the walls.

I take a seat on one of the fluffy couches around the fireplace. I'm still in my school uniform and even though the room is comfortable, I feel chilled, my arms and legs feeling too bare.

Henrik takes a seat in a recliner, watching Ash pace in front of the fireplace with calculating concern. Sebastian lounges on the couch across from me. He leans forward, putting his elbows on his knees, his hands relaxed between him, but his expression is accusatory.

"Tell me what's so interesting about you that a Seraph will risk the council's wrath?"

My attention shifts to Ash, who waves a hand loftily in the air. "Give the Domini tone a rest," he says.

"The longer we wait, the more likely the details get muddy."

"I doubt she'll forget this."

Sebastian stands and this causes Ash to square his shoulders. Henrik sighs, rubbing his temples. "Both of you sit down," he says firmly but gently.

They obey. Sebastian lowers himself slowly, watching Ash as he takes a seat on an ottoman a few feet away from me.

"He's right," Henrik says. "We need all the details and quickly. We have an unidentified rogue Seraph in our custody. There will be a lot of questions, and possibly a query before the council."

Ash gives an almost imperceptible wince.

Callum comes humming into the room, oblivious to the tension, carrying a sandwich on a plate and two water bottles tucked under his arm. He hands one to me on his way to the couch across from me. Sebastian cocks his head back, giving Callum an unmistakably hostile glare.

"What?" he asks. "Midnight recuse missions make me snackish."

"Get out," Sebastian growls.

Callum takes a bite of his sandwich, unperturbed by Sebastian's warnings.

"Come on," he whines, "I already know Ash gave her the Amorial, what's the big deal? I want to hear what happened."

The room holds its breath and Callum rolls his eyes. "Seriously, how stupid do you take me? Don't answer that, Bastian. How else was he able to find her?"

He takes another bite of his sandwich, the sound of him chewing loud in the heavy pause.

"So obvious," he mumbles around his food.

Henrik rubs his forehead as Callum pleads his case. Finally, he gives a little flick of his fingers that say; *fine, whatever, he can stay.*

Sebastian shakes his head, partly for Callum, partly for the whole predicament. "If he can figure it out, we're all dead."

Callum gives him a wounded look but continues to devour his sandwich.

"I'm the only one responsible," Ash says.

"We're not under a query yet," his mother says, sweeping into the room. She's dressed in black skinny jeans and a tucked-in navy t-shirt. She drops her black bag on one of the side tables and bends down to wrap me in a hug. "I'm so glad we found you," she says, her warm hand cupping my face. "Are you alright?"

She takes my measure. The concern there makes my eyes water. I nod, not it's the truth. I don't want to cry in front of a room full of warriors.

She gives me a quick nod, as if she knows everything I'm holding back, and takes a seat at the end of the couch. "We need to know what we're going to tell them," she addresses the room, "get our stories straight."

"Exactly." Sebastian turns to me. "So tell us what happened."

All eyes shift to me and I squirm. I glance at Ash again and Sebastian snaps at his brother, "no, no more protecting her."

"Seriously Bastian, you can get over yourself," Ash says with a dangerous look directed at his brother.

Sebastian balks, "I've risked everything. I deserve the truth."

"So stop interrogating her."

Sebastian quirks an eyebrow and says something in Seraph that makes Ash's eyes flash and heat rise to his cheeks. "It's not like that," Ash says, but Sebastian gives him a look.

"Sebastian," his mother reprimands.

"I'm so glad I stayed for this," Callum smiles.

"Enough," Henrik's voice cuts through the bickering. "Echo," he says to me, "I'm sorry to make you relive this so soon, but we need to know what happened, so if you please?"

I nod, casting a glance at Sebastian to let him know that he should have asked me nicely. I start with what happened at school and end when they showed up. When I get to the part where Alex threatened to shoot Meredith, before I knew she was an impostor, I can't hold back my tears. Ash's mother gets me a blanket when she sees me shaking. I pull the soft fleece up to my neck, using it to wipe away my tears. I feel an overwhelming longing for my bed. To crawl under the covers and sink into sleep.

Ash takes over, filling them in on Alex's deception, starting with Charity and ending with where my story started.

I squirm on the couch as they discuss all my personal details so plainly, but they need to know how we got here and what they'll need to do with all this information. I sip my water and answer when they ask me questions. My eyes feel heavy and my soul weary as the debriefing goes on.

The image of Meredith in the chair, or who I thought was Meredith, still lingers with me. I wish I could call her, hear her voice and know without a doubt she's alive. I wonder how my parents are going to react, and if I'm going to be grounded forever.

Henrik and Sebastian are talking in Seraph. Ash is watching them, running his thumb over his lip and he catches me watching.

"They are discussing how Alex could have a Vestul," he says and then clarifies, "What he called a slave collar."

"A relic from dark times," Henrik muses. "A Siphon creation used to block their connection to the Light. We... adapted it to our own purposes. It translates roughly to void collar, but we haven't used them in a very long time."

"Most were destroyed," Helen adds, taking a sip of water.

"Most?" I ask.

Henrik sighs, looking apologetic. "A few remained in private collections."

I wonder if that includes him. "What about the cage?" I ask, a hint of disgust in my voice. "Are those also in private collections?"

"Both sides used Wolfram cages," Henrik says sadly. "The metal has a high acceptance to charms. And a high melting point. The Siphons use it to contain their criminals." He holds my gaze. "The Domini have a similar dungeon."

"Alex went through a lot of trouble," Sebastian muses, scratching his chin, his gaze moving to mine.

"Whatever he's looking for, he's going through Siphons to find it," I tell them. "He told me there was another girl before me, and when she wasn't what he was looking for, he killed her. The girl that washed up on the beach."

Sebastian casts a cautious look toward Henrik before he asks, "You know, I don't think any of us have seen your little practice sessions with my brother?"

"*Now* Bastian?" Ash snaps. "After what she's been through?"

"Maybe if we knew what she can do, then we'd know what tempted him enough to kidnap a measly Quiescent," Sebastian says and then adds, "if you do not know your enemies nor yourself, you will be imperiled in every single battle."

"Don't quote Sun Tzu. You sound like a pompous ass," Ash says.

"At least he didn't say it in mandarin," Callum mutters, causing Helen and Henrik to share a look.

"I'm trying to understand what would cause a Seraph to break the Olrum Lari'el."

"Why didn't you know Alex was a Seraph?" I ask the Domnius.

"We don't keep a database," Sebastian says with a derisive grunt. "Do you know every Siphon?"

"Births are important to us," his mom says, giving Sebastian a quelling look, "but not everyone can attend the Amoricium Soliel where we declare our offspring."

"And then there are those that keep it secret for a reason," Henrik says, exchanging a look with his wife.

"You think we're dealing with oath breakers, traitors?" Sebastian arches a brow.

"Possibly." Henrik nods as if he already came to the same conclusion. "I think Alex's father, or whoever he claims to be, might be the bigger enemy here." He shares a meaningful look with Sebastian.

"Hard to keep the council out of this for long," Sebastian grumbles, running a hand down his face.

There's dried blood on his arm, trailing from a healed wound. All three of the St. Claire men share similar remnants of the fight. Sleep weighs on us all. I can feel the late hour pressing down on me, but I won't be able to rest until I know what I'm going to do about my parents and I ask as much.

Ash pulls his shoulders back, lengthening his spine as he looks to his father for answers.

Henrik rubs his hand on the back of his neck. "We can't tell anyone about the kidnapping. That'd get the locals involved, poking around too close to Domini business. I'd like to keep this in-house." His eyes flick from me to Ash.

Ash stops rubbing his forehead to add, "I told Adam to tell your friends you were with me so they wouldn't call your parents."

Sebastian is studying some blood under his nails as he says, "The only reason your parents didn't file a missing person report is because they think you're at your friend's house."

Henrik lifts his hands out. "The easiest explanation is that she spent the night here."

I groan, thinking about what Kat and Meredith will say.

Sebastian huffs. "It could be worse. That psychopath could still have you." He stands and stretches. His words tingle along my skin, searing their reality.

Callum drapes his lanky body over the newly vacant couch like an adolescent wildcat. He hums a rather upbeat pop song, his fingers tapping on his belly to the beat.

On his way to the door, Sebastian stops by his father's chair, putting a hand on the back of it. "Oslo is going to want to know why we borrowed some of his people to rescue a Siphon, and why there's a new Seraph in the cells."

Henrik makes a hum of agreement in his throat. He stands, offering his hand to his wife. "We should go get some rest before we're sneaking Echo home or facing down her angry father."

Helen, says with a coy smile, "You can face down all kinds of baddies, but a girl's father scares you?"

Henrik answers emphatically, "Yes."

Ash's parents exit the den. Sebastian gives Ash a sly look on his way out.

Callum lifts his head and says to Ash, "So, your first sleepover with a girl. How was it?"

Ash throws a pillow at him, which only makes Callum laugh.

Ash and I follow everyone's lead and head up to his room. As soon as I enter his bedroom, I drop onto his couch and yawn when he tells me I should try to get a few hours of sleep before the sun rises. I only meant to close my eyes for a second, but the cool room dissolves into darkness.

Alex's there. I can't see him, but I can feel him, that looming presence I've sensed over the past few months. Always watching.

He finally steps out of the shadows.

"Echo, you're the key to all unmaking," he whispers.

I try to fight him, to use my power, but the collar is around me, its weight pushing me down, down, down. I fall through the floor as it turns to sand. Now I'm on the beach and the dead girl is walking towards me from the water. Her light hair flows around her as if it has its own gravity. Her eyes glow hungrily.

"I've waited a long time for you," she says.

Her long spidery fingers grab me up by the collar as Alex did. It digs into my existing bruise and I yell at her; ask her why she's doing this.

"He killed me," she says, and then she devours me.

I wake with a start. The room is bright with the morning sun. It takes a minute for my brain to translate what I'm seeing. Ash is kneeling beside the couch, his hand on my arm.

"You were having a nightmare." His voice is rough with exhaustion.

"Did I wake you?"

He stifles a yawn in answer. "We should probably get up anyway."

There's a change of clothes waiting for me in his bathroom, along with a brand-new toothbrush still in the packaging. The leggings are a little too long, and I have to roll them up at my ankles. The sweater's too hot for October, but it covers the bruises on my arms, and it sits high enough on my neck that with my hair down you can hardly tell I was dragged around by a metal collar. I grimace at my reflection. I've been doing that a lot in the last twenty-four hours.

I finish by washing my face, hoping that it'll be enough to wipe off my haunted look. It's not.

Ash is waiting for me in his room. He's changed out of his dark Dominus fatigues and into a clean set of clothes. He pulls my phone out of his pocket and hands it to me.

I unlock my phone and internally cringe at all the calls and messages from my friends. I rub my forehead as I see one from my parents this morning. Ash leaves me alone as I sit down on his bed and call my mom.

Her voice is cheery on the other end and not how I would expect her to be if she knew I had spent the night at Ash's. She asks how the dance was and I can tell by her tone that she's disappointed she didn't get to see me before I left. She tells me she's glad I had fun and I say I'll be home soon.

Ash leans against the doorway, his arms crossed over his chest, waiting for me to tell him what I want. We share a moment where everything that has happened passes between us and then I sigh.

"Take me home."

CHAPTER 29

S CHOOL BOOKS LITTER my bed; my playlist croons softly as I try to use anything to distract my mind from the messages and missed calls from my friends. I should feel happy and relieved that they still care, that things didn't get ripped into ruins again, but all I feel is numb.

It's already Sunday and I haven't had the nerve to message anyone back, so I'm surprised when Meredith knocks on my bedroom door.

She's carrying a long garment bag, her black hair up in a high ponytail; gold hoops dangle from her ears. She's still dressed in her church dress, and I wonder if she drove here or if I'll see Adam's truck on the curb.

"Hey," I say, closing my chemistry book.

"Hey." Her eyes move over the room as if she hasn't been here in a while, and I realize that's true. She sets the garment bag on my desk chair, her fingers now free to worry each other as she looks around the room. She nervously nods at a framed movie poster for The Rise of the Blue Comet. "You finally got it?"

"Ash got it for me."

Her brows touch her hairline. "Oh? Did you convert him into a fanboy?"

I smile as a memory sweeps me up. "I think he only watches them because I like them."

She nods, her eyes still on the movie poster. Her words are careful as she asks, "And how is Ash St. Claire?"

"Fine, I guess," I say slowly, picking up my pencil and digging my thumb into the eraser.

Meredith is chewing her cheek. Finally, she turns towards me. "I called you. Several times," she says. Her eyes find my phone, still softly playing music.

The accusation and disappointment make my eyes burn. A guilty knot forms in my throat. "I'm sorry."

She sits in my desk chair, the garment bag rustles as she does. For a minute I see her in the warehouse with a cloth bag over her head and Alex pushing a gun to her temple. Everything in me clenches, my heart remembering it vividly as it pounds. I count to ten, slowly coming out of that place, and back to my bedroom.

"I don't want things to get like they were before," she says.

"I don't either," I tell her, "it was horrible not talking to you."

She worries her cheek. "Kat yelled at Charity."

"She what?"

"After you left, Charity was laughing so Kat got in her face, told everyone in the cafeteria that Charity was behind the pictures, that she was spreading lies, and made her admit it in front of everyone."

My head knocks back in surprise. "Wow, Kat did that?" I say, wishing I had been there to see it. "Wait," I say, "Charity admitted to sending the pictures?"

"Yeah."

I'm shaking my head. Charity didn't send the pictures, Alex did, pretending to be Charity. The only thing Charity is guilty of is harassing me in the halls with a curse Alex planted on her. But why would she cover for him? Maybe her devotion to him goes deeper than I thought. Alex boasted enough about it, how he manipulated her. How he was planning on doing the same to me.

Meredith gives me a sideways glance, her hand playing with her earring. "But you knew that?"

"Of course." I swallow. "I'm just surprised she admitted to it."

Meredith snorts. "Kat's pretty persuasive."

"Yeah, she is." We share a smile, but mine quickly fades. "Does that mean she's not mad?"

Meredith shakes her head. "No, and you would know that if you called any of us back."

I wince. "I know, I messed up."

"You should have told us Charity was harassing you from the beginning. We're your best friends. We'll always have your back."

"I know, I know," I plead, hoping she can hear the sincerity in my voice.

Meredith sighs, her hands relaxing in her lap. "We messed up too, handled things badly, but no more; fresh slate." She stands, holding up the garment bag. "I was going to surprise you with this Friday night, but..." She shakes her head and hands me the bag.

I pull the zipper down, moving it out of the way to reveal the ice-blue dress I tried on at the mainland mall. The glittery material of the skirt catches on my bedroom lights, glimmering as I run the fabric through my fingers. "You bought it for me?"

She rocks back on her heels, her grin bright with my reaction.

"Thank you," I tell her, "It's beautiful."

I reach for her and she closes the distance as we wrap each other up in a hug; the dress crushed between us. We break apart, our eyes watery.

Meredith wipes at her eyes, a laugh in her voice as she says, "I'm glad you like it." She watches me hang the dress in my closet. "Too bad Ash didn't get to see you in that dress. There's always next year." She smiles, her eyes devilish. "But I'm sure he saw you in something better?" she says with a knowing tilt to her smile.

"Not even close." I wrinkle up my nose, my face warming as Meredith laughs.

"I hope you'll tell me all about it."

"Soon." I hope I mean it.

She nods in understanding, pausing with her hand on the door. She gives me one last hug before she leaves.

I can't tell Meredith and Kat the truth, maybe forever, but I have hope that we can find some kind of normal again. I'm not naïve enough to think that our friendship can easily resume to how it was before, despite all of us moving past it. I forgive them, but an invisible chasm has appeared between us and that too will take time to heal, but I have faith it will.

Feeling bolstered by Meredith's boon, I text Kat.

While I wait for her reply, I look at my messages from Ash. There's this apprehension that's developed between us now, and I'm not sure how to fix it. Ash and the other Domini saved my life, but Alex's taunts have taken up roost in the back of my mind and I can't seem to let them go. Ash said that they'll begin interrogating Alex soon and then will catch the person or people behind my abductions.

It doesn't comfort me, though.

Alex was looking for something on this island and he knew I was different, knew to bring this dormant power out of me, and he knows I can do things other Siphons can't do. That I'm not hindered by Genevieve's curse as I should be. I wonder darkly what I'm truly capable of. There's a growing dread that I've only just scratched the surface of my power, and it terrifies me.

I'm not sure who I can trust anymore. The Domini are duty-bound to protect the world from Siphons, and I'm not sure I can trust them. The St. Claire's have proven themselves so far, but I don't know when that protection will expire.

My kind, whom I've never met, might not even welcome whatever I am. Alex had called me the Key and I desperately want to find out what that means.

CAGE OF THE CURSED

EPILOGUE

THE HIGH TOWER stood sentry amongst the orange groves. It's peach colored stone meant to blend in to the pastel summer pallet of its surroundings but only accentuates its strangeness.

He parked the car at the mouth of the grove where the well tended pathways seemed to point straight to the prison. He'd have to walk the rest of the way from here. The scent of orange was heavy on the air even though the trees here held no fruit.

During the peak growing season, workers moved through the trees, hand pollinating, pruning and collecting fruit. Never knowing what was underneath the tower.

The ground was hard under his boots, and eerily quiet, not even a wind to rustle the leaves. All he heard was his heart beating. He would have chosen to never visit the tower again, but his current circumstances brought him back to this place of nightmares.

He kept his steps, even knowing the guards would have known his arrival the minute his car made the turn down the dirt road and were watching him now. He had calmed his heart by the time he had made it to the tower doors.

The door was ten feet tall and laced with Siphon-charmed metal that no sound could escape. Apprehension slid along his spine. He could almost hear the screams coming from underground. The desperate sounds of centuries of agony. The soft wailing that get caught up in another, and another until the prison was full of suffering.

It was worse than the sounds of torture, though that too made him hesitate to enter the tower walls again. As his skin touched the sun warmed metal, he thought, not for the first time, that he should never have asked to come back here.

The circular room beyond the door was warmly lit. It looked more like a hotel lobby than the entrance to an underground prison. The facade was to be innocuous and inviting to the wine tour that came through twice a year. Humans were welcomed in and given samples of orange wine and goat cheese and told a story about the tower's creation. A stoic art piece commissioned by the groves' owner in 1902.

Another lie. Another cover.

There was art on the walls. Oil paintings of sunsets, orange trees and birds. Two leather couches sat before a flatscreen on the wall. On one side of the room held a long bar made of Osage wood and opposite that, a desk made of the same wood.

A Domini guard dressed in a peach polo watched the subtitles scrolling along the bottom the TV screen. He felt like he was checking into a hotel or maybe about to play a round of golf, until the Domini shifted, showing the gun at his hip, his green eyes waiting.

"I have an appointment. St. Claire."

The guard gave no reaction to his name, a clear indication he knew who he was before he even said it. He hadn't known a time in his life when the St. Claire name didn't bring about some sort of reaction. Either of reverence or barely contained indignation.

The guard nodded to a door before the bar just as it made a low buzzing sound and clicked open. A wide shoulder guard emerged, his hair shorn on either side. The dark strip of hair down the center was longer than the last time he saw him. He wore the familiar sentry men fatigues. Black pants, gray shirt with the Domini sigil;

golden winds wrapped around a starburst shield and a holster to hold a scabbard and a set of charmed manacles. The dagger was currently missing.

"St. Claire." Titus nodded a greeting, his lips pulling into a sly smile.

He reached out and grasped the younger Seraph's forearm as he extended his own. A greeting amongst their kind.

"Titus," he said, relieved to see a familiar face. "I didn't know you were at the tower."

"You can thank our new guest for the recent transfer." He tipped his chin to the door behind him and what lay beyond. "I imagine why *you're* here."

St. Claire nodded.

"Well, let us descend." Titus dropped his heavy hand on St. Claire's shoulder, making him tense. "I'm sure you're eager to get this over with."

A ring on Titus' hand glowed as he gripped the handle and pulled the door open. They entered an anteroom with less flare and flash compared to the lobby. Titus continued his long strides to the elevator door.

"Not that way."

His voice brought St. Claire back to the present. He had been staring at the other door. Where they took the prisoners down. A tight stairwell void of the warm light of the lobby.

St. Claire entered the elevator, and Titus gave him a small press of his lips. Another St. Claire might have hated the pity, but he felt nothing. He stared at his reflection in the mirrored doors as Titus entered his code, closing the doors and sending them down.

"I'm surprised they approved you an audience." Titus grinned. He didn't hide the deliberate once over he gave him. "Little Sprout."

So am I, he thought.

"I'm hardly Little Sprout anymore," he said instead.

Titus laughs. "Even in a thousand years, you'll still be Little Sprout."

"Everyones little compared to you."

The smile died on his lips as the elevator stopped. The doors slide open to the ground level of the prison. His father had prepared him that they would bypass the visitors' lounge and go straight to the cells, but he couldn't have prepared for the smell.

It was exactly like his nightmares.

Metal and earth, salt and blood. Sick and continuously dying. All floating on air that tasted like ozone and magic.

"Thirty-two," Titus called, leaning against the elevator entrance. When St. Claire paused, he nodded. "You have ten minutes."

He dipped his chin in thanks before he turned, heading down the wide hallway. The cells were empty on either side. Brightlights from the hallway ceiling pointed into the empty cells like animals on display.

Veins of magic pulsed with light in the stone. The ancient Siphon power made them to withstand acts of God. Or Gods. Each cell had a number above the door, and he counted them down as he walked. His boots thudding on the stone like a doomsday clock counting down.

He wanted to tell the other Seraph that he's lucky he gets a sector to himself. In the quiet moments at night, he can still hear the faint sound of some of the more long-term captives. A soft wail in the distance. Or the long haunting cry of an eternally lonely soul only to be carried through the prison. Their song a low but loud blaring that you can't sleep through and your brain won't ever let go.

Thirty-two.

The cell was like all the others, but this one held a boy. A boy who could be seventeen or seven hundred. Sometimes there would be a tell to a Serpahs' age. A faint touch of wrinkles on a young face. Movements or gestures from another time. The slight yellowing in the eyes of a being that should have turned to dust centuries ago. But mostly you could only tell by the stillness.

His earliest memory of his grandfather is the eerie realization that he never blinks. Or the uncanny quick way he looks at you. It can turn your blood cold. Living stone, is what his mother says.

This boy doesn't have the unnatural stillness of the ageless. Even those that have blended in with humans still can't shake the uncanny. Or maybe St. Claire's spent too much time with immortals.

The boy who calls himself Alex Carter lifts his head as he approaches. His lids are heavy and there's a faint bruise on his chin. Looking at Alex is like looking at the past, or maybe he's looking at his future.

They shaved his head like they do for prisoners who don't have famous last names.

"Like it, St. Claire?" he rubs a hand over his head as if he knows what he's thinking.

"And what should I call you?"

"Whats in a name anyway?" Alex muses as he stands. "Only echoes through time, remnants of ghosts."

St. Claire doesn't miss the way Alex falters, catching himself with his hand on the stone. He lets out a hiss of pain. An injured shoulder maybe?

Alex inclines his head to where Titus waits, out of earshot. "I figured your brother would have been the one to come." He folds his shoulders as if disappointed. "Though we both know he wouldn't ask the right questions."

"Who sent you after Echo?"

"Wrong." Alex's voice is hard, echoing in the cell. Harsher than either of them expected. He clenches his hands into fists before releasing them on a laugh. He brushes a hand over his forehead. "You'll have to forgive me," he says, walking up to the bars. "I haven't used my voice much for talking."

Alex grips the bars, pressing his forehead to the metal. His voice is low when he says, "Ask what you really want to know?"

St. Claire swallows before he says, "How do I stop what's coming?"

Alex gives him a knowing grin. His fingers flex on the bars and for a moment St. Claire thinks it's all just another game. The same he played with Echo in the weeks leading up to her kidnapping.

"You can't," he says, backing away. He recites, his tone bored, "the door has opened, the vessel filled. The stars carry a secret, buried the lost key. The burning ones break the last seal and soon all her golden soldiers will kneel. By blood I was betrayed and by blood I will get my revenge."

Alex turns back to face him, his mouth tipping into a dangerous smirk. "You can't stop what's coming," his eyes darken, "not after what you did."

St. Claire cast a quick glance to where Titus waits, his time running up. Alex follows his gaze, quick as it was.

He drops his voice to a whisper. "Secrets safe."

St. Claire grips the metal bars hard enough that he can feel the beginnings of the magic reacting to his blood. The slow tingle along his skin, waiting. "I don't need your protection."

Alex's smug smile has him clenching his hand, remembering what it felt like to hit him.

"You should know there's no truth in prophecies. Only coincidences, potential outcomes, with only fragments of truth."

"Not this one." Alex has wandered back to his cot as if pulled, but reels back to say, "I don't suppose dear old dad told you the last verse?" Alex pulls his arm to his side, cradling it

St. Claire narrows his eyes, seeing the tremble in the other seraphs hand. "There isn't one."

"Shame," Alex says, his gaze losing focus. "I thought you knew better than anyone the treachery of our ancestors."

Alex stumbles back to his cot, dropping heavily to the small bed. A shiver shakes his body, rattling his teeth.

"Tell me then."

"I can't spoil all the fun, now can I?" His dark chuckles echoes in the catacombs. "I'll let you discover that one on your own. And it will be glorious."

St. Claire pushes away from the cell, the adrenaline keeping him from feeling the pain in his hands until later. He cast one last look at the boy who ended up in a Domini prison for eternity.

Alex rest his back on the wall looking like it hurts. No doubt the guards, maybe Titus himself, have been tasked with getting information of out him. Centuries to improve upon their skill and an endless supply of creativity in other parts of the prison.

Before St. Claire can turn to leave, Alex calls out, "You can't stop this, Ash. It has already begun. From Genevieve's lips to our cursed hearts."

ACKNOWLEDGMENTS

I would like to thank my family, who listened to all my excited tangents and anxiety-ridden doubts while I wrote, edited, and published this book, and for giving me pep talks when I wanted to give in to the impostor syndrome.

Thanks to Reece for reading multiple drafts, and late night critique sessions. Thanks to Avalon for helping to keep the wildling boys under control so I could work on finalizing this book. Thank you to the boys for understanding that morning coffee time is quiet time, and to my Daniel for always coming along on my wild rides, even when you couldn't see the destination, you still fully supported the journey.

I want to thank Lace for telling me when a character wasn't working, and to my beta and sensitivity readers for their guidance in shaping this story.

And thank you, dear reader, for giving my words life.

ABOUT THE AUTHOR

NICOLE LIGHTWOOD was born and raised in Florida, where a lot of her stories take inspiration from. Now she lives on a small farm in the bluegrass region of Kentucky with her husband, five children, two cuddly Dobermans, and way too many geese. When she's not writing, she can be found haunting old bookstores, making art, or exploring her new home state with her family.

YOU CAN ALSO FIND HER HERE:
www.nicolelightwood.com

@nicole.lightwood   @nicolelightwood

THE STORY CONTINUES IN BOOK 2

COMING SOON

SUBSCRIBE FOR EMAIL UPDATES ON THE LEGACY OF LIGHT SERIES AND UPCOMING RELEASES BY AUTHOR NICOLE LIGHTWOOD,

Sign-up here:

Milton Keynes UK
Ingram Content Group UK Ltd.
UKHW011829061123
432058UK00018B/304/J